All the Drowning Seas

Historical Fiction Published by McBooks Press

ALEXANDER KENT
Midshipman Bolitho
Stand Into Danger
In Gallant Company
Sloop of War
To Glory We Steer
Command a King's Ship
Passage to Mutiny
With All Despatch
Form Line of Battle!
Enemy in Sight!
The Flag Captain
Signal–Close Action!
The Inshore Squadron
A Tradition of Victory
Success to the Brave
Colours Aloft!
Honour This Day
The Only Victor
Beyond the Reef
The Darkening Sea
For My Country's Freedom
Cross of St George
Sword of Honour
Second to None
Relentless Pursuit
Man of War

DOUGLAS REEMAN
Badge of Glory
First to Land
The Horizon
Dust on the Sea
Knife Edge

Twelve Seconds to Live
Battlecruiser
The White Guns
A Prayer for the Ship
For Valour

DAVID DONACHIE
The Devil's Own Luck
The Dying Trade
A Hanging Matter
An Element of Chance
The Scent of Betrayal
A Game of Bones

On a Making Tide
Tested by Fate
Breaking the Line

DUDLEY POPE
Ramage
Ramage & The Drumbeat
Ramage & The Freebooters
Governor Ramage R.N.
Ramage's Prize
Ramage & The Guillotine
Ramage's Diamond
Ramage's Mutiny
Ramage & The Rebels
The Ramage Touch
Ramage's Signal
Ramage & The Renegades
Ramage's Devil
Ramage's Trial
Ramage's Challenge
Ramage at Trafalgar
Ramage & The Saracens
Ramage & The Dido

ALEXANDER FULLERTON
Storm Force to Narvik
Last Lift to Crete
All the Drowning Seas

JAMES L. NELSON
The Only Life That Mattered

PHILIP MCCUTCHAN
Halfhyde at the Bight of Benin
Halfhyde's Island
*Halfhyde and the
  Guns of Arrest*
Halfhyde to the Narrows
Halfhyde for the Queen
Halfhyde Ordered South
Halfhyde on Zanatu

V.A. STUART
Victors and Lords
The Sepoy Mutiny
Massacre at Cawnpore
The Cannons of Lucknow
The Heroic Garrison

The Valiant Sailors
The Brave Captains
Hazard's Command
Hazard of Huntress
Hazard in Circassia
Victory at Sebastopol
Guns to the Far East
Escape from Hell

R.F. DELDERFIELD
Too Few for Drums
Seven Men of Gascony

DEWEY LAMBDIN
The French Admiral
Jester's Fortune

C.N. PARKINSON
The Guernseyman
Devil to Pay
The Fireship
Touch and Go
So Near So Far
Dead Reckoning

*The Life and Times
  of Horatio Hornblower*

JAN NEEDLE
A Fine Boy for Killing
The Wicked Trade
The Spithead Nymph

IRV C. ROGERS
Motoo Eetee

NICHOLAS NICASTRO
The Eighteenth Captain
Between Two Fires

FREDERICK MARRYAT
Frank Mildmay OR
  The Naval Officer
The King's Own
Mr Midshipman Easy
Newton Forster OR
  The Merchant Service
Snarleyyow OR
  The Dog Fiend
The Privateersman
The Phantom Ship

W. CLARK RUSSELL
Wreck of the Grosvenor
Yarn of Old Harbour Town

RAFAEL SABATINI
Captain Blood

MICHAEL SCOTT
Tom Cringle's Log

A.D. HOWDEN SMITH
Porto Bello Gold

All the Drowning Seas

ALEXANDER FULLERTON

THE NICHOLAS EVERARD
WORLD WAR II SAGA, BOOK 3

MCBOOKS PRESS, INC.
ITHACA, NEW YORK

Published by McBooks Press 2005
Copyright © Alexander Fullerton 1980
First published in Great Britain by Michael Joseph Limited

Cover illustration adapted from an image by Chris Mayger.
*Every effort has been made to secure permission
from copyright holders to reproduce this image.*

Library of Congress Cataloging-in-Publication Data

Fullerton, Alexander, 1924-
  All the drowning seas / by Alexander Fullerton.
      p. cm. — (The Nicholas Everard WWII saga ; bk. 3)
  ISBN 1-59013-094-4 (trade pbk. : alk. paper)
  1. Everard, Nick (Fictitious character)—Fiction. 2. Great Britain—History,
Naval—20th century—Fiction. 3. World War, 1939-1945—Fiction. I. Title.
  PR6056.U435A78 2005
  823'.914—dc22

                                                        2004030

Distributed to the trade by National Book Network, Inc.
15200 NBN Way, Blue Ridge Summit, PA 17214
800-462-6420

Additional copies of this book may be ordered from any bookstore
or directly from McBooks Press, Inc., ID Booth Building,
520 North Meadow St., Ithaca, NY 14850.
Please include $4.00 postage and handling with mail orders.
New York State residents must add sales tax to total remittance
(books & shipping). All McBooks Press publications can also be ordered by
calling toll-free 1-888-BOOKS11 (1-888-266-5711).
Please call to request a free catalog.

Visit the McBooks Press website at www.mcbooks.com.

Printed in the United States of America
9 8 7 6 5 4 3 2 1

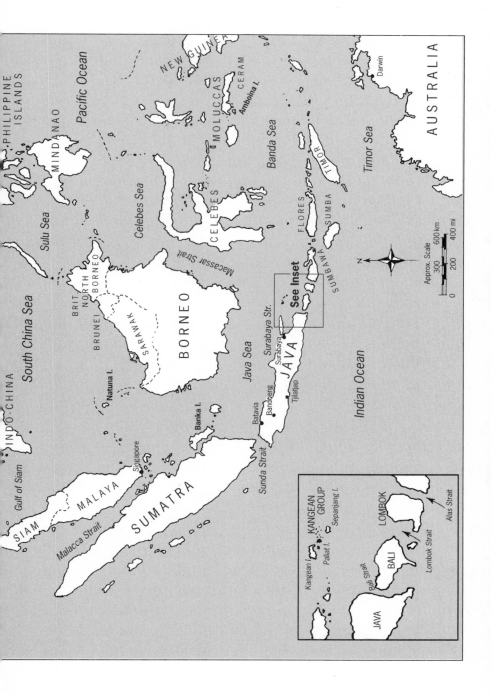

CHAPTER ONE

· · ·

The Surabaya Strait was a blue wedge glittering between the greens of Madura Island and the Java mainland, and as the squadron closed in towards it *Defiant's* camouflage-painted steel ploughed water already churned by the two Dutch cruisers and the Australian and the other British one, *Exeter.* Astern of *Defiant* came the American, *Houston,* and then the mixed bag of destroyers—two Dutch, six American and three British—in a slightly ragged seaward tail.

Every damn thing, Nick Everard thought, was slightly ragged. Slightly hopeless. You had to pretend it wasn't, you had to seem to believe in this attempt to stem an avalanche that had rolled clear across the south-west Pacific in just ten weeks . . .

Farting against thunder, Jim Jordan of the USS *Sloan* had called it.

The slaughter wasn't finished yet. Even this force now—this scratch collection of ships—well, they were steaming back into Surabaya now, but only for the destroyers to refuel. Then they'd be sailing again, to meet the invasion fleet that would be arriving within a day, possibly within hours.

De Ruyter, Rear-Admiral Doorman's flagship, had put her helm over to port a few moments ago, and her next-astern, *Java,* was following her round now. They were leaving the Jamuang rock to port, turning around it to follow the channel into that funnel-shaped approach. Nick became aware of Chevening, his navigating officer, waiting with an eye on him, wanting to know whether Nick would take over the conning of the ship now they were in pilotage waters.

The hell he would. There were still twenty miles to go, to Surabaya itself, and he'd be lunching anyway, as soon as his servant brought the tray up. He told Chevening, "Carry on, please." A very proper, formal-mannered man, was Chevening, like many of these big-ship people; and it was conceivable that some of them might see their new command-ing officer, Captain Sir Nicholas Everard DSO DSC RN, as something of an interloper. A destroyer man who'd been out of the Navy alto-gether between the wars certainly wasn't a typical cruiser captain; for some of them it might be difficult to imagine an RN officer leaving the Service voluntarily, unless there was something pretty odd about him . . . Chevening was a senior lieutenant, tall and prematurely bald-ing: his light-coloured eyes reflected the sea's brightness as he waited at the binnacle for the moment when he'd turn *Defiant* in *Exeter*'s wake. Like a bloody old heron, Nick thought, watching *Perth,* ahead of *Exeter,* begin her turn. The Aussie cruiser was an old friend—from the Mediterranean, which was where he'd brought this ship from a few weeks ago. In the Med, before his own destroyer flotilla had been so reduced in numbers that it had virtually ceased to exist, he'd shared actions with *Perth* time after time: in the Greek operations, Crete, on the desert coast, in Malta convoys, she'd been through the thick of it.

Exeter, veteran of the Battle of the Plate, was turning now. But they were all, men and ships, veterans now.

Nick heard Chevening steadying *Defiant* on her new course. He lit a cigarette, squinting aft over the flare of the lighter to see *Houston,* the American, pushing her stem around inside the out-curving wake. *Houston*'s guns were eight-inch, as were *Exeter*'s; *Defiant* and the other four cruisers were armed with six-inch. With ten destroyers, they were not by any means a negligible fighting force: *would not have been,* he thought, if it weren't that they'd never fought together or even exer-cised together, had no joint tactical plan and no common signal code. They could communicate just about well enough to be able to follow each other around. Whereas any Jap force they came up against would be highly trained and integrated. They'd have air reconnaissance too, and their ships wouldn't be old crocks, already worked half to death.

What it came down to was that any Jap force of roughly equivalent strength would be able to swallow this lot whole.

He prowled across the bridge and trained his glasses on the Java coastline, on Panka Point and the hill behind it. That strip of coast was about eight miles away, and with the binoculars you could see how the inshore waters were thickly groved with fishermen's stakes. They made what amounted to underwater corrals, by driving in bamboo stakes and lacing them together with lighter branches . . . The Japanese would take Java, all right, even if the Dutch did fight to the last man as they were promising. The Allied command had been dissolved two days ago, and General Wavell had flown back to India, leaving the island in the hands of its Dutch commanders. There was no doubt about what was going to happen now. The Japs had taken Bali to the east, Timor beyond it and Amboina north of that, and they'd raided Port Darwin in north Australia; they were in Sumatra to the west and Borneo and the Celebes to the north, they'd got Malaya and Sarawak and fighting had just about ended in the Philippines. They'd won footholds farther afield as well, at Rabaul in New Ireland and Lae in New Guinea; but the main thrust of the assault now was a pincer movement closing in on Java, which they had already isolated and which they'd want in order to close the ring on all the Indies.

It was a good thing, Nick thought, that Wavell had flown out. There was nothing he could have done here. The Japs had to be kept out of India and out of Australia: if they could be held inside that huge perimeter there'd be time to reorganize, rebuild. With the Americans in it now you could reckon that in the long term things would turn out all right. Here and now, things looked bloody awful.

There'd been an "order of the day" issued by the Dutch governor-general. Its text ran: "The time for destruction and withdrawal has now ended, the time for holding out and attacking has come . . . The foreign troops which are here will remain and will be maintained through a regular stream of reinforcements . . ."

It was a nice thought, but the truth was there'd been an order that no more troops were to be landed in Java. Nick flicked his cigarette-end away down-wind and moved back to the port side of the bridge. Chevening had just ordered an increase in speed; and *Defiant* was indeed too far astern of *Exeter.* She'd lost ground somehow during that turn, he supposed. He told Chevening, "Bit more than that, I'd say." The navigator ducked to the voicepipe again and ordered another ten revolutions per minute, to get her back where she belonged more quickly. The last thing you wanted was a Dutchman telling you to keep proper station.

Now that was Leading Seaman Williams's voice, its Welsh lilt easy to identify, as he acknowledged the order through the voicepipe. Williams was new to the ship: he'd been drafted to her from shore duty in Singapore, and he'd left a wife there. Not many days before the end, when *Defiant* was bringing the last Australian reinforcements up through the Sunda Strait, Williams had requested a private interview and begged to be allowed ashore when they arrived. Nick had allowed it, although he'd been aware he shouldn't have; there was no question of granting shore leave, and he'd have to have *Defiant* well clear before daylight. He'd told Williams, "I'm trusting you to be in the boat when it comes back. Whatever the situation is ashore, whatever you find out. All right?"

"Aye aye, sir. Very grateful, sir."

Grateful, for the privilege of seeing to his own wife's safety. The town and dock area were already in chaos, thronged with desperate people who had no way out. Williams's wife was Eurasian, and the Japanese weren't behaving any less brutally to people—women particularly—of mixed blood than they were to whites, in the places they'd already over-run. The killick had come back as he'd promised he would, but in a worse state than when he'd landed: he'd failed to contact her or get any news of her. Most telephones were out of order, and the dockyard office where she'd worked had been empty, apparently ransacked. Facing Nick, he'd been stammering, helpless, a man in a waking nightmare. Nick told him that it surely meant she'd got away some-how, over to Sumatra or south to Java. Williams couldn't accept it: there was no way she could have got out, and she was there somewhere, in that panic-stricken rabble. Nick had appreciated how he'd have felt himself if Kate had been ashore there: and all he'd been able to do was tell Forbes, the chaplain, and the doctor, Sibbold, to keep an eye on him. Soon afterwards, two weeks ago, Singapore had fallen to the Japanese.

In his mind he could still smell the burning oil tanks, which had been set alight a week before the surrender. Even with Singapore island under siege, the enemy triumphant in Johore, Allied ships including *Defiant* had still been bringing troop convoys up through the Sunda Strait. You couldn't use the Malacca Strait because the Japs had estab-lished a crushing air superiority early in the battle for Malaya, and those waters were impassable. Without air power, you lost control of the sea; without that, you couldn't prevent enemy landings. The vicious circle tightened. The last troops into Singapore were the Aussie 18th Division, brought in so late they might as conveniently have marched straight into the POW camps. Evacuation had become a rout, a panic rush in anything that floated, and with Jap warships hunting close inshore. By that time there'd been a smoke-pall over Sumatra too, as the Dutch blew up their oil wells and refineries; the glow of the fires around Palembang had been visible in the sky from hundreds of miles out at sea. Nick had seen it when he'd been taking *Defiant* to meet a convoy of refugees who were being brought south from Natuna Island, a place the Japanese hadn't bothered to stop at in their first wave of assaults. The civilians had been ferried there from Miri in Sarawak and Labuan in North Borneo, just ahead of the enemy landings in those places, and at Natuna they'd been packed into a Dutch steamer which sailed with an escort of one Dutch and two American destroyers. The Dutch destroyer and one of the Americans had been sunk by Val dive-bombers before *Defiant* could reach them, and on the morning of the rendezvous the steamer was hit and set on fire and had to be abandoned. *Defiant* and the surviving American, USS *Sloan,* picked up most of the refugees and then fought their way down to Tanjung Priok— the port of Batavia, Java's capital—under recurrent air strikes. It had felt very much like the Crete battle: the frequent bombing, lack of air support, awareness of defeat, retreat.

A few days ago in Nick's cabin in *Defiant,* when they'd been licking their wounds in Tanjung Priok prior to sailing to join Doorman's Combined Striking Force at Surabaya, the USS *Sloan*'s captain had remarked, "Darned strange, when you look at how things are right now, how none of us doubts we'll end up winning. Wouldn't you say so?"

Bob Gant, Nick's second-in-command, had glanced at Jordan in surprise. He and the American were both commanders, Gant a year or two older than Jim Jordan.

"Just as *well* nobody doubts it, I'd say."

He'd pushed back his chair: "If you'd excuse me now, sir. Rather a lot to see to." Getting to his feet, Gant tried to look as if the effort didn't hurt him. He was a small man, with hair already grey although he was still under forty. He'd been in the carrier *Glorious* when she'd been sunk off Norway in June 1940, and he'd suffered some sort of damage to his spine. He wouldn't admit to it, but Surgeon Lieutenant-Commander Sibbold had said he was probably in pain twenty-four hours a day; he wouldn't admit it because if he had they'd have moved him to a desk job ashore.

Which *some* people might have preferred, Nick had thought, watching him leave the day cabin, to being where Bob Gant was now. Jordan was right: you didn't have to be defeatist or a pessimist, but you didn't have to be blind or stupid either.

Jim Jordan, Commander USN, was a square-built man with ginger hair and a face that broadened at the jaw. His eyes moved back to Nick as the door shut behind Gant.

"D'you have any doubts of it yourself, Captain?"

"That we'll win, eventually?" Nick shook his head. "None at all."
Jordan said, "Present circumstances are not exactly auspicious."

"Oh, I don't know. I mean, so far as Java's concerned." Out loud, one tended to resist the truth. "If the Dutch can hang on ashore . . ."

"*If* . . ." Jordan shook his head. "What worries me, frankly . . ."

He'd cut himself short. Nick waited: resuming, Jordan spoke more quietly. "*Everything.* As of this moment, I can't see we have a damn thing going for us. However . . ."

He'd checked again. Nick smiled. "As you say—*however.* Let's drink to that."

"In this whisky," Jordan nodded at it appreciatively as his fist closed round the glass, "I'll drink to just about anything."

He'd come aboard to discuss details of their move to Surabaya, and stayed at Nick's invitation to sample a malt whisky, some Laphroaigh that Nick had acquired in Alexandria. He added, sipping the end of it, "I never tasted one as smooth as this."

"Let's have one for the gangway, then."

"No opposition . . . You married, sir? Family?"

"I'm not married now."

He didn't want to have to think too much about it, either. There was a girl in London, Fiona Gascoyne, a young widow, to whom he felt he was more or less committed: to whom he'd *wanted* to be committed, before he'd got to know Kate Farquharson. Kate was Australian, an Army nurse, and he'd brought her out of Crete on board *Tuareg,* his destroyer. If it hadn't been for Fiona in the background he'd have proposed to Kate before she and her unit had been shipped home to Australia. In the circumstances, perhaps it was a good thing she *had* been sent home; but it was a complicated and unsatisfactory state of mind to be in.

He told Jordan, "But family—yes. I have a son who's sort of part adopted American."

"How come?"

"My former wife remarried, to an American. He's an industrialist, millionaire I'm told, lives in Connecticut. She had custody of our son Paul, and when the war started he ducked out of college over there and came across to join the Royal Navy. As a sailor, lower deck, but he's commissioned now and a submariner." Nick pushed the cork back into the Laphroaigh bottle. "Last I heard, he was being sent to Malta, to the submarine flotilla we have there." It was the main reason he hadn't wanted to leave the Mediterranean. With Paul in the 10th Submarine Flotilla they might have had a chance to see each other occasionally.

He'd sent Chevening down to get lunch in the wardroom; he'd already had his own, up here on the bridge. It had been corned beef, as usual. Ormrod, one of the watchkeeping lieutenants, was at the binnacle, and Nick was on his high seat in the port for'ard corner of the bridge. Glancing round, he saw Bob Gant coming forward from the ladder. Gant was in Number Sixes—tight, high-collared whites; Nick wore loose-fitting white overalls which he'd had made in Alexandria.

"Suppose we'll only get a few hours in there, sir?"

"If as much." He offered the commander one of his black cheroots, and Gant's refusal seemed a shade defensive. Nick told him, "They aren't as bad as they look, Bob."

"I'll stick to my pipe, sir, thanks all the same."

The Combined Striking Force had been patrolling north of Java since yesterday afternoon, looking for an invasion force that had been reported up there somewhere. They'd found nothing: lacking air reconnaissance, it was a matter of luck whether you bumped into an enemy or missed him. And the destroyers, with endurance strictly limited by the capacity of their fuel tanks, needed to be kept topped-up against the moment when you *might* run into the invaders.

Not "might," though. *Would*, undoubtedly. Doorman's object would be to intercept at the earliest possible moment, and break up the convoy.

To get at it, at the troopships, you'd have to sink or drive off the escorting warships first.

Gant observed quietly, stating what he knew Nick knew already but feeling he had to mention it all the same, "Ship's company could do with some rest, sir."

The old, old story. Exhausted men, worn-out ships. The Jap ships would be new and fast and their crews fresh, high-spirited with all the momentum of their sweeping victories. Nick asked, leaking cheroot-smoke as he glanced round to see what the officer of the watch was doing, "Is Sandilands happy?"

Gant smiled. At the idea of Sandilands, the engineer commander, being *happy* . . .

Defiant was twenty years old. She'd been laid down as part of the War Emergency Programme—the *first* War's . . . Gant said, moving back to avoid some of Nick's smoke, "If he can keep the wheels turning for just a while longer," he moved one hand, indicating the other ships as well, "we ought to give a pretty good account of ourselves, wouldn't you agree, sir?"

"Of course." He wondered whether the commander was expressing confidence or fishing for reassurance. Remembering again the conversation with Jim Jordan, and wondering whether there was really any point in their being here at all. When there was no chance of them winning anything, except—oh, that old intangible, honour? And when you were already so short of ships that you had to keep antiques like this one running, was "honour" worth six cruisers, a dozen destroyers?

Gant called suddenly, breaking into what was becoming a depressing line of thought, "Yeoman!"

Pointing: at a light flashing from *Exeter*'s signal bridge. Ruddle, yeoman of the watch, had responded with a yell of "Aye aye, sir!" and a leading signalman at the port-side lamp had already sent an answering flash.

"Captain, sir?"

Nick took his eyes off the fast sequence of dots and dashes. A messenger was beside him, with a sheet of signal-pad. He recognized the sloping scrawl of Instructor Lieutenant Hobbs, "Schooly," who'd have deciphered this wireless message down in the plot, immediately below this bridge. Before he'd had time to read it, Ruddle called, "Squadron stand by to reverse course in sequence of fleet numbers, sir!"

"Pass it to *Houston.*"

"Aye aye, sir!" PO Ruddle had a high screech of a voice, acquired from years of bawling down to flag-decks against high winds. *Defiant*'s lamp was already calling the American cruiser astern of her, and Nick was reading the decoded signal—which Doorman would have received in Dutch, from his Dutch senior officer at the other end of Java. There was a British rear-admiral there too, working with the Dutchman. Nick looked up from the signal, and told Gant, "Two assault groups coming this way. Our bird's the eastern bunch. Said to be eighty miles offshore now."

The flagship, *de Ruyter,* had begun to swing to starboard, initiating the about-turn. No fuelling for the destroyers, after all. There wouldn't be time for it, of course. With the two forces steaming to meet each other at an aggregate speed of, say, nearly forty knots, it would be only a couple of hours before they met. He glanced again at the signal. The escort with the eastern group was reported to consist of four cruisers and fourteen destroyers. Behind them, of course, not in company with them but near enough to be whistled up when required, would be heavy striking units, battleships and carriers. However much damage you did to start with, therefore, you wouldn't be left long to gloat over it.

But—as Jim Jordan had so aptly put it—*however . . .*

CHAPTER TWO

· · ·

From the motor vessel *Montgovern's* boat deck, with one shoulder against a lifeboat's davit for support as the ship rolled, Sub-Lieutenant Paul Everard RNVR gazed around at the crowd of ships bound for Malta. *Montgovern* was second in the port column of merchantmen; there were four columns, each of four ships, and all except one of them were carrying mixed cargoes consisting mainly of food, ammunition and cased petrol. The food was mostly flour. The exception, the *Caracas Moon,* was an oil tanker, and the cased petrol distributed among the other ships was there in case, with her load of aviation spirit, she did not get through. They'd all of them be targets for the Luftwaffe and for submarines' torpedoes, but tankers did tend to attract particular attention.

Ahead of the *Montgovern* steamed the *Warrenpoint,* nine thousand tons, and abeam of her, leading number two column, was the *Blackadder,* carrying the convoy commodore. Astern of the commodore's ship and thus on the *Montgovern's* starboard beam plodded the long, low shape of the big *Castleventry.* They and the other twelve were all fine, fast ships of good capacity, specially chosen for the task ahead of them. They'd passed through the Gibraltar Strait at dawn yesterday and they were now well into the western basin of the Mediterranean, roughly south of the Balearics, steering east with rather more than six hundred miles to go.

The strength of the naval escort was a fair indication of the importance of the operation. Ahead of the solid block of merchantmen, three cruisers in line abreast stooped and swayed to the grey-blue swell. Astern of the columns another cruiser in the central position was dwarfed by two battleships, one on each side of her. Back on the starboard quarter, not visible at the moment from here on the *Montgovern,* three aircraft carriers with three more cruisers in close attendance formed a separate group. While all across the convoy's van and down its sides were the destroyers, several as close escort on each side of the square of merchant ships and another twenty forming an A/S screen on a radius of about three miles. The whole assembly covered many square miles of sea and made, Paul Everard thought, a very impressive picture.

There was a fourth carrier too, but she had a special job to do and wasn't part of the convoy's escort.

The enemy knew, by this time, that the convoy was on its way. They might have known a long time ago, when it was on its way south from the Clyde: but their spies in and around Gibraltar would certainly have reported the sudden traffic through the Strait and the warships, dozens of them, steaming in to refuel and hurrying out to sea again. On top of which there'd been several submarine alarms yesterday, contacts by destroyers out in the deep field, and a few depth charges dropped, and the submarines would have wirelessed sighting reports when they'd surfaced astern of the convoy and after nightfall. More annoyingly, and just to clinch it, yesterday evening an Algeria-bound French airliner had overflown the convoy with its radio chattering excitedly.

"Bless their little Vichy hearts!" Mackeson, naval liaison officer in the *Montgovern,* was a soft-voiced, easy-going man. Humphrey Straight, the freighter's master, had been very much more forthright. He'd growled, "Fucking frogs . . ." and spat to leeward, which had happened to be in the direction of Algeria.

"Weather's not much cop, eh, Paul?"

Mick McCall, the freighter's second mate, was beside him, steadying himself with a hand on the lifeboat's rudder. He nodded skyward. "Clearing, isn't it?"

It was, unfortunately; as daylight hardened you could see that grey areas were fewer and smaller than blue ones. At this time of year, you'd think you could have reckoned on some decent cloud cover . . . It was damned cold, anyway: Paul hunched into the turned-up collar of his greatcoat as McCall asked him, "Service all right, still? Food up to standard? Sleeping well, are you? No rude noises in the night to wake you?"

Sarcasm: because Paul was a passenger and McCall had work to do, watches to keep. It was only half joking, too: part of it was the Merchant Navy man's resentment of the "fighting" navy, the men who—McCall would have said—won all the applause, the glamour. It was an understandable resentment too: sitting on this eight-thousand-ton steamer with her explosive cargo, knowing that very soon a powerful enemy would be doing his best to see that it did explode, you could understand his point of view.

Paul told him, "I'd have you know I was on the bridge for more than an hour last night."

"My God, hadn't you better turn in again?"

"You're a riot, Mick . . ."

The whole convoy was altering course, turning to a new leg of the anti-submarine zigzag. Convoy manoeuvres, emergency turns and formation changes had been practised over and over again on the way down from the Clyde to Gibraltar; the merchantmen had acted like a herd of recalcitrant cows to start with, but the admiral had drilled them until their masters must have been stuttering with Merchant Navy-type fury, and they were handling themselves quite well now. McCall said, "I'd best be getting up there. And you ought to get below while there's still some breakfast left . . . Just look at that bloody sky!"

Paul glanced up, and agreed. The Luftwaffe would be in luck, if this weather held.

In the saloon, he found fellow passengers and ship's officers crowding the table. At first glance it looked as if he'd have to wait for someone to finish; then Mackeson called, "Here you are, Sub!" and Paul saw there was a vacant chair beside him. He helped himself to coffee from the urn, murmured a general "Good morning" as he squeezed in: someone pushed the cornflakes along, and Mackeson nudged the milk-jug his way. Condensed milk, of course; by this time any other kind would have tasted peculiar. Mackeson jerked a thumb towards Paul, and told a grey-haired, wingless RAF officer across the table, "I knew this lad's father in the Navy twenty years ago. Small world, eh? Would you believe it, there are three damn generations of his family at sea now?"

The air-force man raised his eyebrows, let them fall again, chewed for a few seconds and then swallowed; he muttered, "Remarkable."

The three generations were Paul, his father Nick, and Nick's uncle Hugh. Admiral Sir Hugh Everard had come out of retirement to become a commodore of Atlantic convoys: a fairly arduous job, for a man of seventy. Nick Everard was—well, Paul wasn't sure where he was. Until quite recently he'd had a destroyer flotilla in the eastern Mediterranean, but in the last letter Paul had had from him he'd given his address as HMS *Defiant* and hinted—or seemed to hint—that he was taking her elsewhere.

It had been on Mackeson's invitation that he'd spent some time on the freighter's bridge last night. Several times since they'd sailed from the Clyde the older man had said something like: "Must have a yarn, Everard, when we get a minute's quiet. I want to hear the news of your family." He'd known Nick in the Black Sea in 1919, and he'd known *of* Hugh Everard in the same period. He—Mackeson—had gone to sea as a midshipman RN in 1918, left the Service a few years later and rejoined as an RNR lieutenant-commander in 1939. So he was about forty-two now, Paul supposed, to Nick's forty-six.

Egg and a rasher of bacon appeared suddenly: powdered egg, as usual. The plate curved in from nowhere and more or less dropped in front of him: Paul looked round and said "Thank you" to the retreating steward's back. Devenish, the *Montgovern*'s chief officer, advised from Paul's left, "Wouldn't bother with the courtesies, if I were you. He's a bolshy sod . . . Did you get that Mention in Despatches in submarines?"

"No." Devenish was squinting downwards at the small bronze oak-leaf sewn to Paul's reefer jacket. Paul told him, "I haven't been in sub-marines very long. Hardly operationally at all."

"He was at Narvik." Mackeson spoke to Devenish across him. Mackeson seemed proud of the Everards, or of his old friendship with

Nick. He added, "Ordinary Seaman, gun's crew in one of the H–class destroyers. That's where he got it." He asked Paul, "Sunk, weren't you?"

Paul nodded as he began to eat. He'd been through all this last night, and the egg mixture was getting cold.

Last night in the darkened bridge, with Pratt, the third officer, in charge of the watch and Mackeson there to back him up while Captain Straight snored in the chartroom, Mackeson had suggested that Nick Everard might have taken *Defiant* to join the Eastern Fleet.

"It's as likely as anything." He'd taken another pull at his pipe. The ship was moving rhythmically to the swell, creaking as she rolled, and the night air was cold enough to mist the glass side windows. He'd removed the pipe from his mouth again; it made a popping sound as he took it out. "Unless he's taken her home for refit, of course. And if you're right and she'd left the station at all. If he's still out here and you run into him, though, give him my very kind regards, will you?"

Paul said he would, of course.

"Bongo, they used to call me. Bongo Mackeson. I was a few years junior to him, of course, but I dare say he'll remember . . . I wouldn't envy him, mark you, if that's where they've sent him now. Japanese are all over us, and what've we got to stop 'em with?"

Paul really needed to see his father. Not just for the pleasure of a reunion: there was a very personal and unpleasant situation back in England which Nick Everard had to be told about, and Paul was the only person who could tell him. It wasn't anything to look forward to, and it wasn't the sort of information you'd want to put in a letter for some censor to read, either.

"Are we expecting things to warm up today, Mackeson?"

Paul emerged from his thoughts. The question had come from the other end of the table, in the high, thin tones of Lieutenant-Commander Thornton RNVR. Thornton was some kind of cipher expert: code-breaking, something of that sort. He'd made it plain that his particular expertise, for which he was urgently needed in Malta, was too secret and important to be discussed. The boy on his left, toad-like in thick spectacles, was an RNVR paymaster sub-lieutenant named Gosling; he was shy and hardly ever spoke to anyone. Thornton was staring at Mackeson, dabbing at his mouth while he waited for an answer to what Paul thought had been a damn-fool question.

Mackeson said easily, pushing his chair back from the table, "Depends if we're referring to the weather or the enemy. Damned if I know either way."

Thornton looked offended. "Bongo" Mackeson was on his feet, bushy-browed and noticeably bow-legged: at fifty paces you'd guess he'd spent a lot of his life on horses. Leaning over his chair, he was telling anyone who cared to listen that the aircraft carrier that was doing the ferrying job would be flying-off her load of Spitfires later in the forenoon, and that there'd probably be a view of it from the *Montgovern*'s boat deck.

It was still cold up there at noon, when the passengers came drifting up to watch the fly-off. The ferrying carrier had hauled out to the convoy's port quarter, with two destroyers in attendance; she had forty-two Spitfires which were to fly from here to join the RAF in Malta, then this evening she'd turn and head back to Gibraltar, her job done. The other three carriers—fighter patrols from them were up and guarding the convoy now—would carry on eastward, providing air cover, Paul guessed, until the convoy came into range of the Malta squadrons. Or as near to that point as possible. And come to think of it, there'd have to be a gap, a period when there'd be *no* fighter cover, and the convoy would be at its most vulnerable then. But the carriers' Sea Hurricanes had drawn first blood this morning: just after boat drill had finished, Mackeson had sent down a message that they'd shot down a shadowing Junkers 88.

Dennis Brill, a young Army doctor, had murmured as he stirred a mug of Bovril, "So we're being shadowed . . ."

There was no surprise in it. Brill looked thoughtful, more than surprised, and Paul understood the reaction. It was only that this confirmation of the enemy's interest in the convoy brought home the reality, the certainty that before long they'd be attacked.

He and Brill had come up to the boat deck together, and Brill had stopped near Thornton and Harry Woods. Woods was a captain in the Royal Artillery and in charge of the *Montgovern's* Army gunners. Thornton, the cipher expert, sniffed and murmured, "Place is getting like Brighton pier." He made room for them at the rail, though. He was tall, an inch or so taller than Paul, and he had an irritatingly high voice.

Woods pointed. "You're just in time."

The first Spitfire lifted from the carrier's deck, and curved skyward. Thornton turned his back on the scene, as if he now knew all about it. He asked Paul, "Are you going to Malta to join one particular submarine, or—"

"Yeah." Paul nodded. "Just one." The second Spitfire swooped away. Another stupid question, he thought. Talking to people like this one made him feel more American, more like he used to sound before the re-anglicizing process began two and a half years ago. It wasn't intentional, the reaction simply occurred, an instinctive raising of some psychological drawbridge. It reminded him, when he thought about it, that his father had said in his own younger days that *he'd* had a lot of difficulty getting along with some of his superiors.

"Not simply to the Malta flotilla for an unspecified appointment, I meant." Thornton said it sharply, as if he thought he'd been snubbed. He had been, too. Four Spitfires were airborne now. Paul explained, "I was in a submarine called *Ultra*. I went sick just when she was sailing for the Mediterranean, and now I'm rejoining her."

He'd developed appendicitis a day or two before *Ultra* had been due to cast off from the depot ship in Holy Loch, where they'd been based during their work-up period. He'd had a pain in his gut and tried to ignore it, but then it had blown up and he'd had no option. After the long preparation, months of training and practising for the time when they'd be judged fit to go "operational," it had been intensely disappointing. But his CO had come up trumps: he'd taken a spare crew sub-lieutenant out with him as a temporary replacement, and promised Paul his job back if he could get out there reasonably quickly. This convoy had been the first chance of a passage: there'd have been three weeks' wait in Gibraltar for the next supply submarine's trip to the island—even if he could have got himself to Gib and then wangled the passage in her. He was scared, even now, that if he didn't get there soon his replacement might have taken root, proved to be more useful than Paul Everard. Any submarine skipper would want the best team he could put together—particularly in the 10th Flotilla, who were fighting an extremely tough campaign in very difficult conditions. And another reason for concern was that he thought there'd probably be some spare submarine officers kicking their heels at the Malta base: several boats had been sunk or damaged in harbour by the bombing, so there'd be experienced men without sea billets.

By wartime standards Paul wasn't experienced at all. Since the submarine training course at Blyth he'd spent six months in a training boat, then the work-up months in *Ultra*. At the end of the work-up they'd done operational patrol in the North Sea—it was standard routine, a shake-down patrol—and in the course of it they'd sunk a U-boat, and that was the sum total of his submarine experience.

Woods said, watching the eighth Spitfire climb to join the others, "That'll be the first flight. Short break for refreshments now. They go in eights, I'm told." He asked Paul, "What's its name?"

"What?"

"This submarine, what's—"

"*Ultra.*"

Thornton proclaimed, looking up at the Spitfires, "Those are the only chaps who can be reasonably certain of getting anywhere *near* Malta."

The Spits had formed up, and were flying east. They'd be on the ground in Malta in about a couple of hours . . . But this ciphering character was, truly, a jerk. You could know the odds without going around shouting them . . . Brill murmured, as Thornton stalked away, "He's right, isn't he?"

"Is he? I guess I'm an optimist."

"You'd have to be, wouldn't you?" Woods, the gunner, made a face. "I mean, *submarines,* for God's sake."

A lot of people reacted in that way, because they didn't know about submarines, what it was like and how it got into your blood, how you'd have hated, now, to be anything but a submariner. It wasn't worth the effort of trying to explain. He asked Woods, instead, "D'you stay in this tub? Go back in her?"

"I stay in Malta. Relieving some character who'll make the trip home in her. Same with my blokes."

His soldiers, he meant. He had about a dozen of them to man the four-inch gun on the stern. As well as soldiers there were some naval DEMS ratings on board to look after a forty-millimetre Bofors—it was on this boat deck, in a raised steel nest abaft the funnel—and some Oerlikons. DEMS stood for Defensively Equipped Merchant Ships. Other extra personnel on board included Mackeson's staff—an RN signalman and a W/T operator. The same kind of set-up applied in all the other ships as well.

Brill pushed himself upright. "Anyone for a stroll?"

Woods declined. He had work to do, he said. Paul set off with the doctor, who'd been a medical student until very recently. He wondered, as they paced around the midships superstructure, up one side and down the other, how many miles of this deck he'd covered in the past week. "Taking passage" was a dull business, after the first day or so; hence the interest in watching something as repetitive as one fighter after another taking off from a distant aircraft carrier . . . He had a novel half-read down in his cabin, but he'd found that reading palled too. It was a combination of boredom and nervous anticipation, he thought, that prevented your mind really settling to anything.

That, and a sense of impatience, the fact that all he was really interested in was getting to the Malta flotilla and *Ultra.*

After a few circuits they stopped, and leaned on the timber rail at the after end of the boat deck. There were life-rafts here between the big grey-painted ventilators, and a ladder each side led down to the after-well deck and the hatches to numbers four and five holds. Three Jeeps and a truck with RAF markings were chocked and lashed down there between the hatch-covers; in the port-side gangway off-duty crewmen were squatting to throw dice. Brill offered Paul a cigarette: "Did old Mackeson say *three* generations of your people are at sea?"

"He missed one out. There's a sort of in-between that makes it up to four." He stooped, shielding a match for their cigarettes. Then, straightening, "There's me, my father, and the old guy who's a convoy commodore. That's the three. But also my father has a young half-brother called Jack. Young enough to be his son, but happens to be his half-brother—less than two years older than I am, for God's sake . . . Look, more Spits."

A second batch had begun to take off from the carrier. She was broad on the convoy's beam now as the block of merchantmen swung to the port leg of the zigzag. There was a white embroidery on the sea: not bad conditions, Paul realized, from a submariner's point of view, with that camouflage for the feather of a periscope and the swell too low to make depth-keeping difficult. What with that and the largely clear sky that would help the Luftwaffe . . . Then he noticed something else: that the spaces between destroyers in the outer screen were wider than they had been earlier. Counting, and allowing for similar spacing in the sectors he couldn't see, he thought there weren't more than a dozen destroyers out there altogether.

The others would be fuelling, presumably—as some had done yesterday—from the oilers that were following a few miles astern. There were two fleet oilers with their own destroyer escort, and Mackeson had told him they'd be turning back for Gibraltar tonight.

He swung around, leaned on the rail beside the doctor. Brill asked him, "Is this Jack relation in the RNVR, like you?"

"Is he hell. He was at Dartmouth. Lieutenant RN, now. He was in a cruiser that got sunk off Crete a year ago, but he got ashore and then worked with the partisans, guerrillas or whatever they call themselves.

There were soldiers on the run to be got out, and weapons and stuff to be brought in for the resistance effort, and Jack was in and out of the island a couple of times by caïque. Cloak-and-dagger stuff. They gave him a DSC for it—either for that or for whatever went on earlier."

"*Another* bloody hero."

Brill sounded disgusted. Paul smiled, looking at him. The doctor had a triangular-shaped face, pale and with rather large, dark eyes in it. A bit like Mickey Mouse, really. Paul's smile faded as he thought of telling him, *Jack Everard's a shit. If he's a hero, give me cowards* . . . Instead he said, "He's back in England now. Some small-ship job."

And preparing to take part, in whatever small ship it was, in some fantastically hazardous operation. In London a couple of months ago Jack had let Paul glean that much, then he'd clammed up. And turned his attention to quite different interests.

Jack Everard, Paul thought, was a twenty-four-carat bastard: and Mrs Fiona Gascoyne, who was tipped to marry Paul's father, was a bitch of roughly the same quality.

If his father had left the Mediterranean, Paul thought, he'd *have* to put it down in writing. When you were the only person who could tell him, and personal survival couldn't exactly be guaranteed, you couldn't just wait for a chance meeting.

But of all the lousy jobs . . .

"Those aren't Sea Hurricanes, surely?"

Brill was pointing. With the convoy on this leg of the zigzag you could see back through the lines of ships, past the oil tanker *Caracas Moon,* which was number three in column three, and the American freighter *Santa Eulalia* next to her, to the group of aircraft carriers and cruisers following astern. A fighter had just taken off from one of the carriers, and a second was following it into the air now.

He told Brill, "They're Grumman Wildcats."

You learnt aircraft recognition with your trousers down. "Own" and enemy aircraft shapes were displayed inside all lavatory doors in ships and training establishments, so you had them in front of your eyes for at least several minutes every day. He looked over at the ferry carrier, out on the beam: the second batch of Spitfires was high above her, formed up and departing. He said, "Funny to think those guys'll be in Malta in time for tea."

And we, he thought, had better be shuffling down for lunch. He glanced down to check the time, and his eyes were on his wrist-watch when the deep *thump* of an explosion reached them. It had a muffled quality: an explosion under water was his first guess. Depth charge, maybe?

A second one, now—a duplicate of the first. And smoke was spreading over one of the big carriers astern. A third explosion, and a fourth. Four torpedo hits on that one carrier? She was listing, smoke pouring up. He couldn't see where the cruiser had got to, the C-class anti-aircraft cruiser that had been with the carrier. Behind the smoke, maybe. He wished he had binoculars. He muttered, trying to make his eyes do binoculars' work, "Four hits . . . Christ, *look* at her!"

Brill was staring, gripping the rail. The smoke cleared enough to show the big ship right over on her side; then it drifted across the line of sight again like a curtain. All distant, soundless and somehow unreal: it was more like watching a film, a newsreel or something, than seeing something happening in real life. Over there, at this moment, men would be dying: burning, drowning. You leaned on a rail and watched it, because there wasn't anything else you could be doing.

Smoke clearing suddenly: and it had cleared, he saw, because the carrier had gone. Sunk—just like that . . . Other passengers were crowding to the rail and asking questions. Brill asked Paul, watching a swirl of destroyer activity back there, "How many men would there have been in her?"

"I don't know. More than a thousand." He added, "I guess a lot'll be picked up."

"God, let's *hope*—"

"Yeah." He thought, *Let's* . . . There were six hundred miles to go, and the battle had opened with the convoy losing about one third of its air defences.

CHAPTER THREE

· · ·

The Java Sea was a blue-tinted mirror reflecting heat, and the steel of the cruiser's bridge was hot to touch. Nick took his eyes off the ship astern and turned to face the leading seaman who'd been waiting for him here behind the lookout positions on the port side of *Defiant*'s bridge.

"Well, how's it going?"

Williams had a long, narrow jaw and a high, similarly narrow forehead. Deep-set brown eyes, rather close together, held Nick's steadily.

"Going on all right, sir."

"I thought we might have a chat, before we get too busy."

A smile . . . "Can't happen too soon, sir, far's I'm concerned."

"How d'you mean?"

"Well. Get a crack at the bastards this trip, won't we, sir?"

Nick had told them so, in a broadcast he'd made over the Tannoy. And he could understand Williams's personal desire to hit out, kill some Japanese . . . He said, "I've been thinking about it quite a lot—about your wife, I mean—and I keep coming to the same conclusion. I honestly think she *must* have got away. When they shut down the dockyard offices they'd have cleared out to Sumatra probably, then Batavia or Bandoeng."

Bandoeng, in the interior of Java behind Batavia, had been Wavell's headquarters and it was the Dutch headquarters now. Nick went on, "Then they'd have evacuated—civilians, surely—from the south coast. From Tjilatjap. The odds are she's in Ceylon now, or Australia. I'd guess Ceylon."

"She'd've left word for me, sir. I know that."

"*If* she'd had the slightest notion that you'd be back. But for all she could have known we might've been in Australia by that time. *I* couldn't have said for sure we were coming back."

"She'd still have left word, in case, like."

"She might not have been given time to. Anyway, who was left—to leave word with, I mean? Must have been panic stations by that time. You saw for yourself how it was ashore then."

Williams nodded. "Wish I never *had* seen it . . . I'd like to see it your way, sir, but—"

"Try allowing yourself to. You aren't helping her by torturing yourself—isn't that what it amounts to?"

"Padre said something like that, sir. But it's what's in your mind, not what you'd *like* in it. It's—well, seeing things like they *are*, sir."

"I think you should allow yourself to admit the possibility that you're wrong. Stop thinking, and just damn well hope. The way things are out here at the moment—well, for God's sake, it's not *only* you and your wife—"

"It is to me, sir."

It would be to me, too, if I thought Kate had been stuck in Singapore. By Christ, it would . . .

If she'd been there and disappeared, been left behind, he'd have gone half mad. Imagining it, he could admire Leading Seaman Williams's restraint. And there was substance for a different, personal reflection in that. If when you approached bedrock, the level of bare survival as a goal, it was B and not A who kept coming into your mind, didn't it tell you something?

If you let it?

Well, Kate was in this half of the world, and Fiona was ten thousand miles away. And Kate was an Army nurse who'd been on active service, she *could* have been in Singapore, so in any connection of that kind she was naturally the person you'd think of.

And here and now, in any case, it wasn't of much consequence. Williams's state of mind was, because Williams was one of about five hundred individuals in this ship for whose welfare he, Nick Everard, was responsible. He was one of five hundred moving parts of one machine.

Back in the bridge, he unslung his binoculars from the back of the high seat and put their strap over his head. There'd been no sign of an enemy yet, but there would be soon. Doorman had wirelessed a request for air support: Nick thought he might as well have asked Father Christmas for it. Some of these cruisers had carried spotter aircraft when they'd arrived out here, but they'd all been landed weeks ago. In some places if you gave the garrison an old seaplane you doubled the local air defences. But this force's first sight of the Japs' eastern assault group might well be an enemy spotter plane scouting ahead of their ships.

And none of these Allied ships had RDF, either.

Doorman had stationed the three British destroyers ahead of the cruisers, and he'd put the Americans and Dutch astern. The cruisers were in line ahead. With inter-ship communications as limited and slow as they were, it was the simplest formation for him to control. He was leading, in his flagship *de Ruyter;* then came *Exeter,* then *Houston, Perth, Defiant, Java.* So the admiral had the two heavier-gunned ships astern of him.

"Signal, sir."

Hobbs—"Schooly"—had brought this one up himself. Wanting a breath of air, no doubt—understandable, because all the below-decks compartments were stiflingly hot, and the plot below this bridge, where he did his coding and decoding, had the sun beating on its steel walls from dawn to sunset. Some ovens might be cooler . . . The signal was an English-language repeat of an answer to Doorman's request for air support. All available fighter aircraft had been sent to cover a torpedo-bomber strike against the Jap transports, the troop convoy whose escort was somewhere just over the horizon now. Nick could guess what was meant by "all available fighter aircraft"—half a dozen American-built Brewster Buffaloes. Slow, clumsy, easily out-manoeuvred by the Zekes. The Buffaloes hadn't been built for the tropics either, and in Malaya they'd suffered from carburettors that oiled up when their engines were gunned for take-off. To counter this, some bright RAF engineer designed a home-made filter stuffed with Tampax. The RAF bought up all the Tampax from all the chemists in Singapore, then, explaining that they needed it for Buffaloes.

He passed the signal back to Hobbs.

"Comfortable down there, are you?"

Schooly's sweat-running face creased in a smile. "No danger of frost-bite, sir."

Nick beckoned to Gant, as Hobbs left. He told the commander, "No air support is available to us."

"I *am* surprised, sir."

"At least we know that anything we see is hostile."

"Ah." Gant nodded. "That's a comfort."

"See that Haskins knows it, will you?"

Haskins was the captain of marines, and at action stations he controlled the ship's air defences. The paymaster lieutenant who'd had the job when Nick had taken command hadn't been too bright at it, so there'd been a reshuffle of some action duties. Haskins had a detachment of about fifty Royal Marines under him.

"Cup o' tea, sir?"

Able Seaman Gladwill, Nick's servant, was beside him with a tray of tea and biscuits. The china, Admiralty issue, was white with pink roses around the edges; Gladwill's thumbs, hooked over the ends of the tray, were spatulate and black-rimmed. He was a bird-fancier, and kept canaries in the lobby outside the cuddy. He muttered, as Nick got up on to his high seat, "Warming the bell a touch, sir, but I thought while the going's good, like."

Behind Nick and to his right, on the step at the binnacle, was Charles Rowley, a lieutenant-commander who was the ship's first lieutenant and senior watchkeeper. His shaggy brown hair needed cutting; grey eyes in a deeply tanned face were watching *Perth,* their next ahead. The sea was churned white but still quite flat here in the dead centre of the other ships' wakes: *Defiant* was so steady that the only danger to the tea in the cup was the old girl's shaking, the constant vibration in her steel.

There was a certain incongruity, to be sitting here sipping tea from flowered china when there was a fair certainty of being in action within the hour . . .

"Signal, sir."

It was the chief yeoman, this time, CPO Howell's ruddy complexion and prematurely white sideboards. The rest of his hair was shiny black. Howell had played rugger for the Navy at one time.

"Thank you, Chief Yeoman." He put down the cup with its awkward little handle, and now he read the signal. It duplicated a Dutch original announcing that the Jap troopships had turned away northeastward.

Only the convoy: not the cruisers and destroyers. The transports were being kept out of danger while the warship escort cleared a path for them. The report would probably have originated with the RAF torpedo-bombers that had been sent out earlier. It was a pity they had been, really.

There'd been one signal that he hadn't shown even to Bob Gant. It was an Intelligence report which had reached Doorman before they'd sailed from Surabaya yesterday, and Doorman had apprised his captains of it when they'd met on board the flagship. It had indicated that two Jap carrier divisions had been coming south towards this area and that one of them was thought to be steering for the Sunda Strait, presumably to pass through it and operate *south* of Java. If this was so, there'd be enemy surface and air patrols blocking any chance of escape south to Australia or northwest to Ceylon.

A buzzer sounded, and a light was flashing on the W/T office telephone. The chief yeoman had jumped to it, pushing a messenger aside. Now he swung round to face Nick.

"From *Electra,* sir—'Enemy in sight, bearing north!'"

He glanced round. Gladwill materialized, like a rubbery-faced genie, to remove the tray. Gant, who'd been smoking his pipe on the other side of the bridge, took it out of his mouth as he pivoted and Nick told him, "Close the hands up, Bob." The pipe had vanished. One of Gant's hands, unbidden, rested in the small of his back, on that damaged spine of his; the other was on the red-painted alarm button sending the morse letter "S"—"S" for surface action stations—reverberating through all the ship's compartments. Nick saw a string of bunting run to *Perth*'s yardarm: the flags were almost edge-on from this viewpoint but there was enough flutter in them for him to read them as flag "N" with the numerals 3-6-0 below it: "N" meaning "enemy in sight" and the numerals standing for the compass bearing, north. He told Rowley, who was still officer of the watch until Chevening arrived to take over, "Warn the engine-room." He saw Greenleaf, known as "Guns" but more formally as the PCO, principal control officer, and told him, "We're likely to be up against four cruisers and fourteen destroyers."

"Aye aye, sir." Lieutenant Greenleaf was a tubby, cheerful-looking man. He'd turned away, to climb up the ladder into the director control tower on the foremast. And Haskins, the marine, had arrived now neck-and-neck with Chevening. Moustached and burly, Haskins was also going up the ladder, to his ADP, air defence position, an open-topped platform below Toby Greenleaf's director tower. Other men, the crews of both positions, were also scrambling aloft.

Chevening had taken over from Rowley, who'd gone below to take charge of damage control. All through the compartments certain doors and hatches would be shut and clipped, hoses unrolled, emergency lighting checked, fire-fighting gear set ready.

A telephone buzzed beside the torpedo sight, and Lieutenant-Commander Swanson, arriving in the bridge at that moment, skidded across to snatch it up. Swanson was blond and bearded, a short and stocky, pugilistic-looking man. With the telephone in one hand he used the other to remove his cap, substituting the tin hat that had been hanging below the sight, and displaying in the process the bald, sun-tanned back of his head. He listened to a report, then hung up. He told Nick, "All tubes' crews closed up, sir." He had twelve torpedo-tubes, in four triple mountings. He asked Nick, "Depth charges, sir?"

"Yes. Clear the traps."

Depth charges in the chutes aft were a danger, if an enemy shell should land on them. Mr North, the torpedo gunner, would set their pistols to "safe" now and release them. They'd be sinking harmlessly towards the bottom as *Java* passed over them.

CPO Howell suggested, "Battle ensigns, sir?"

"Not yet." Only the destroyer *Electra* had seen the enemy as yet, and *Electra* was a good five miles ahead.

"Flagship's going round to port, sir."

Chevening reported it. Nick looked ahead and saw the turn beginning, *de Ruyter*'s rather upright-looking, single-funnelled profile lengthening as her rudder gripped the sea and hauled her round. Doorman would keep the ships in this formation: all they'd have to do was follow where he led, and there'd be no need of signals. It would be limiting, though, on his choice of tactics . . . *Exeter* was following him round now. You could guess from this change of course that Doorman must have sighted the enemy and that the Jap course was something like south-westward: *de Ruyter* had steadied on three hundred and twenty degrees.

Houston, two-funnelled, and at just over nine thousand tons nearly twice *Defiant*'s size, had put her helm over; that rather strange-looking flare-topped foc'sl was slanting into *Exeter*'s white track, gleaming in the sunshine. Greenleaf reported by telephone, "Main armament closed up and cleared away, sir."

"Very good." From his high seat, Nick reached to put the telephone back on its hook. Greenleaf and his crew up there, with stereoscopic binoculars and stabilized telescopic sights, would be straining for a first glimpse of the enemy; but there were still ships ahead, and funnel-haze, to obscure their view. It would be clearer when *Perth* had turned, though, and she was swinging now as the American ahead of her steadied on the new course.

Sure enough, the director telephone was calling. Nick reached for it: "Captain."

"Enemy in sight, sir. Four cruisers: two heavy, and two smaller. And two groups of destroyers, roughly six in each but it's hard to count them yet. Bearing three-five-five—"

He heard Chevening order, "Port fifteen." Greenleaf was continuing his report: at this extreme range he was only looking at the enemy's upperworks, masts and fighting-tops above the curve of the horizon, and it would be a while before even the eight-inch ships, *Exeter* and *Houston,* could be in gun-range of the enemy.

"Signal, *speed twenty-five,* sir!"

Flag "G," numerals two and five: Nick said, "Very good." Chevening's face was already at the voicepipe, ordering the increase in revolutions, and it was Leading Seaman Williams, down in the wheelhouse, who'd be passing that order to the engine-room. Twenty-five knots was two knots short of this ship's maximum.

Japanese heavy cruisers, Nick thought, would have eight-inch guns. Almost for sure. So the forces were fairly evenly matched. Except that the Japs, with more modern ships, would have a speed advantage. Ten or twelve minutes, he worked out roughly, would bring the heavy cruisers into range of each other. *Defiant* and the other six-inch ships would be inside the Jap cruisers' range without any hope of hitting back. There'd be a frustrating period to live through, until they got in closer.

Bob Gant said, without taking the binoculars from his eyes, "There, sir. See their foretops."

Chevening was steadying her on the new course. Nick had his glasses at about forty degrees on the bow, and he'd got them suddenly, the fighting-tops of two heavy cruisers in line ahead. None of the smaller ships was visible yet from this level: but all right, he thought, here we go . . . He lowered his glasses and called over to Howell, "Battle ensigns, chief yeoman."

"Battle ensigns, hoist!"

Two of them had been bent on and ready on the flag-deck, and PO Ruddle was passing the same order aft by telephone. White ensigns ran swiftly to both mastheads, to the mainmast gaff and the port yardarm.

You put up that many in case one or more should be shot away. With four ensigns flying, there'd have to be a hell of a lot of damage done before the ship displayed *no* colours. *Perth's* were already hoisted, he saw. Astern, *Java* was settling into line; her slender foretop made the twin funnels look more massive than they were. He checked the time: eleven minutes past four. Any minute now, someone would try the range. He reached for his tin hat, glancing round at the same time to see that everyone else was wearing them: his own helmet was blue with four gold stripes on it, artistry by AB Gladwill.

Greenleaf called again on the DCT telephone. "Enemy has a seaplane up, sir. Green six-five at the moment, looks like it's working its way round astern of us."

In a minute, he'd got it in the circle of his binoculars. It looked from here like a black, very slow-moving mosquito, so slow that even one of the cranky old Buffaloes could have knocked it down. It was going to be a great advantage to the Jap gunners to have a spotter wirelessing fall-of-shot to them. He looked round at the OD who manned a group of voicepipes, including one to the ADP: "Tell Captain Haskins there's a seaplane moving down the starboard side and if it comes into range I want it shot down."

The communications number was bawling it up the pipe. When he'd finished Nick added, "Tell him it's worth a bottle of gin."

His gin was quite safe, he thought. Unfortunately. That seaplane would keep its distance, if its pilot had any sense.

"Enemy's opened fire, sir!"

Sixteen minutes past four. His eyes were on his watch when *Exeter's* guns crashed out a salvo. Two seconds later, *Houston* fired. Cordite smoke and smell drifted back along the line of ships. Nick called the DCT and asked Greenleaf what the range was.

"Twenty-six thousand yards, sir."

Thirteen miles . . .

Shells scrunched overhead. Looking out to port, he saw the splashes rise like white pillars that turned grey as they hung momentarily and then collapsed. They'd fallen well over and quite a distance ahead, probably too far right for line. But with that seaplane spotting for them the enemy gunners wouldn't need to get their salvoes in line before they could correct for range; without a spotter you did have to, because until you had the splashes in line with the target you couldn't tell whether they were short or over.

Exeter fired again. As the noise faded, Bob Gant began, "Flagship's—"

Houston flung off a broadside. Gant was pointing, and Nick saw *de Ruyter* swinging, starting a turn to port. He'd be weaving, perhaps, "snaking the line," which was a way of taking avoiding action—and confusing the enemy's observations—while still keeping the ships in line ahead. He'd hardly be turning parallel to the enemy at this extreme range—when only two of his ships could use their guns?

Being shot at wasn't fun. Being shot at when you couldn't shoot back was extremely trying.

But perhaps there was some wisdom in it: if the enemy line had been in a position to "cross his T"—bring their full broadsides to bear on the flagship as one narrow, bow-on target—Doorman would have seen that he'd be running into trouble, and this turn would have avoided it. More Jap shells: the whistling, rushing noise of them. They went into the sea well over again, but not as far over as the first lot. Doorman was turning towards the fall of shot, which was a well-used, logical tactic: the enemy would be shortening his range setting now, while his target veered out towards the range at which the last salvo fell. *Exeter* and *Houston* had both fired, *Exeter* well out to port now in the flagship's wake; Doorman had gone round by about twenty degrees and he seemed to have steadied on that course. *Houston* had put her helm over, turning her bow into the drift of smoke from *Exeter*'s last salvo.

The flagship wasn't weaving, though. Doorman did intend, apparently, to stay out at this range. Whatever reasons he might have for it, one's own strong inclination was to get in closer, into the fight. Nick held his glasses on *de Ruyter*'s stern, hoping to see it move, see the

Dutchman begin a turn towards the enemy. He was steady though, holding that course. Then there was a flash and a burst of smoke somewhere amidships: the flagship had been hit. Other shells splashed in short. Then *Exeter* fired, and *Houston,* and a yellowish haze of cordite smoke hid the flagship. *Houston* steadied now, *Perth* turning astern of her. Nick glanced round and saw Chevening ready to order *Defiant's* wheel over. The DCT telephone called, and Gladwill passed it to him: Greenleaf reported, "Destroyer attack developing, sir. Six of them have turned towards us on green five-oh."

"You may get a target or two, then."

"Certainly wouldn't mind one, sir."

If Doorman didn't order *his* destroyers out to meet the attack, and let them foul the range. Nick was thinking that if he'd been running this show he'd have divided the cruiser force, kept the two heavy-gunned ships at about this range and sent the other four in closer, probably in two separate groups of two ships each, making three in all. Not only so as to get their guns into the action, but also to divide the Jap gunners' attention. The snag was, of course, that communications weren't up to coping with any complicated manoeuvring: Doorman would be scared of losing control. If there'd been a prearranged plan and a chance to practise it, though, that would have been the answer, and in Doorman's shoes one would have chanced it anyway.

He wasn't sending the destroyers out, at any rate. *Exeter* and *Houston* were shooting steadily, and about twice a minute an enemy salvo splashed down. There'd only been that one hit, on *de Ruyter,* so far as one could tell from *Defiant,* and despite the spotting aircraft hovering on the quarter now the fall of shot seemed haphazard. Whether the enemy ships had been hit at all one couldn't know. Nick got up higher, with his heels jammed in the strut that linked the seat's legs, and trained his glasses on the bow where the destroyer attack was supposed to be coming in. The enemy heavy cruisers were easy to see, and one light cruiser's upperworks were in sight astern of them. The smaller ships would be flanking the big ones, he guessed, one on each quarter.

"Captain, sir!"

Director telephone again: Greenleaf said, "Destroyers closing on green eight-five, sir. Permission to open fire?"

"Open fire."

Perth did so at that moment. Splashes from Jap eight-inch shells lifted the sea astern. In the DCT Greenleaf said into the mouthpiece of his headset, "All guns with full charge and SAP load, load, load!" "SAP" meant semi-armour-piercing, as opposed to "HE" for high-explosive. He told his team, "Target the right-hand destroyer." On his left Mr Nye, the gunner, began passing information over his telephone to CPO Hughes, chief gunner's mate, down in the transmitting station. He was giving him figures for enemy course and speed. Mr Nye was the rate officer, and on his estimates the rate of opening or closing range was calculated. All kinds of other data was reaching the TS and being set on dials on the Admiralty fire-control table, which would transmit its own conclusions to the guns. Below Greenleaf the director layer and trainer held their telescope sights on the enemy, the foot of his foremast being the standard aiming point, but the guns themselves would be aimed-off by the amount that had been computed from all the facts and figures fed into the machine in the TS, which was a tank-like cell of a compartment well below the waterline. Greenleaf was watching his gun-ready box, and when he saw the lights in it all glowing, a light for each of the six gun mountings, he ordered "Shoot!" Firegongs double-clanged as the director layer, with his eye still pressed to the rubber eyepiece of his telescopic sight, squeezed his trigger.

Defiant's six 6-inch guns fired: cordite smoke washed back along her decks, curled mustard-coloured over the white wake. All six guns were on the centre-line: two for'ard of the bridge, one for'ard and one aft of the twin funnels, and two aft. They were guns with shields, not turrets. *Perth* had fired again. Then the deeper rashes of broadsides from the bigger ships ahead of her. And Nick had the oncoming destroyers in his glasses, small, jumpy images in the heat-haze low on a dazzling sea, mirage-like and distant. He saw shell-splashes momentarily super-imposed, a small flickering of white that vanished as suddenly as it had appeared. *Defiant* and *Perth* both fired again.

A pressure against his forearm was Gladwill offering him the director telephone. He took it and said into it, "Captain."

"They're turning away, sir. I think they've fired torpedoes."

At that range? Over the line he heard the PCO's order: "Shoot!" Then, as the echoes of the salvo died, "Check, check, check!"

It was said that the Japanese had torpedoes called "Long Lance" which were far better than the Royal Navy's, but however marvellous they might be they'd been wasted by being fired from such a distance. Particularly as Doorman was now altering course again. Nick hadn't been aware of it happening, but looking astern he could see the elbow in the wake and *Java* following *Defiant* round.

Exeter and *Houston* were still engaged in their long-range action. And Doorman's new course was still more or less parallel to the enemy's . . . Might Nelson, Nick wondered, have used the excuse of that torpedo attack to turn his own ship towards the enemy? The move might have been excused, explained, if with his blind eye he'd seen torpedo tracks, and turned to comb them. But *Java* wouldn't have followed Nick Everard; mightn't even have followed Horatio Nelson. And Waller of *Perth* would have had no option but to stick to *Houston's* tail, so there'd have been only one advancing ship for the enemy to concentrate his guns on. So—no, Nelson would *not* have. It was still galling to be kept out here, non-combatant. It wouldn't improve the ship's company's morale, either. Earlier in the afternoon, soon after the force had turned and headed back out to sea from Surabaya, he'd talked to his crew over the Tannoy broadcast system, explaining what was happening and leaving no doubt that *Defiant* would soon be in action. The enemy force was about equal to their own, he'd said, and with a bit of luck and straight shooting they ought to wipe the floor with them.

There'd been cheering on the messdecks. Some of them might be wondering now what there'd been to cheer about.

What might Doorman be hoping to achieve? To have *Exeter's* and *Houston's* guns knock out the big ships, leaving the rest—and the convoy—as easy meat?

It wasn't happening. The time was just on 5 PM, they'd been in action for three-quarters of an hour, and the only hit Nick had seen had been that one on *de Ruyter*. He asked Greenleaf over the telephone, "Have you seen any hits on the enemy?"

"I think so, sir. Two earlier on, and one a minute ago. Can't be positive, but—"

"All right." He took the phone from his ear, but Greenleaf caught him with a sharp "Captain, sir . . ." He reported, "Looks like a new destroyer attack starting from fine on the bow."

Enemy shells splashed down, short. *De Ruyter* at once began a turn to starboard. *Exeter* had loosed off another broadside: and now *Houston* . . . Nick heard shells arriving, that distinctive rushing, ripping sound . . .

Exeter was hit.

She'd been out to starboard, following the flagship round and far enough out to be in sight from *Defiant*. He saw the shell strike, the flash and puff of debris and dust as it went in, and then the explosion, eruption inside the ship. *Exeter's* helm went over the other way, reversing the direction of the turn.

Houston's guns had fired; and now she was following *Exeter,* turning to port although *de Ruyter* was going the other way, had steadied after a swing to starboard. *Exeter,* Nick realized, was slowing, losing way quite fast; he could see her bow-wave dropping as speed fell off. *Houston* must have recognized his mistake and also seen the danger of ramming the British cruiser, and she was keeping full rudder on, in order to turn inside her, under her stern. *Perth* was following *Houston*.

Shambles . . . Nick was at the binnacle, displacing Chevening, who moved to the director telephone to maintain contact with the DCT.

"Starboard five."

"Starboard five, sir . . . Five of starboard wheel on, sir!"

Just enough wheel to take her clear of all that mess. An enemy salvo thumped into the sea, short. He called down, "Midships." *De Ruyter* had held on. *Houston* and *Perth* had turned with *Exeter,* but they should not have. Nothing had been all that good so far, but now it had become much worse. Only two ships had been in action, and one of them had been crippled while the other had waltzed off on her own. Another salvo scorched over and raised spouts on *Defiant's* bow. He called down, "Port ten." He'd passed clear of the scrimmage and now he had to get her up astern of the admiral. *Exeter* seemed to have stopped; destroyers were circling her, laying smoke to hide her from the enemy, whose rate of fire seemed to have increased. Those were the American destroyers: the three British ones were ahead and on the flagship's bow to port, while a Dutchman was moving up on the engaged side—to starboard. Shellspouts lifted in the gap between *Exeter* and a smoke-laying American destroyer. The smoke would have very little effect, Nick realized, when the spotter was airborne and well above it; but perhaps, in this sort of mess, every contribution helped . . . He said into the voicepipe, "Midships."

Houston had extricated herself from the scrum: she'd opened fire again. *Sloan,* Jim Jordan's ship, was one of those laying smoke.

"Steady!"

"Steady, sir . . . Two-six-five, sir."

"Steer that."

It would be suffocating in the wheelhouse. The heat came out of the voicepipe in a stream you could have smoked a herring in. Flagship going round to port . . .

"Destroyers attacking from ahead, sir!"

Chevening had that report from Greenleaf in the tower. It might account for the flagship's sharp swing away: Doorman would be turning so as to bring his guns to bear. There were ships all over the place: *Houston* still firing steadily but *Exeter* right out of it, away off on the quarter and wreathed in smoke, destroyers standing by her. He stooped to the voicepipe: "Port fifteen." It was necessary to cut the revs too, so as to drop back and let *Houston* get in astern of *de Ruyter*. Enemy shells fell in a clump to starboard; *Houston* was shooting over her port quarter as she came up into the re-forming line. Chevening put a hand over the mouthpiece of the DCT telephone: "PCO requests permission to engage destroyers on bearing 330, sir!"

A glance checked that bearing. "Open fire." Into the voicepipe: "Midships."

"Midships, sir . . . Wheel's amidships, sir!"

Defiant's guns let rip, over her quarter. *Perth* edging in astern of the American. *Exeter* was under way again, steering southeast with a Dutch destroyer making smoke astern of her. Nick called down for increased revs, to maintain station now on *Perth:* the Australian had opened fire, joining *Defiant* in discouraging the Jap destroyer attack. *Java* was in action too. Chevening reported, "Enemy destroyers have turned away, sir." They were still being shot at, anyway, but if they'd turned away you could bet they'd have fired their torpedoes on the swing. He was thinking that, and looking round at the positions of other ships, when he saw a torpedo hit a Dutch destroyer out on *Defiant's* beam. A column of dirty water shot up over her, then smoke rose in a cloud to hide her. He heard the *boom* of it, and when the smoke dissipated he saw she'd gone. A Jap salvo fell short of *Houston:* the course was northeast now, Doorman leading his surviving cruisers across the line of *Exeter's* retreat. Destroyers were still laying smoke, but only *Houston* was firing. Chevening told Nick, "PCO reports destroyer targets obscured, sir." And CPO Howell reported from the W/T office telephone, "The admiral's ordered our three destroyers to attack with torpedoes, sir."

The three British destroyers were *Encounter, Electra* and *Jupiter.* But they were widely dispersed: one a long way off on the beam, one moving over to look for survivors from the torpedoed Dutchman, and one close astern. All three were turning now, bow-waves lifting and foam piling under their sterns as they built up speed to obey Doorman's order. Widely spaced as they were, though, the attack would amount to three individual charges, which was not at all a realistic destroyer tactic. Doorman should have given them time to concentrate and make a coordinated attack. Nick thought, knowing precisely as a destroyer man himself how it would be for them, *He's throwing them away* . . .

Exeter was well clear now, retiring at half speed on a course that would take her to Surabaya, with one Dutch destroyer to keep her company. With her departure the odds had worsened: in the long-range fight it was now one—*Houston*—against two.

The Jap commander seemed no keener to get to grips than Doorman was. He'd be thinking about his convoy of troop transports, of course: his job first and foremost was to protect them, get them to the Java coast and see they got their troops ashore. If he lost his cruisers he'd lose the convoy too: so his plan would be to hold Doorman off, damage him if possible but only at minimal risk to his own ships. While Doorman's thoughts would also be concentrated on the need to destroy that convoy; and he could only achieve it by remaining afloat and intact, so he wasn't keen to take risks either. On the other hand this so-called Striking Force didn't have the speed to get round the enemy and find the convoy: the speed advantage was on the Japs' side, not Doorman's.

Doorman should have split his force, and gone for bust. He'd had no luck for the simple reason that he'd taken no chances. On the other hand, it would be starting to get dark, before long: in the dark, if he got lucky and really chanced his arm, it might just be possible to slip past these Japs, find the transports.

"Pilot. Ask—"

An explosion, some distance astern. Nick's first thought was for *Java*, but it was farther away than that. Chevening had the DCT telephone at his ear: nose like a marline spike under the tin hat's rim as he looked downwards, listening. Now he'd pushed the telephone back on to its hook. He told Nick, "*Electra's* sunk, sir. The other two are rejoining."

And Doorman was turning to starboard: leading them southward, maintaining his distance from the enemy. Nick thought, *Turn towards the bastards, not away. Go in and support those poor bloody destroyers.* He thought it during one slow blink. With his eyes open again and no emotion showing in his face he told Chevening, "You'd better check on how the plot's going, pilot. Put on a good DR while you're about it." He looked at Gant. "Keep an ear open to the tower meanwhile, Bob?"

"Aye aye, sir."

CPO Howell reported, "Admiral's ordered the American destroyers to attack, sir!"

Houston ripped out a broadside, thunderous over her quarter and some of the blast-effect coming back along the line of cruisers. She'd been in action for the best part of two hours now and her ammunition was likely to be getting low. A messenger standing near the W/T telephone jumped to it as it buzzed. He answered "Bridge!" Listening, he glanced round as the chief yeoman moved towards him asking, "What's it about, then?" The messenger said into the telephone, "Aye aye." He reported, "Orders to the American destroyers cancelled, sir. They've been told to lay smoke instead."

Now it was dark and they'd lost contact with the enemy. The cruisers were following their Dutch admiral northwestward. Doorman had turned east under cover of the smoke-screen, and after about five miles he'd led them round to port, back up towards where the enemy had been—but almost certainly would not be now.

Hoping to slip past them, probably, and find the important target, the troop convoy.

At seven Nick handed over the conning of the ship to Chevening; he checked the plot and the latest signals, and then settled down on his high seat. Doorman, he thought, could only be looking for the troopers now: but the same thing would be equally obvious to the Jap admiral. The convoy wouldn't be in easy reach and it wouldn't be unprotected either.

Houston had reported that she had very little ammunition left.

Gladwill asked him, "Tea, sir? Coffee? Kye?"

"Coffee, please." Gladwill made excellent coffee. Bob Gant came back. You could smell him—or rather his pipe—before you saw or heard him. Nick called after Gladwill, "And a cup for the commander, too."

"Much obliged, sir . . . Any idea what we're up to now?"

"Looking for the invasion convoy, I imagine. Trusting to luck."

"We might be about due for some, at that."

They'd certainly achieved nothing yet, beyond delaying the assault on eastern Java. It could only be a temporary delay, with a weak force trying to impede a strong one, which was the situation here. Before long Java would be attacked and occupied. Any Allied ships still afloat by that time would have no base or fuelling facility, or much prospect of escape. The Java Sea would have become a Japanese lake entirely surrounded by Jap bases in Jap-occupied territory.

"Flagship's going round to starboard, sir!"

The report came from Swanson, the torpedo officer. He'd settled himself in the starboard for'ard corner of the bridge, as an extra lookout.

"Your coffee, sir."

"Put it down there, would you?" He had his glasses on the ships ahead. He called over his shoulder to Chevening, "Follow round, pilot."

"Aye aye, sir."

No difficulty in following, in the phosphorescent wakes. Doorman brought them round to a course just south of east, reckoning, Nick supposed, that he'd come far enough north to have by-passed the enemy cruisers and that a cast to the east might bring him up against the convoy which could have been disposed a few miles astern of them.

Could have. Could have been any damn place at all. Could have been on the Java coast by now. You could be sorry for Doorman. In Doorman's boots you might well be sorry for yourself.

An hour felt like two hours, dragging by.

"Captain, sir?"

Schooly, up from the plot with a decoded signal. Nick heard the voice of Leading Seaman Williams reporting up the voicepipe to Chevening that the ship was steady on the course he'd ordered. Williams would have been giving the chief quartermaster frequent spells on the wheel down there: at least that little oven of a wheelhouse would be cooling off by this time . . . He told Hobbs, "Read it to us, will you?"

To himself and Gant, he meant. He didn't want to spoil his night vision by going to the chart table with it. Hobbs said quietly, "It's a Most Immediate, sir, to the effect that the enemy has reinforced his eastern assault force. Cruiser and destroyer reinforcements, it says, but no details other than that."

"All right. Thank you."

The Japanese eastern assault force was the group this force had been sparring with. Nothing was getting any better.

Darkness like warm velvet. The ship's rattles, her engines' thrumming, the rush of sea along her sides and wind-noise in stays and shrouds, voices night-quiet at the back of the bridge where lookouts were being changed. It was a familiar backing to one's thoughts, to the hours of waiting and expectancy and the tension that ran through them, in your nerves and brain. It had always been like this but tonight there was more, there was a feeling of being trapped, an instinct that if the night lasted long enough to end as all the other nights had done—with daylight—then the bars of the trap would be plain to see, whichever way you looked . . . He caught a whiff of pipe-smoke: Gant was still near him, propped against the side of the bridge with binoculars at his eyes. Nick asked him, "If you were in Doorman's place, Bob, what would you be doing?"

"The answer's rather vulgar, sir."

"Seriously."

"Well." Gant moved closer, and answered in a murmur that only Nick could have heard. He said, "I'd make a dash for Surabaya, fill up with oil, then go flat-out for the Sunda Strait. Hoping to get through before they block it. Sunda or Lombok."

It was a programme that might be hard to fault, Nick thought. But it was also, for the time being, impractical; while at any later time—as Gant had rightly pointed out—it would be impossible. He said, "Doorman can't do it, unfortunately. He's a Dutchman, and the Dutch have said they'll defend Java to the last man."

"Just our luck, sir, isn't it?"

"Aircraft over us, sir!"

He'd heard it too, that throbbing engine sound. Then a flare broke overhead, a sudden glimmer that expanded to flood the sea and the ships on it with blindingly white light.

He had the DCT telephone in his hand and he was asking Greenleaf whether he could see anything from up there. The thought in his mind being that the ships from which the flare-dropper was operating might be close at hand.

"Horizon's clear, sir."

The engine drone faded. But the pilot would be using his radio, triumphantly telling his master, the Jap admiral, what he'd found and where. Nick wished to God he had RDF in *Defiant.* Even destroyers were getting sets now. *Defiant* was well overdue for refit: if her docking hadn't been delayed she'd have been fitted with one by this time. All new-building and refitting ships were getting it. The Americans called it "Radar."

Moonrise would be in about an hour. Well—an hour and a half . . . But if that flyer could keep them marked with occasional flares till then, they'd be tracked right through the night.

Perth, ahead, ploughed on, floodlit. *Houston,* gleaming as if she had snow on her decks but with a slant of black shadow across her after-part as the flare drifted lower on the bow and silhouetted her, blocked any sight of the flagship beyond her. *Java*'s bow-on shape, astern, was low and solid-looking. He could see two of the American destroyers: there were two on each quarter and one right astern, and the two surviving British ones were out ahead.

The flare dwindled like fading candle-light as it approached the sea; then it was out and you were blind, night vision lost. You could as well have had your head in a bucket.

"Can't hear it now. Can you, Bob?"

Gant was back from the after end of the bridge, where he'd been exhorting the lookouts to greater efforts. He paused, listening . . . Then he nodded. "I'm afraid I can, sir."

Nothing anyone could do about it. That was the worst, the sense of impotence. Having located them, it was possible that the Jap airman would be able to see the ships' phosphorescent wakes and have no need of more flares. In any case he'd have counted and classified the ships, reported their course and speed. It was like being blindfolded in a room full of clear-sighted enemies.

"Can't hear it now, sir."

"Flagship's altering to starboard!"

Chevening had seen it, from the far side of the bridge, and he was telling Rowley, the first lieutenant, who'd taken over from him at the binnacle. Chevening had been down in the plot for the last half-hour. Nick put his glasses up again, watched *de Ruyter*'s black profile growing as she swung out.

"How far have we run east, pilot?"

"Ten miles, sir."

Doorman might be hoping to get lost again, while the Jap airman wasn't looking. *Houston* turning now: the flagship had steadied on a southerly course. Nick asked Chevening, "How far are we now from the Surabaya Strait?"

"Forty miles, sir."

Two hours' run, say. But they were about to steer south, and the course for Surabaya would be more like southeast. The enemy troop convoy and the augmented cruiser force covering it could be north, south, east or west by this time: but the Jap admiral knew precisely where this squadron was. He could keep his transports well out of the way, and send his cruisers hunting—probably in more than one pack, now he had more of them. Nick thought again that he didn't envy Rear-Admiral Doorman his job.

Perth was in her turn, and Rowley would be putting *Defiant*'s helm over in a minute. The two American destroyers on the port quarter would be increasing speed, and the pair to starboard slowing, in order to maintain station through the turn. Doorman would have passed an alter-course signal by light, probably, to *Jupiter* and *Encounter* ahead of him.

Behind him, Nick heard Rowley's low-voiced order, "Starboard fifteen." And then, sickeningly, the drone of an aircraft engine. *Defiant* was heeling to her rudder when the flare broke, high up and ahead.

Bob Gant said, "Suppose our best hope's for the bugger to run out of petrol."

But if he did, Nick thought, there'd be another to take his place. And for that matter, what about these destroyers running out of fuel?

Cat and mouse: a seedy mouse, and a cat that knew exactly what it was doing.

At 9 PM, five miles off the Java coast, Doorman led them round to starboard: westward. At the same time he detached the American destroyers with orders to put in to Surabaya. *Sloan* had reported engine defects from a near-miss, and they were all dangerously short of oil. The Combined Striking Force now had only two destroyers, the British pair.

There'd been no flares dropped, and no sound of aircraft, since about 8:30. With any luck that snooper *had* been forced to go home and refuel, and it was just possible he'd have thought they were retiring to Surabaya. Doorman, Nick guessed, would be hoping for just that.

"Kye, sir?"

Petty Officer Ruddle, yeoman of signals, was offering him a mug of cocoa. "Compliments of the communications department, sir."

"Thank you, yeoman."

It was thick, strong, sweet and hot. Thick enough to make one suspect there'd been a little custard powder mixed into the paste of cocoa, condensed milk and sugar. It was an old sailor's trick, aimed at producing a mug in which a spoon would stand vertically without support. The matelot's ideal "kye" would also be laced with rum: this brew was non-alcoholic, but in all other respects distinctly *Cordon Bleu*.

"You wouldn't get kye like this at the Savoy, yeoman."

"Ah—thank you, sir!"

This very night there'd be people dining and dancing at the Savoy. It was a peculiar thought, from here in the Java Sea and at this moment. He found a picture suddenly in his mind of Fiona, Fiona dancing in the arms of—he asked himself, angered by the quick flare of jealousy which was quite irrational, *Why shouldn't she dance with anyone she pleases?*

She always had gone out with anyone she wanted to go out with. She'd never made any bones about it; since her rich and much older husband had died and thus released her from a marriage in which she'd felt trapped and miserable, she hadn't wanted or pretended to be a one-man girl. It had suited him well enough, for a time. Then, about a year ago, or a bit more than that, both his and her feelings had begun to change: hers had changed, for instance, to the extent that dancing and dining was about all she *would* do, with other men. At least, this was what she'd implied, what he thought she'd implied . . . But in black and white, he'd committed himself, and she hadn't—not as unequivocally as he had. There'd been one letter which as he remembered it could have been taken for commitment. But it could have been interpreted less positively too—knowing Fiona, and not having the letter now to look at again and reassess. He didn't have it because it had gone down in his destroyer *Tuareg,* halfway between Malta and Alexandria.

She'd have implied that change of attitude rather than made any clear statement of it, he realized, because to be more forthright about it would have been to admit how she'd been handling her life up to that point, and it would have been out of character for Fiona to have made any such admission. This would account for the element of vagueness, and it had allowed him to accept it as meaning what he thought she'd meant. By that time he'd known the Australian girl, Kate Farquharson, but not as well as he'd known her a few months later. He'd never told Kate that he was in love with her. He'd wanted to, but Fiona had got in the way of it, twisted his tongue and made him feel stupid to be in such a mess. Now—well . . . He thought, training his glasses slowly across the hazy line of the horizon on the bow, that in present circumstances it wasn't likely to make a pennyworth of difference to anyone at all. Perhaps this very fact was what allowed one to look at it squarely and recognize one's own blunder.

Blunders, plural. He couldn't claim to have made any roaring success of his emotional life. He'd done a fairly good job for the Navy, off and on, but he'd done very little for Nick Everard. In the personal sense—facing it *very* squarely—very little for anyone.

And *that* kind of thinking didn't help much, either.

At 9:20 they were ten miles offshore, north of a place on the Java coast called Tuban. The course was two hundred and ninety degrees. Chevening, just up from another visit to the plot, identified a dark shadow of land on the bow as Aur Aur Point, or rather high ground just inland of it. If they held to this course they'd be passing within four miles of the headland.

At 9:25 an explosion, ahead and to port, shattered the recent quiet. Greenleaf told Nick over the DCT telephone, "It's *Jupiter,* sir. A mine, I think." There was flashing ahead, the flagship signalling either to the stricken *Jupiter* or to the other destroyer, *Encounter.* But there were ships between *Defiant* and the flashing light, and the snatches of it that one saw weren't readable. The squadron held on, at twenty-five knots. Bob Gant and Swanson were on the port side of the bridge. Chevening was taking over at the binnacle from Rowley, who was going down to his damage control headquarters. Swanson muttered, with glasses at his eyes, "She's sinking . . ."

"Flagship's altering course to starboard, sir."

That dark patch—on the beam now as they passed—wasn't a ship at all, it was smoke. Broken water gleamed there too: and—boats? He had time for no more than a quick look, because he had to know what was happening ahead. All he'd seen had been vague and smoke-wrapped, and they'd passed it now, swept past and left it on the quarter. He heard Swanson ask, "D'you reckon those are boats, sir, or floats?" He was asking Gant: but the cruisers and the one remaining destroyer were turning north, not even *Encounter* was being allowed to stop for survivors.

If that had been a mine there'd as likely as not be a whole field of them, and Doorman was right not to risk another ship in it. Particularly if *Jupiter*'s people had got boats or floats away, and with the Java coast in easy distance. But another passing thought was that if there was a minefield here it would be a Dutch one and it would have been laid in the last forty-eight hours. Didn't the Dutch tell their admirals where mines were being laid?

Doorman was steering north, with *Houston* already settled astern of the flagship and *Perth* turning now. *Jupiter* had been a fine, modern destroyer, with a complement of nearly two hundred men. Launched as recently as 1939. And now this "Striking Force" had just one destroyer. The enemy assault group had had fourteen, and had since been reinforced with more.

He thought of Jim Jordan's musings a few days ago: *however . . .*

They lost *Encounter* half an hour later.

The moon had come up, and by chance Doorman had led his ships into an area of sea dotted with survivors from the Dutch destroyer which had been torpedoed during the action earlier. He ordered *Encounter* to pick them up and then take them down to Surabaya. The five cruisers continued northward, in line ahead and with no destroyers to scout for them now, across a moon-washed sea. Moon to starboard, still low but silvery-bright.

Pitching slightly: *Perth*'s quartermaster had let her swing off course, and as she turned back to regain station *Defiant* had the ridges of the Australian cruiser's wash to plough through. Her bow slammed into them, one after another in quick succession, and after each impact spray swept back across the foc's'l and rattled on the gunshields. Then she was through it, settled again, and *Perth* was back in station dead ahead.

"Time now?"

"10:29, sir."

He wondered what Kate was doing: whether she was still at home, or working in some military hospital again by now. The hospitals would be busy, he guessed, with wounded who'd been lucky enough to be brought out of places the Japs had over-run. Kate's home was a ranch in the west of Australia, not far inland from Freemantle. That was the address he'd been using for his letters. He was closer to her now than he'd been since she'd left Egypt. If she was at home now she'd be— he guessed—a mere fifteen hundred miles away.

"Alarm port, cruisers, red—"

A crash of guns from ahead as *de Ruyter* and *Houston* opened fire drowned the lookout's yell. Nick had the DCT telephone in his hand. He heard Greenleaf's order "Shoot!" and then the firegongs, and *Defiant's* six-inch thundered. Gun flashes puncturing the darkness to port were the enemy's: a lot of them, and they had this force silhouetted against the moon.

"Flagship's hit, sir!"

There was a glow of fire on *de Ruyter* and she was swinging away to starboard while *Defiant's* guns blazed in a smooth and rapid rhythm. *Houston* belching out shells too as she followed the flagship round. Swanson, at the torpedo-control panel, was shouting over his telephone to Mr North, the gunner, who'd be down at the tubes. *Perth* turning now: Nick told Chevening, "Follow round!"

"Aye aye—"

Gunfire smothered the acknowledgement. One hit on an enemy ship—on the quarter, a blossoming glow in that blackness: then, astern of *Defiant* as she approached the turning-point in *Perth's* wake, a heavy explosion. *Java:* and if that had been a torpedo, he thought, the sooner they got round and stern-on to any more that were coming, the better. Turn now, independently? Aft, in *Defiant,* a shell struck: he'd heard a salvo coming and he'd been thinking about *Java* and torpedoes from the Jap cruisers, and then his own ship shuddered to the hit which had sounded like a muffled *thump* below decks and somewhere amidships. Gant was roaring into the telephone to damage control HQ, wanting to know the position and extent of the damage. Astern, a shoot of flame reached skyward and the blast of an explosion was solid, buffeting: a shout from the after end of the bridge was CPO Howell, chief yeoman, reporting that *Java* had blown up.

Defiant was slowing: engine rhythm dying, and the way falling off her. Her guns were still firing, all of them, Nick thought, hearing Chevening in a moment's comparative quiet shouting down: "Starboard fifteen!" But ahead—impossible to know immediately which ship it was, when from this angle the leaders were so bunched together—another eruption, a burst of flames and a roar of sound. Greenleaf told him over the telephone, "Flagship, sir. Looked like a magazine going up." Gant chipped in, at Nick's side and raising his voice high to beat the racket of the guns, "Shell burst in number two boiler room, sir."

A large-calibre shell struck aft. You felt the blow of it, heard the whine of ricocheting fragments in the echo of the explosion. There was a major fire back aft. Gant yelled, "Permission to go aft, sir?" He'd gone without waiting for it. Chevening reported from the binnacle, "Losing steerage way, sir." Nick told him, shouting through the noise of another salvo, "They'll have her moving again in a minute." In *some* minutes, he thought. He *hoped* Sandilands would get her moving. He hadn't heard that bit of Gant's report. He heard more Jap shells coming—for a second or two before gunfire drowned the unpleasant sound of them—and he knew, knew more than guessed, that this would be a straddle over the forepart of his ship. The salvo came from abaft the beam; one shell was a near-miss, short; three went over; one burst on the foc'sl and wiped out "A" gun's crew; the last one crashed in through the port side of the bridge superstructure and burst in the plot, most of its explosive power blasting laterally into the wheelhouse and upwards through the thin deck-plating of the bridge.

CHAPTER FOUR

·   ·   ·

Dusk came to the Mediterranean six hours later than it had darkened the Java Sea, and clouds low on the horizon in the west were turning pink as the sun sank down into them; against the spreading brightness Paul had watched the two carriers, astern of the convoy, turn into the wind and fly-off a stream of fighters which, when they'd gained height, had moved out northward. The two carriers were back on course now. There was a lot of activity still in the destroyer screen, though: the fleet destroyers had spread themselves into a wider and more distant arc, while the smaller Hunt class had moved in closer to the four columns of merchantmen—to provide close protection with their AA weapons against the bombers when they came.

He was in the open port wing of the *Montgovern's* bridge. So was Gosling, the little paymaster sub-lieutenant. Mackeson, who was allocating action duties to all the passengers, had told them both to wait out here.

Some of the fleet destroyers were still hurrying back after visiting the oiling group astern. At full speed, racing to overtake the convoy and get back into station ahead before the Luftwaffe arrived, one of them passing now up the port side was throwing a high, curved bow-wave tinged pink from the reflection of the western sky. Too pretty, really, to be true . . . Convoy and escort—battleships, carriers, cruisers and destroyers—were at action stations, although no alert had been sig-nalled yet. It was coming: it might have been expected anyway, this far into the Mediterranean, but in fact there'd been a warning signal dur-ing the afternoon: intercepted enemy radio messages had made it clear that an assault was being mounted.

Gosling said, blinking at Paul through the pebble glasses that made him look like a frog, "I wonder what jobs he's going to give us."

"I'd guess we'll be extra lookouts."

"What, out here?"

Mackeson had had the passengers assembled in the saloon at tea-time, told them about the probability of a dusk attack and added that he'd be expecting them to lend a hand in the ship's defence. He'd co-opted Thornton, the cipher expert, first of all, and put him in the chartroom to decode signals. But looking out, Paul thought, was about all he and Gosling could be useful at: and the short-sighted little pay-master wasn't likely to be very good at that, even. Might be better helping Thornton, he thought: not that one would wish that on some-one who hadn't done one any harm . . . He asked him, "What were you doing before you joined?"

"Accountancy. Actually I'd just qualified."

"You've something to go back to, then."

"Haven't you?"

"I was at college. In the United States."

"I *thought* you sounded a bit American."

"Admiring the sunset, lads?"

Humphrey Straight, the *Montgovern's* master, had come out of the enclosed bridge behind them. He was a blocky, grizzled man: he had a way of staring with his head lowered, glaring at you under his eye-brows like a bull trying to decide whether or not to charge. Paul told him, "We're waiting for Commander Mackeson, sir."

"Oh, aye." Straight's eyes looked bloodshot with that western light in them. "Grand sight, eh?"

"Beautiful."

"Aye. Beautiful . . . If you could paint that, and get it just right, folks'd say you'd laid it on too thick." He stared around at the destroy-ers; then ahead, past the column leaders to the cruisers. "Mack had best hurry up. The buggers'll be at us directly." His eyes moved to Paul. "Seen action, have you?"

"Some. Not air attack, though."

"You?"

Gosling shook his head. "None at all, I'm afraid."

"Afraid is what we all get, betimes." Straight rubbed the side of his jaw reflectively. "It's never so bad as you expect, though. Least, it's as bad for them as it is for us. Helps to bear that in mind, see."

Mackeson came out of the side-door from the bridge. Straight asked him, "Left all this a bit late, haven't we?"

"Well, perhaps . . . Now—Gosling . . ." He asked him sharply, "Where's your tin hat?"

"Here, sir."

"Well put it on, boy. And take this." A lanyard, with a whistle on end of it. "Round your neck. That's it. All you have to do is stay right in the wing here, and keep a sharp lookout. If you see an attack coming that the guns haven't got on to, point at it and blow that thing like hell. Understand?" Gosling nodded. Mackeson asked him, "Wearing your lifebelt, are you?"

"Under my coat, sir."

"Right. That's you settled, then. Now, Everard." He pointed for'ard. "I want you up there on the foc's'l. You'll find a bunch of bloody-minded DEMS characters lolling around the Oerlikons. I want you to keep 'em on their toes, generally act as OOQ and help to put 'em on to targets. Keep an ear open for this lad's whistle, and the other one for our tame flying officer who's in the other wing. All right?"

Paul nodded. "Except once it's dark I won't be able to see which way they point."

With the guns in action, he doubted whether he was likely to hear whistles anyway. He didn't want to aggravate Mackeson with too many objections to his arrangements, though. Mackeson told him, "By the time it's dark, Everard, the show will be over. That's the usual form, anyway."

Humphrey Straight loomed closer. He said dourly, "My second mate looks after DEMS gunnery lads."

"Oh, yes." Mackeson glanced round at him. "But he can't be in more than one place at a time, can he? Don't we want all the help we can get?"

The master shrugged, and walked away. Mackeson murmured, "He's very talkative this evening. Don't know what's got into him."

Paul nodded. "Minute ago, he was talking about painting the sunset."

"Good God!"

He went down the ladderways through the bridge superstructure, out into the ship's-side gangway, down into the for'ard well deck and across it, and up the ladder to the foc'sl-head. One glance, as he reached the top of it, showed him that one of the two Oerlikon guns still had its canvas cover on.

Keep them on their toes, Mackeson had said. A covered gun—at action stations?

A red-headed sailor, about Paul's own age, stared at him inhospitably. Beyond him a heavy-set, pale-faced man of about forty was fiddling with the Oerlikon that had been uncovered. There were several drums of the twenty-millimetre ammunition in a bin nearby.

Paul told the older man, "My name's Everard. I'm taking passage to Malta, but I've been detailed to lend a hand up here. Spot targets for you, all that."

DEMS personnel, he was remembering, were Merchant Navy men who signed on under a special system called the T. 124 agreement. They wore naval uniform—at least, they were supposed to, although the one at the gun was wearing a checked shirt under a donkey-jacket—but weren't subject to ordinary naval discipline. They got better pay, for some reason.

The fat man had acknowledged Paul's presence with a nod. The young, red-headed one was staring at the fat one as if he was waiting for a lead. The fat one said, "Leading 'and 'ere's Ron Beale." He nodded towards the covered gun. "That's Ron's. Be up in 'alf a mo'." He stooped, and hefted a drum of ammunition; he gasped, "I'm Withinshaw. This lad—" the young one had gone to help him—"McNaught, this is."

"Easy now, Art . . ."

Arthur Withinshaw, then. Possibly from Liverpool, Paul guessed. Art pushed the red-headed boy aside, or tried to, with an elbow. "Gerrout of it!"

"*There* . . . All right?"

Boots scraped on the ladder from the well deck: with them came a leading seaman cradling an ammo drum in his arms. A younger sailor behind him also carried one. Paul told him—Beale—who he was. Beale looked round at the young one: "Get that fuckin' cover off, Wally boy." He looked back at Paul: "Where's Mr McCall, then?"

"I expect he'll be along."

The wind across this unsheltered deck was bone-cutting, and it would get worse when the sun was down. He hoped Mackeson was right that the Luftwaffe went home when it got dark. It would be about fifteen minutes to sunset now, he guessed, and that would make it about zero-hour for an attack. Astern, the whole sky was crimson. He pushed his fists deeper into his greatcoat pockets, and asked Beale—who'd clamped an ammo drum to the other gun now—whether they'd been told about that signal, the warning that an attack was coming. Withinshaw said, "Stands to reason. Why we're 'ere, like." He stared at Paul: at his rank insignia first, the single wavy stripe on each shoulder of his greatcoat. Then at his face. He asked him, "Had a basinful before, 'ave ye?"

"Not in the Med. Up north. Narvik, that business . . . You?"

"We done a few trips, me an' Ron, Malta an' back once. Other pair's green as grass. Bloody babes in arms, right, kiddoes?"

The red-headed one growled and spat. Beale, the killick, asked Paul, "Fuck-up, weren't it, Norway?"

"In part, I guess it was." The two older men were at their guns, getting their feet spaced right, then leaning into the shoulder-rests, weaving a little to test their stance, settling comfortably, the gun barrels traversing and arcing. Then they were resting, waiting, and the younger men were using spare ammunition drums as stools to sit on, McNaught chewing with his mouth open, like a dog. Paul added, "Can't say I knew much about what was going on, though. I was an OD Gun's crew."

Withinshaw murmured, "Stone the crows."

Beale asked him, "Did all right then, did you?" Beale was about thirty, Paul guessed. Rather mean-looking. Probably good at his job so long as he was left to do it on his own. It was undoubtedly an advantage, he thought, to have served on the lower deck in action conditions. He knew these people, understood them; to him they weren't some different form of life, incomprehensible and sometimes a bit worrying, which was how he suspected some commissioned officers tended to view them. The secret—or part of it, he thought—was to accept them as they were, appreciate and make use of the qualities they had, instead of expecting to find ones they *didn't* have.

The one called Wally jumped up suddenly, and pointed. "Flag's up. Stand by, gents."

A red flag for red alert—but in this light even a white one would have looked red. Mick McCall came up the ladder: it was obvious, from his look of surprise, that he hadn't known he'd find Paul here. He gave him a hard, questioning look before he turned to the Oerlikon gunners.

"You blokes all set?"

Beale's answer to the question was a wink. Withinshaw's was: "Be better wi' a few pints inside us." But they were ready, alert, watching the sky, the two at the guns and the others standing by with the spare drums at their feet. McCall looked at Paul again: "Someone tell you to come up here?"

"Mackeson. Idea is to keep us all busy, I suppose. The skipper did say it was your part of ship."

Beale muttered, "Extra pair of eyes can't do no 'arm, can it?"

McCall visibly relaxed. Paul blessed the instinct that had made him keep his mouth shut when he'd noticed that gun still covered. If he'd been Thornton he'd have made a fuss about it, and he'd have got nowhere with this bunch.

McCall said to him, "What a sunset, eh?" Then, somewhere out on the convoy's port bow—northeastward—a destroyer opened fire.

There was nothing to see, from here. Just the sound, the hard, cracking thuds of four-sevens. And the recognition that the attack was starting. McCall said, "Here we go. Least, here *I* go . . . I'll be up at the Bofors, Beale."

Ahead of the block of merchantmen, a cruiser opened fire. Then a second joined in. Here on the *Montgovern*'s foc'sl-head the two Oerlikon gunners jerked back the cocking handles on their weapons and waited with their left shoulders towards the blaze of the dying sun.

The shooting ahead, on the bow, was thickening, but those destroyers were three or four miles away from the convoy and there was no way of knowing what their target was. The cruisers had fired a few rounds and then ceased fire, and nothing had appeared anywhere near the convoy. Slow minutes crawled by: you felt an urge to be in action, get to grips with it. Paul asked Beale, watching the sky, "Do you have tracer in those drums?"

"One in six."

One tracer round in every six: the others would be high-explosive or incendiary.

The cruisers ahead and the Hunts to port and astern opened fire simultaneously, their gun barrels poking out on the beam, to port. The noise of it smothered the more distant sound of the barrage from the destroyers in the screen, but obviously there were two quite separate attacks being made. Now the racket astern doubled and redoubled as the two battleships and the cruiser between them added their HA armaments to the party. Most of the warships would have RDF, Paul realized: it would have been an RDF contact on approaching bombers that would have initiated the air raid warning in the first place.

High on the port side of the convoy shell-bursts were opening like black fists against the pink-flushed sky.

Beale shouted, "There. *There,* Art. You on 'em?"

Black against that bright background, twin-engined bombers, Junkers 88s. They were coming straight towards the convoy, undeterred by thickening groves of shell-bursts in front of them and around them. Wally muttered, "*'Undreds* of the bastards!"

There were dozens, though, not hundreds. Perhaps forty, Paul thought. Beale was watching them over his sights: it would be a while before close-range weapons would have any part to play. Beyond Beale and

Withinshaw at the guns was the grey steel of the foc'sl with its ordered
clutter of cable gear, and the gleam of surrounding sea and, a couple
of hundred yards ahead, the big lumbering stern-on shape of the motor
vessel *Warrenpoint,* leader of this number one column. To port, tracer
was rising from destroyers in the outer screen, and the noise of gunfire
was still mounting as ship after ship joined in.

Glancing over his shoulder, Paul could see figures motionless behind
the glassed-in front of the bridge. Straight, that would be, and his first
officer Devenish, and Mackeson no doubt. A small, pimple-like silhouette in the extremity of the port wing would be Gosling; a taller
figure was visible on the other side. Mackeson's idea might have seemed
good in principle, Paul thought, but either of those two could have
blown their lungs out through the whistles without a single peep being
audible down here.

"Stand by, Art!"

Beale had shouted the warning. The leading flight of Junkers were
diving shallowly towards the convoy's centre. Others behind them, Paul
saw, were banking away to their right, towards the rear. Gunfire was a
solid roar and the multi-coloured tracer was thickening too, streams of
it criss-crossing and converging towards the front-running bombers as
they drove in, diving, holding straight courses into the explosive centre of the barrage. One was beginning to turn away, though. You saw
a wing tilting as it banked; then another—and another. But others were
still coming on, and Paul's nerves jumped as Beale squeezed the trigger of his gun and Withinshaw immediately followed suit, both Oerlikons
blazing out intermittent, ear-shattering bursts and the tracer-streams
soaring, curving. One bomber—not one that *Montgovern's* guns were
shooting at, but one that had turned and was flying towards the convoy's rear—had smoke streaming from one engine. The tracer seemed
to arc away as it approached its target: the whole sky was streaked and
patterned with it, multi-coloured streams of fire and, astern, the setting
sun's bonfire-like glow. A bomb-splash—the first of a stick of several,
probably, but he saw only one and paid no attention to it—had risen

on the quarter, between this and number two column. He was looking around, remembering that his job here was to spot new targets, not
simply watch the action, when he heard the commodore's siren from
ahead, the lead-ship of column two, ordering an emergency turn to
port. More bombs splashed in between the lines of ships, mounds of
dark water leaping. The *Montgovern's* own siren let out a preliminary
hiss and then found its voice, a deep bellow of sound repeating that
order: all the ships' hooters echoing it as their helms were put over
and the entire convoy, lumbering merchantmen and the warships surrounding them, turned in unison with all the guns still racketing. More
bombers weaving in: on the bow now instead of the beam, black and
evil-looking, bombs clumping into the sea here and there and the aircraft lifting, banking away and climbing, putting their tails to the explosive streams that were reaching up for them. The barrage over the
convoy was so intense that you wouldn't have thought there'd be a
space a bomber could pass through without being hit: and it did, on
the whole, seem to have kept them out on its fringes. But it was eas-
ing now, and shifting, most of it astern, in the general direction of the
sunset. It had become a moving barrage, in fact, as the remaining
bombers circled, probing for easier targets or gaps in the defence, the
warships' guns following them around like a boxer with a long straight
left, keeping his opponent on the end of it.

Beale and Withinshaw were standing back from their guns while
their assistants changed the ammunition drums. The red-headed boy,
McNaught, was needling Withinshaw: "I didn'a see so many comin'
doon in flames."

"I'll see *you* in fookin'—"

Siren, for a turn back to starboard. All the ships acknowledging. The
long days of practising such manoeuvres, in the Atlantic on the way
south from the Clyde, were paying off: the convoy was in good formation as it turned back to the mean course. Firing still quite heavy
astern and on the quarter. Paul was trying to look all ways at once,
knowing there were still enemies around and that this failing light was

perfect for surprise. The light was going fast now, leaking away as the source of the red glow retracted and dimmed . . . Gunfire ahead, suddenly: and he saw the attacker as he turned. A bomber low, wing-tilted, swooping upwards from wave-top level where it had slipped between the cruisers, who were the ones that had opened fire. The German had flames streaming from one wing's leading edge, flickering back all over it. It passed over at masthead height, the Oerlikons starting up with an aiming-point too far astern and the midships Bofors, where McCall was, only managing three or four barks at it, much too late. Tracer rising again astern, the Hunts back there giving it all they had. There was a sheet of yellow flame like the flare of a huge match, and the guns abruptly ceased firing. The barraging was all on the starboard quarter and beam now; in this area, there was peace again. Withinshaw said, "That sod bought it, Ron. See it, did you?"

"No fault of ours, if he did." Beale watched the sky, which was losing its last shreds of colour. The barrage was moving up the convoy's starboard side. But the convoy was back on course, no ships had been hit, so far as anyone could see, and progress was continuing Malta-ward. Beale muttered, "I don't reckon that last 'un for an 88, any road."

Paul didn't think it had been, either. In the few seconds that it had been over them he hadn't had time to think about it, but in retrospect it seemed to have been a Heinkel and almost certainly a torpedo-bomber. That would account for the low level at which it had come in, and it might also explain that emergency turn. The action had started with a barrage from the destroyers on the bow to port, and that could have a torpedo-bomber attack developing. They'd have been turned away by the barrage, but they'd have hung around, waiting for a chance to press in again when the escorts might be busy fending off the attack by Junkers 88s. The convoy would have been turned to avoid torpedoes, and that last effort would have been a late comer sneaking in for a solitary, surprise attack.

It hadn't done him any good. He'd almost certainly perished in that burst of flame . . . But from a position like this you could only see pieces of the action as they happened from minute to minute and in your corner of the fight; you could only guess—in lulls or when it was over—at the broader pattern of events. It was much as it had been for him as a sailor in a destroyer gun's crew: he'd hardly ever known what was happening or which way they were going or what for; he'd simply helped to serve the gun, a creature with a voracious appetite for fifty-pound shells . . . And there was a feeling of enclosure, at this level: of being surrounded, hemmed in ahead and astern and to starboard by the bulks and high bridge superstructures of the other freighters. Rather like being a cow in a herd of other cows, plodding on with that feeling of being hidden in the mass. It was an illusion, of course, because to the attackers each ship was separate and a target to be got at, and any hunter worth his salt picked his individual quarry and went after it. The comforting feeling of partial invisibility also failed when you looked out to port and saw only darkness, glimmer of sea with the shadows of the night across it. It *was* almost night now, and the only sound of guns came faintly, distantly from astern. They might be attacking the oiling group back there, he thought.

Withinshaw mumbled, "They weren't tryin' all that 'ard, I reckon."

Beale had pulled the drum off his Oerlikon. He dumped it into McNaught's arms and turned back to begin overhauling the gun. He worked fast and deftly, Paul noticed, working more by feel than by sight. Neither of the guns had jammed even once, as Oerlikons tended to do, and it might have been because they were well maintained.

McNaught had a spare ammo drum ready, and he'd put the two part-used ones aside; it would be his job to refill them now. He was singing quietly, about Saturday nights in Glasgow: the song broke off abruptly as a new storm of gunfire broke out astern. In seconds the Oerlikons were reloaded and the gunners were standing ready, one facing out on each quarter. Tracer astern was heavy, and far brighter now the light had gone, and as well as the interlacing streams of red, blue, green and yellow the sky flickered with the yellowish flashes of time-fused AA shells.

It stopped as suddenly as it had begun.

Withinshaw grumbled, "What the fookin' 'ell . . ."

McCall arrived, heaving himself up the ladder from the well deck. "All right, lads?" He put a hand on Paul's shoulder: "Okay?"

Paul was still watching the sky astern. He said, "Apparently it's not over yet."

"It is, you know. That was the Fleet Air Arm coming back. Trying to get down on their carriers. Nice sort of welcome, I must say."

The atmosphere in the saloon was already heavy with pipe and cigarette smoke. Brill said, waving some of it away, "Wouldn't imagine this was a hospital, would you?" Until about ten minutes ago he'd had the place to himself; at action stations the saloon became his first-aid centre and operating theatre.

Mick McCall fetched two cups of coffee from the sideboard, and came to join them. He said, accepting a duty-free cigarette from Paul, "Very gentlemanly introduction, that."

"Be worse tomorrow, will it?"

"Christ, what do *you* think?"

"I've no idea." Paul sipped coffee. "Never been on a thing like this before."

"I'd better educate you, then." McCall used a stub of pencil and the back of a brown OHMS envelope to make a rough sketch of the western Mediterranean. "We're about here. Halfway, roughly, from Gib to Malta. And this—" he drew a large oval shape to the northeast of their position—"this, believe it or not, is Sardinia. By tomorrow forenoon we'll be passing to the south of it, through the narrows here with the Sardinian coast about fifty miles to port. The Germans and the Eyeties have air bases on Sardinia, don't they?"

"I suppose they would have."

Those narrow waters would be an obvious place to have submarines waiting for them, he thought. McCall didn't mention submarines, though. He told them, "By tomorrow evening we'll be through that stretch. With any luck, we will be. Touching wood, etcetera . . . So—tomorrow night, *here,* the battleships and the carriers leave us and turn westward, and we carry on into the Sicilian narrows. Between Sicily here to port and Cape Bon on the North African coast to starboard. Through the Skerki Channel, and down here past Pantellaria—where E-boats are based, incidentally. And Sicily, of course, is virtually one large Luftwaffe base . . ." He put the pencil away, and reached for his coffee. "It all starts tomorrow, really."

CHAPTER FIVE

. . .

Bob Gant had rattled down four flights of ladderway from *Defiant*'s compass platform to the level of her foc's'l deck and turned aft to get to the next ladder, down to the upper deck and aft—get to the fire, get it out before the enemy found it too useful as a point of aim. *De Ruyter* and *Java* had both blown up, which left only three targets for the Jap cruisers out there in the dark: and this ship was slowing, stopping, as a result of the hit in number two boiler room.

He'd reached the ladder and started down it when number three gun—the six-inch mounting between the foremast and the funnels—fired, on a bearing just for'ard of the beam. The blast knocked him backwards, flash from "flashless" powder blinded him, and for a moment he was witless, lost. He'd cannoned backwards into his "doggie," Ordinary Seaman Pinner, who'd been following close behind him. It was Pinner squawking in his ear, "Are you all right, sir?" that brought him back to his senses. The sheer silliness of the question—it seemed silly at the time, anyway—penetrated and triggered annoyance, put him back in touch with events around him. Flames aft, voices shouting, the shouting drowned in gunfire: *Defiant* wallowed, rolling in the troughs of other ships' wash. A salvo came in a hoarse rush and the top of the for'ard funnel glowed red and disintegrated. He had to get aft, see about the fire that was somewhere near the after tubes on the starboard side. He was starting down the ladder again, with Pinner in close company behind, when he heard shells going into the sea nearby. Metal whirred and whined, clanged into the ship's side and superstructure; then a shell struck and burst for'ard, and just as *Defiant*'s own guns sent away another salvo she was hit again: up in the bridge superstructure, above him.

The bridge, he realized . . .

Back the way he'd come. Up the foc's'l break ladder, in the screen door, and climbing again. Dreading what he'd find . . . The top ladder was loose, twisted, the bulkhead of the lobby outside the lot was bulged and split, its white enamel paint blackened. Shouts for help, wounded men moaning, a first-aid party with Neill-Robertsons, hardly knowing where to start. In seconds, everything had gone, changed. You were in a different century, another world. Gant was in the after end of the bridge, which was completely wrecked. Haskins, the captain of marines, saw him and came over to him. He had come down from the ADP because all its circuits and communications had been cut so there'd been no point staying up there; he and his ADP crew who'd come down with him were trying to help the wounded, find the living . . .

The bridge deck had been blasted open from below. Rescuers were at work down there: voices and torch-beams, and the stink of smouldering cortisone. Gant didn't want to use his own torch—it was on a lanyard attached to his belt—up here in the open. He shouted, towards the for'ard end of the bridge, "Captain, sir?"

Haskins said, "He'd have been right where the blast came through."

One gun fired. Number two—sometimes referred to as "B" gun—the mounting immediately for'ard of the bridge. It was crewed by Royal Marines. Gant hadn't at this stage caught on to the fact that he was now in command, possibly because not wanting it to be so his mind rejected the obvious truth. He only remembered later being struck by the thought that Everard couldn't have been killed, because it would be too much sheer bad luck to have history repeat itself after only this short an interval. *Defiant's* previous captain had died in that same corner of the bridge only a few weeks ago. They'd been off Mersa Matruh on the desert coast when they'd been jumped by a lone Messerschmitt fighter-bomber that had come whistling out of the sun and strafed the bridge with cannon-fire. The skipper had been the only casualty. It had been Everard's inheritance of some of the same rotten streak of luck—in retrospect you could see it as one sequence of events—that having just had a destroyer sunk under him he'd been available to replace the cruiser captain.

"In the for'ard corner there." Haskins had started by shouting, but he'd found there was no need to, suddenly a normal tone of voice was perfectly audible . . . "I've seen—first thing I did was—anyway, there's no point, sir, I'm sorry but—"

"All right." He'd check for himself though, all the same. Haskins seemed to be taking personal responsibility for his captain's death. Shock, perhaps. The ship was lying stopped, rolling very slightly, and none of her guns was in action now. Gunfire from other ships was distant and sporadic. The battle had passed on, and *Defiant* was alone. Haskins stopped beside the binnacle, which was still vertical and seemed intact. He stooped, wary of what it was that he'd found here, and Chevening told him, "I'm all right. I think I was knocked out."

Getting to his feet. Haskins said, helping him, "It's the navigating officer, sir. Binnacle must have sheltered him. And the deck isn't holed here. Here, steady . . ."

"You're right, I was behind the binnacle. Is the captain—"

"Not a hope . . . Look, are you sure you're okay?"

"Bit dizzy, that's—"

"Well, you're damn lucky." The marine tried a voicepipe: "Bridge, wheelhouse!"

"SBA Green down 'ere, sir. And a stretcher party." The reply had come from the void below them: and that voicepipe led nowhere, as Gant's torch revealed. He'd been unwilling to switch it on until now, when it was plain there was no enemy anywhere near them. The beam of light flickered over bodies and parts of bodies enmeshed in twisted steel. The plot was open to the bridge. A pair of shoes were jammed in torn deck-plating, their soles upward: if there was a man still in them he'd be hanging head-downwards in the lower compartment. A voice from the rear of the bridge asked gruffly, "Captain, sir?"

Mr Nye, the gunner. Down from the director tower. Gant told him, "The captain's dead, Mr Nye. What's the state of things in the tower?"

A low groan led his torch-beam to a body and an upturned face. It was PO Ruddle, one of the signals yeomen. Gant had already seen what was left of the chief yeoman, CPO Howell. Nye told him, "Only communications link is with number three gun, sir. PCO's sent me and Colour Sergeant Bruce to get the lads out of the TS—the circuits is all gone, sir, see—and put the other guns in local control. Not much else we *can* do, sir. Except the ACP *might*—"

"All right, carry on." Gant called down, "We need stretchers up here. And morphine." Morphine for Ruddle. Gant couldn't imagine there'd be anyone alive on that lower level, where the shell had burst. "You still there, Green?"

"I'm coming up now, sir!"

He told his "doggie," Pinner, "Go down to the lower steering position. Know where it is?"

"Platform deck, sir, just about under 'ere."

"Good man. Tell them I'll be testing communications to them from the after conning position. Then I can decide whether to steer from there or from the after position."

Haskins joined him as he picked a way forward through jagged edges of torn plating, wreckage, bodies you didn't need to look at twice and could not afford to allow to imprint themselves on your mind. They did, however hard you tried not to let them into your consciousness; and in later days, nights and years you'd see them again, these and others . . . The full force of the shell had blown up through the middle, under these men's feet . . . He remembered, like something in a dream, Sandilands, the commander (E), saying there'd been a shell in the top of number two boiler room. It had cut steam pipes, smashed other gear, killed or wounded most of the men in the compartment. Number two was the larger boiler room, with four boilers in it, and Sandilands had said he'd be able to provide steam from number one—steam for slow speed—in roughly half an hour. But how long ago that report had been made was hard to remember: an hour, ten minutes, it was what happened in any given space of time that counted, not the time itself.

He told Haskins, "Job for you, soldier. There was a hit aft, starboard side, and it started a fire. I want to know whether they've put the fire out, and the extent of the damage and what's being done about it. Rowley may be there. Find him anyway, and tell him I want a situation report made to me in the ACP. All right?"

"Aye aye, sir." ACP stood for after conning position. It was abaft the funnels, near the mainmast, on a platform which also supported the searchlights.

Haskins said, "Here, sir."

The captain's wooden seat had been smashed against the forefront of the bridge. Splinters of its wood were mixed with the slumped body in its overall suit that had been white but was now bright red. It was in the corner, in a heap suggesting bonelessness, and the head was like raw meat.

He'd taken the torch-beam off it. Haskins had been right when he'd said there was no point in looking. The beam moved back—as if the torch had moved his hand, more than the other way about. There was a smear of blood all down the front of the bridge, over a nest of telephones and the captain's action-alarm button and a fuse-box, right down to the body, and at the top the glass windscreen had been shattered. He must have been hurled on to it, and the half-inch glass, jagged now and bloodstained, had just about decapitated him.

"Captain, sir?"

Gant's torch-beam swung around, to blind the doctor, Sibbold. Sibbold's whites were bloodstained too. A broad, solid-looking man, capless and dishevelled, peering blinking at the torchlight and the man behind it. Morphine ampoules in his top pocket were like a railway clerk's fountain pens.

"There he is." The light-beam acted as a pointer. "I wouldn't think there's the slightest chance of—"

"Stretcher here, please. Quick, now!" Sibbold dropped down beside the body. Gant said, "Not a hope. My God, *look* at him. He's *dead*, damn it."

He'd had to state the fact, oblige himself to face it. He didn't want Everard's job, this command, this rotten, hopeless situation. All his life he'd funked command. Now it was being thrust on him, and in the worst of all worlds. He told Sibbold, "Petty Officer Ruddle's over there, and he's alive, so—"

"One thing at a time." Sibbold shouted, "Green, are you—"

"Coming, sir, coming!"

You could sympathize with the doctor's refusal to accept the truth, that Everard was dead. But he oughtn't to be wasting time that might have been spent on men with a chance of living . . . Well, it was Sibbold's business. Gant turned away, knowing that *his* job now was to get *Defiant* under command and moving, get her away before the enemy returned.

"Another quarter of an hour should do it." John Sandilands's voice was hoarse-sounding over the telephone between engine-room and ACP. "But then you must let us work her up very gradually. I can just about promise you revs for five knots. If we're lucky and it looks good we *might* get her up to ten."

Gant hesitated for a moment before he answered. Anxiety made him want to shout. It was an effort to speak normally. He said, "It's fifty miles to Surabaya, chief, and we have to get there before dawn. That calls for ten knots as an average if we were to get cracking now, this minute."

"It wouldn't help anyone if the repairs don't hold, Bob. And they won't if you go and—"

"Now listen . . ." Everard had asked him, an hour or two ago, what he'd have been doing if he'd had Doorman's job. Now Doorman was probably dead, but the job he'd got was Everard's, not the Dutchman's, and it was just as bad. You had to shut your mind to the hopelessness of it, just get on with what had to be done immediately. Such as, now, persuading Sandilands to see the wood as well as the trees. They'd been patching steampipes, or rigging jury ones, from the for'ard boiler room through the after one where they'd been holed by blast or splinters. It was an engineering problem, Sandilands's, not *his*. He had God knew how many of his own—insoluble, overwhelming problems . . . He told Sandilands, his voice thin with anxiety, "If we don't get into Surabaya before daylight, we're finished. Ten knots, John. I'm not asking you, I'm bloody well *telling* you, d'you understand?"

He hung up. His hands were shaking, from that flare of temper. No: from taut nerves, not temper. If Sandilands had insisted that ten knots was an impossibility, he'd have been beaten, stumped. He hadn't, thank God. So it was all right, for the moment, you could press on—to the *next* problem . . . This telephone was working only because its line went straight down through the deck under the after conning position, and it hadn't therefore been cut by that shell-burst near the tubes. There was no communication from here to the lower steering position, for instance. None to the after steering position either, the ASP being a closet-sized corner of the steering-engine flat. Helm orders, when they got her moving, would be passed down to it from this conning position by voice, from man to man via a chain of sailors who were already in position. And steering would be by magnetic, since although the gyro itself, which was down on the platform deck for'ard, was all right, its repeaters weren't functioning.

What if Sandilands rang back now, said no, he couldn't do it?

Christ . . .

The hit below the bridge, or the upward blast of it, had cut all the gunnery control circuits except for the telephone connection between the tower and number three gun. As the TS was isolated, this one link wasn't of any value from the point of view of gunnery control, but it was being made use of all the same, linking the tower as a lookout position with the upper deck, and, by messengers, with the other guns and with the ACP.

Number one gun, on the foc's'l, had been knocked out in the same salvo that had wrecked the bridge.

The hit aft had killed the crew of the starboard after torpedo-tubes and wrecked that triple mounting. Luckily none of the torpedo warheads had exploded. Flying debris had smashed the starboard searchlight, torn holes in the armoured side of this conning position, and the shell had blown a hole through the upper deck, cutting leads and communications to the two after guns and jamming the ammunition hoist to number four. Artificers were working on that now, but meanwhile shells were being brought up by manpower through the hatches and stockpiled near the gun. The fire which Gant had seen from the bridge hadn't been an upper-deck fire at all. Its flames had been shooting like a blowtorch's through the hole in the deck, but it was an internal fire, in the lower deck. Charles Rowley and his damage control parties had it under control now, but it had taken a lot of water to subdue it and the water couldn't be got rid of until there was steam-pressure to run the pumps.

He kept mentally cataloguing damage and the measures that were being taken to deal with it. As if there was a danger of losing some element of the overall picture and, through oversight, making some colossal blunder in a moment of emergency.

In number two boiler room, seven men had been killed and two wounded. The latest count of casualties was nineteen dead and fourteen wounded. Everard was being counted as one of the fourteen, but Sibbold wasn't holding out much hope for him. He'd glanced round from a man whose leg he'd been amputating and told Gant, "The presence or absence of life can be a technicality, you know." He'd proved Gant wrong in the basic fact that Everard had been alive—technically, whatever that meant—when they'd got him down to the sickbay. Since then, he'd been ready to accept the inevitable. He was single-handed and struggling to meet all the demands that were being made on him; he'd had an assistant, a younger RNVR doctor, but he'd been landed at Batavia to look after wounded British and American naval personnel in a Dutch hospital where nobody spoke English.

There wasn't much room in this ACP, and Chevening's bony length wasn't any help. The navigator squeezed out past Gant now, emerging from the little cubby-hole that held a chart table. He said, "Course will be south forty-eight west, sir, if our DR's reasonably accurate."

"What's the compass error?"

"Two degrees west, sir. Variation and deviation just about cancel each other out."

Gant had only asked the question to see what sort of an answer Chevening might give him. The navigator's manner was peculiar, as if he hadn't completely regained contact with his surroundings. Perhaps he'd always been like that: but Gant hadn't noticed it before.

"Pinner?"

"I'm 'ere, sir."

Ordinary Seaman Pinner was on the ladder outside the ACP, slewing himself aside from it when anyone needed to go up or down it. Out of the way, but in earshot, which was the ideal disposition for a "doggie." Gant was impressed by young Pinner, who'd shown a lot of common sense during the past hour's unpleasant moments. He told him now, "Go down to the sickbay, and ask the PMO that same question."

"Aye aye, sir."

Pinner dropped off the ladder. It was the only entrance and exit, as the starboard one had been blown off at the same time that the searchlight on that side had been smashed.

Gant asked Chevening, "Time now?"

"Eleven twenty-two, sir."

Sandilands's quarter-hour would be up at about 11:30, he supposed. There'd be time to tour the upper deck, visit the guns' crews and have a word to Greenleaf. He told Chevening, "Hold the fort here now. If the engine-room pipes up, or anything else, send a messenger after me. I'm going to walk around the guns."

"Aye aye, sir."

He added from the ladder, "Keep Pinner here when he gets back. Use him to find me if you need to."

The ship lay motionless in black water dappled where moonlight filtered through strips of cloud. She felt dead, spiritless, and the stink of burning still hung over her. Sandilands, he thought, had better get a move on. It was getting to the point when every passing minute mattered, if they were to reach Surabaya before daylight.

What might happen after that—with the ship crippled and a Jap invasion imminent—didn't bear thinking about. At this very moment they could be ferrying their troops ashore . . . Thinking didn't help anything at all. You had to go through the motions, but when you forced your mind past them to where they'd get you in the end, you came back to that nightmare of the no-way-out. The only trick he'd found that did help him to stave off the sense of pointlessness was to ask himself, *What would Everard be doing now?* The answer was simple, each time: Everard would have been dealing with each problem as it arose, with the situation as it was at any given moment, in this minute or the next—and so on, step by step. And he'd have looked to the future, the longer term, in the same way, deciding to cope with new developments as they cropped up.

Gant found he could only look a few hours ahead. Because beyond that, eventually, he knew he'd be on a cliff-edge; and he'd have brought a whole ship's company to it with him. *That* was the thing that froze him when he let his mind loose.

The one objective that was rational and achievable—with luck— was to get the ship to Surabaya. Surabaya and not Batavia, because it was the nearest and because Sandilands's repairs obviously couldn't be relied on for more than a short distance. And there was the need to get there quickly, not to be caught at sea, alone and in this semi-wrecked condition, in daylight.

There'd be air attacks on Surabaya, of course. There'd been raids since the beginning of the month, but they'd be intensified now because the Japanese worked to a set pattern of heavy bombing before a sea or land assault. But there'd be some collective defence, with other ships there—*Exeter* and *Encounter* and the American destroyers.

Except they'd almost certainly be ordered to run for it, now . . .

One's mind flitted, sometimes recoiling from what it found.

"All right here?"

He'd stopped at number three gun, the one that had a telephone to Greenleaf in the director tower. He'd passed by number four, the gun with the jammed ammo hoist, because the telephone link made this the key position now.

CPO Hughes, chief gunner's mate, told him, "Top line, sir. Standing by, and no problems."

No problems, Gant thought. Weren't there? Really, *none!*

From his jaunty tone, Hughes might have been outside a drill-shed on his native Whale Island, the Navy's gunnery school. From memories of the course he'd done on Whale Island in the remote past when he'd been a sub-lieutenant Gant still shuddered mentally at the thought of it. Whale Island produced gunnery specialists, in Gant's imagination, as primeval swamps produced pterodactyls.

"Let me have a word with Lieutenant Greenleaf." He took the telephone headset from the sightsetter, removing his own tin hat so he could slide the earphones on. "Greenleaf?"

"Yes, sir!"

"All right, up there?"

"Well—the horizon's clear, sir . . ."

"We'll be getting under way in a few minutes, I hope. With luck we'll be in Surabaya before sunrise. But I'll have you relieved before long."

"Any news of the captain, sir?"

"Not yet." The question had taken him by surprise, like a blow below the belt. In an attempt to sound brisk and optimistic he'd forgotten Everard, for that moment. He told Greenleaf, "When there is any, I'll let you know." He handed the gear back to the sightsetter, and put his tin hat back on. "I'll be taking a walk around, chief. Is Mr Nye—"

"Mr Nye's aft, sir, looking after five and six."

"I'll see him there, then . . . You chaps all right?"

"Aye, sir." The gunlayer, Jackson, answered from his seat inside the shield. "But—the captain, sir—do they reckon he'll—"

"PMO can't say yet, Jackson. It's touch and go."

Everard had been alive when they'd got him down from the bridge, but he'd been in a coma, lifeless-*looking,* and Sibbold had admitted that the odds were against his coming out of it. Minor damage consisted of an arm broken in two places and a lot of cuts and punctures, but the main injury was to his head where he'd been flung on to the glass windshield. And since then, well after that, Sibbold had made his remark about the presence of life being no more than a technicality. Meaning that a man in coma was alive but he didn't necessarily have to wake up? Gant had had no time, and nor had Sibbold, for any longer session of questions and answers: the simple fact was that he didn't know, could only wait and see.

Gant went for'ard, round the side of the bridge superstructure, to number two gun. Haskins was there, talking to his colour sergeant.

"How are the old donkeys, sir?"

The engines, he meant. Gant told him, "We should have half speed any minute now . . . You chaps all right here?"

"Satisfactory, sir . . . Any gen on the skipper, sir?"

"Not yet. PMO won't even guess."

"Let's 'ope it's a case of no news is good news, sir."

Colour Sergeant Bruce had a voice to match his build. A very large man, taller and wider than Haskins, who was himself no lightweight. Bruce was the marine detachment's senior NCO, and as Haskins had no subaltern this made him second-in-command. He looked a bit like a Saint Bernard, Gant thought.

"Soon as I hear, I'll pass the word."

How marvellous it would be, he thought as he went aft, to be number two again, to have Everard on his feet and making the decisions. Second-in-command was the best job of them all: you had as much responsibility and authority as any reasonable man could want, without carrying that *ultimate* burden. As a number two, one should have been more consciously aware of one's good fortune. If he got out of this and had that kind of job again, he'd revel in it!

If . . .

Number four gun: he'd passed number three and the for'ard torpedo-tube mounting, and under the raised platform that carried a four-inch AA gun on each of its wings, and now he stopped at the gun with the non-functioning ammunition hoist. He leaned with one hand on the edge of the gunshield and the other fist pressed into the small of his back, where the pain was.

"Who's in charge here?"

"I am, sir. Petty Officer Longland, sir."

"Any progress on the hoist, GM?"

"ERAs are still at it, sir."

"Meanwhile you've a good stock of ready-use charges and projectiles, have you?"

"Enough to be getting on with, sir. Wouldn't want too much layin' in the open, like."

Inevitably, then, came the question about Everard. The question, and the unsatisfactory answer. Gant was providing it when a whistle shrilled from number three gun and CPO Hughes bawled "All quarters alert! Alarm port, bearing red two-oh!"

Mr North, at the for'ard tubes, was yelling to his team at the after ones to get them turned out. From the guns, Gant heard the clangs of loading-trays slamming over, breeches thudding shut, the calls of "Ready!" He was back at three gun, taking over the headset. The gun was loaded, trained on the alarm bearing . . . "Commander here. What is it, Greenleaf?"

"Two ships, sir, look like cruisers, coming straight towards. They're in line abreast but they could be *Perth* and *Houston,* I can't—"

"All right." He passed the headset into the sightsetter's hands, and ran aft, passing over the tops of the out-turned torpedo-tubes. "Yeoman!"

He'd reached the ladder to the ACP. "Stand by to challenge on bearing red two-oh!"

"Searchlight, sir, or—"

"Aldis." The searchlight would show too far. Even if the ships approaching were *Perth* and *Houston,* there could still be Jap ships around. And after that damage aloft and most electrical circuits out of commission you could be sure the yardarm challenge-and-reply system, the coloured lights, weren't working.

"Port bow, ship challenging, sir!"

They'd got in first, then. Two red lights and a green: it had flashed on, off again: on-off—

"Correct challenge, sir!"

"Give him the correct answer, then. By Aldis." There was a challenge and reply using morse letters as well. It changed every few hours, just as the masthead lights system did. "Pinner, tell three gun to tell the tower they're friendly."

It could only be *Perth* and *Houston.* Anything else afloat now in this sea would be Japanese. Petty Officer Morris was clashing out the letters ZS, ZS, ZS. The other ship acknowledged, and then began again: "Defiant *from* Perth: *How are you fixed?*"

Gant had read the morse for himself. He told Morris, "Make to him: *Have action damage to boiler room and bridge. Am about to get under way with maximum speed probably ten knots and steering from aft. Hope to reach Surabaya before daylight.*"

That said it all, he thought. All that needed to be said, anyway. The yeoman was scribbling it down, inside where a dim light glowed on Chevening's chart. Still scribbling, Morris told Leading Signalman Tomsett, "Call 'im up, an' I'll give it you word by word."

"Commander, sir?"

"Who's that—Pinner?"

"Yes, sir. Message from the surgeon commander that the captain's still in coma, sir. Still can't say more, sir."

Sibbold was scared to make guesses, Gant thought, for fear of guessing wrongly. Surely by this time he'd have *some* notion . . . Pinner added, "Petty Officer Ruddle's died, sir."

So now there were twenty dead. Gant had expected Nick Everard to become the twentieth. And he hadn't: so perhaps there was hope? But even if he survived, he couldn't possibly take command . . . The telephone squeaked: there was a whole bank of them but the only one working was the line to the engine-room. Gant said into it, "ACP, commander speaking."

"We can move now, Bob. Sorry about the delay."

"Wait a minute." That signal was still being passed to *Perth*. Then he thought, *Why wait, for God's sake?* He told Sandilands, "All right. Half ahead together. Or slow ahead if you like, but I must have a minimum of ten knots within five minutes."

"We'll do our best. But I don't suppose you'd particularly want me to blow the——"

"I don't suppose you want to be caught out here and blown out of the water, either. Get on with it, John!"

"From *Perth*, sir: *Agree Surabaya is your best bet. I am continuing with* Houston *to Batavia. See you at the*—word we're not sure of here, sir—*Galleface?*"

"It's a pub in Colombo."

A couple of thousand miles away . . .

Captains Everard and Waller were old friends, of course. Gant was glad, for a moment, that he hadn't said anything about Everard. Then he wondered if he had any right to withhold the information from a senior officer who, however informally, had asked for a report on *Defiant*'s present state. He decided he did not have, that it was a vital part of the whole picture: and secondly, that he'd continue to withhold it. The message still formed itself in his mind: *Captain Everard seriously wounded and principal medical officer is in doubt whether he will recover consciousness. Commander R. Gant Royal Navy acting in command.* It was more an instinct than a decision not to make such a signal, and he couldn't

have explained, at that moment, what the reasons were for it. *Defiant*
began to tremble as her engines and screws turned. The important
thing was that they should continue turning, and turn faster—much,
much faster . . . He checked the ship's head by magnetic and called to
Pinner on the ladder, "Starboard twenty!" The order was repeated first
by Pinner and then by a sailor ten yards farther aft; and again, more
faintly as one heard it here, by a man on a downward-leading ladder:
to ensure there was no slip-up he'd got Flynn, one of the watchkeeping lieutenants, back there to monitor the passage of the orders. When
he'd let that first one get a certain distance, he thought probably to its
destination by this time, he sent another after it: "Steer south forty-
eight west."

"Signal from *Houston,* sir: *Good luck.*"

Houston was commanded by a Captain Rooks USN. Gant had met
him once, when he and some other captains had come aboard for a
meal with Everard. He told PO Morris, who was now the senior surviving signal rating, "Reply: *Thanks and the same to you.*" About as banal
as one could get, he realized; and phrased as if it might have been Nick
Everard answering, not a man one rank junior to the American. Once
you embarked on a deception, you had to stick to it. And having kept
one's mouth shut, a deception was what it had now become.

Chevening cleared his throat. "Should we not—er—do you think
we should tell *Perth* about the captain, sir?"

"What?"

Defiant was making five or six knots, and the quartermaster in that
very cramped space down aft and below the waterline was steadying
her on the ordered course. The other two cruisers, steering west, had
already crossed astern. And there were quite a few things to be seen
to now . . . Gant poked his head out of the port-side hatch, and found
his "doggie" still there on the ladder.

"Pinner, go and find Lieutenant-Commander Rowley for me. Tell
him I'd like a word."

Chevening tried again: "Sir, d'you think we ought to report that—"

"That the captain's wounded? No, I don't . . . Are you sure *you're* quite all right now, pilot?"

"Absolutely, sir. Full working order. But I just wondered whether—"

"Is that rev counter working?"

Chevening stooped, mantis-like, to check it.

"Yes, sir. Revs on now for—seven to eight knots."

"Let me know how we're doing in five minutes' time."

With *Perth* and *Houston* heading for Batavia, *Exeter* badly damaged in Surabaya, *Java* and *de Ruyter* sunk and *Defiant* crippled, the so-called Combined Striking Force no longer existed. All that survived was a ragbag of ships in various states of disrepair scattered about the archipelago and waiting to be finished off. Or to attempt escape. Nothing had been achieved, because nothing had been achievable. He'd suspected this from the outset, and he thought Everard had probably seen it too. So had the American, the captain of USS *Sloan*. *Sloan's* captain had come near to stating it out loud, and at the time Gant had felt shocked. It had been in his own mind, but at that stage only as a private thought which he'd been trying to dismiss.

Now the proof of the pudding was in the eating, and the results were in his—Gant's—lap. Whether Everard lived or died, that was the plain fact of it: this ship was in an entirely hopeless position, and it was up to him, Bob Gant, to—

To do *what,* for Christ's sake?

Well. Get the boiler room mended, then run for the Sunda Strait, or the Lombok Strait. A lot would depend on what sort of a job Sandilands would make of it.

"Commander, sir?"

Charles Rowley's head and shoulders were framed in the open hatchway. Rowley looked as if he'd been down a coalmine.

"Bloody awful about the skipper, sir."

"Yes. But he may pull through."

"PMO thinks it's unlikely, sir."

"When did he say that?"

"Ten minutes ago. I was passing—"

"Did you see the captain?"

"No, just Sibbold, but—"

"Did he say if he was still unconscious?"

Rowley nodded. "Also that he's weaker. Loss of blood and something about his heartbeat."

"Well." Gant took a deep breath, as if he needed more air than he was getting. "Listen, Charles. First, you are now executive officer of this ship, and you're to act as such . . . I take it the damage control picture's satisfactory?"

"Everything's under control, sir."

"Well, what the ship's company must have immediately is a meal. Soup and sandwiches, something of that sort, and action-messing routine."

"The galley's working on it now, sir."

"Excellent. Second thing is to relieve Greenleaf in the tower. Any of the watchkeepers—it's simply a lookout job now, with a telephone link to number three gun, and that's all. But I want lookouts for'ard, and on the four-inch gundecks too. Also, stand down one gun's crew at a time, give them each a half-hour stand-easy. Then the PMO—I want a casualty list from him, as well as a report on the outlook for the captain. And finally—for the moment, that is—the dead have got to be buried, and it must be done now, before we're much closer inshore. Tell Mr Nye to organize a burial party, put someone else as OOQ on five and six guns and ask the padre to come and see me . . . Where is he, d'you know?"

"He was—er—ministering to the wounded, sir."

"Tell him to come and see me, anyway."

"Aye aye, sir. We're going into Surabaya, sir, is that right?"

"Yes. ETA about dawn. And that's another thing: we can expect air attacks, when we get there, and Haskins had better sort out his AA control system. The ADP's out of action, same as the tower, and the TS isn't operating, so it'll be local control . . . Greenleaf can work out a system, with Haskins."

"Right." Rowley waited in case there was more to come. Then he asked, "After we make Surabaya, sir, what'll the programme be?"

"We'll get orders. Probably to make emergency repairs and then leg it to Ceylon."

"From what I'm told, sir, there's at least a week's hard work to be done in that boiler room. And if the Japs are about to invade?"

"The Dutch are confident of holding out, Charles." He thought, hearing his own voice say it, *What a stupid bloody statement* . . . He was annoyed at being faced with a question he couldn't answer, when it had become his job to produce answers and there was no one else who could provide them. And he'd let Charles Rowley see both the dilemma and the irritation . . . Anyway, to call it a week's work was ludicrous: in much less time than that, Java would be Japanese.

"That's the lot, Charles. Get on to it, will you?"

He asked Chevening, "How are the revs?"

"Coming up steadily, sir. We must be making nearly ten knots now."

"We shan't be in the anchorage before daylight, though, would you say?"

"I'd guess we'll be in the Strait, sir."

And it mightn't be such a bad thing, to have some daylight to help them through that quite tricky passage. He'd leave the pilotage to Chevening, anyway . . . He asked him, "Will you be all right on your own here, pilot, for about ten minutes?"

He was sick of getting no answers out of Sibbold. He'd decided to go and see for himself.

Chevening said, smiling, "Oh, I believe so, sir."

The navigator had a good opinion of himself, Gant had noticed. He hoped it might be justified, at that, because he was going to have to depend on him quite a lot. He told him, "I'll leave Pinner here. If you need me you can send him to get me. I'm going to the sickbay."

"Aye, sir."

"And when there's a spare moment, pilot, you'd better ask the PMO to check you over."

On the way for'ard he stopped to chat to the tubes' crews: his last tour of the upper deck had been interrupted by the arrival of the other cruisers. He visited the two port-side mountings first, then crossed over to starboard where he also paused for a word with shipwrights working on repairs to the thirty-foot cutter. The boat's stern, rudder and transom had been damaged by flying splinters from the shell-burst further aft . . . And that hit aft, the same one that had taken the lives of four torpedomen, had saved his own life. If he hadn't been hurrying aft he'd have been in the bridge . . . The whole thing was a toss-up, and you had no control over it at all. He went on for'ard, in through the door at the foc'sl break and past the seamen's galley. Bacon was frying appetizingly in enormous pans. He asked one of the cooks—a skinny man with anchors tattooed on both forearms—"Is that for sandwiches, Gresham?"

"It is, sir. Care for a bite?"

"Not just now, thank you."

"Cap'n be all right, sir, will he?"

"I'm on my way to find out."

The sickbay was a large compartment with a curtain across the centre of it. In normal times the curtain divided the area that had cots in it from the outer section where medicines were issued and minor ailments treated, but now there were camp beds in this half too. There was a reek of ether and disinfectant. One SBA was working at a desk, another was winding bloodstained bandage round a stoker's torso, and Padre Forbes, who was young and fair-haired, boyish looking, was squatting beside another of the beds. He stood up when he saw Gant.

"Hello, sir."

"Padre." He was looking at the men in the camp beds, and they were mostly looking back at him. "Johnson, *you* swinging the lead again?"

"Seems so, sir." Johnson was an Asdic rating. The SBA got up from the desk and came over. He said, "Broken ribs, sir. And there's some metal in 'is back. Mr Sibbold'll be 'aving a go at him in a minute." He glanced round as a messenger came in: he was a writer whose action job was in one of Rowley's damage control parties. He looked taken aback when he saw Gant; he said, "I was to tell Mr Forbes the commander wanted a word with him."

"Yes. All right." Gant explained to Forbes that he'd asked Rowley to send a message, before he'd decided to come along himself. He said, "I'll see you in a few minutes, padre."

Burial arrangements might be better discussed elsewhere than in the presence of wounded men, he felt. The messenger said, "I was to ask for a casualty list too." He'd nodded towards Gant. "For—"

The SBA said, "I was just making it out, sir." Then Sibbold came out, parting the blue curtain. He said, "Come through, sir."

All six berths, three double tiers, were occupied. Nick Everard was in a lower bunk, flat on his back and dressed in a sickberth nightgown. He looked like a corpse in a shroud, Gant thought: there was no difference between the colour of his face and of that garment. His left arm, splinted above and below the elbow, was strapped to his chest; his head was wrapped in bandages and a thick surgical dressing had been plastered to the left side of his face.

Sibbold told Gant, "He was practically scalped. Concussion's his main problem, if he does come out of it. The arm would be all right. Whether or not he *will* emerge from coma I simply cannot say." The doctor looked challengingly at Gant. "I may add I've been asked at least a hundred times."

Gant nodded.

"There are a couple of dozen stitches in his face, under that pad. It was open to the cheekbone and down as far as the corners of his mouth. Starting near the eye. About thirty stitches in the scalp. It's very fortunate the skull isn't fractured: I don't believe it is. I suppose because the glass broke. If it hadn't, his skull would have. And of course I've no way of knowing what internal damage there may be: that's the major question."

"If he comes out of the coma, will he be—well, normal? I mean mentally?"

"I don't know."

"Can you estimate how long it may be before there's *some* kind of change?"

"As I said"—Sibbold shut his eyes. He looked as if he was trying not to scream—"I do not know what damage may have been done to the brain. It is impossible, at this stage—"

"All right." Gant sighed. "I'm sorry . . ."

"*I'm* sorry. If I could find reason to make optimistic noises, I'd be making them—very happily indeed. But for the time being—frankly—the best we can do is what we're doing already, plus maybe say a prayer or two."

Gant realized that all this time he'd been stooping, bending forward so as to look at Everard's face. He realized it because now, as he straightened, his back felt as if there was a fire in it. Sibbold was looking at him from close range, and it was an effort to keep the pain from showing in his face. He asked him, looking at the figure in the upper berth of this tier, "Who's this?"

"Leading Seaman Williams. Quartermaster."

"But—he was in the wheelhouse—"

"Very lucky to be alive, aren't we, Williams?"

"I'd like to write a letter, sir. Before she starts doin' her nut."

"Well, there won't be a mail landed for some time yet, old chap. And you'd write a better letter if you waited until you were stronger. I'd just rest, if I were you."

He told Gant, as they moved away, "He's a concussion case too. Plus some bits of wheelhouse in his legs. He had the luck to be on the far side of the chief quartermaster, who was between him and the blast. The chief QM was a very large man, as you know. Wasn't much left

of him: what there was—" He frowned, shook his head. "Williams's
concussion's nothing to worry about. But the letter he wants to write
is to that wife of his who got lost in Singapore. His memory'll come
back to him in a day or two—possibly even in an hour—and when it
does it won't be good for him at all. Now here we have one of our
prize exhibits." The doctor's voice had risen: "Stoker Petty Officer
Arnold, sir. First degree burns: but we'll soon have him chasing the
girls again. Eh, Arnold? Here's the commander to see you . . ."

A few minutes later, in the other part of the room, they gave him
the list of casualties. The dead included AB Gladwill, the captain's servant; Yeoman Ruddle and Chief Yeoman Howell; Alan Swanson the torpedo officer, a bridge messenger and two signalmen and one lookout;
Hobbs the schoolmaster and Newcomb who was a CW candidate and
Hobbs's assistant in the plot, and Paymaster Sub-Lieutenant Bloom; four
torpedomen including a torpedo gunner's mate; and the stokers who
were in the boiler room. In the wheelhouse the chief QM, a stoker
petty officer and an able seaman had brought the total to twenty-two.

Gant showed Padre Forbes the list. "This is what we have to talk
about."

"Yes." Forbes nodded, blinking. "Of course."

Gant went back through the curtain, for another quick look at his
captain. He said in his mind, staring down at the bandaged, bloodless-
looking face, *Come on now, come on* . . . And then, remembering Sibbold's
suggestion—which might have come better from young Forbes, when
one thought about it—he whispered, *Please God, may we have him back
with us, well again?*

He had to admit then—and if he was in contact with a Supreme
Authority his mind would anyway be open to inspection—that he was
making the request for his own sake, more than for Everard's. He and
the ship and all her officers and men needed Everard alive—needed
his experience and leadership and luck. He had a reputation for getting into sticky situations, and for getting out of them too—so possibly, if he could remain alive and even get back on his feet . . . Gant

asked humbly and self-consciously, knowing he wasn't much of a hand at the supplication routine, *If you could see your way to helping, please— to help us all?*

Reaction set in as he turned away. He wasn't a praying man: he was a churchgoer only because the Navy made it compulsory and because at home his wife expected him to set an example to the children. If God existed, He'd know this: and why should He take notice of an appeal from an agnostic, when He had real believers sending up forty thousand prayers a minute?

Gant thought that perhaps Everard had been in too many tight corners. No man's luck could last for ever . . . He nodded to Sibbold. *Defiant*'s principal medical officer was in his middle thirties, dark-jowled and brown-eyed, Mediterranean-looking. He could easily have been taken for a Greek. Gant asked the chaplain, "Coming?"

CHAPTER SIX

. . .

Something had Paul by the shoulder, pushing and pulling at it. Then Dennis Brill's voice broke through: "What does it take to wake you up, for God's sake?" He *was* awake: remembering where he was and that this was the day the Luftwaffe was likely to pull the stops out.

"What's the time?"

"It's alive, then. I was beginning to wonder." The doctor told him, "Five o'clock. Just after. Half an hour to action stations, right?"

Twenty-five minutes, actually. There'd be coffee available in the saloon, it had been mentioned. Paul let himself down from the bunk—it was the top one, with Brill's under it—and began to get dressed while the doctor shaved.

"You going to be all morning with that basin?"

"So far, I've been thirty seconds."

The hell with shaving, anyway. Who'd care—Leading Seaman Beale? Paul muttered, buttoning his battledress trousers, "Likely to be a tough day, according to the experts."

Brill said, glancing at him in the mirror as he scraped his Adam's apple, "There was some news last night, after you'd left us. I'd have told you, but I didn't like to spoil the rhythm of your snores . . . Aren't you shaving?"

"Later, maybe. What's this news?"

"RAF Beaufighters from Malta made a bombing raid on some Sardinian airfield—in aid of this convoy's easier passage, one gathers—and either on the way in or on the way back they flew over Cagliari Bay and saw Italian cruisers leaving Cagliari and steaming east."

It would have been on their way back, Paul thought. If they'd still had bomb-loads they'd have dropped them on the cruisers, surely. But the news didn't seem to him to add up to much. He glanced up from pulling on his halfboots: "That's it?"

Cleaning his teeth now, Brill nodded.

"Well, thanks for not waking me last night."

"Steaming east, Paul, suggests they'd be on their way to rendezvous with other Italian ships. And as the Italian fleet hardly ever does leave its harbours, I'm told the natural conclusion is they're assembling a force to put between us and Malta."

Paul smiled. "What time does your brain start working, Doc?"

"I beg your pardon?"

"We have battleships with us, remember? And carriers?"

"But they'll turn back tonight."

"They part company with us, sure. But McCall didn't say it all. Mackeson told me that what the big ships do then is hang around somewhere to the west, and the escort that's taking up to Malta—cruisers and destroyers—see us into Valletta but don't come in with us. They turn around and steam back to rejoin the heavy mob, who'll be waiting for them. Bit further west still, just outside flying range of the Sardinian fields, they all join up with the fleet oilers, and away they go. Because otherwise the destroyers would have to refuel in Malta, which doesn't have enough oil for itself . . . Anyway, the point is that while they wait out here somewhere the battlefleet's a threat to any Italian ships that did think about coming south."

"A long way from us, though?"

"Near enough to put the wind up the Italians. They like to have the sea to themselves before they stick their necks out." He'd pulled on a sweater, and now he reached for his battledress jacket. Brill wasn't even half ready yet. Paul had had a lot of practice, of course, in turning out fast to get up on watch: and in conditions a lot less comfortable than these. A destroyer's messdecks in foul weather—well, to an outsider it wouldn't seem possible that men could live like that. Brill, fresh out of medical school, wouldn't have believed it if he'd seen it. A lot of people wouldn't. Brill was standing on one leg getting into his khaki trousers. Paul took the opportunity to slap him on the back, and he went staggering across the cabin. "See you, Doc. I'll be where the coffee is."

Mackeson was in the saloon, and so was Thornton and the middle-aged flying officer. Thornton, in the early morning, looked to Paul like a turkey with an egg stuck halfway out. Amused at the thought, he smiled at him, and Thornton seemed disconcerted. You could guess he wasn't accustomed to being smiled at. Paul said "Good morning" to Mackeson, and asked him, "Is it true there are Italian surface ships on the move, sir?"

"Seem to be." Mackeson was loading his pipe. "But their destination may be the eastern basin. That'd be my guess."

"Why would they be going east?"

"There's a dummy convoy, a diversion to take some enemy attention off this one, persuade them to hold a few squadrons of Stukas in Crete, for instance, rather than concentrate the lot on us. The dummy consists of four ships out of Port Said in ballast, with a light escort joining them from Alexandria. Might look tempting to the intrepid Latins, eh?" "Bongo" smiled, patting his pockets in search of a match. He asked Paul, "How did you get on with the DEMS characters?"

They were on the dismal, frozen foc'sl-head, with their Oerlikons loaded and ready, when he got up there just after 5:30. Light was seeping up from the eastern horizon, silhouetting the dark bulk of the MV *Warrenpoint* ahead of the *Montgovern*. To starboard the *Castleventry* was a grey ghost-ship hissing along on a cushion of white foam, while to port a Hunt-class destroyer was visible only by her bow-wave.

Beale said, by way of greeting, "Nice an' peaceful."

The four gunners were muffled in scarves, overcoats and balaclavas. Paul said, "I always thought of the Med as a *warm* sea."

"Gets fookin' 'orrible when it wants to." Withinshaw took his hands out of his pockets and beat them together. "Am I right in guessin' you're a Yank—sir?"

He'd trotted the question out so quickly that it was obvious they'd been discussing him. And it was the first time any of them had used the word "sir" to him. Compensation, probably, for the directly personal question. But he didn't give a damn, one way or the other. He told Withinshaw, "I'm British, but I was at school in the States for a few years. Sounds like it, does it?"

"Well, not all *that* bad." He was being fookin' patronizing now, Paul thought. "How come you was in Yanky-land, then?"

It was because my mother's Russian and she and my father didn't get along . . . He wasn't about to explain all that to Withinshaw, though. He said, "Family reasons . . . Where are you lot from?"

Withinshaw had started life in Birkenhead but lived in Yarmouth. Beale had a wife and baby daughter in Nottingham. Wally was a Londoner whose parents had moved up to Preston, Lancs, and McNaught was a Glaswegian.

Bloody cold . . .

Light was increasing, reaching upwards from the horizon ahead. He wondered what might be showing on the warships' RDF screens. It was a fair bet the enemy would have reconnaissance flights out by this time, and bombers lined up on Sardinian airstrips waiting for the convoy to be pinpointed. Some of those bombers would be taking off for the last time, and some of these ships might not be afloat by sunset; but there'd be very few airmen or sailors reckoning on it being their own last day. That was strange, when you thought about it: because conversely, if you had a ticket in a lottery you *did,* surely, consider the chances of winning.

He wished he'd written to his father.

Steady pounding of the freighter's engines, swishing murmur of the sea. It was like waiting for a curtain to go up. He wondered what the odds really were, on any one of these ships in the convoy getting through. Sixteen ships: if you reckoned on four of them arriving, you might have it about right?

Funny they'd sent passengers in them, really. Except there wasn't any other way to get there. To be flown to Malta you'd need to be an admiral or a politician, and even that wouldn't be anything like safe transport.

Such an enormous effort, to sustain that one small island. The reason for it, he supposed, was that if Malta fell there'd be no base from which to attack Axis supply convoys to the desert. So they'd be able to build up their forces to any strength they needed and then keep them supplied without interruption, so they'd sweep through to take Cairo and the Canal. Then the rest of the Middle East, including the Gulf and its oil; and up into the Caucasus to link with their armies facing the Russians there. They'd have the world strangling in a Nazi noose. When you stretched the imagination that far it became understandable that the Admiralty and the War Cabinet and the Chiefs of Staff should be satisfied if just a few of these sixteen ships survived to reach Malta. You could understand it yourself, even when you happened to be sitting on top of one of them.

He doubted whether the Admiralty would sweat blood, exactly, if Sub-Lieutenant Paul Everard RNVR didn't make it to the island, either.

If he'd mustered the resolution to write that letter before he'd left England, what would he have said in it? How did you raise a subject like this one, to your own father?

He left the DEMS group and paced for'ard, into the eyes of the ship, the narrowing stem with its furnishing of heavy anchor-and-cable gear and the waist-high steel bulwark. He stood in the curve of it, right in the very bow, and tried to frame a letter in his mind.

I wish I didn't have to tell you this, but I hope you'll see why I do have to. If I could wait until we met it might be easier to say it than to write it— well, I don't know about that either, but the fact is I'm the only person you could hear it from, and if anything happened to me before I saw you, you wouldn't ever know. Not until it was too late. So, here goes.

You'll remember telling me and Jack about the Gay Nineties Club, and that you asked Mrs Gordon to make us members of it if we went along and saw her. Well, Jack and I met in London and we did just that, and she— Phyllis Gordon—introduced us to Mrs Fiona Gascoyne . . .

Phil Gordon was a very good-looking woman and a great personality: very smart, bright, outgoing. The Gordon family, Paul had gathered from what his father had said, was well-known in the hotel business, and this probably explained the fact that here in her own club she used her maiden name, although she was actually the wife of Eric Maschwitz, the man who'd written "A Nightingale Sang in Berkeley Square." He was in the club too on the evening Paul and Jack Everard called in, but he wasn't around for long. He had some job in or near that same square, and his wife's club was in Berkeley Street so it was very convenient for him. A tall man, genial and easy to get along with; he was in SIS or Military Intelligence, one of those outfits. He'd spent a few minutes with them, then excused himself to go through to the dining room—where the menu was chalked, in a very stylish handwriting, on a blackboard on an easel.

Phil Gordon perched herself at the bar, and patted the stools on each side of her.

"Up you get, boys." She told the white-coated barman, "We'll have those again, Terry."

"Large ones, Miss Gordon?"

"Naturally." She smiled at Paul: her eyes did most of the smiling. "I'd have known you for a son of Nick Everard's even if you hadn't told me." She shook her head at Jack. "Not you, though."

"Perhaps because I'm *not* a son of his?"

Jack was a powerful, hard-looking man now, and the way he looked at Phil suggested that the twenty years' difference in their ages wouldn't have stood in his way if he'd been in the mood. That was very much the impression he gave: that he'd take what he wanted, when he wanted it. Paul was to remember afterwards that he'd had this thought in his mind less than half an hour before Jack went right ahead and proved it . . . But the two-year interval since they'd last met had changed Jack Everard completely. Even if it had been *ten* years you wouldn't have expected such a difference. It wasn't only that he looked so much older. At Mullbergh, at Christmas of 1939, Paul had thought he was supercilious and spoilt, with a sneering, snobby manner that wasn't easy to put up with. He'd been pampered by that rather forbidding, bloodless mother of his, Nick's stepmother Sarah. And defensive, unsure of himself.

Now, the lap-dog had turned wolfish.

Phil Gordon seemed wary of him too. She'd talked mostly to Paul. He'd asked her, "You must have known my father quite a while?"

"So much of a while I'd rather not dwell on it. How *is* the old darling?"

"Fit and strong, going by his letters. He has a destroyer flotilla, you know, out in—"

He'd stopped, before it slipped out. "Careless Talk": there were posters on a lot of walls about it. Phyllis said, "Wherever he is, give him my love."

"I sure will."

"And kisses."

He wondered, sipping his drink, whether they'd be a brand of kisses already familiar to his father, from some time in the pre-war era. The old man could have shown worse taste, at that . . . Phil might have guessed how his thoughts were running. She'd laughed, murmured, "Not in front of the future Lady Everard, though . . . Have you two met her?"

Neither of them had known of the existence of any such creature. Phil told them, "Well, if you pop in here often enough I'll see you do. She's one of our regulars."

"Well." Paul shook his head. "Bombshell, if there ever was one."

Jack asked, "Who is she?"

"Fiona Gascoyne. *Mrs*—a widow. Very pretty, young, and rather rich." She'd added, "Perhaps just a *little* young for him . . ." In the short silence that followed, Paul thought he could see her claws retracting again. She said suddenly, "Oh, dear. Perhaps I should have kept my trap shut. If it's a secret from the rest of the family . . ."

Jack was looking quite put out, as if the idea of Nick Everard remarrying was an affront to him. Paul suggested to Phil, "If you introduce us to her, it might be best that none of us mentions it. Then if *she* does, you're off the hook."

"That's a *very* smart idea." She patted his hand where it rested on the bar. "Thanks. And before I let any more cats out of bags, I've a few chores to see to. So I'll leave you for a while. Remember, tonight you don't pay for any drinks."

"It's very sweet of you, but—"

"Any argument, you don't get membership. Right?"

"We surrender."

Jack nodded. *"Force majeure."*

"You said it." She slid off her stool. "Look after these two, Doris." Doris was the second bartender. "Terry knows—their drinks are on the house, because I'm crazy about their father." She looked at Jack: "Sorry. Half-brother. Enjoy yourselves, now."

Paul remembered Jack looking after her as she threaded her way out through the crowded room. From the back, with that cloud of red hair and her slim figure in the grey silk dress, she could have been in her twenties. Jack murmured as he turned back, "Old Nick has an eye for them, all right. I'd have said he *had* an eye for them, but apparently . . ." He frowned, without finishing the sentence. Two years ago, Paul was remembering, he'd hardly been able to look you in the eye. Now he had eyes like stones; they looked as if they wouldn't have blinked if you'd stuck your fingers in them.

He wondered why Jack disliked the idea of Nick remarrying.

Well, a fairly simple theory was that if Nick Everard was killed, he— Paul—would succeed to the baronetcy and to Mullbergh, the house and the estate. And if *he* then drowned—or whatever—that would leave Jack in line. It wasn't such a remote possibility, at that. In wartime people did get killed, and Nick Everard was invariably in the front of things. Submarining mightn't be the safest way of earning a living, either. But on the other hand, if Nick married and started a new family—well, any baby son would stand to inherit after Paul.

Something like that?

He mightn't have thought of it, except that two years ago at Mullbergh he'd had quite a strong impression that his presence and existence didn't exactly thrill either Jack or Jack's mother, Sarah.

Jack murmured, "Must say, I'd like to catch a glimpse of the so-called 'future Lady Everard.' Are you sure you didn't know it was in the wind?"

"Not a bit of it . . . But listen—you were telling me about your time in Crete?"

"I've said everything that's worth telling."

He'd said it irritably. Bored with the subject, because he had something else on his mind now. Paul said, "I was finding it very interesting."

"Did I mention that my beloved half-brother, your parent, was present in his destroyer when I was sunk in *Carnarvon*."

"Dad told me all about it, in a letter."

Jack took a swallow of his drink. Pink gin. "He didn't hang around for long. Did he tell you that too?"

"He described it all. It must have been pretty damned awful for him."

"It wasn't exactly fun for the rest of us . . . Cigarette?"

"I just put one out, thank you. Care to tell me what this job is you're doing now?"

"Be difficult. I wouldn't, if I could, anyway; but to be honest I don't know *exactly* what it's in aid of—except it's something fairly extraordinary . . . I wonder who this bloody woman is?"

"Sounds like it's a special op of some kind . . ." It had to do with MLs, motor-launches; and Jack had been employed in cloak-and-dagger work in Crete, of course . . . "Hey, we aren't talking about the Second Front, are we?"

"We aren't talking about anything at all." Jack emptied his glass, and pushed it forward to be filled again. "But when you hear about it over the BBC one of these days, you'll know what I was talking about." He shrugged. "So will I . . . Let's change the subject, shall we?"

Paul tried to, without much success. Jack had turned moody, and he was drinking faster. It was a relief when Phyllis Gordon came back. With her, was one of the most attractive women Paul had ever set eyes on.

"Now then, Everards, pay attention!" She slid an arm round the girl's shoulders. "Fiona darling: this is Paul, Nick's son, and this is Jack, the half-brother. Jack, Paul, this is Fiona Gascoyne."

Jack said, getting off his stool and with his eyes fixed on the girl, "Oh I *know* you!"

Her black dress was sleeveless, and he'd taken hold of her arms.

She glanced round at Phil. "I never saw him before in my—"

"I know *you*, though! You don't know me yet but I do know *you!*"

Fiona was the only one who didn't seem embarrassed: just amused. Then a wing commander came up on Fiona's other side, asking, "Who are these far-from-ancient mariners, now?" Fiona looked round at him, and turned away again: Jack asked her, "Want to hear *how* I know you?"

"Oh, everyone in London knows Fiona. Everyone who's anybody, that is." The RAF man had an inane laugh, Paul remembered, and Phil had cut into it, telling him, "Harry, I only borrowed her for a moment. Take her away, will you?"

"All right." Fiona moved back a pace, and Jack's hands slid off her arms: you could see the marks where he'd been holding her. "I give up."

"Your portrait. In Nick's cabin in a destroyer thousands of miles away. About a year ago, it was."

"But how sweet of him to have had—"

"The hell with *him! I've* lived with your face in my mind ever since! Now I know you're real, and it's incredible. I'd begun to think you were a figment of my imagination—or Nick invented you, or—"

"You're not at all like him, are you?"

"No." He inclined his head, like someone acknowledging a compliment. "I'm not."

The roar of an aircraft engine blotted out the daydream. Paul and the four OEMS gunners stared upwards as a fighter swept over. No guns were firing, and there was just enough light to make out the shape of a second one as it hurtled over behind the first: they'd both been Fulmars. Memories of that evening in the Gay Nineties were like bits of an old film that he could rerun at will in his brain. And the shot of Jack as he'd uttered those three words, "No, I'm not," became a still, the camera holding on an expression that was a mixture of excitement and vindictiveness.

Beale said, "Patrols goin' up."

The two that followed were Sea Hurricanes. One pair of fighters from each of the two carriers, probably. Paul checked the time, as the noise of the last one faded: 6:22. The escorting warships would almost certainly have enemy formations on their RDF screens by now, and two of the cruisers, Mackeson had said, were equipped as fighter-direction ships, able to vector fighters on to approaching bombers.

Daylight growing. Waiting, watching. Wally and McNaught chewing gum: even in this half-light you could see the rhythmic chomping. Withinshaw yawned like a great fat cat.

The commodore's siren had blared for an emergency turn to starboard, and out on the wing of the screen destroyers were hunting and dropping depth charges: so it was obvious what the emergency turn was for. No bombers had appeared yet, but it was almost fully light and the red air-raid alert signals were flying, indicative of there being RDF contacts on the big ships' screens.

The *Montgovern*'s Willet-Bruce moaned, repeating the emergency-turn signal. Mackeson had swung round for a quick look at the destroyer activity on the bow, but his glasses were trained out on the quarter again now, at the carriers who'd turned into the wind to fly-off a batch of Sea Hurricanes. Reinforcements to those already airborne, and another sign that enemy formations couldn't be far away.

Humphrey Straight was beside his quartermaster at the steering position, conning the ship round to starboard.

Thornton came into the bridge. He'd stopped just inside the door, with a look of surprise, as if he'd expected to be welcomed. Now he'd come over to Mackeson. He cleared his throat, as the siren wheezed itself into silence, and told him, "Signal. About a concentration—as you were, *two* concentrations—of U-boats on our track."

He'd announced it rather pompously, as if the information derived from his own private sources.

"They're right here, never mind on our track." Mackeson lowered his glasses and perused the signal. He murmured, "Galitia Island, northeast and northwest of it. That's about where we'd expect them to be thickest, isn't it. But it's—what, ninety miles ahead." He took the message over to show the master. "I'd say it's a case of sufficient unto the moment are the U-boats thereof, captain."

Straight told his quartermaster, "Steady as you go." The pipe in his mouth had gone out but he was still sucking at it. He glanced at his chief officer, Devenish, and muttered, "I'd say it's a case of fuck the lot of 'em." Thornton's eyebrows were raised as he left the bridge. Out on the convoy's port beam some destroyers had opened fire: before the turn, of course, that had been the bow. Now a more solid build-up of AA fire as battleships and cruisers and the Hunts on the quarter let rip too. Young Gosling, out in the exposed port wing of the bridge, was pointing astern and he had his whistle in his mouth. He was blowing it, presumably, but he might as well have been sucking it for all the use it was. Shell-bursts were gathering in the sky, which was silver-bright now from the rising sun ahead, and black-brown-grey puffballs of the exploding time-fused shells had edgings of gold and silver. To the bomber pilots they'd be plain black, and more deadly than decorative. The bombers were Junkers 88s again, a pack of a dozen or fifteen planes with a similar-sized group astern of them. They were high, and they gave the impression of climbing against the background brightness as they came in, most of the shell-bursts below them at first but getting closer: in fact they weren't climbing, they were flying straight and level, giving warships' HA control systems the kind of shoot they'd been designed for and didn't often get. Bursts were appear-

ing under the Junkers' noses and all around them: and either they were
dodging now or it was the percussions of the shells jarring them this
way and that. Still coming, though—black wings, black crosses on
white backgrounds, slicing through the drifting smoke of the shell-
bursts as they held on towards the centre of the convoy.

A signalman—the naval V/S rating who was one of Mackeson's
team—was pointing out to starboard: "Sir, that—" It was drowned in
sharper, closer noise as the *Montgovern's* Bofors guns opened fire. The
signalman had been pointing out at the RAF man in the starboard
wing. He in turn had been trying to draw Mackeson's attention to
something in the sea on the starboard bow, but now he'd given up, he
was leaning over to watch the "something" as it passed.

Devenish muttered, "Torpedo track." There wasn't much else it could
have been. But it was as well they'd turned: the escort commander must
have told the commodore that torpedoes had been fired. From the
Blackadder now another siren-signal was wailing, ordering a return to
the mean course, and at the same time every gun in the convoy and
in the warships surrounding it was blazing vertically or near-vertically
at bombers overhead. Humphrey Straight leaned close to his quartermaster's ear and growled, "Port fifteen degrees." Bombs were raising
dirty-looking heaps of sea between ships in the rear half of the convoy
as they began the turn. Then, from the quarter, an explosion was deep,
solid-sounding . . . Mackeson, still out in the wing—he'd gone to see
what had been exciting the Air Force man out there—saw several
bomb-splashes between the rearmost merchantmen and the battleships:
it looked as if the battleships had been the targets for those bombs. But
that deep *boom* hadn't been the bomb-burst: he was almost certain
someone had been torpedoed. He had his glasses trained on the quarter as the whole convoy turned back towards its mean course: and one
ship back there was turning the wrong way. It was the freighter on the
far side—the starboard side—of the tanker *Caracas Moon*. The last ship
in column four. She was swinging out to starboard, away from the rest
of the convoy and across the bows of a Hunt-class destroyer which was

taking sharp avoiding action. That ship was also listing. Gunfire, which had slackened, was building to a new crescendo as the second half of the bomber force came over. Mackeson, turning to go back inside the bridge, happened to glance down at the foc's'l and saw young Everard grab one gunner's arm and point. Then both Oerlikons were spitting fire. These Junkers, unlike the front-runners, had gone into shallow dives, flying faster because of that and dipping through the barrage of AA fire and across the forepart of the convoy. *This* part. But they weren't in Oerlikon range yet, he thought. Everard lacked experience, but that DEMS killick should have known better and held his fire. He went inside, shutting the bridge door quickly to keep some of the noise out. Humphrey Straight was telling the quartermaster, "Ease to five degrees of port wheel." He glanced around, stared bull-like at Mackeson, who told him, "End ship in column four. Torpedo. She's dropped out."

Straight scowled, looking at the convoy diagram on the bulkhead. "*Agulhas Queen*. Old Vic Kerrick."

He stared aft in the hope of a sight of her: then he'd turned back. "Midships the wheel." He muttered, "Bastards." A stick of bombs came slanting, and sea rose in a mound of white and grey not far off the port bow. The other three of the stick hit and smothered the *Warrenpoint*: sea leaped from near-misses right against her hull, and one bomb landed in her after well deck. There was a spurt of smoke and debris, then a second afterwards an explosion near the waterline on her port side. Smoke gushed out of her, enveloping her afterpart.

Humphrey Straight was leaning forward with his blunt nose almost touching the glass front window of the bridge. He ordered "Port fifteen degrees. Two short blasts."

Devenish moved that way, but the bosun was ahead of him with a hand on the lever that operated the siren. He jerked it down twice, sending two short, strong wafts of steam through the whistle, two blasts meaning, "I am directing my course to port." The ships astern would follow his lead.

It was close enough. The *Montgovern*'s stem was hidden in the smoke pouring out of the ship ahead. Swinging through it, swinging faster now: and they would almost certainly have carried away the *Warrenpoint's* Cherub speed log, coming that close under her stern. Straight had ordered the wheel to be centred, then put the other way, so as not to swing his own ship's stern in a swiping blow at the *Warrenpoint* as they pounded by her. The *Warrenpoint's* guns were still in action: all of them, even a Bofors on her stern with Army gunners manning it. You could see the rapid winking stabs of flame as it flung up its forty-millimetre shells. In her after-well deck men were struggling with hoses. The smoke seemed to be coming up from her number five hatch. Mackeson, out on the bridge wing as the *Montgovern* passed her, saw a big gash with jagged, out-turned edges just above the waterline. So that bomb must have exploded on its way out, after it had passed almost right through the ship. They'd got by her now: she was dropping astern between columns one and two. While about a mile astern of the convoy—he used his binoculars, looking back between the columns and out past the battleship on the quarter—a long way back now a Hunt-class destroyer was nosing around the bow of the *Agulhas Queen*. She was leaning right over and he could see boats in the water, and a Sea Hurricane dipping protectively overhead. So the *Agulhas Queen* was being abandoned; and from the condition of the *Warrenpoint* as she'd been when they'd passed her he wouldn't have betted on her survival either.

As he went back inside, Humphrey Straight had just ordered five degrees of starboard wheel, to edge her over into station at the correct distance from column two; he'd also glanced at the bosun and shaken his head, a negative to the man's readiness to give one short blast from the siren. He'd take her in gradually, not swerve in. He told Devenish, with a nod towards the engine-room telegraph, "Up a touch, mister." Devenish gave the telegraph handle a jerk, one clang of the bell in the "ahead" direction, a private signal for a couple more revs per minute. They had a voicepipe to the engine-room, fitted specially for the requirements of convoy manoeuvring, but they weren't accustomed to it and Mackeson had noticed that they hardly ever used it. The *Montgovern* had to move up now to take the *Warrenpoint's* station as a column leader on the commodore's port beam.

Gunfire had died away, except on the bow where a mutter of it was still following the attackers round: they'd be circling that way to get back on to their northeastward course for home.

They'd be back later, Paul supposed. Or others like them.

Ahead of the convoy a parachute drifted slowly seaward. Beale said, "One of our lot. On 'is own, must be." He was probably right: the 88s had a crew of four, so from any of them there'd have been more than one parachute. Wally Short said, stepping back with an empty or part-empty Oerlikon magazine and swinging round to dump it in the bin, "I seen four Gerries down."

Paul had seen three bombers hit and in trouble, but only two actually go down in the sea. The others might have crashed, but they hadn't done so in his sight. Not much of a swap anyway, for two ships . . . Another depressing fact was that although they'd fired off a lot of ammunition, these Oerlikons hadn't had any targets low or near enough to have had much chance of hitting.

When they'd been choking in the *Warrenpoint's* smoke he'd thought *There but for the grace of God* . . . and then, *But there's still lots of time.* For the grace of God to be less in evidence, he'd meant. And it had become real now, it was happening just as one had been told it would. When you were lectured on things like previous convoys' losses and what was therefore certain to be in store for this one you heard it and believed it, but somehow without seeing it as applying to you directly. Until you saw it happening it was theory, talk, speculation. But it was real now. Or it *had* been, for a few minutes . . .

There wasn't anything to do now except wait, and it was a different kind of waiting. You were waiting for something you knew about, something you'd seen the shape of.

The *Montgovern* had become the leader of the port-side column, with the *Blackadder* to starboard flying the pennant of the commodore and three cruisers ahead across the convoy's front. One, a ship of the *Mauritius* class, was about four thousand yards on the port bow of the *Montgovern,* and the smaller ship in the centre of the trio—about the same distance on the freighter's other bow—was one of the old C class who'd been converted as anti-aircraft ships. She would be just about identical to *Carnarvon,* in which Jack Everard had been navigator when she'd been sunk off Crete. And off the far (right-hand) corner of the convoy, out on the starboard beam of the C-class cruiser, was a contrastingly modern ship of the *Newcastle* class, nearly ten thousand tons of her.

Those three cruisers would be coming on with the convoy tonight when the battleships and carriers and their attendant cruisers turned back.

Paul walked for'ard, up into the narrowing stem again. With his back to the bridge and with the foremast and a cargo-derrick nicely in the way, he lit a cigarette. Mackeson might not approve of naval personnel smoking, he thought, at action stations, and he didn't want to upset old Bongo . . . He wondered what might be happening astern, with the *Warrenpoint* and that other casualty. He hadn't seen that torpedo hit. He'd heard it, and Beale had muttered, "Some poor sod's 'ad it," and McCall had told them about it when he'd come visiting. But with the convoy plugging on eastward and the gaps where those ships had been already filled, he realized with a touch of shame that casualties tended to drop out of mind about as soon as they dropped out of station. Perhaps because these fourteen now—he was trying to rationalize it to himself—holding on for Malta and waiting for the next stage of the whittling-down process to start, were the ones that mattered . . . But would one feel like that about it if—or when—it was the *Montgovern* falling back, sinking or burning? Might this feeling that what mattered was carrying on, pushing *some* part of the convoy through, be only a manifestation of the famous sailorlike response of *Fuck you, Jack, I'm inboard?*

Translated, it meant "I'm safe in the boat, so the hell with *you* . . ."

The odds were, he knew, that he'd get a chance to find out. So for the time being, damn the introspection too. He dropped the half-smoked cigarette, and trod on it, then made his way back to the others. Only three of them. Beale explained, "Ginger's gone for char."

Phyllis Gordon had broken up Jack's play for Fiona Gascoyne (or Jack's and Fiona's play for each other: she could easily have brushed him off, made a joke of it and then ignored him) by virtually pushing her into the arms of the moustached airman, the bemedalled character called Harry who'd seemed, Paul thought, pretty ineffectual . . . Harry had found Fiona's arm linked into his, because Phyllis had put it there, and they'd gone off to the dining room because she'd directed them to it. If they were hoping to get a meal tonight, she'd urged them, they'd better take up their reservation *now.*

But she hadn't realized, as Paul had, that Jack had been doing anything more than mildly flirting. Paul had sensed it: and met Jack's glance and then *known* it . . . Phyllis told Jack, after Fiona and the airman had moved off, "Don't overdo the charm, my boy. Nick mightn't go much on it."

"Oh, come *on!*"

As if he couldn't believe that anyone could even *imagine* he'd make a pass at his half-brother's future wife . . . And Phil accepted it on that level: as a joke they'd shared, nothing to be taken seriously. She'd patted Jack's hand, and told him, "Nick's very much in love with her, you know."

"Who wouldn't be?"

He'd glanced sideways at Paul. Wanting him to know, for some reason. A personal triumph over Nick Everard? Or—more simply—just because the girl attracted him?

Jack had picked up his glass and emptied it. He said, "We'd better go and eat too, Paul."

In order to follow the Gascoyne girl into the dining room, Paul guessed. Phil Gordon stopped that one anyway: they hadn't booked—couldn't have, in fact, as they weren't members—and the place was full. She advised them, "When you're members, do make sure of booking. Lunches are easier, but—"

"It doesn't matter." Paul told her, "I hadn't thought of eating here."

"Might as well have one for the road, then," Jack added. "My round. We can't possibly go on cadging—"

"Non-members can't buy drinks, they *have* to cadge." She beckoned the barman. "Terry?" He was coming over. Jack said, "How *very* kind you are. But—if you'd excuse me, a moment—where's the heads or gents', around here?"

She told him. Then she was alone with Paul. She said, "Bit of a card, your . . . half-uncle?"

"I barely know him. Since childhood—we haven't met in years. Two days two years ago was the last time, and before that I honestly don't remember when it was."

"Mrs Gascoyne wasn't encouraging him, you know." Terry was waiting for the order: she twiddled her finger at the three glasses. "I wouldn't blame her, Paul."

"Blame her for what?"

"I had the impression you didn't like her much."

"I don't know her. But if my father wants to marry her, she must be a very nice person." He added, "As well as very pretty."

"It's quite natural that she and Nick's own brother should be interested in meeting each other, anyway . . . Here's your drink, son of Nick."

"You're very kind." He glanced at Terry. "Thanks."

"Here's to all the Everards—past, present and future."

"Hah." Rejoining them, Jack picked up his glass. "I'll drink to that. This is a *very* nice club, Mrs Gordon."

"I'm glad you like it." She asked Paul, "Do you really have to go now?"

"Go?" Jack seemed surprised. "Did we say we were going?"

"To eat. This was the one for the road, remember?"

"So it was." Jack laughed, for some reason. "I'd quite forgotten. But—how about a meal at the Wellington?"

"I don't know it."

"It's not a bad dump. I'm a member."

Phyllis Gordon said that if they wanted membership of the Gay Nineties, now they'd seen it, she'd make the arrangements. They both said yes, they'd very much like to join, and she suggested they might look in tomorrow or the day after. Jack told her, "I'm going to almost live here, from now on."

"Don't you have a war to fight?"

"Oh, there are plenty of people to keep that damn thing going."

They were laughing as she walked away. Paul was beginning to wonder if he could have been wrong, if he'd over-reacted, earlier. He'd never liked Jack much, and perhaps his snap judgement had been influenced by this.

Jack settled himself on a stool, and lit a cigarette.

"The Wellington's towards Knightsbridge." He sipped his drink. "So we'll go along and have a snack. Sign you in as a member if you like it. It's open on Sunday nights, meals and dancing, which is useful sometimes."

"Okay. Thanks."

"But afterwards—well, I don't know what you plan to do with the rest of the evening, Paul, but personally I'm going nightclubbing. I'm joining Wing-Commander Thingummy and Mrs Gascoyne at the Embassy."

Paul sat leaning on the bar, looking at him sideways.

"You are *what?*"

"Did you really imagine I was in the heads?" Jack fingered a card out of the top pocket of his reefer jacket. "He invited me, believe it or not. They're in a big party, so an odd number won't really matter. *She* pointed that out. Tell you one thing, half-nephew—*I* won't be the odd man out." He was studying the card. "This is where she lives. Eaton

Square, hum hum. Tell you another thing—*I* reckon she's a push-over."

Paul put his glass down. He asked him, "You don't really imagine I'd eat with you, do you?"

Jack shrugged. "Please yourself." He held up the visiting card. "Better than a hole in the ground in Crete, eh?"

"Want a wet? Sorry, sir, want—"

Withinshaw was offering him a tin mug of steaming, dark brown liquid. He had a cigarette sticking to his lip. Beale was smoking too.

"Thanks."

Paul had been sitting on the ammunition bin. He stood up now, stretching, and glancing around at sea and sky. There'd been some aircraft around during the past twenty or thirty minutes, but each time they'd turned out to be Fleet Air Arm machines either leaving for or returning from patrol. Fulmars, Martlets and Sea Hurricanes.

The tea tasted as if someone had washed his socks in it, but he could feel its warmth trickling down inside. He asked Withinshaw, "Are you a family man?"

Beale burst into guffaws of laughter: he was staring out towards the horizon in the north, out past a nearby Hunt. The two younger DEMS men were laughing too. Withinshaw ignored it all: but he was looking at Paul in a cautious manner, as if he wasn't going to be caught out by any trick questions. He nodded. "Aye."

Beale said without turning round, "Ask 'im *'ow many* families."

"Huh?"

Withinshaw advised him, "Don't want to take no fookin' notice o' silly fookin' sods like Ronald bleedin' Beale."

"Great Yarmouth is where he keeps one lot." Beale glanced round now, to wink at McNaught and Short. "But what do they know in Yarmouth about the little loved ones in Durban, Union of South Africa? Eh, Art?"

"You can shut your fookin'—"

"Hey, up!"

Beale had turned back, and he was pointing out on the port quarter. Aircraft: fighters like silver toys closing on two larger planes. A trail of smoke was like a thin tail from one of them. It was diving, the smoke blackening and painting a curve on the sky as it went down into the sea and the fighters lifted like swallows, banking away after the other enemy, who'd turned away. Paul couldn't see that one now. But faintly, there was a second stammering of cannon-fire.

"One down, anyway. Fleet Air Arm are keeping it all away from us. No wonder we're getting a quiet forenoon."

Beale said, "Them'll just be recce flights, most likely, keepin' tabs on us. When they really come, they'll not be stopped that easy."

"You said you'd been in a convoy like this one before. Malta and back—in this ship?"

"Not in this bastard, no." Beale cocked an ear; and Paul heard it too, depth charging, on the other bow.

"Did you get hit by anything on that convoy?"

"Not a scratch."

"Fookin' lucky we was an' all." Withinshaw stood up. " 'Ere we go again . . ."

Another emergency turn—to port, this time. Turning away from that submarine while the destroyers' depth charges kept it deep.

Withinshaw murmured reflectively, "We was fookin' lucky, though, that trip. Eh, Ron?"

"You oughter get a sign painted, Art."

"What you on about now, then?"

"A notice you could 'old up when Gerry's comin' over. Big letters sayin': 'Mercy—two families to support.' "

Gunfire, out in the destroyer screen, three miles ahead . . .

Paul went towards the bow, to get a clearer view. Behind him, the DEMS men went on teasing Withinshaw, Wally asking him how many papooses he'd got so far out of each squaw in his separate wigwams. Paul could see the smoke-haze of the destroyers' barrage fire ahead, but not what they were shooting at. Then two Fulmars belted over from astern, flying in that direction: and the commodore's siren bellowed like a moose at rutting-time, ordering a turn back to starboard. McCall came up the ladder from the well deck, and Paul went back to meet him.

"What's all that about?"

"Torpedo-bombers, apparently. Italians." Beale and Withinshaw became more alert, less chatty, standing to their guns and looking out over the port bow as the ship swung to starboard. McCall added, "Fighters from the carriers back there have shot down two Eyetie recce aircraft in the last half-hour. Savoia Marchettis."

"Fine."

"Sods are just keeping an eye on us, for the moment. Getting set for something big."

"D'you think so?"

"Well." Staring out towards where that action was, shielding his eyes against the sun, McCall said, "That bit's over, by the looks of it." He answered Paul, "Very close to Sardinia, aren't we? They aren't going to just sit on their fat arses and watch us sail by, are they?"

"I guess not."

"Right . . . Meanwhile the *Agulhas Queen's* sunk, and the last we heard of the *Warrenpoint* was a signal telling the destroyer that was standing by her to take her blokes off and then sink her."

Paul looked at him, and nodded. "Come to cheer us up, have you?"

"Why should you need cheering up, for Christ's sake?" He offered Paul a cigarette, and they both lit up. Everyone did smoke at action stations, apparently. McCall was a medium-sized man with a hooked nose, deep-set blue eyes and wiry dark hair: about as Celtic-looking as you could get, Paul supposed. The second mate added, "We've got off very easy, so far. Aren't I right, Beale?"

The killick nodded, watching the sky across the convoy's van. McCall pinched his cigarette out, and flicked it over the side. It was only half smoked, but with duty-free at twenty for sixpence you didn't have to bother much. He nodded: "See you later."

•   •   •

Forenoon wearing on . . .

There'd been several more emergency turns, and more depth charging out in the deep field, and once the Mauritius-class cruiser on the port bow of the convoy had gone hard a-port to avoid torpedoes which had narrowly missed a Hunt outside her. The Hunt had turned too and dashed out along the torpedo-tracks, picked up a submarine contact and attacked with depth charges, but by the time another destroyer had joined her the contact had been lost.

McCall had told Paul he wasn't bound to spend the entire day on the foc's'l-head, and he'd been aft to his cabin for a shave, then down to the saloon for coffee. He'd found Brill in the saloon, reading a P.G. Wodehouse novel. There was an oilcloth cover on the mess table, and Brill had a lot of medical gear laid out on it. He'd complained, "Trade's slow. Thought you might've been a customer."

From the boat deck you could see that the merchantmen had been rearranged following the loss of those two ships. There were only three freighters now in columns one and four, and four in each of the two centre columns. The *Caracas Moon,* the tanker, had shifted up to become second ship in column three, so she was now on the starboard beam of the *Castleventry* and protected by having other ships all around her.

Back on the foc's'l, Paul found the DEMS team lying around smoking, dozing, chewing gum. There was no alert, no red flag flying: and in the three cruisers ahead would be RDF sets that would pick up any enemy aircraft pretty well the minute it left the ground, with Sardinia no more than seventy-five miles away.

Getting towards noon, too. Noon, according to McCall, being danger-hour, or thereabouts. Paul shut the lid of the ammunition bin and sat down on it, facing out over the port bow, northeastward. Out to starboard, abaft the beam when the convoy was on this leg of its zigzag, two destroyers were following up an A/S contact, but it was too far away to see what was happening.

Warmer now. He took his cap off, and opened his greatcoat. Remembering how, two evenings after that first one in the Gay Nineties, he'd gone there alone, primarily to check up on the membership situation. He'd called in first at Hatchet's on the north side of Piccadilly, to visit the bar—one flight of curving stairs down towards the restaurant—and check in the submariners' book they kept there. If you were on leave in London and at a loose end you put your name in it, and where you were staying or where you'd be that evening. But none of Paul's friends was in the capital, apparently, or had bothered to record the fact. He had a beer, then went up the stairs into Piccadilly again and headed west towards Berkeley Street. The tarts were already competing for pavement space, and there were some very smart-looking girls among them. A lot of them worked in munition factories, he'd heard, in daylight hours, and now the massed bombing raids seemed to be over they flocked into the West End every evening. It was about half-seven when he got to the Gay Nineties. He called in to the office first, saw Phil Gordon and collected his membership card, then went to the bar, and he'd just got a drink when Jack arrived and joined him.

Paul wanted to ignore, forget what had happened the other evening. Jack had only been putting on a show, either to impress him or to pull his leg. If one could shut it out of mind, it might blow over, have never happened. And she—Mrs Gascoyne—with or without the help of her RAF friend might have put Jack in his place. *That* would be the best outcome of all.

Paul told him that his card was in the office, to be collected.

"Good." Jack checked the time. "I won't bother with it now, though. Fiona'll be along at any minute. In fact I was late, and she's later."

There was a silence, while Paul thought about it. He cleared his throat. "Is—er—does she really intend to marry my father?"

"I gather he's set on it. Don't blame him, either." Jack smiled. "In some ways, I mean."

"And what's your relationship with her?"

"Oh, grow up, Paul!" He shook his head. "What d'you imagine she's been doing with the bloody Air Force?"

"She's going to marry him, but she's prepared to play around mean-while?"

Jack shrugged. "Takes all sorts, doesn't it?"

"Where do you fit in? I mean, if my father's—"

"Now, or after?"

"After what? Their marriage? You don't surely imagine he'd still—"

"I don't care all that much."

"Have you considered what happens when he hears about it?"

"You mean when you tell him?"

"If no one else does first, you can count on it."

"Well, *she* wouldn't like that. Personally, I don't give a damn."

"You want him to hear about it, is that it?"

"It doesn't matter to me, Paul. I don't bloody *care*. Can't you under-stand that?" He was staring at him, across his glass. "It's pretty damn simple, if you'd—"

"Yeah." Paul nodded. This wouldn't be a good place to start a brawl, and in any case he thought Jack could probably take him on one-handed, and enjoy it too. He muttered, "It's just I never imagined an Everard could be such a total shit. I wouldn't have thought *anyone* could—"

"Takes people different ways. Some men leave other men to drown, some help themselves to other men's women. Which brand's the shit-tiest might be a matter of opinion . . . Oh, here she is!"

Fiona Gascoyne, wreathed in fur. Jack slid off his stool, and took her hands. "Wow. Such glamour . . ."

"Only because the old bags won't let us wear our uniforms in dives like this one. Otherwise I'd wear it all the time. Day *and* night." Paul remembered the way she'd smiled up at Jack: then she'd glanced at him. A different kind of smile: "Hello, Paul." He was remembering it now through other movement, action building round him, the immediate surroundings in visual if not mental focus. He remembered Jack saying blandly, "She does look terrific in the MTC uniform. For some reason it's *verboten* when they're off-duty. Not that I'm complaining . . ." He was showing Fiona the face of his watch, then: "Look, we've got to skid along, I'm afraid. I mean right away."

"Oh, damn it all!"

In hindsight and memory you could sort the exchanges into a rational sequence. At the time, it had been a blur, confused by the way he felt. Fiona complaining to Jack that she'd have liked to spend longer here, talk to Paul and get to know him, and Jack answering that if she arrived half an hour late it wasn't *his* fault . . . Paul told him, "My leave's up tomorrow. I'll be on an early train north."

"Too bad." Jack nodded. "Good luck, anyway."

"It might be a good thing if we could talk together about that drowning angle."

It was totally irrational, he thought: no more than an excuse . . .

"We do truly have to run, unfortunately." Jack's hand was in the crook of Fiona's elbow, turning her away. A lot of men looking at her: she really was quite sensational . . .

"Fookin' soddin' bastards!"

No need to look round to know who'd yelled that. Paul was on his feet between the two guns, Beale and Withinshaw closed-up at them and the loading numbers standing by. There was a red alert and the commodore's siren was calling for an emergency turn to port, there was a pack of bombers right ahead with a fighter escort weaving against the sky above them, and a big force of Junkers 88s approaching on the beam. They had fighters over them too. They'd need them, with Sea Hurricanes, Martlets and Fulmars streaming up from the two carriers astern. He'd been watching the pattern of a multiple attack develop— destroyers abaft the beam to port had just opened fire, a low-level barrage which could only mean there'd be torpedo-bombers moving in on that quarter—he'd been seeing it and reacting to it while the close-up of Fiona Gascoyne, dazzlingly attractive, faded from his mind.

CHAPTER SEVEN

·   ·   ·

The noise bewildered him. Searching for voices in it he found one
inside his head, Fiona's voice telling him, "Of *course* I'll marry you, you
great oaf!" She was naked: she was striking poses, wearing his new cap,
strutting around in it, playing the fool and looking absolutely sensational, shouting things like "Hard a-port! Are *you* hard a-port again
yet?" He'd been urging her to come back to bed. The cap had arrived
yesterday by parcel post from Messrs Gieves of Bond Street, who'd
sent it to him at this pub where they were spending a few days of his
leave. It was muddling, because it seemed to be happening in the
wrong war: the cap had gold oak-leaves on its peak, which made it a
commander's although he was still a junior lieutenant. He'd only come
back—*been brought* back—from the raid on Zeebrugge in which he'd
commanded his old "oily-wad" destroyer *Bravo:* he'd been wounded,
on *Bravo*'s bridge, in the course of towing another destroyer, *Grebe,* out
of trouble, and this was why he was in bed now in Sister Agnes's private hospital in Grosvenor Gardens.

The clattering and hammering made no sense either. Unless they
were tearing the lead off the roof. Which wasn't likely, he thought . . .
Actually, she was a Mrs Keyser. Her patients called her "Sister Agnes,"
and she was a personal friend of the King. His Majesty had given her
a key to some private entrance to the palace gardens, someone had told
him. It might have been Sarah, his stepmother, who'd mentioned it.

Getting muddled again now. Because if he was in Mrs Keyser's
establishment, how could Fiona have been here with him?

Christ, the din . . . Connected with it was an ache in his head like
a slowly turning knife.

The pub was in Sussex. But that had been a leave in the *second* war.

And if Sarah wanted to persuade Mrs Keyser to discharge him, it could only mean that—

Well, he'd *dreamt* the bit about the pub. That was it.

But—damn it, if this was 1918 . . .

He was panting, his own heartbeats shook him like blows inside his chest. It was the sheer effort of thinking this out, trying to get events in their right order, trying to reason with it all, make sense . . . He warned himself, *One thing at a time, now* . . .

Sarah wanted to have him in her care at Mullbergh while he recuperated. He wanted this too. Except he also knew it should be avoided, because he had some fore-knowledge of what would happen at Mullbergh, if he was alone there for long with Sarah. He didn't want it to happen. His feelings for her were protective as well as adoring: and she was his father's wife. Besides, Fiona—who'd looked tremendous in his cap, who was one of those girls who'd been designed not to wear clothes—wouldn't approve of it either. He'd told her, "You have the most beautiful breasts I ever saw."

"Kiss them, then."

Cap flat-aback, soft hair flowing around her bare shoulders, which were also beautiful. She had large eyes set slightly aslant above prominent cheekbones. He'd asked her, "What if Sarah comes?"

So she *had* been here!

He wished to God they'd stop that hammering . . .

You got to it eventually, though, if you took it step by step and didn't rush it. Everything fell into place quite naturally and simply then. The afternoon was the time for visits, and Sarah had come specially to London to get him out of Sister Agnes's place and take him to Mullbergh. He rather liked the idea of Mullbergh, because his father wouldn't be there. Sir John Everard was in the Army, in France. Fiona asked him, "Who's Kate?"

"She's in Australia. But if I'm going to marry *you*—"

"Will Sarah object?"

He didn't see what Sarah had to do with it. It was his having married Ilyana, Paul's mother, that had turned Sarah into a block of granite . . . He *thought* that was what had done it; that more than anything else. But Kate was in Crete, where the Stukas had come in screaming packs in a day-long, day-after-day-long bedlam. *Orion* had been hit again: smoke was gushing out of her and the whole armoured top of one for'ard turret had been blown off, the gun-barrels twisted and blackened, and every man in that gunhouse would be dead. He hadn't known it at the time but her captain had been dying on his bridge at that same moment. Her steering had gone and she'd swung right around, reversing course and heading back towards Crete with a new Stuka swarm coming up from Scarpanto. She was the flagship and they'd crippled her, and now they'd concentrate on her and do their damnedest to finish her. You had to stay close to her, keep the bastards high, give her a chance to draw breath and fight her fires, shift to emergency steering and get back on course. All the destroyers were turning with her, closing in around her. She'd been packed with the troops they'd lifted out of Crete and he'd guessed then what it would be like inside her, in those crowded messdecks to which Stukas' bombs had penetrated, and he'd guessed right because they couldn't make much of a job of cleaning her, in Alex. They sent her for refit, reconstruction in the States, and when she stopped at Cape Town she smelt so badly they wouldn't let her dock. She had to anchor, outside.

He told Sarah about it, when she came to take him up to Yorkshire. Sarah had brown hair and hazel eyes and an intriguing mouth: vulnerable, adorable. He told her, "Jack's cruiser was sunk by dive-bombers, off Crete. I couldn't stay to pick up survivors because—well, you *couldn't* stop, if you did the Stukas had you nailed. If I'd have stopped I'd have only killed *more* men—"

"Did you kill Jack, then?"

"He's alive. He got ashore, and—"

"No thanks to you. And David drowned, didn't he? At Jutland? He died like a hero, trying to save other—"

"He died in a blue funk. Off his head."

"You're lying, Nick! You killed your own father with that lie!"

"It's the truth. I heard it all from a man named—"

"You killed your own father, Nick!"

It was Sarah but a different Sarah. Transformed totally. Bitter, tight-faced, shrewish. Cold, harsh eyes hating him . . . "You'd have let Jack drown, too—your father first, then your—"

"No."

It wasn't true. Ordering his destroyers away had been an agonizing, terrible decision. The sea full of swimmers and the German aircraft dipping to machine-gun them in the water, murder them as they tried to swim away: you'd see a man stop swimming and lie still in the water while it turned pink around him. Jack's face, blood-stained, staring up at him from the water. Jack screamed, *"I'm your son!"*

"Steady. Steady, now. You'll be all right, now. Easy does it . . ."

A different voice asked quietly, "Could we get him aft to his own cabin?"

"I suppose we could move him without doing any damage. Trouble is, looking after him. He can't be left alone, and with this lot here I can't spare an SBA."

"His own steward full-time, plus visits from you?"

Beyond the curtain, a sailor muttered something in a voice like a groan, and an SBA told him, " 'Ang on, Lofty. With you in a mo'."

"Well, I suppose that's possible . . ."

The voices had dropped lower, and with the clanging and general racket from up top he couldn't hear what they were saying. It hadn't made much sense anyway, but he'd been glad to hear the voices. Such a ghastly bloody din up there: it was like being in a destroyer in dry dock, with workmen banging around here, there and everywhere . . . There was no engine vibration, he realized, her screws weren't turning. In intervals between bouts of hammering from above he could hear the whirr of a fan, but there was no draught from it that he could feel.

All he could feel was the pain in his head and a sort of confused sadness involving Sarah and Jack, the whole mess that was the past but still contaminated the present and in some way seemed to threaten the future too.

"Will I be allowed to travel up to Mullbergh?"

Silence . . . Except for the row elsewhere. Then: "Mullbergh?"

"Sarah's running it as a sort of recuperative centre."

Sibbold looked at Gant. "Sounds very suitable." He didn't smile. He paused before he added, addressing his patient, "To start with we'll move you to your own quarters, sir."

Whatever *that* meant.

Tired. But he didn't want to sleep if it meant slipping back into the nightmare of Sarah's accusations. It wasn't the same Sarah whom he'd loved, whose screams had woken him in the night, brought him out of bed and hurrying down that long, icy corridor. He'd been a boy then, a child: remembering it, he was a child again, dropping off to sleep. There'd been rows before, time and again he'd lain awake trying not to hear his father's drunken raving and Sarah's quiet, defensive reasoning, pleading. Misery would hold him doubled in the bed, cold from the old house and colder still inside, helpless despite his urge to protect, to love Sarah as much as his father seemed—inexplicably—to hate her. Head under the bedclothes, praying for it all to end . . . But that night she'd screamed, he'd heard a crash and another scream and he'd thought, *He's murdering her:* then he'd been running, bare-footed and shaking with cold and fright . . . Sarah's dress had been ripped open, downwards from the neck. She was trying to hold it together with one hand and the other was out defensively towards Nick's father, who was in evening clothes and raving, mad-bull drunk. The top half of Sarah's bedroom door had been smashed in—he'd done it with a heavy shoe-case, which was lying among the broken wood. For years and years, her voice had echoed in his skull: "It's all right, Nick. Truly. Go back to bed."

"Why are we stopped?"

He wondered why they didn't answer him. And then, why he was down here anyway. What the noise was, what was going on . . . He was below decks: he could feel that—sense it, smell it. Besides, all the hammering and rasping was overhead. And—that smell was ether, a hospital smell . . . Well, of course, he'd been dreaming, he'd *dreamt* he was at sea . . . He asked, "Has my stepmother been in today?"

He wondered whether Kate might come: whether anyone had told her he was here. But he didn't like to ask about Kate, because the people here wouldn't know who he was talking about.

He wondered whether he'd told Fiona about Kate. He didn't think he had.

"All right, sir, are we?"

"Who's that?"

"SBA Green, sir. PMO'll be back in two shakes."

"Why are we stopped?"

"Stopped, sir? Oh. Well—we're at anchor, sir."

"Where?"

"Surabaya, sir."

Surabaya. Java, in the Dutch East Indies . . .

Combined Striking Force. They'd sent him to join China Force and he'd got rumbled with this fellow Doorman . . . And—it came to him suddenly—there was to be a conference, a captains' meeting in the Dutch flagship *de Ruyter*, and he had to get to it. God almighty, he'd be late!

"Help me up, would you? Are my clothes here? Come on, give me a—"

"Steady on now, sir. PMO'll be back any minute, he'll explain—"

"I can't *see!*"

"Because of the bandage, sir, that's all it is. Here—easy does it, just lie back again, sir, lie still a while and—that's the way . . ."

Hands on his shoulders were holding him down.

"Look. I have to get over to the flagship. Otherwise—"

"Hello, hello." Different voice. The first one began to whisper: then the newcomer murmured soothingly, "All right. All right, now, all right . . ." There was something familiar about the voice, despite its tendency to repeat itself like a stuck gramophone record. Nick said, "I have to get up and dress, because Sarah's coming for me. She's arranged it with Sister Agnes: I'm going up to Mullbergh, to recuperate."

"That's a first-class idea, sir."

He felt the slight pressure of the antiseptic swab and then the prick of the needle.

"There. Relax now. Rest's your best medicine now." Sibbold straightened up. So did Green, who'd been holding Nick down on the cot. Leading Seaman Williams, on the upper berth, had his head turned to the right and he was eye to eye with the doctor. He asked, "In a bad way, is he?"

"Not necessarily, Williams. If we're lucky, it'll turn out to be quite a temporary condition." He pointed upwards. "Hear that?"

"Couldn't hardly *not* hear it."

"They're straightening out your wheelhouse for you. All we've got to do is get your legs healed up, and you'll be right back on the job."

"D'you know how long we're staying here, sir?"

"Just long enough to get essentials working, I'd guess. Commander Gant's ashore, seeing the rear-admiral. We'll know more about it when he gets back."

"Repairs'll take a while, sir, won't they?"

"I think just patching up, jury-rigging—"

"Any other ships in Surabaya, sir?"

"Oh, yes. *Exeter, Encounter,* five or six Yank destroyers . . . Williams, old chap, I'm sorry, but I've got to get around the other patients now. You're feeling a lot better, aren't you?"

"Except I'd as soon be dead."

He'd said it flatly, unemotionally, and turned his head away to stare up at the deckhead, which was white-enamelled with heavy I-sectioned girders crossing it.

"Listen, Williams. Here is one fact. There is no reason or evidence to believe that your wife did not get away from Singapore. Here's another. If she did get away, she'll be as anxious to find you now as you must be to find her. You'd be no use to her dead, and precious little use alive if you adopt that kind of attitude. Aren't you giving up a bit too easily?"

"I'm sorry." His eyes stayed on the deckhead.

"Damn it, she's going to need your help, man!"

The head turned. Williams nodded. "Sir."

Sibbold hesitated. Then he turned away, beckoning Green to follow him out through the curtain. He told him quietly, "Keep an eye on that one. I don't want him left alone for any length of time."

Gant was still ashore when the first air attack came in. They were Val dive-bombers with an escort of fighters. They went mostly for the harbour front, with only a few desultory passes at the ships—like afterthoughts, as if they hadn't been briefed to expect anything afloat here and didn't have bombs to waste on them. The shore guns put up an extremely effective barrage, too, and it kept all the attackers high. Repair work in *Defiant,* even the work on the bridge, continued without interruption while her four-inch AA guns joined for a short while in the barrage; the only notice the men working with cutting-torches in the bridge paid to the enemy was to put on tin hats.

There was damage to some buildings and to an oiling jetty, where a fire was started, and there was a nearish miss on an American destroyer in dry dock. Then it was over, and the ERAs took off their tin hats. They were cutting away the wreckage, as much as needed to be removed before new beams and plates could be riveted and welded on. LTOs—electrical ratings—were re-rigging telephone and gunnery-control circuits, and shipwrights, mechanics and ordnance artificers were all working flat out, backed up by teams of less skilled assistants. The biggest job of all, of course, and the most important, was in the boiler room.

Gant returned aboard at noon. Lieutenant Flynn RNVR was officer of the watch on the quarterdeck. Gant asked him, stepping off the
gangway and bringing his hand down from the salute as the thin wail
of the bosun's call died away, "Any news of the captain?"

"He's been moved to his cabin, sir. Last I heard, he was still unconscious."

Flynn was short, dark and dapper; he was a yachtsman, one of the
pre-war weekend reservists. Rowley arrived, apologetic for not having
been on the quarterdeck in time to meet him.

"Sorry, sir, I was down in the—"

"This is no time for standing around gangways, Charles . . . Did any
bombs come near us?"

Rowley shook his head. "They seemed to be more interested in the
hotels."

"I know. I was in one of them, talking to the admiral." Gant looked
round at Flynn. "Send your messenger to the engineer commander, tell
him I'll be in the cuddy and I'd like to see him if he can spare a
minute. Same message to the PMO, please."

Harkness, the captain's PO steward, came out to meet him. He murmured, "No change, sir. He hasn't moved a whisker."

It was half dark in the sleeping cabin, and curtains were drawn over
both the scuttles. Nick Everard was lying on his back, motionless as a
corpse. Gant asked Harkness, "Has he said anything?"

"No, sir."

When he'd been up for'ard, he'd been mumbling to some imagi-
nary woman about her breasts. With half the ship's company listening
to every word. Gant said, "He was delirious, earlier on, talking nonsense. If you hear any—you know, personal stuff—"

"I got cloth ears, sir."

Sibbold, the PMO, tapped on the door and came in. He stopped
beside Gant, and stooped to look closely at the patient. He explained,
"We changed the wrapping, you see, so when he comes round he'll
be able to open his eyes. One of the question-marks, after a crack on

the head like he had, is whether his sight may be affected. Hence
drawn curtains, in case the light's too much for him at first."

"Harkness here says he hasn't moved or spoken."

Nick recognized that voice. It belonged to—Bob Gant. And Bob
Gant was . . .

Damn . . .But it would come. Just for the moment, it had slid away
from him. He could see the face in his mind and match it to the voice,
but he couldn't follow it beyond that. He lay still, keeping his eyes shut,
wanting to listen to the voice and let it trigger his memory.

There was a lot of noise—clattering and banging and scraping—but
it was farther away than it had been before, and it didn't torture his
skull like it had. The pain was less intense now anyway, more of an
ordinary headache.

He'd had a nightmare, about Jack. "Half-brother" Jack . . . Sarah had
been talking about him. And about Nick's father, John Everard, who'd
died after a series of strokes which had been triggered by Nick telling
him the truth about Jack's drowning: how he'd had to leave him—and
about five hundred others—and how the German pilots had been using
swimmers for target-practice.

No. Wrong, again. That had happened—one year ago. And Nick's
father had died in—oh, 1931 . . . It was David, then, he'd told him
about. David at Jutland. Nick's elder brother David, who right from the
nursery had had a great deal wrong with him and who'd cracked, gone
round the bend before he drowned. A quarter of a century ago. History.
History meant pain, for some people. And complications. It was important to keep Paul clear of all that, to keep the sins of the father *to* the
father. Or fathers, plural.

David had looked very much like Jack. Sarah had always denied it,
but it was a fact and there was an oil painting of David in her Dower
House at Mullbergh to prove it. She denied it because she knew the
truth about David, although she denied that too. She certainly *had*
known the truth: but she possessed this extraordinary ability to change
the truth even as it existed in her own mind, turn black into white

because that was how she wanted it. And having changed it, stick to the *manufactured* truth, admit no other view, no doubt . . . That way, you built your own surroundings, your own history, you justified the loyalties you wanted to give and the hates you *needed* . . . Make-believe was reality, to Sarah. Although she'd admitted, finally, that Jack was their son, hers and Nick's.

No—she had not. That was the dream he'd had, the nightmare. Sarah would never, not even if she were tied to a stake and burning alive, admit to Nick's having fathered her son. She'd wiped all that out of her mind, washed out completely any memory of how she'd loathed and feared John Everard and in one moment's—oh, weakness, aberration, love—turned to her stepson. Who hadn't been—wasn't—all that much younger than herself.

That dream, though: Jack's dead face, and the sea reddened, washing over it . . .

Nightmare. There'd been no alternative to leaving him and the others in the water: to have stayed and tried to pick them up would have done them no good at all, would only have thrown away his own ship and ship's company. And Jack was alive, anyway, and he didn't know he wasn't John Everard's son. Only he, Nick, and Sarah knew it. Sarah *had* known it.

Paul must never know it: never have an inkling of it.

He said, "I must write to Paul."

Sibbold leant forward, listening. He'd sent Harkness out for a smoke, and Gant was in the day cabin talking to Sandilands. Sibbold had pulled a chair near the head of the bunk. He got from it now and leaned over to peer through the semi-darkness at his patient's closed eyes.

"Feeling a little better, sir?"

"Who's that?"

"Sibbold, sir. PMO."

"Oh. Sibbold."

Silence . . . The pulse-rate was all right. He tried again: "How do you feel now, sir?"

"Not bad." The right hand moved, pointing. "Head aches, but it's better."

"You had a very nasty bang on it."

"What about this arm?"

"Your left arm's broken in two places. I've set it and splinted it, and it's strapped to your chest to keep it still. I don't expect any problems with it."

"Did I miss the meeting in the flagship?"

"No, sir, you—"

"Admiral Doorman's conference?"

"You attended that meeting, sir. You've had a knock on the head, you see, and it's left you with concussion, so your memory's confused. What I'd like you to do, sir, is just lie still, relax, sleep if you can. Commander Gant—"

"Did you say I *did* attend Doorman's conference?"

"Yes. And we sailed—the whole squadron—soon after that. Now we're back in Surabaya."

He didn't see how this was possible. Sibbold explained: the conference had taken place two days ago. They'd sailed that same day, turned back yesterday to refuel the destroyers, but an enemy report had sent them hurrying north again. This time, they'd found the enemy.

"Where am I?"

"In your sleeping cabin, sir."

He hadn't asked yet how he'd sustained his injuries. There were still loose connections in the mental processes.

"What—time of day is it?"

"Early afternoon, sir."

"Well, my God, I'd better—"

"Please, you really *must* lie still, sir!" Sibbold eased him down again. "You have to rest—you have a badly damaged head and some minor wounds as well. The only way you can do anyone any good is to stay there and rest, get your strength and memory back. Now, *please* . . ."

"Why are those curtains drawn?"

"So you'd rest better, sir."

"Where's Gant?"

It was amazing how quickly a brain that had been jolted off its gimbals could get back on them again. Even though it would, obviously, still take a while to settle, you could see and hear awareness growing every minute. Sibbold told him, "He's been ashore to see the admiral, sir, and now he's talking to Commander Sandilands about the repairs to the boiler room. I expect he'll be in to see you in a minute—he was here earlier, but you were asleep."

"No, I wasn't. I heard his voice."

He hadn't picked up that mention of repairs to the boiler room. But he might at any moment, as his mind mulled over what had been said. And any such extension to what had already been a lengthy question-and-answer session would keep Sibbold even longer from his other patients . . . "Look here. I just walked clear through the ship, didn't I? I mean, to get here. If I can do that, why shouldn't I turn out now?"

"You were brought aft on a stretcher, sir. Unconscious."

"I've just told you, Sibbold, I came on my own two feet!"

"You're concussed, sir—"

"Who's this?"

The door had opened, and shut again very quietly. Sibbold, glancing round, was glad to see Harkness back again.

"Your PO steward, sir."

"Petty Officer Harkness?"

"Ah, you're a lot stronger now, sir!"

"I'll be turning out, in a minute. Where's Gladwill?"

"Gladwill, sir?" Harkness looked round for Sibbold, but the doctor was retreating stealthily towards the door. Nick said, "I can see two of you, Harkness . . . What did you say about Gladwill?"

"I—er—been seeing to 'is birds, sir. Singing away fit to bust, that littlest one is. They've eaten all their grub, though, would you believe it? Every time you look, they've wolfed the lot!"

"Why can't Gladwill look after his own canaries?"

Sibbold had come back to the bunkside. He asked Nick, "You said you could see two of Harkness, sir. Can you see two of me now?"

"Yes."

"Double vision. It's probably only temporary, but I'd like to take a look at it. We'll need to have those curtains open—you may find it a bit bright, at first. Harkness, would you—"

"You haven't answered my question about Gladwill."

The curtains were open, and he was blinking at the sunlight.

"We were in action, sir." Sibbold held up his thermometer in its metal case in front of Nick's eyes. "Watch this, please. Follow it with your eyes as I move it . . . We were in action last night. We were hit just under the bridge, and in number two boiler room. There was a hit aft as well—starboard side here, by the after tubes. It was the shell in the bridge that did this damage to your head. Actually you smashed the glass windbreak with your forehead, and it was the glass that cut your face too. I'm sorry to say just about everyone else up there was killed. Including Gladwill. I'm *very* sorry to have to tell you this, sir . . . How many of this object are you seeing now?"

Gant told Sandilands, "You've got until sunset tomorrow. No matter how much still needs doing then, we sail as soon as it's dark."

A siren was howling, ashore, signalling another air-raid alert. This time, perhaps, they'd be going for the ships. *Defiant*'s alarm buzzers were sounding, but her AA armament was already closed up and for the moment there was nothing Gant could be doing. There wasn't anything to be seen, either. He turned back from the scuttle.

"Including tonight, it gives you twenty-eight or thirty hours. Can you finish in that time?"

Sandilands was personally supervising the boiler room job. He was in overalls, oil-stained and unshaven. He was a rugged-looking character, but here and now he also looked just about exhausted.

"In present circumstances I couldn't finish in twenty-eight *days,* let alone that many hours. We need a dockyard and shoreside facilities.

There were bits falling off before any of this happened, you know . . . All I can say is we'll do what's physically and mechanically possible. If all goes well I'll have two of those four boilers back on the job."

"Four altogether, you mean?"

Sandilands nodded.

It was better than he'd expected. He told him, "*Sloan's* captain wanted to spend an extra day here. He's got engine parts coming by rail from Tjilatjap."

"So?"

"We can't wait that long. Everyone's of the same opinion. Even Jordan agreed, finally. What will our own best speed be, John?"

"Twenty-three or twenty-four."

"You'll have done damn well, at that . . . I'd say you needed some rest, though. Did you get any, last night?"

"Christ's sake, how could I?"

"You don't have to turn every nut and bolt yourself, John. You've got Murray, Holbrook, and young Benson, not to mention—"

"The boiler room isn't the only job we've got. But I will—I'll get my head down, later . . . *Sloan's* troubles came from a near-miss, you said?"

He nodded. "Pretty bad, too. She ground to a halt, apparently, out there in the Strait. One of the others towed her in."

"If they don't get the spares they're hoping for—"

"They don't. But they'll manage twenty-five knots, as opposed to more than thirty. They've had artificers from all the other destroyers working with them, I gather."

"Some people get all the luck, don't they?" Sandilands pointed upwards, as a thudding of AA guns came to them. "Here's some more of the other kind."

Gant followed him outside. The Jap raiders were high, over the land in the west. He couldn't see them at first, but bursts of AA shells led his eye to them, to half a dozen mosquito-like objects flying north or northwest. The smoke bursts were already fading, gunfire tailing away. Looking for'ard he saw the crew of the starboard four-inch, on the raised gun platform that straddled the ship from one side to the other between her funnels. They were already securing the gun and discarding tin hats and anti-flash gear. It was likely those aircraft had been attacking some military target inland; the enemy had been bombing road and railway junctions, so he'd heard ashore, and there'd been raids on Tjilatjap on the south coast of the island as well as on Batavia and Bandoeng. They were preparing for the military invasion by disrupting Dutch lines of inland communication.

Pinner was waiting, at ease, near the entrance to the cuddy. He had rather a self-satisfied look about him, Gant thought. Perhaps he was thinking of himself now as the commanding officer's doggie, a step-up from being only the second-in-command's?

"Pinner, find Lieutenant-Commander Rowley, please. Tell him I'll see heads of departments in the wardroom at 1800 hours."

Nick had been tired by his talk with Sibbold, and he'd fallen into another deep, dream-filled sleep. Kate had been with him, somewhere or other, and he'd been trying to explain why he had to go through with the idea of marrying Fiona. Kate had argued, "You and I hadn't met at that time, had we?" It wasn't easy to explain his view that the point was irrelevant, that a man had to stand by his word. There was more to it, as well, an attitude of mind much harder to put across to her because it had roots that led right back into his youth. It was the fact that he'd already done a lot of harm to several individuals, and the prospect of adding to the list of injured parties by breaking his word to Fiona was anathema to him. He'd never set out to harm anyone, it had simply resulted from things he'd done. This time he could see likely consequences, and choose for himself.

"Do you really think you can make amends for bloomers you've made way back by messing up your own future now—and mine?"

He wasn't sure whether he was asleep and had dreamt of Kate asking him this, or whether he'd imagined it, put the words into her mouth in his own imagination as a way of arguing with himself.

Thinking about Kate was soothing to the spirit, anyway.

When she'd been with him in Alex and Cairo—after he'd brought her out of Crete—she'd never even hinted at any such thing as marriage. The Cairo interlude had been when he'd had a few days' leave, with *Tuareg* boiler-cleaning in the dock at Suez. Ostensibly, he'd gone up to see the pyramids, and that was what she'd told her people she was doing, too. And they *had* looked at them, once or twice . . . And he, Nick, had talked about the future, peacetime, and hinted at the idea of marriage. He'd felt guilty about it, having Fiona in the back of his mind and wishing he did not have; and Kate had totally ignored the openings he'd given her.

"It's too late now, isn't it? I *am* committed. I'm sorry, Kate, I'm truly—"

"A bit late to be sorry!"

He was asleep; Sarah, not Kate, had said that. They were on the steps leading up to the front entrance at Mullbergh, which had been Sir John Everard's house and had just become Nick's. They'd just come from his father's funeral. He'd said, "I feel as if I'd killed him." Sarah had stopped, and her dead-white face had jerked round to him, her eyes venomous. *"Didn't you?"*

He told Kate, "I killed my own father." He saw the contempt in her expression before she turned her back on him. Turning slowly, like a dummy swivelling on a central pivot. Then her back was towards him: that long, slim neck and the tawny hair, her tall, slim figure. Receding, leaving him.

"Kate!"

She was going, getting smaller, leaving not only physically, in terms of distance, but out of his life for ever. Well, he'd as good as told her to. And the thought of that was suddenly horrifying, like a new crime on his conscience: he shouted, "Kate, please, come back?" She was tiny, as if he was looking at her through the wrong end of a telescope, and the concept of her being totally and permanently out of reach was too frightful to accept. He shouted, "Kate, I love you!"

He woke with the shout ringing in his skull. Harkness, the PO steward, said, "Ah, you're awake again, sir. Nice little sleep, you had."

"Was I yelling something?"

"Only muttering a bit, sir. Not what you'd call comprehensible like . . . The commander, sir, was wanting a chat. He said I was to let him know when you found it convenient. Should I—"

"Yes, please. I'd like to see him."

Paul and Kate would get on well together, he thought. They were the same sort of people: direct, straightforward . . . He wondered where Paul was now, at this minute. If he was in the Mediterranean—as he would be, by now—there'd be a time-difference of about—what, six hours between them?

That didn't tell him much. He didn't even know what the time was here in Java.

Harkness had gone to the door. "Shan't be gone a minute, sir."

Nick lifted his free hand and held the forefinger in front of his eyes, like Sibbold's thermometer. He saw two fingers instead of one. Annoyed, he let the hand flop. It was called double vision, Sibbold had said, and the odds were that it would disappear in a few days.

That wasn't good enough. It was now, today, he needed all his faculties. Somehow or other, the process of recovery would have to be speeded up. Better talk to Sibbold again. Perhaps aspirin, or some such thing. Or just keep one eye shut. And use a telescope instead of binoculars . . .

But now, before Bob Gant arrived, he set himself to remembering what Sibbold had told him about the action—last night's, or the night before that—and the damage to the ship. There'd been—*three* hits. One under the bridge, in the wheelhouse or plot: and a mental note here, *See Leading Seaman Williams as soon as possible* . . . Second hit—back here, near the starboard after tubes. Holed the upper deck and started a fire, and cut most communications from the ACP. Work in that area would account for much of the noise that he could hear now . . . Third hit had been—

Blank.

Damn.

Well, force yourself, stretch your brain . . .

Boiler room!

He relaxed again, sweating from the effort. Major damage in number two boiler room, which had cut the speed to about ten knots. And as speed was of the essence if *Defiant* was to have the faintest chance of getting away from this place, Sandilands had teams of his best men working on it flat out.

Twenty-two dead, and fourteen wounded.

Java and *de Ruyter* had blown up and sunk. Sibbold thought they'd been hit by torpedoes from Jap cruisers. *Exeter* badly damaged. *Electra* and *Jupiter* sunk.

If ever there'd been a time when a man needed to have his brain in working order . . .

"Well, sir! *Delighted* to hear you're so much better!"

Nick raised the movable hand.

"Pull up a chair, Bob. Light that foul pipe of yours if you want to."

Gant murmured as he sat down, "D'you know, sir, we all thought you were a goner?"

"So Palliser's leaving?"

"On Helfrich's orders. Soon as the rest of us have cleared out. But they hadn't foreseen this delay to ourselves and *Sloan,* so in fact he'll be away before us. By air to Australia."

Rear-Admiral Palliser was the senior British naval officer in Java. As long as he was here he was under the orders of the Dutch admiral, Helfrich, who was at Batavia and who had been Doorman's boss.

Gant said, "I was asked whether it would be practicable for you to be flown to Australia with him, sir."

Australia. Kate was in Australia . . . He caught himself thinking about Kate, and pulled himself together. Keeping the mind drifting off on its own was one of the things he was going to have to work hard at. He told Gant, "There's no question of it, of course. I imagine you told them so?"

"I said I thought you were too groggy to be moved, sir. Frankly, it never occurred to me you'd come out of it so quickly. I said I'd have a word with the PMO, then confirm it one way or the other."

"You can forget all that. By tomorrow I'll be on my feet and *compos mentis*. Even if there's still a touch of this bloody double vision."

" *Truly,* sir?"

Nick nodded. "I'll be up and about, and you'll be out of a job again, you poor chap!"

"Well, my God, if you *could* be—"

"You'd like that?"

Gant smiled. "I most certainly would, sir!"

Nick wondered about him. *Why* he'd be so eager to relinquish the responsibilities of command . . . If he, Nick, had been in Gant's shoes he'd have welcomed the opportunity to take over, he'd have grabbed at it and he'd have been bitterly disappointed, privately, to be done out of the chance once he'd thought he'd got it.

Gant wasn't feeling any disappointment, though. And it wasn't concern for Nick Everard, either. He was genuinely anxious to get "out from under." Looking at him intently, interestedly, seeing two of him, Nick realized that his second-in-command was very much a background figure, self-effacing, thoroughly reliable at putting someone else's orders into effect, but—scared of the idea of command? Distrustful of his own abilities?

If the job was forced on him, he'd probably have set his teeth and eventually grown into it. But crisis-time was *now:* and a second-in-command ought to be ready, eager to step up.

"Hard luck, Bob."

"What d'you mean, sir?"

"Weren't you looking forward to becoming your own boss?"

Gant shook his head. "Straight answer to a straight question—no, sir. If you're fit enough, I'm as pleased as Punch!"

"You can start celebrating, then."

Even if he wasn't as fit as he hoped he'd be, tomorrow, he'd have to pretend he was, *make* himself be so. It would be better for the ship to have a captain who was slightly boss-eyed and occasionally dizzy than one who was scared of the job.

Gant was studying *him,* now. Wondering whether he was up to it probably. That answer had been an honest one, all right. Gant had probably reconciled himself to the idea of command, stiffened his dicky spine to it. But he was relieved now—at least, hopeful.

"Tell the admiral, Bob, that I'm much better and intend to reassume command before we sail. In the meantime I have to rest, and therefore hope he'll excuse me from calling on him. And thank him for that very kind offer."

Gant nodded. "I'll tell the ship's company too, sir. Should have the Tannoy working soon, and I was intending to give them a pep-talk. This'll cheer them up no end . . . I've called a heads-of-departments meeting for 1800, by the way."

"Like me to attend it?"

"Wouldn't it be better to rest, sir, as you say?"

"What?"

He'd begun to think of something else: Gant had to say it again. It was embarrassing . . . He agreed: "You're right, of course . . . Now—thinking of future plans . . . By tomorrow morning we and *Sloan* will be the sole occupants of Surabaya?"

"Except for the Yank destroyer in dock, sir. They're going to blow her up and wreck the dock as well."

"Tell me about the other sailings."

"Well. Four American destroyers will leave as soon as it's dark tonight. Eastward—via Madura and the Bali Strait."

"Good luck to them."

"Yes. Indeed . . . *Exeter* will leave about the same time, with *Encounter* and the USS *Pope. Exeter* draws too much water to leave by the eastern exit, of course, and Palliser's routing the three of them northward and then west. The idea is to get well clear of the coast—to avoid Jap invasion forces—and then make for the Sunda Strait."

Sunda was at the western end of Java, between Java and Sumatra. Five hundred miles away.

"Has *Exeter* made good her damage?"

Gant shook his head. "Sixteen knots, sir."

"Long way, at that speed."

"Yes." But there weren't any soft options. Gant took his pipe out, looked at it and put it away again. Nick said, "I don't mind if you smoke."

"Thanks. Trying to cut down a bit."

"Now, about ourselves, Bob. The idea ashore is we should sail tomorrow night, and it's up to us to decide which way we go?"

"Yes, sir. Point being that the situation could change dramatically between now and then. And we'll have heard how the others have got on. The admiral's arranging for Bandoeng to keep us informed."

That was good. And the freedom of action—within limits which would be established by geography, ships' speed and the enemy's deployments—was very welcome. In recent weeks there'd been no such latitude, and every move they'd made had been not only disastrous but foreseeably so. He muttered, "Yes . . ." Tiring, losing the track again, and Bob Gant obviously worrying that he might not be up to it . . . Nick got hold of his powers of concentration again. "I think we might have a council of war tonight, Bob. Here. I'll send an RPC to Jim Jordan—well, you do that for me, will you? Make it 1900 for 2000, and tell Harkness I've a guest for supper. Two guests—you've got to be in on all of it, in case I keel over again. All right?"

"With much pleasure, sir."

As a signal, that would have been sent out as WMP. The RPC to Jim Jordan stood for "Request the pleasure of your company."

"And have Chevening standing by with some charts . . . Chevening was damn lucky, wasn't he, getting off without a scratch?"

"Very lucky indeed."

"You did a good job, bringing the ship back."

"That wasn't difficult, sir. But we did truly think you were dead, at first. I suppose because there was so much blood . . ."

Blood. Thoughts wandered. Nick's right hand came up, and his fingers touched the dressing on the left side of his face. Sibbold had admitted he'd have a scar from that eye to the corner of his mouth; there were a lot of stitches in it, apparently. Nick wondered whether Kate would be revolted by it: but probably not, she was a nurse, she—

Now stop that . . . He asked Gant, "Has Sandilands said what speed we're going to be capable of?"

"He reckons twenty-three knots, sir. Maximum twenty-four."

"And *Sloan?*"

"They hope twenty-five."

Gant told him—he'd meant to earlier—that Jim Jordan of *Sloan* had sent a personal message, enquiring about Nick's progress.

"Very kind of him." Nick was thinking *Twenty-three or twenty-four* . . . Even after a crack on the head he knew that engineers could invariably do better than they promised. Then they got congratulated instead of cursed. And if Jim Jordan's destroyer could make twenty-five knots, he wasn't going to ask him to make less than that for *Defiant's* sake. Getting out of this hole was going to require a lot of luck, a lot of nerve and every knot that anyone could squeeze out.

He interrupted Gant.

"Sandilands is always a bit over-cautious. And we can't use the Madura Channel either. *Sloan* might: she wouldn't draw more than nine or ten feet, I'd guess?"

Sloan was one of the Selfridge class: not much under two thousand tons, with five-inch guns, and launched in about 1935. Those ships had been designed for thirty-seven knots, and on trials some of them had knocked up nearly forty. So Jim Jordan, who was proud of his ship, had told Nick that evening in Batavia, the evening they'd drunk Laphroaigh. A week ago? Something like that . . . But this question of speed: he covered his eyes with his free hand. His brain felt heavy, he

had to drive it hard to make it work. He knew, too, that he was thinking in the dark, at this stage. Without a chart in front of you, all the
distances and depths and tides, the whole thing was guesswork. But the
fact remained, you'd still need every ounce of steam you could get.

"Bob, listen. If *Sloan's* likely to make twenty-five knots, that's what
I want for *Defiant* too. Tell Sandilands, will you—twenty-five, *at least*."

"Well, sir, I'm not sure—"

"*Make* sure. Just *make* sure, Bob."

"Aye aye, sir."

"He'll have to do better than he thinks possible, that's all. Twenty-
five, tell him."

Gant nodded. He was looking at Nick as if he thought he mightn't
be thinking straight yet.

"*Perth* and *Houston*—did you tell me they *have* got to Batavia?"

"Yes, sir. The signal arrived when I was there, ashore. They got in
at 1400 hours, and Admiral Helfrich has ordered them to sail at 2100,
via Sunda to Tjilatjap."

"Why not tell them to clear out altogether, I wonder?"

"I gather there are some small ships at Tjilatjap, sir, and refugees to
be evacuated. He may be putting a convoy together."

Nick's thoughts had jumped back to the speed question. He told
Gant, "If there's any argument from Sandilands about giving us twenty-
five knots, bring him here to see me."

"Aye aye, sir."

The commander looked relieved: he had someone to fall back on . . .
Nick told himself, *I was right* . . . Then he'd lost that train of thought
and he was wondering what the chances were—for *Perth* and *Houston,*
for *Exeter* and the two destroyers going with her, or for the four
American destroyers who'd be making a dash for the Bali Strait tonight.
The Bali Strait was a lot closer than any of the other gaps—and as
those destroyers could slip out over the Madura shallows, the short cut
eastward, it was closer still—but it was less than two miles wide and
Bali was swarming with Japanese invaders now. They had an airstrip

working too, on Bali . . . There was one fact, anyway, that was beyond dispute: however slim any of those ships' chances might be tonight, *Defiant's* and *Sloan's* twenty-four hours later would be slimmer.

It had all been so obvious, so inevitable . . .

"Of course, we don't have all the information that Helfrich must have."

Gant was stuffing his pipe, at last. While out of memory like a dream Nick was re-reading a signal which Admiral Doorman had shown him: about Jap aircraft carriers operating to the south of Java, across all the lines of retreat to Australia or Ceylon.

Australia, where Kate was . . .

Think about the carriers, not Kate!

He'd muttered something, angrily. Gant, thumbing loose tobacco off the top of the pipe's bowl, had glanced up and was now embarrassed, pretending he hadn't heard. Nick told himself, *Better still, don't think about the bloody carriers either* . . . What he had to coerce his wobbly mind into concentrating on was how to get this ship and Jordan's out through the straits. Through either Lombok, Bali or Alas. *If* you made it that far, then you could start worrying about Jap carrier groups. Reaching this conclusion, he nodded to himself: and at the same moment realized that he and Gant had been staring at each other . . . Gant had looked down at his pipe, obviously embarrassed again, for the second time in a minute, doubtful of Nick's fitness. And he had good reason to be doubtful, too . . .

But he could still do the job, Nick thought, better than Bob Gant would do it. Because however technically competent Gant was, he lacked confidence, lacked trust in himself at least as much as he lacked it—at this moment—in Nick Everard.

CHAPTER EIGHT

. . .

A freighter in column four was on fire. Junkers 88s had come in from the bow, flown down the port side of the convoy and then circled round astern; then they'd turned inward and passed over high from the other quarter, releasing their bombs as they flew homeward, northeastward. The ship that had been hit was still in her station, but she was leaking a trail of smoke. One bomber had been shot down by gunfire from the warships astern, and the last attackers, when last seen from the *Montgovern's* bridge, had had Fleet Air Arm fighters on their tails.

Wind and sea were on the port bow, and the ships had quite a bit of movement on them. And stage two of this assault was developing now ahead: something new, by courtesy of *Superaereo.*

Mackeson said, using binoculars and trying to make out what was happening, "Mines, of some sort." He had his glasses on parachutes that were drifting down ahead of the convoy, out ahead of the destroyer screen. Italian bombers, s84s, had approached from ahead during the last stages of the Junkers' bombing run, and until the parachutes blossomed it had looked from here as if they were dropping huge bombs on the destroyers. Now, through binoculars, Mackeson could see that the objects were barrel-shaped, rather like depth charges, and that they were going into the sea well ahead, beyond and not *on* the fleet destroyers. The destroyers had engaged the bombers first, but now they'd shifted target to the dangling secret weapons: and to add to their problems fighter-bombers had just appeared. Small, stubby-shaped biplanes, diving on them.

"Commodore's flying forty-five degree emergency turn port, sir!"

Turning his ships to steer them clear of the mines—or whatever those things might be. Mackeson's signalman had reported it through the window from the bridge wing; part of his job was to watch the

Blackadder's yardarms for signals. There were attackers coming in from other directions as well but it was this unidentified threat ahead that had to be taken care of first. Siren, now, a hoarse screaming to implement the flag-signal for the turn. Straight told his quartermaster, in a flat tone as if the whole thing disgusted him, "Port fifteen degrees."

An Italian bomber was flaming down into the sea. It wasn't anywhere near any of the ships, and it looked like a kill for the Fleet Air Arm, who were making interceptions at longer range, clear of the convoy's guns. The guns were as bad for the Sea Hurricanes as they were for Junkers or Savoias, but in any case the fighter pilots' object was to break up attacking formations long before they reached the convoy.

The *Montgovern* was under helm now, her motion changing as she turned head-on to wind and sea, the whole convoy swinging round to avoid the unknown danger in its path. Devenish said to Mackeson, "Something new, strange but true." Quoting something, presumably. Mackeson murmured, "Secret Woppery." Bomb-splashes near destroyers in the screen ahead seemed to be small ones, and those aircraft which had been acting like fighter-bombers—they were already invisible in the haze thrown up by the destroyers' AA barrage—had looked old-fashioned, like First War fighters.

Ships' guns were getting noisy in other sectors now.

"Midships the wheel."

Devenish, back from a visit to the starboard wing, told Straight, "That was the *Neotsfield* caught one. Fire'll take some putting out, I'd say."

With the amount of smoke that was coming out of her, any U-boat waiting for this convoy would see them coming from fifty miles away. And there'd be some U-boats waiting, all right.

Torpedo-bombers had begun an approach from the quarter—which because of the turn to port had now become the beam—but they'd split up now. It had seemed at first that the destroyers' barrage-fire in the sector had broken up the attack, but in fact they'd divided into several groups each of five or six aircraft and then begun to circle outside the range of the destroyers' guns, before long the separate groups

would make simultaneous attacks from different directions. The battleship on the convoy's port quarter opened up at some of them now,
using her sixteen-inch guns: the percussions were so enormous that you
just about felt them as well as heard them, even from this distance. The
splashes looked as high as Nelson's Column, rising grandly somewhere
inside the radius of the circling Italians. Another flight was ahead of
that one, had passed round astern and would now be moving up on
the other quarter; groups who'd turned the other way were hanging
around on the port beam and bow.

And all turning inwards . . .

Now, Mackeson thought, it would start to become real. So far, he'd
felt like a spectator. You were in the middle of it all, part of the vulnerable target, but it had all been happening at a distance and on the
periphery. Like being in the middle of a bar-room brawl and for some
odd reason no one hitting *you* . . . But now, matters were about to
change and involve one personally: of those five separate threats spread
over an arc of about a hundred and eighty degrees some, surely, would
get through. They were Savoia Marchettis, he thought. This whole
effort seemed to be Italian: and the air bases in Sardinia *were* Italian, of
course. Any Germans that showed up, like those Junkers, would be
from the Sicilian bases. He remarked to Humphrey Straight as he
passed behind him to take a look out on the other side, "Nothing but
Eyeties, we have now." Straight squirmed his facial muscles as if he was
about to spit, but that was as far as it got. Destroyers all round from
the port bow to the starboard quarter were engaging the on-coming
torpedo-bombers, and so were the big ships astern. The inner screen,
the Hunts, were staying in close to the block of merchantmen; they
had their guns trained out on their own sectors, ready to engage any
of the Savoias that got in this far.

Straight had steadied his ship on the new course. On the quarter
smoke still blew thickly out of the ship that was on fire. On the starboard bow the secret-weapon-dropping had finished. It would be very
annoying, Mackeson thought, to the backroom boffins and others on

the Italian side to see the convoy simply stepping round the fruits of
all that labour. And they'd surely have meant all the different kinds of
attack to go in at once: he guessed that the Fleet Air Arm had probably disrupted their co-ordination for them. But five attacks were on
their way in now, and that was enough to be going on with. Gunfire
was thickening and spreading as the action drew inexorably in towards
the centre, the merchant ships and their cargoes which formed the
bull's eye of the target.

Devenish touched his arm, and pointed. Ahead, high against clear
sky, were—he got his glasses on them—more Junkers 88s. At first he
saw only one small bunch of them, but then he realized there was a
wide, loose scattering of such groups, threes and fours and sixes; and
above them, fighters.

One torpedo-bomber had got through the fleet destroyers' barrage
on the port bow of the convoy. Suddenly it was inside the screen, an
enemy at close range and determined. Humpbacked, thick-bodied, ugly,
low to the sea and being shot at now by the Hunts on this side and
by the Mauritius-class cruiser which was fine on the *Montgovern*'s bow.
Beale and Withinshaw were on their toes at the guns, catching slit-eyed
glimpses of it through shell-bursts, watching it over the sights of their
oily-black, wicked-looking weapons. If it kept coming, at that height,
it would be lovely for the Oerlikons.

Paul saw it lift as its torpedo fell away, tilted tail-down and flopped
into the sea. By the time the splash went up the aircraft was already
well ahead of it. The commodore's siren was shrieking for yet another
emergency turn—and none too soon, with at least one torpedo in the
water. To his right, on the bow, Paul saw a second attacker trailing smoke
from one engine but still coming, low and deadly. The cruiser was blazing away at it: and the first one was hauling away to the right, nose up
as it banked, and tracer from a Hunt's Oerlikons seemed to lick its belly.
Beale saw his target escaping before he'd had a shot at it, and he tried
one burst that didn't have a hope of hitting. Paul yelled in his ear,
"Watch out for that Hunt!" The Hunt destroyer had been moving up,

engaging the bomber with everything she had, and as the convoy swung to port she was about to pass across these Oerlikons' field of fire. Beale might have raked her bridge with his twenty-millimetre explosive shells before he'd known what he was doing. He'd ceased fire now, and Withinshaw hadn't fired at all.

On the bow, the aircraft that still had its torpedo under it blew up. Bits of plane and torpedo sang over, ringing off the *Montgovern's* steel and peppering the sea with splashes. Obviously the torpedo's warhead had exploded. The echo of it was still ringing when the second crash came: deeper, softer-sounding. Paul's eyes or mental eye still registered the fire-ball of the exploding bomber as he swung round and saw the *Garelochhead* hit—a torpedo-hit, that first one probably, the one he'd seen launched. The *Garelochhead* had been next astern of the *Montgovern* but after two emergency turns to port she was on the beam now. A spout of seas shot up across her foc'sl; but he wasn't looking at her now, he was remembering what he was here for and doing it, looking round for new attacks. He heard Withinshaw yell at Beale, "Let's go 'ome Ron!"

"*Which* 'ome?"

Wally Short had shouted that. Everyone except the fat man was laughing. The volume of gunfire was decreasing: there was still some action somewhere astern but the torpedo attack, at least, seemed to have played itself out.

Then he saw bombers: high up, and to starboard. He thought they were 88s. You got used to recognizing each different type without consciously looking at the details of its shape: it became like looking at a face, you just glanced at it and knew it. He hadn't realized this before, and he had to look back at them to check that his quick impression had been right. Siren blaring: the commodore was turning his convoy back to starboard. At present it was ninety degrees off course, steaming directly towards Sardinia, with wind and sea consequently fine on the starboard bow, the ship rolling as well as pitching, a ponderous corkscrewing motion that wasn't violent but still made you take care of your footing and hold on to things. He'd drawn Beale's and Withinshaw's attention to those bombers, and now he was free to look around, take stock.

Earlier on, there'd been a bomb-hit on one of the ships in column four. It had started a fire and there was still a lot of smoke back there. But one ship in each of the outer columns made a total of four casualties so far, although the ship on fire was still keeping up—so far as he could see. Turning, now. The *Garelochhead* was out of sight, lost among the crowd of freighters astern. As the convoy swung back towards its easterly course she'd be somewhere between columns two and three, and then she'd slip out astern as the rest of them forged on. So—three drop-outs, one burning; and now—gunfire from the cruisers ahead reminded one—the Junkers 88s were about to make *their* effort.

The bombers were coming over high and in their separate groups. He thought there were fewer than when he'd last looked at them. All the warships firing steadily, surrounding them with shell-bursts which the wind quickly tore to shreds. They were at ten or twelve thousand feet: you got the impression, from their appearance of remoteness, that they were only passing—like migrating geese . . . Mick McCall was beside him, staring up at them. Paul hadn't noticed him arriving.

"Fleet Air Arm gave their mates a clobbering. There were half as many again, before they got stuck in." He jerked his head. "We get a good view of things, up top."

"Shot them down, you mean?"

"Just broke 'em up. You could see the bomb-loads going, and they'd skip out of it. They've got the legs of our lot when they put their noses down."

The bombers were still flying southwestward. It was the rearmost groups that the cruisers and battleships astern were shooting at now, and one was turning away to port, an engine smoking . . . Wally and McNaught cheered, and McCall said, "Every little helps."

Paul said, "Going down in Tunisia, I suppose."

"Maybe." McCall told Short, "Don't want to cheer too soon. It'll get worse before it gets any better."

Withinshaw muttered, "Be 'appier if we was carryin' wheat." Paul asked why. The fat man said, "Keeps you afloat, like." McCall explained, "Wheat expands when it gets wet. So if you get holed when you're carrying it in bulk it's like having your 'tween-decks full of kapok."

"It don't explode, neither."

"There." McCall sighed. "Buggers are turning. They'll be at us now." He asked Withinshaw, "Had a load of wheat on that Atlantic trip, did you?"

"Aye. Out of Halifax. Laffin', we were."

"Does a lot o' laffin', does our Art." Beale glanced round at McCall, then back at the 88s. "Won't be laffin' when they catch 'im, though."

The bombers were circling astern, maintaining the separate groups. Paul asked McCall, "A ship on fire, is there, back there?"

"The *Neotsfield*. Last ship in column four. Her skipper reckons they're getting on top of it, though this wind can't help."

"How about the one that was astern of us?"

"*Garelochhead*. All we know is she was holed and flooding for'ard. She won't be coming on with us, that's for sure." He nodded, with his eyes on the bombers. "Here we go. Here *I* go." He told Beale and Withinshaw, "Shoot 'em all down, lads. Wait till you see the whites of their eyes, then plug 'em up the arse." He went to the ladder and rattled down it, on his way back to the midships Bofors. Paul checked the time: it was 1:35. Beale said, "Stand by, Art." Up astern, from something like ten thousand feet, the first of the 88s were putting their noses down, aiming their dives into the centre of the convoy.

You waited. There was always such a lot of waiting, Paul thought. In submarines there was a lot of it too. They sent you to patrol an area or a position where it was hoped targets would appear, and you sat and waited for them. Just as submarines on this convoy's track would be waiting now. But they'd know something was coming, they couldn't doubt it, whereas sometimes you could wait for two or three weeks, the whole duration of the patrol, and see nothing. They called those "blank" patrols.

Here, now, you waited for bombs. For bombers diving, with men his own age at their controls. He wondered what it felt like and looked like from up there. But for those Germans the wait was over, the attack had been launched and time-fused shells were exploding in their faces.

Withinshaw was narrow-eyed, open-mouthed. You could see his thick torso heaving as his breath came and went in short gasps. Paul wondered if it was true about his double life. He walked behind him, passing between Wally Short and the ammo bin, to the rail on the port side; he leaned out over it, looking astern. A freighter had closed up in the place of the *Garelochhead,* and that one and the *Montgovern* were now the only two ships in column one. Firing was heavy astern: battleships', cruisers' and carriers' AA guns all plastering the sky with high-explosive, dark smoke-flowers opening in tight bunches that quickly loosened and smeared, disintegrating while fresh clutches of them appeared like magic under the noses of the diving bombers. He was back in his place between the guns. That was Mackeson out in the bridge wing, staring aft, up at the approaching aircraft. If Beale or Withinshaw got careless they'd wipe old Bongo off his perch. Gosling was there too, and the signalman. A stockier figure behind the glass-enclosed front of the bridge could only be Humphrey Straight.

Gunfire spreading as well as thickening. The close escort of Hunts had joined in, and Bofors from ships at the tail-ends of columns two and three. It was one roar of noise but you could pick out the different elements in snatches of solo sound: the harsh rattling stabbing fire of Oerlikons, the measured thump-thump-thump of pompoms from the Hunts and the distinctive Bofors bark, and over all of it the hard thunder of four-inch.

Explosion astern. It had sounded like a bomb hitting. Then before he'd expected, like great black bats howling across the sky—

Oerlikons jumping, pumping their din into your skull. Tracer soaring, and the sky a mass of shell-smoke. Withinshaw a jellyfish shaking from the pulsing of his gun, shaking like a fat woman in a slimming machine, and used shell-cases cascading. The sea rose hummocking on his left—to starboard—with the top streaming off it like confetti, and a second later, as a separate stick came down, the back end of the *Castleventry*'s bridge went up in a sheet of flame.

There were three—four—bombers over the convoy, all just about finishing their dives, pulling out, sea leaping in mounds between ships and columns, and the bone-jarring crash of another hit somewhere on the quarter. Paul wasn't looking at the *Castleventry* but that huge gush of fire was still blinding, brain-scorching, as the belly of a Junkers 88 obscenely exposed itself, black crosses on white panels and one of its engines smoking, a lick of bluish flame from the wing behind it and smoke colouring with fire all out along the wing. It was Beale's gun hitting, Beale screaming joy, and Withinshaw's tracer arcing to another one, fire-beads curling away behind its tail as it roared over, lifting out of the mess of bomb-bursts and gun-smoke. Half a dozen separate streams of tracer were converging on it but it still rose, banking to port across the *Empire Dance*. Beale shouted, "I got 'im! See me get 'im?" The first one, he meant, and Paul nodded and gave him a thumbs-up sign, but he hadn't seen it. He'd seen Beale hitting and the machine in flames; he didn't doubt that it had crashed but he hadn't seen it. There were some moments now in which to breathe, look around, confirm that this ship was still intact, still plugging on: it was simultaneously reassuring and surprising. The noise had lessened and there were no enemies for the moment within Oerlikon range; ships astern were barraging at the next flight as it started down but here in the convoy there was a surprising pause. The *Castleventry* was out on the quarter, several cables' lengths away. He was looking at her, at the flames enshrouding her superstructure and right back as far as the after well deck, when she blew up. The heat as well as the shock-wave of the explosion hit them solidly, from a distance of about half a mile. Then the *Empire Dance* and the *Blackadder* and the freighter who'd moved up into the

Castleventry's station all opened fire. Some of the merchantmen had Brens and other light machine-guns mounted in their bridge wings and flying bridges, as well as Bofors and Oerlikons. Withinshaw had opened up, but Beale's gun had jammed as soon as he'd pressed the trigger, and he and Short were working to clear it all through that attack. They were still at it, cursing, when the third bout started. Another Junkers had gone flaming into the sea ahead, and the Hunt-class escort who'd been standing by the *Castleventry* and must have had her paint blistered in that explosion had ranged up close to port of the *Montgovern,* adding her own close-range weapons to the protective bar-rage. Two tin-hatted sailors on her foc's'l were ditching what looked like wreckage—probably bits of the *Castleventry* blown on to her. Paul could see her guns' crews and bridge staff—busy, smoke-wreathed, somehow like parts of the ship herself, men and weapons and ship forming one live creature. He was reminded of destroyer action of his own, of the smell and sound of it and the sudden transition to swim-ming with a half-dead man on his back, then swimming alone, realiz-ing he didn't know whether he was swimming towards the shore or away from it. He'd lost his sense of direction but after an initial surge of panic it didn't seem to matter much . . . He grabbed Withinshaw's thick shoulder, and pointed. Withinshaw swung round like a heavy-weight ballet dancer twirling, old twinkle-toes himself. He had his sights on the underside of the Junkers as it flattened and its bombs thumped into the sea somewhere in the middle of the convoy. The gun began its fierce clattering roar, Withinshaw a-tremble with it as he slid his thick body round, hose-piping with the tracer. Then a shell from the Hunt burst under the bomber's tail and it was a cloud of out-flying debris around the bright nucleus of its exploding petrol tanks.

Mackeson said, "Not so good, that shemozzle." Humphrey Straight, who'd been adjusting engine revs to maintain station on the com-modore's beam, only glanced at him and sniffed. Devenish, who'd moved up front in case the master wanted him to take over the conning of the ship now that bit of action had finished, muttered, "*And we've got tonight ahead of us.*"

Tonight they'd be turning down into the Skerki Channel, towards the Sicilian Narrows. And before dark—apart from whatever might be thrown at them in the interim—there'd be the evening, sunset performance.

Mackeson thought, *And we're lucky, at that.* Because the *Castleventry* people, amongst others, did not have an evening or a night ahead of them.

The destroyers were busy with a submarine contact out on the convoy's bow. Three of them had converged there, and they'd dropped two patterns of charges. The escort commander had sent his two reserves—Hunt-class ships which he'd stationed ahead of the cruisers for this purpose—to fill the temporary gaps in the screen.

Gunfire from ahead. Mackeson raised his binoculars. It had come from destroyers, but it had already stopped. He caught a glimpse of a single aircraft, flying low to the sea and coming in towards the convoy. He'd tensed, but relaxed again when his signalman said, "Fulmar, sir."

"You're right." Devenish had his glasses on it too. "And it's in trouble."

It was trailing smoke, and struggling to stay airborne. But if it went down now, a destroyer would get the pilot out, with any luck—unless he was badly wounded. Quite a few of the fighters returning from intercepting enemy formations had been in difficulties, struggling to reach their carriers. And when they did make it, since this last fracas they'd found they all had to get down on just one of them, because the other had had a bomb on her flight-deck. It was an armoured deck and the bomb hadn't penetrated, but it would be a while before that carrier could operate normally. A side-effect was that the other one would be so overcrowded that her flying operations would be hampered too.

"He's going in."

The Fulmar was belly-landing into the sea, within fifty yards of one of the Hunts.

The *Castleventry* had blown up. Like the *Montgovern,* she'd had her quota of aviation spirit stowed in her bridge deck, which was where the bomb had struck and burst. It must have blown out through the for'ard part of the bridge as well—or sprayed burning petrol right through the superstructure—because she'd gone out of control immediately, swinging off-course and under the stern of the *Empire Dance,* and by that time the whole of her afterpart had been wrapped in flame. You'd been looking at a fire, not at a ship. When she'd exploded, burning wreckage had landed on a Hunt who'd been close to her; the same Hunt was now abeam to port and had signalled the commodore via the *Montgovern* that she'd picked up two survivors.

The *Kinloch Castle,* leading column three, had been hit for'ard. Some of her deck cargo of landing-craft had been blown overboard and there'd been internal damage, in her foc's'l and 'tween-deck spaces for'ard, but she was still in station and her master had said he was all right. The Clan ship that had been number two in column four had been less fortunate: she'd dropped out, with engine defects following a near-miss. And a couple of miles astern a destroyer who'd been badly hit was being abandoned and would then be sunk.

"Emergency turn starboard, sir!"

To give a wider berth to the submarine which they were still hunting out there on the bow. Turns like this were the commodore's decision. The escort commander told him what was happening ahead, and the commodore took such action as he personally considered necessary. The flag-hoist dropped, and the siren hooted. Humphrey Straight nodded to his chief officer, and moved away to the side of the bridge; Devenish told the quartermaster, "Starboard fifteen degrees."

More depth charges exploded as the convoy swung away. In this column there were still only two ships, the *Montgovern* and the *Empire Dance,* but there were three in each of the three others. A rearrangement since the end of the last bombing attack had involved moving one ship, the *Miramar,* from column three to column four, where the

Clan ship had fallen out and the *Neotsfield*—her fire was out now, and the smoke was greatly reduced—had moved up into second place astern of the *Blair Atholl*.

Mackeson counted on his fingers: out of sixteen starters, five had gone, either sunk or dropped astern. Droppers-out very often ended up by being sunk anyway. But near enough one-third of the convoy had been lost. And the worst, admittedly, was still to come, as they moved in close to the Luftwaffe bases in Sicily and the submarine and E-boat ambush territory, the narrow waters south of the Skerki Bank. But if one-third of the original convoy could be brought into Malta, he thought, it would be a triumph. One-third would mean half the number of ships surviving now.

A triumph: and perhaps a pipe-dream too. Decodings of some Malta RAF reports indicated that a strong Italian cruiser force had assembled at sea and was steering south. The two cruisers from Cagliari and the Third Cruiser Squadron out of Messina and the heavy cruiser *Trento* had been mentioned. Mackeson had decided not to think about it: and he'd told Thornton to keep the information to himself.

"By 'eck, look there!"

On the beam, a submarine had shot to the surface. The long finger of the fore-casing was sticking up out of the sea, and the stubby conning-tower was awash like a half-tide rock.

"Ease to five degrees of wheel." Devenish had given the U-boat one quick glance, and turned back to his job. The Hunt to port of the *Montgovern* had opened fire: she was under helm, bow-wave rising as she picked up speed. Mackeson hurried out into the bridge wing. Looking aft, he saw the Army gunners with their four-inch on the ship's stern. They'd got the gun trained round but they couldn't fire because the Hunt was in the way. The Hunt's own for'ard four-inch were firing as she tore straight in towards the submarine. She'd fired again: and splashes had gone up, over by a hundred yards. There were men visible in the conning-tower, which could only have been a couple of feet above sea-level. He'd certainly seen *one* man, and now the

Hunt was in the way . . . The *Montgovern* and all the rest of the merchantmen were steadying on the new course, the Hunt and the submarine abaft the beam now. The Hunt seemed to jump in the water as she rammed, her stem smashing into the enemy craft's hull, opening it to the sea and riding over it, thrashing over and now moving slowly, wallowing, down by the bows in a welter of churned foam. The submarine had gone.

There were cheers from the gunners, Army and DEMS men. Mackeson thought the ramming had been unnecessary and rather stupid. The U-boat had already been in bad trouble, presumably from the depth-charging, and a few well-aimed shells would have finished her. Alternatively, she might have been boarded. The glimpse he'd had of at least one man in the tower had given him the impression that her crew had been about to abandon ship. It hadn't been necessary at all, he thought. A perfectly good escort destroyer had been put out of action. She might limp back to Gibraltar and eventually be repaired, but in the meantime this convoy, which needed all the protection it could get, had lost one escort. Thinking about it as he turned to go back into the bridge, Bongo Mackeson was angry. Part of it lay in the fact that while he would gladly have seen every living German and Italian burn in hell if it saved Allied lives or helped to beat them in the war they'd started, a completely unnecessary taking of lives seemed incompatible with his own ideas of why the war had to be fought anyway: and he was face to face with Humphrey Straight, who must have been standing right behind him. Scowling: reflecting Mackeson's own scowl . . .

"That were a daft bloody thing to do." Straight stared at him challengingly, his head lowered like a bull's. "I'd courtmartial that bugger!"

Mackeson heard himself responding to the challenge, defending his own Service.

"The submarine might have slipped under again. He just made certain of it, that's all."

"I thought destroyers were along to look after us, not play silly buggers like—"

"That's what he was doing, captain. If that thing had got down again it might still have got some torpedoes off—or even just got away, fished you on your way home to Gib next week, or—"

"Bloody 'ell—"

Siren: for the turn back to port . . .

There'd been submarine alarms and emergency turns all through the afternoon, and now with dusk approaching it was time for the air assault to start up again. The convoy had re-formed, into two columns instead of four. The reason for it was that when they turned down into the Skerki Channel destroyers ahead would be streaming their TSDS minesweeping gear, and the merchantmen had to be in a narrower formation to keep inside the strip of cleared water.

This pair of ships, the *Montgovern* and the *Empire Dance,* had dropped back and tagged on to what had been column two. But the C-class cruiser had inserted herself in the line as well, so there were three merchantmen, then the cruiser, then the *Montgovern* and the *Empire Dance.* The starboard column consisted of the three ships who'd comprised column four—the *Blair Atholl,* the damaged *Neotsfield* and the *Miramar*— with the *Kinloch Castle,* the tanker *Caracas Moon* and the American freighter *Santa Eulalia* completing the line of six ships.

So the *Montgovern* now had a cruiser ahead of her and the tanker abeam to starboard. Two other heavy cruisers led the columns, and a third, who'd been with the battleships earlier on, was centrally placed astern with a Hunt-class escort on each side of her. The minesweeping destroyers were in the lead and there were three others down each side, all inside the area of swept water.

New air attacks were coming, and in strength. Mackeson's W/T operators had been listening to the chitchat between Fleet Air Arm pilots and the fighter-directing cruisers, and the Sea Hurricanes had already run into some opposition. They'd reported big formations of Italian and German bombers already up and circling in waiting areas.

The Hurricanes had scored some successes and they'd suffered losses too, and among the formations they'd encountered had been some of Ju87s, Stuka dive-bombers.

Beale spat down-wind. "Stukas is *all* we bloody need."

"I heard they're sitting ducks to fighters."

"Won't be no fighters, will there? Not when the flat-tops turn back."

The carriers and their own cruisers, and the battleships, would be reversing course in about an hour's time. The light was already weakening, and by then it would be dark. The hope, Mackeson had explained, was that the enemy might not realize the forces had split until tomorrow's daylight.

Paul was hungry. Lunch, in mid-afternoon, had been corned beef and pickles, and there'd been sardines for tea. Devenish, who presided over the saloon and the messing arrangements, had said the evening meal would probably be soup and corned beef sandwiches. He'd added, "What we're missing, thanks to you lot, is a decent breakfast." Thanks to having passengers on board, he meant. When they had the saloon to themselves, apparently the ship's officers breakfasted on steak and onions, which rations didn't allow for now.

Withinshaw said, "Can't abide fookin' Stukas."

Paul told him, "Your turn to knock one down, this time."

"I 'ad one *last* time!" The fat man was indignant. "I was all over the sod an' some bastard blew it in fookin' 'alf before I could shittin' finish!"

"Yeah." Beale laughed. "I bet. Just because I got one an' you didn't come inside 'alf a mile—"

"He did, though." Paul confirmed it. "I saw it. He was hitting, and a shell burst right under it."

" 'Ear that?"

Withinshaw was delighted. Beale said, "Bein' kind to you, ain't he? On account o' you're so cultural . . . What's time now?"

Paul checked. "Just on six."

"Light's going. If they're coming, they'll come now."

"Fookers'll come, don't you worry!"

Paul wondered where his father was. BBC news of events east of Suez wasn't encouraging, particularly if you listened to what they didn't say. He hoped *Defiant* had not been sent east . . . But whether she was there or still here in the Mediterranean he wondered how his father would like it, commanding a cruiser when he was so very much a destroyer man. Funny, really: Nick Everard, destroyer man, driving a cruiser, and Paul Everard, submariner, a passenger in a freighter . . . He put a hand up and touched his forehead—an old schoolboy habit, "touching wood," for luck. He shut his eyes: *Please let me get to Malta.*

Double-think, he knew it: prayer or wish? He doubted whether either was likely to change the course of events. Destroyers opened fire, out to starboard in light that was turning milky. The scattering of gun-fire thickened into a steady barrage. Torpedo-bombers were probably the target: there were no shell-bursts in the colour-washed sky, so it was a low-level barrage which almost certainly meant torpedo-carrying air-craft. This in turn was likely to mean Italians.

Sirens were wailing for an emergency turn, and he guessed torpe-does might have been dropped. Waiting again, wondering what was happening, trying to put the clues together. He'd learnt one thing: that after you'd waited a while, things did happen . . . Like the whistle which he heard now above the sound of the guns to starboard. Gosling was in the bridge wing, pointing upwards, and Beale, watching the sky ahead and to port, shouted, "Stukas, Art!"

The destroyers ahead—cruisers too now—were engaging them. Two formations, Paul saw, at about ten thousand feet. Or eight, or maybe seven . . . If they attacked from that direction they'd be diving with the setting sun right in their eyes. Gold and pink and violet, too pretty by half, and there was a watered-down reflection of it in the sky behind the Stukas. They were on the port bow as the convoy altered course. Withinshaw was muttering at them resentfully as he settled at his gun. Paul was glad, in one way, to be seeing them. His father and Jack had written and talked about the dreaded Ju87s in connection with the

Crete evacuation last year, and now he'd experience them for himself. He didn't want too much of them, just enough so that when someone started shooting a line about Stukas next time he could cut in with his recollections of this convoy.

To have any, though, you had to stay alive. To get to Malta or see your father or write a letter you didn't know how to write, you had to get through this. The first Stukas were in their dives: there were three of them, with two more behind, in this group. Flipping over sideways, rolling over and shoving their noses down . . .

No screamers: they were supposed to have sirens on their wings, and these hadn't. Gone out of fashion, he guessed, thinking of how he'd put it in a letter to his father: *Stuka sirens are now old hat . . .* The noise was the racket of their engines and the surrounding roar of gunfire. Tracer added to the overhead colour, lacing and criss-crossing its brilliant streaks, garish against the subtler colouring of the sunset through a sky that was being spoilt and dirtied by the shell-bursts. For seconds at a time bombers would be hidden in them, then reappear intact, still diving, coming . . . Beale had opened fire, now Withinshaw. Both guns snarling, shaking, jetting fire: and bombs away . . . It was exactly as it had been described to him and as he'd seen it in his mind, except for the absence of the siren-shriek that was intended to affect morale. A merchantman in the other column was firing some kind of rocket that soared vertically to meet the dive-bombers and then exploded, smoke and fragments bursting outwards. He saw there were several of these things in use, now. An anti-Stuka device he hadn't heard of before. From the merchantmen alone there must have been fifty or sixty Oerlikons and a couple of dozen Bofors in action, plus a lot of lighter weapons, and when you added all the warships' four-inch AA guns and close-range weapons to that you had a sky so full it was surprising the Stukas could get through it without being torn apart. Bombs were splashing in ahead and between the columns, and he saw another go in to port, beyond the AA cruiser's bow. The action was shifting back, though, nearer the tail-end of the convoy: the second rush of Stukas seemed to be going for the cruiser. Withinshaw's gun jammed, and Beale's was temporarily silent too as Short changed its magazine. It didn't matter, the barrage was slackening, the next batch of attackers still high. And now Beale had the new magazine on and the gun cocked, ready. Paul moved over to watch the fat man and McNaught clearing their snag. They were busy at it, and on the other side Beale was staring upwards, watching for Stukas, when gunfire flared suddenly to starboard and an aircraft came lurching over the other column at only about masthead height. It was a Savoia, one of the Italian torpedo planes. It passed over the tanker, the *Caracas Moon,* with its nose coming up as its pilot fought to gain height, and all the tracer was curving away astern of it—gunners taken by surprise, shooting *at* it instead of ahead of it. Withinshaw was screaming obscenities as he wrestled with his Oerlikon. The Savoia roared over ahead of the *Montgovern* and Beale was shooting behind it, but the AA cruiser's guns were ready and right on it, blasting it as it rose across her. More Stukas had started down by this time, and Beale had shifted target to them. But the Italian was in flames, and out of the side of his eye as he turned back to pay attention to the dive-bombers Paul saw it belly-flop, burning, into the sea. That one had clearly been the cruiser's bird. But Stukas were the threat again now, four or five of them coming down together, and again every gun—including Withinshaw's, at last—blazing up at them. One was pulling out high, and looked as if it had been hit, but the others came on in near-vertical dives, and like the last few they were going for the convoy's rear. But there were others suddenly—a pair he hadn't seen until this second, although Withinshaw had been on to them, aiming at the centre: they were greenish-khaki coloured and they carried the green-white-red Italian markings. He hadn't taken it in before, but all these Stukas were Italian. Pulling out, bombs on their way, black eggs tumbling slowly at first, then accelerating, and you didn't see them after that until they splashed in or hit. More Stukas were diving now behind that pair: others swarming over high . . . The diving bombers and the stammering guns merged into one enclosing, deafening and blinding blur of action: it was more mind-dulling than frightening, it swamped your consciousness, identity, sense of time. His own problem, he knew, was mostly *in*action, and he envied the two men at the Oerlikons. If you had a weapon in your hands the whole thing became much easier—your mind as well as your hands had that weapon to hang on to, to become a part of. The weapon became an anchor holding you to reality. The Oerlikons had ceased fire, though, McNaught and Short changing ammo drums while the gunners stood back and flexed their fingers and hands, loosening taut muscles.

There was a freighter on fire, Paul saw suddenly, at the rear of the other column.

Beale was telling the two younger men to take some of the empty magazines below and bring up full ones . . . But that ship had been hit, just a few hundred yards across the water, without him having seen it happen. He wouldn't have thought that was possible. It was the ship astern of the *Caracas Moon,* who was abeam of the *Montgovern.* Straining his eyes through the rapidly fading light he saw that her flag was the Stars and Stripes: and there was only one American in the convoy, so that was who she was, the *Santa Eulalia*. The fire was in her for'ard well deck, and a Hunt had ranged up alongside with a hose jetting water over it. With night coming on—it would be dark within minutes—and enemies of various kinds lying in wait ahead, prospects for a ship with a fire to light her up wouldn't be too marvellous. They wouldn't be all that good for the other ships with her, either.

There was a new outbreak of firing ahead. High-angle gunnery from the cruisers leading the two columns and from the destroyers ahead of them. Shell-bursts thickening up there: a fresh assault arriving, evidently, with the last of the evening light. A hand grasped his arm: Mick McCall asked, "All right, are we?"

Paul said, "That American isn't all right."

"You're telling me. She's got ammo down for'ard . . . I was coming to spread the news that it's the intention to remain closed up at

action stations." He jerked a thumb upwards. "Now we have more vis-
itors anyway . . . See that Savoia getting chopped?"

"What's this lot, then?"

The new attack, Beale was asking about. He didn't want to talk
about the Savoia, which had been an easy target that he'd missed.
McCall told him, "Stukas again. From the Sicily direction, and the carrier boys said there were Hun Stukas as well as Wop ones, so these'll
be the other kind, most likely."

Gunfire was closing in again as the enemies droned over, high. Paul
asked McCall, "Was that the only hit they scored?" On the American,
he meant. McCall yelled, "Destroyer. One of the fleets, astern."

"Sunk?"

He'd nodded. "A Hunt got some survivors."

That was the engine note of diving Ju87s, now, lacing through the
noise of the guns. Quite a different note was the commodore's signal
for a turn back to port. All the heaviest firing was from astern. Then he
saw the burning American open fire, and from the volume of it you'd
have guessed she had a gun on every square foot of deck-space. All the
merchantmen's guns opened up again as a single Stuka, its dive com-
pleted, came racketing over from astern, lifting through streams of tracer,
straining towards the sanctuary of the surrounding dark. With luck there
might still be some Sea Hurricanes waiting for stragglers out there. The
ships were all under helm, coming round to port. Heavy firing astern
and the intermittent snarl of diving bombers, the rising note and then
the full-throated roar as they flattened out and sped away . . . Paul was
out at the ship's side, at the starboard rail, from where he hoped that
if any other Stukas came this way out of the action astern he'd get an
early sight of them and warn the gunners. Back there in the tracer-
streaked, flash-pocked near-darkness he saw a flash bigger than all the
other flickering, a flare of yellow spearing into an orange-coloured fire-
ball that spread and then snuffed out abruptly: it had lasted about three
seconds. Then, from the general roar of action astern, there was one
much heavier explosion.

McCall shouted, "They're after the carriers!"

Paul had thought the second mate had left them. He went over to him. "Did you mean we'll be at action stations all night?"

Perhaps he hadn't heard him. The fire on the American freighter was a bright glow that brightened as the darkness gathered, and the bridge superstructure of the fire-fighting Hunt was blackly silhouetted against it. Astern, gunfire faded and died away. As your ears came back to life, you could hear the pounding of the ship's engines and the swish and thump of the sea around her stem.

With Bizerta thirty miles to starboard, the convoy had altered course to enter the Skerki Channel. Ahead, destroyers streamed minesweeping gear, and astern the heavy escort of battleships and carriers had turned back westward.

There was a sense of total commitment at this point. In fact the convoy had been committed to its purpose from the moment it had left the Clyde, and more deeply so again when, passing through the Gibraltar Strait into the Mediterranean, it had been joined by its heavy naval escort. But now, with only three cruisers and a dozen destroyers remaining, it was actually pushing its head into the noose—the Sicilian Narrows, where there'd be U-boats and E-boats to contend with as well as German air bases on Sicily and Italian torpedo aircraft from Pantellaria.

For the moment, things were quiet, and Paul went aft to get something to eat. The guns were to be manned all night, but the DEMS men would have stand-off periods with their number twos—Short and McNaught, for instance—taking over. Paul, unconvinced of his own value to the community on the foc's'l-head, didn't think his absence was likely to upset anyone.

The atmosphere in the saloon was cheerful, laced with tension, awareness of the crucial stage they'd reached. There was satisfaction, too, in the fact that losses so far had been light. To have eleven ships still in convoy at this point was better than anyone had expected.

Brill, the doctor, offered, "Beer?"

"I think a large Scotch might fit the occasion better."

"Oh you do, do you!"

"So would you, if you poked your nose out into the cold. It's freezing, up on that damn—"

The ship trembled to the deep *crump* of an explosion.

He thought first, *Mine?* Because with the sweeping gear out ahead you were conscious of the danger of them, now the convoy was in narrow waters. A second thought was that it might be the *Santa Eulalia,* her fire reaching the ammunition in her for'ard holds.

Matt Harrison, the *Montgovern*'s second engineer, began, "Best get up top, boys, or—"

A second explosion was closer, much louder. Movement towards the door became a rush. Up till now most of them had been listening and wondering, waiting for an explanation and not keen to leave their food and drink. Paul was on his way up to the boat deck when the third bang went off. He and Brill and John Pratt, the third mate: they'd been the last out of the saloon. The ship was under helm. He'd thought about the *Santa Eulalia* because although it had looked from the outside as if her fire had been put out, it could still have been alive inside her; but at the second crash he'd thought, *Torpedoes* . . . And the third seemed to confirm it.

Then suddenly he was up on deck, in the open, and off to starboard the *Caracas Moon* was a sheet of flame. To port of the *Montgovern,* as she swung under helm to starboard, the AA cruiser—the old C-class ship who'd been ahead of them—lay stopped with her stern deep in the sea and her bow lifting as she flooded aft. Humphrey Straight was swinging his ship around her, handling the clumsy merchantman as she'd never been designed to be handled. The whole seascape was lit by the burning tanker. She was stopped, and the *Santa Eulalia* had had to put her engines astern to avoid running into her.

They'd passed the cruiser. There were ships all over the place, as helms were flung over to avoid collisions. And on the bow another cruiser— a big one, Mauritius-class—was circling to port with a heavy list.

It was incredible. Two cruisers—out of a total of three—and one tanker, the convoy's *only* tanker, full of the stuff Malta needed most . . . In one salvo of torpedoes? There'd been three freighters between those two cruisers. If it had been just one salvo, picking out those particular ships and thus denuding the convoy of its protection—protection against surface attacks, *Italian* cruisers, for instance—some German or Italian submarine captain had been extraordinarily lucky. And the *Caracas Moon* was in the other column—she *had* been, she wasn't in any column now, she was a mile astern and burning—so the fish that hit her must have passed through this port column, probably between the cruiser and the *Montgovern*.

Unless that one had come from the other side, a simultaneous attack by a different submarine . . . Brill was asking him what he thought had happened. He told him, "We've taken a beating, that's what." Torpedoes from E-boats? It didn't seem likely: and they'd have been seen, or at least picked up on the warships' RDF screens. There'd been no alarm, no gunfire, just three hits at fairly regular intervals. It *had* been one salvo . . . He saw McCall coming down the ladder from the bridge, and moved to intercept him.

"What was it?"

"U-boat, apparently. That's the flagship and the anti-aircraft cruiser gone. The only two fighter-direction ships we had!"

So when fighters from Malta had the convoy in range, they wouldn't be able to communicate with them?

The convoy was in a mess. Ships in all directions, and they were pointing in all directions too. Some had turned one way and some another, some had put on speed and some had slowed. They were strung out and widely separated, in single and small groups. Depth charges went off somewhere astern. A destroyer passed at high speed, bow-wave and stern-wash foaming high, close under the *Montgovern*'s stern. It was a Tribal-class destroyer, big and two-funnelled, and it was heading towards the heavy cruiser—the flagship—which was still circling slowly around out on the quarter. You could see it all in the yellowish flickering light

from the burning *Caracas Moon*. Another destroyer creaming up now—
you saw the bow-wave first, then the ship, and this was one of the
Hunts. Its captain's voice, magnified by a loud-hailer, boomed across
the gap of dark water between that slim hull and this stout, lumbering one: "Will you step on it a bit, *Montgovern?* Close up on the
Woollongong please, captain?" An answering shout, unamplified but stri-
dent enough to carry, was Bongo Mackeson's: "Where *is* the bloody
Woollongong?" But the Hunt was already surging ahead again, heeling
with her rudder hard a-port as she cracked on speed, heading to round
up another member of the flock, herd the stragglers together. If the
enemy had an attack ready to come in now, Paul thought, they'd make
hay with us . . . He'd been intending to put on an extra sweater, and
he hadn't done it. Nor, he realized as he went for'ard to his action station, had he had even a sniff of whisky. He'd have settled, now, for just
one good sniff . . . It was colder. And Withinshaw was belly-aching,
complaining that if the destroyer screen had been doing its job that U-
boat wouldn't have had such an easy shot. Paul explained that there
was no A/S screen on the convoy's beams now. There couldn't be,
because destroyers as well as freighters had to be inside the strip of sea
that had been swept for mines.

Withinshaw still griped. Beale snarled at him to shut his face. "*You've*
come to no 'arm, 'ave you, you great fat—"

"No thanks to *them*, I 'aven't!"

Gunfire: it was on the port bow and ahead. Astern, there was much
less flame visible from the *Caracas Moon:* enough, though, to silhouette
the convoy for the benefit of any enemy attacking from ahead. Paul
blew up his lifebelt, and suggested to the DEMS men that they should
do the same. The firing was thickening. And a Hunt came up between
the columns at high speed, making about thirty knots and heading for
where the action was. The ship ahead of them now was presumably
the *Woollongong*. The one astern didn't look like the *Empire Dance*,
who'd been there earlier. Abeam of the *Montgovern* now was the *Kinloch
Castle*, and ahead of her—he thought—was the *Neotsfield*, and that was

the *Santa Eulalia* bringing up the rear of the starboard column. So what was left of the convoy seemed to have got itself fairly well together, after all. Most of the gunnery that was in progress ahead would be from the cruiser that had been leading the starboard column, and the minesweeping destroyers and two or three other escorts . . . Then suddenly they were *all* in it—all the ships, all the Oerlikons, pompoms, Bofors, rockets, Brens, the sky hung with skeins of tracer, flashing and flickering with shell-bursts. The attackers were Junkers 88s in low-level, shallow dives. A stick went down across their next-ahead—*Woollongong,* if that was her. There was a bomb-splash close on her port side, then the crash and flash of a hit amidships and the usual, now-to-be-expected leap and spread of flames; and more splashes on her other side. The *Neotsfield* had fallen away to starboard, outwards from that other column, with smoke gushing from her and the *Woollongong*'s flames illuminating it. The *Montgovern* was hauling round to port to get past the *Woollongong;* and the *Woollongong* blew up, in a spurt of fire and an ear-splitting roar of detonating explosives, debris flying through the tracer-laced darkness while bombers dipped overhead and soared upwards out of havoc. The *Montgovern* was back on course, steaming through littered water into which the Australian freighter had disintegrated. There were torpedo-bombers coming in now, as the Junkers finished. They were approaching on the other bow, and Paul saw the wide, blurred shadow of the first one like a great evil bat lifting over the lead ship of the starboard column. He knew what it must be, immediately, because it obviously wasn't an 88, and logic did the rest. Tracer was hosing at its nose and then pompoms or Bofors or both were hitting. It was a Heinkel with its port wing on fire, the black crosses of Nazi Germany floodlit as it stalled, turned nose-down and dived into the sea between the columns of merchantmen in a great fountain of black water. But a second Heinkel was over the centre too, Beale's gun amongst fifty others flinging coloured beads of explosive to meet it. Its torpedo fell away, splashed in, and the big aircraft was lifting, in a hurry to get up and away now while gunners in a dozen different ships tried to make sure it didn't. Humphrey Straight's loud-mouthed Willet-Bruce let out one short blast, meaning he was shoving his helm a-starboard. Paul thought he'd be too late if that fish *was* on course for the *Montgovern.* The ship had barely begun to swing when it hit her, abaft the stem on the starboard side.

It felt as if she'd steamed full-tilt into a stone quayside. Sea that had flung up was raining down on them now. He'd been thrown across the foc's'l and grabbed the wire rails to stop himself going over the side. Only Beale and Withinshaw, clinging to their guns, had stayed on their feet. Beale was yelling at Withinshaw to watch out for new attackers, and to the other two to stand by with more ammo. Beale was a hell of a good hand, Paul thought. The *Montgovern's* engines had stopped, and she was settling by the head. Looking down over the side he couldn't see much except that the water seemed closer to him than it had been before. A freighter was passing, almost close enough for him to have reached out and touched her, or to have jumped, cadged a lift to Malta. She'd been their next astern but now she was overhauling them and would close up—by two spaces, one for the *Montgovern* and one for the *Woollongong*—on the leaders. Paul remembered, as the ship rolled sluggishly in the other one's overtaking wash, that he'd wondered what it might feel like to be dropping out while others—*the ships that mattered now,* was how he'd thought of them—pushed on. Now, he'd find out.

CHAPTER NINE
· · ·

Gant came in and shut the cabin door. Nick told him, "Come and sit down, Bob. Like some coffee?"

"Thank you, sir, but I just had some. That was a hell of a barrage again, wasn't it?"

They'd just been visited by Val dive-bombers. *Defiant* and *Sloan* had been the targets, but the Dutch AA gunners ashore had put up such a solid umbrella barrage over them that no bombs had come anywhere near.

Now it was 7:20, and Nick was eating breakfast. Making himself eat, although he wasn't hungry. Last night's grim events were in his mind—in Gant's face too, as the commander pulled back a chair and eased himself down into it, like a dummy being let down on a rope—on account of that back of his, which he swore had nothing wrong with it.

The repair work to the boiler room and bridge superstructure had been going on all night, and you could hear them banging around now in the ACP.

Gant said, "Let's hope no news is good news, sir."

News of the other ships, he meant: of *Exeter* and the two destroyers with her, and of the four Americans. Nick had been up and dressed since 5:00, waiting for it. He knew he should have been resting, and he'd every intention of leaving all today's problems to Gant, but you couldn't just lie there and wait. Perhaps some men could have. Perhaps, he thought, he ought to have more self-control. But old dogs got to know what they could or couldn't do.

Jim Jordan of *Sloan* had accepted Nick's invitation for dinner yesterday evening, and Gant had joined them. They'd known that *Perth* and *Houston* had been due to sail from Batavia at 9 PM, and when the meal had ended, at about that time, Nick had proposed a toast to them, to their safe passage through the Sunda Strait to Tjilatjap.

"*Perth* and *Houston.*" Gant put down his empty glass. It was the last of the Laphroaigh. Jim Jordan said evenly, "May God go with them." He was a very direct, plain-spoken sort of man, and you could tell that for him it hadn't been any mere form of words or pseudo-pious hope, that he'd meant literally, "God, please look after them."

God hadn't heard. Or he'd had his hands full elsewhere. Soon after 11:00 a telegraphist on duty in *Defiant's* W/T office picked up a signal from *Perth* to the Dutch admiral at Batavia. She and *Houston* had run into a Jap invasion fleet in Banten Bay, troop transports with a covering force of heavy cruisers and destroyers. After that, messages were sparse and brief, scraps of information sent in the heat of battle with increasing damage and ammunition running low. What it amounted to, when that distant radio had fallen silent, was that *Perth* and *Houston* had fought like tigers and gone down still fighting. *Perth* had sunk first—just after midnight—and *Houston* had followed her within half an hour. From some of the earlier messages it seemed likely they'd taken quite a few of the transports to the bottom with them; but not even a hundred Jap troopships could make up for the loss of those two cruisers.

In the case of the American destroyers who'd run for the Bali Strait, Nick thought, it *might* be a case of no news being good news. Because that strait wasn't far, and if they had *not* got through one would surely have heard something by now. But *Exeter* and *Encounter* and the USS *Pope*—well, some time today, probably this forenoon, they'd be trying to pass through Sunda, where HMS *Perth* and USS *Houston* had been overwhelmed last night.

Gant sighed. "They could have better luck. The fact there was a Jap cruiser squadron there last night doesn't mean it'll still be there now."

Nick thought he was talking nonsense. The troopships had been putting men ashore in Banten Bay, at the eastern entrance to Sunda. They wouldn't get themselves unloaded in ten minutes, and while they were there they'd have warships to protect them.

And it didn't have to be in the Sunda Strait that it happened, either. There could be an encounter anywhere. Since the invasion of Java had now started, the entire coastal region was likely to be infested with Japanese, and the air would be thick with them too . . . You could only wait, hope, guess; and there was no way of guessing how far the three ships might have got at this stage. *Exeter* had sailed with a known capability of sixteen knots, after repairs here to her damage, but her engineers had been hopeful of working her up to quite a bit more than that. She'd been hurt badly, but she was a very tough old bird. At the Battle of the Plate, in December 1939, she'd played the leading part in running the *Graf Spee* to earth, and in the process she'd stood up to an incredible amount of battle damage. With two turrets out of action from direct hits by the *Graf Spee*'s eleven-inch shells, with her bridge and control tower wrecked, no internal communications and no W/T or electric power, on fire below decks and several feet down by the bow and listing ten degrees to starboard, she'd stayed in the fight— with only one turret in action, finally, and with her captain using a boat's compass to steer by.

That was what he thought of when he thought of *Exeter*. That, and the fact that she was somewhere in the Java Sea now, with Japanese forces closing in from all directions and the only exit that twelve-mile-wide Sunda Strait . . . He'd eaten all he could. He put the plate aside, and reached for a cigarette.

"I want a third funnel, Bob."

Gant looked at him oddly. Speculatively. The doubt, suspicion in that glance was irritating. Nick said tersely, "We have two funnels, don't we? You said the for'ard one's under repair?"

Gant had coloured. "We're patching the top of it, yes, sir."

"Right. And now I want a *third* funnel. It'll have to go on number four gundeck." He pointed: "If you'd bring over that copy of *Jane's*, I'll show you what I want us to look like."

The shipwrights had their hands full already, of course. Gant would probably remind him of it in a minute. But this wouldn't be an intricate or delicate job of work . . . Gant brought the book, *Jane's Fighting Ships,* and Nick opened it at the page where he'd left a marker, earlier this morning.

"There. You'd better let Raikes have a sight of this, so he'll know what he's doing." Raikes was the chief shipwright. "Timber and canvas, hinged so it can be hauled up into place when we want it. It'll need to be done after dark and without showing any light, so the rigging must be as simple as it can be."

He'd been thinking about it, in between periods of dozing, during as much as had been left of the night. Dozing, and struggling to think instead of dream, most of the time ending up with a cross between the two . . . But adding a third funnel would change the ship's profile from that of a Dauntless-class cruiser to a fair likeness of one of the Japanese Natori class.

Last evening he'd gone through a period which, looking back on it, he could only have described as hellish. A waking nightmare . . .

When he'd finished yesterday afternoon's conference with Gant he'd gone back to his bunk, slept heavily, and woken with the doubt already in his mind—an instinctive feeling that things weren't going to work out. It was as if it had been in his mind all the time and he'd just seen it, recognized it. He'd sent Harkness to collect a chart and some instruments and reference books from Chevening. The navigator had brought them along himself, but he'd sent him away again because he'd needed to look into this alone.

That instinct had been right. Speeds, times and distances combined to confirm the unpleasant truth that *Defiant* was locked in.

Sandilands had agreed, under protest, that he'd provide engine revs for twenty-five knots. So that was the speed you could count on, and the first basic element in this calculation. (It would have been pointless to have demanded more than twenty-five knots, because even before the recent action damage their best speed had been twenty-seven.)

The second basic was that he couldn't take her out of Surabaya before dusk. If he tried to move her in daylight and she was spotted, they'd know which way she was going and they'd be in or near the Strait, waiting for her. In effect, this meant she couldn't get under way earlier than 9 PM.

Point three was that whichever of the straits you picked on, you'd need to have passed through it and got far enough south of it by first light to have some chance of not being found and attacked at sunrise. A ship caught on her own wouldn't have a hope of surviving, because the enemy had numerous aircraft and the Allies had none.

(Well, they did. They had two, based at Bandoeng and used for reconnaissance. He thought they were Beauforts.)

Now: you had to relate those three basic points to the distances from Surabaya to the various exits. The nearest was the Bali Strait, through which the Americans were hoping to pass: and those four destroyers would get to it by the short route through the Madura Channel, the eastern way out of Surabaya, south of Madura Island. This channel was impassable to *Defiant,* because she drew fifteen feet of water. At the top of the tide she might just about have made it, but the time of high tide would have to fit in with a dusk departure, and the tide tables showed clearly that in the next few days it would not. So *Defiant's* only way east would be around the north side of Madura; and the distances involved were such that at twenty-five knots she'd be right in the Bali Strait, or still this side of the islands if he picked on the Lombok or Alas Straits, at sunrise.

Then ship and ship's company would live—what, half an hour?

Sloan, Jim Jordan's destroyer, drew only about ten feet of water, so she could use the Madura Channel. She'd be all right. For *Defiant,* it wasn't easy to see any way out at all.

When he'd checked the distances and times again, he sat back and thought about it. He was sweating, and he could feel his pulse and heartbeat racing. The wounds in his head, face and arm pulsed too. The

fear wasn't personal, it was the nightmarish suspicion, rapidly harden-
ing, that he wasn't going to be able to get his ship out of the Java Sea.

He took some long, slow breaths, to slow the pulse-rate, and told
himself to be calm and rational. There *had* to be a solution.

Think about going west, as *Exeter* was about to do?

She'd be sailing as soon as it was dark, in about two and a half
hours' time. It wasn't a good prospect, he thought—not even for *Exeter*
now, and certainly not for *Defiant* later. As time went on and the
enemy built up naval and air strength down here it became less likely
with every passing hour that an Allied ship could survive in daylight
north of Java.

He murmured aloud, *"However . . ."*

Jordan's philosophic acceptance gave no comfort now, though. And
Jordan would be arriving on board soon. Nick wanted desperately to
have some sort of answer to the problem before he found himself having to talk about it.

He was trying too hard, perhaps. Panicking. So relax, think it out
logically and calmly . . .

Well, if you discarded the idea of using the longer, western route,
the choice narrowed to one of the three eastern straits. It would have
to be either the narrow Bali Strait, or the much wider one between
Bali and Lombok, or the more distant, medium-sized one, the Alas
Strait, between Lombok and Sumbawa. And whichever one you chose,
Defiant's track would have to be to the north of Madura.

Those were conclusions, facts, solid and unchangeable. You could save
yourself the trouble of looking for alternatives to them, because there
weren't any. Another fact—the one that crushed you—was that *Defiant*
would not be able to make the trip inside any period of darkness.

He shut his eyes. It could be, he thought, that his brain wasn't working properly, that there was some oversight in his calculations.

There *had* to be!

He tried again. Checking the route on the chart first, looking for
short cuts. No short cuts . . . Until now he'd assumed that the run

along the north coast of Madura to the Bali Gap was within his reach. He didn't know now *why* he'd made any such assumption. Trying to think back to any earlier state of mind was like thinking about another person, one whose mental processes he didn't understand and—worse— had no faith in.

There were five hundred men in this ship—nearly five hundred— all getting on with their jobs and relying, as they were entitled to do, on their captain's competence to direct their efforts sensibly, professionally, in ways that gave reasonable chances of survival. How would they feel if they knew he was sitting here sweating with fear, *seeing no way out?*

Perhaps Gant's doubts were well-founded, and he was unfit for the command now. If he couldn't find a way out of this trap, he *was* unfit for it.

Give up? Hand over to Gant?

His head hurt, and he felt sick.

Sunda, after all? A hundred to one against making it, but the only chance there was?

No. Sunda was a locked door now. Even if it wasn't yet—you had to allow yourself to hope that *Exeter, Encounter* and *Pope* would get through—it would be barred and bolted by this time tomorrow.

Lombok, then. Sail at dusk. No—a little before that. Let them see her heading west. Then turn north in the dark, and northeast, spend the following day out of sight of land and away from obvious routes, and hope to God not to run into anything or be spotted by aircraft. Then, the following evening when it got dark, turn southward, fast, through the Lombok Strait.

Well, what alternative was there?

He stared at the chart. It would be only about twice as risky as a game of Russian roulette. It depended entirely on the sheer luck of remaining undetected throughout one whole day at sea. The odds were very heavily against any such thing being possible: but long-odds bets *had* been won, before this. And it would be less foolhardy than trying to get away through Sunda . . . Ask Jordan to take *Defiant*'s wounded with him in *Sloan?* And others too: cut down to a skeleton crew, enough men to steam her and man her guns and tubes, while the rest took passage in the destroyer?

Five minutes later, still concentrating on this possible way out, he'd heard *Sloan*'s captain being piped aboard. No alternative had occurred to him, and the chances of remaining invisible for a whole day in an area that would probably be carrying a lot of enemy traffic, seaborne and airborne, were so slim that it was going to be embarrassing to spell out the plan. Another consideration was that with several thousand miles to go, Jordan wouldn't want to be cluttered up with passengers. He might take the wounded, and perhaps Sibbold or an SBA to look after them . . .

Nick gave him a pink gin. A proper one, made with iced water, no lumps of ice in it to melt and turn it into dishwater.

"All set for tomorrow night, Jim?"

"Well." Jordan rubbed his wide jaw. "I guess we will be."

"Bali Strait?"

The close-cropped, ginger head nodded. "If our guys get through it tonight, that seems the obvious way to go." He frowned. "Only thing is—"

"I'd say you're right. Flat out through the Madura Channel, sharp right past Bali, and you're home for breakfast."

"Almost." The American smiled, briefly. "But how about you, sir?"

"I can't get over those shallows, unfortunately."

"That's what I thought. I've been trying to work out what you might do, and frankly I don't seem to get very far."

"Well, let's deal with your intentions first. Incidentally, Bob Gant's joining us for dinner, and afterwards my navigating officer will be available if we want him. I thought we could have half an hour's private chat first, though."

"Sure . . . It's a—er—peculiar drink, this."

"Don't you like it?"

"Oh, I *like* it—"

"An acquired taste, I suppose. But the malt whisky comes later."

"Did you see me wondering about that?"

They both laughed. Nick thanked him for having sent enquiries about his state of health when he'd been lying unconscious in the sick-bay. Then he came back to the subject.

"I take it you'll sail at sunset, via Madura to the Bali Strait, at—did someone say twenty-five knots?"

"Right." Jordan flicked a light to his Chesterfield. "Only thing is— well, okay, we have to get the hell out, first chance we have. I know it. I just wish I had another twenty-four hours."

"What for?"

"So my ship could be near as good as new." He blew smoke at the deckhead: the draught of the fan caught it, sent it swirling . . . "Twenty-eight, maybe thirty knots I'd have. There's some engine spares we need, coming up from Tjilatjap by railroad, due here tomorrow afternoon. If I had the time to get some bits and pieces fitted—well, listen, sir. Twenty-five knots, the way I am now, if I sail at 2100 hours by sun-up I'm out of the Bali Strait, sure, but I'm only forty miles south of that airstrip. Okay, that's the best there is, I'll do it. But if I waited, had another five knots out of her, I'd be *seventy or eighty* miles south!"

"How did you happen to have spares at Tjilatjap?"

"Another Selfridge-class ship there. Or was, yesterday. She had 'em. We swapped a couple of signals, and I struck lucky."

Nick was nodding at him, but he'd barely heard that explanation. An idea—the germ of the possibility of an idea—had just stirred into being.

"Excuse me, Jim. I want to take a quick look at the chart."

He pushed himself up, one-handed. Jordan asked him, "Are you all right, to be moving around this soon?"

"Better every minute, thanks."

He was standing, looking down at the chart, with one eye shut to cut out the double vision. And, incredibly, hope stirring. It was Jordan's idea of taking an extra day that had triggered it. It wasn't totally different, in general principle, from his earlier idea, but it was a hell of a lot sounder. He was checking now, with the dividers—one-handed, of course. You only needed one, though, except in rough weather . . . If this was a valid, pursuable plan, he'd been blind and daft during the last half-hour. Double-checking, now . . . Then he dropped the brass dividers on the chart, and went back to his chair. He picked up his glass. He knew he couldn't possibly be showing the degree of relief that he was feeling.

Not that it was going to be easy—or anything approaching easy. He raised the glass. "Bless you, Jim. You've saved my bacon."

"I have?"

"And I think you'd do well to wait for those spares. After all, if the Dutch can put up barrages like we've seen today and yesterday, we don't have to worry much, about air attack in here."

"No, we don't. But—well, only thing is, if they start their invasion. Paratroops ashore here—maybe surface ships outside—we could find ourselves in a real jam."

"If you want your extra day, taking that risk's the price of it."

"I guess I'll take it. But how does it help you?"

"I don't think it necessarily makes much odds to me, Jim. But just to clear your side of it first—obviously your plans will depend on what we hear of your people in the Bali Strait tonight. If they get through—fine, no problem. But if it goes wrong—well, I suppose with thirty knots you might just make it via Lombok."

"Maybe. Cutting margins so fine I'd get the shivers. But for now, I'm *assuming*—"

"Yes. Assuming the Bali Strait looks good, that's your choice. I believe mine is the Alas Strait."

"But that's a hell of a long way!"

Nick nodded. "From here, it is. But Surabaya won't be my starting-point. It can't be, can it?"

"I—don't quite follow—"

"You'd seen the snags for yourself, before you came over. I can't do more than twenty-five knots, I can't alter the distances or extend the hours of darkness. On the other hand I have *got* to get this ship out through one of those holes. The only variable factor, therefore, is where I start from."

"You plan to hole-up some place?"

"Exactly." He nodded towards the chart. "In the Kangeans. Just off the cuff, I like the look of an island called Sepanjang. We'll check all that later, in the Sailing Directions, but it looks like deep water—give or take a few rocks . . . But you see—I'll sail tomorrow, as intended, at sun-down. I'll have the ship hidden—tucked away, anyhow—before daylight, somewhere among those islands. I *hope* the Japs won't be looking for us: and we'll be a damn sight less visible than we would be out at sea. Then we—and you—Push off the night after. You from here at thirty knots, and me from the Kangeans at twenty-five. You go through Bali, I'll take Alas."

"Might you not as easily make it to the Bali Strait, rendezvous there with me?"

"I don't think so. Which gap one chooses is a toss-up; but making a rendezvous that close to the enemy on Bali, one of us perhaps having to hang around and wait for the other—*and* I'd slow you down . . . No, that doesn't appeal to me much. Lombok I don't like, either. It's too obvious, the one they'd expect us to pick on. Don't you think?"

Jordan nodded. "But your scheme may not be as easy as you make it sound. With respect—"

"I'm not suggesting it's going to be easy, Jim."

"No . . . Would we rendezvous down south, after we both get through?"

"I'd like to, yes. We'll make for Perth, I should think. It's a long way, and two's company. It's not impossible that in the early stages there could be air attacks—remember Doorman had information about carrier groups moving to the other side of Java?" The American nodded. Nick suggested, "We might work out some details after we've eaten. My navigator can do the work—it's what he's paid for. He isn't seeing double, either."

"You are, sir?"

"It's only temporary. But the rendezvous—I'd imagine we'll naturally converge about two hundred miles south, some time around noon. Then we could afford to slow down a little—we'll need to conserve fuel."

"It'll be a great moment, making that rendezvous."

"Yes . . . But listen. I hope to God we'll have good news early tomorrow about your four Bali Strait ships. But if it is *not* good, then you'd better forget about the spares and sail with me tomorrow evening. Otherwise you'll be in the trap *I* could've been in."

He was tired, now. But he was also excited. Nobody would ever know, and he himself would be glad to forget, the state of mind he'd been in only an hour earlier.

Gant was taking another look at the photograph of a Japanese Natori-class light cruiser. He'd been out and told the chief shipwright what was wanted; now he was back again, in Nick's day cabin. He said, "It's quite startling, sir. Add that funnel and we'll look very much like this. Except for the seaplane catapult on her stern."

The disguise wouldn't have to stand up to close inspection anyway. The main thing was that when *Defiant* sailed tonight he wanted any enemy, or enemy agent ashore, to think he was steering west; and when he turned her the other way after dark it would help the illusion if she looked like a different ship. It could be useful later on, as well. The deeper the water, the more readily you clutched at straws.

"How are the repairs going, Bob?"

"The bridge is finished, sir. Some parts are planked—timber bolted to the steel beams—but otherwise it's near-enough normal. Telephones and voicepipes have all been refitted, and gunnery circuits will be fixed by this afternoon. By sailing time anyway. You agreed we wouldn't try to refit the wheelhouse."

"Did I?"

Gant gave him that suspicious look again.

"Yesterday afternoon, sir. I proposed that we should make do with the lower steering position, with telephone communication. Because of certain practical difficulties, and priorities elsewhere, and you concurred."

"I don't remember any such conversation."

Gant said, after a pause, "The only other defect we can't do anything about is the starboard searchlight."

"We can manage without it." He looked round, as Harkness knocked and entered. The PO steward said, "Yeoman of signals, sir."

"Come in, Morris."

"Signal from *Exeter* to Bandoeng, sir. Enemy report."

The news they'd dreaded. *Exeter*'s only hope had been *not* to run into any enemies.

He took the log from Morris, and read the top signal in the clip. It was a report of sighting enemy cruisers. He handed it across the table to Gant. There was nothing to do but wait for the rest of it, for what you knew would be happening in the next few hours. Facing a superior enemy force, *Exeter*'s only hope of survival would lie in avoiding action. But she was already crippled, so she couldn't make much of a run for it, and in any case the only way she could run was into the trap of the Sunda Strait.

He nodded. "Thank you, yeoman."

"It's good to see you so recovered, sir." Morris was on his way to the door. Nick asked him, "Have we got a Japanese ensign on board, Morris? Rising Sun thing?"

"Yessir, we have."

"Look it out, would you, and keep it handy."

He wondered whether *Exeter* could have adopted a plan such as he had in mind now for *Defiant*. But yesterday, the escape route westward hadn't looked so hopeless. And if the Japs hadn't picked Banten Bay as their landing-place, right on the entrance to Sunda, the other two might have got away. Hindsight changed viewpoints: twenty-four hours ago, if it had been his own responsibility, *he* might have sent *Exeter* westbound. And if *Defiant* had been seaworthy then, she'd have been there now, with *Exeter.*

"Bob, tell me—if I'd remained comatose, and you had the command, how would you be getting us out of this place?"

Last night, Gant had been thoroughly alarmed at the thought of trying to hide in the Kangeans. Even when Chevening had checked in the local Sailing Directions and confirmed that there'd be water enough behind Sepanjang, he'd still looked scared of it. Nick had asked him, "Worried, are we?"

"I was only thinking, sir—it's less than eighty miles from Bali, there'll be aircraft about, and we don't know until we see the place how much cover there'll be or how—"

"Pilot." Nick told Chevening, "Read out that description of Sepanjang."

Chevening found the place, in the *Indonesia Pilot Volume II.* He read aloud, ". . . second largest island of the Kepulauan Kangean . . . wooded, and approximately two hundred feet high near its middle . . . the north coast consisting of mangroves with deep creeks forming islands—"

"That's enough." Nick looked at Gant. "The north coast's our billet. Doesn't it sound tailor-made?"

"Yes, on the face of it . . ."

"Do you have any alternative suggestions?"

He'd been questioning himself as much as Gant. How could you tell whether your brain was functioning as it should: how could you trust it, when it was the brain itself that told you it was trustworthy? The only thing that mattered was that *Defiant* should get away. It didn't matter a damn who did the job. It was his own responsibility to do it if he was capable of it, but alternatively to see that it was done by someone else. By Gant, for instance. He thought that he, Nick Everard, was the best man to do it: but again, the belief came out of his own brain. He asked Gant, "Well, Bob?"

"I hope I'd have come eventually to the same conclusion you've arrived at, sir. I'm not sure, though. I *might* have opted for the Sunda Strait—taking a gamble on the situation having changed by the time we got there."

"You'd have been wrong, if you had."

"I agree, sir. Before, it wasn't as plain."

One aspect bothered Nick a little. In the Crete evacuation he'd solved a problem by capturing an island and holding it for a day. One long, hot, sleepy day. If his mind was cranky now, might a symptom be that it was throwing up an old answer to a new problem?

But in fact it *wasn't* the same answer. The Milos operation had involved a deliberate penetration into enemy territory, whereas in this case they were in potentially enemy territory already and trying to get out of it. The Kangeans would be a halfway house on the way out. The similarity was that Sepanjang and Milos were both islands. Beyond that, it was a superficially similar solution to an entirely different situation.

He had to be sure. Because his mind *had* been playing tricks. And several hundred lives and this ship, possibly Jordan's as well, depended on it functioning properly.

"Do you see any weakness? Something I haven't thought of and nobody's mentioned yet?"

"No, sir, I don't."

"You realize that if I drop dead you'll have to see it through?"

Gant nodded. "Yes."

"So you're happy with it?"

"I was in the chartroom at six this morning, with Chevening, and we went over every possible alternative. There isn't one that stands a hope."

He nodded. Thinking, *You can stop dithering, now* . . . "While we're at it, Bob, there's another question I've been meaning to ask you. About the exchange of signals you had with *Perth* when she and *Houston* came back for you after the night action. When poor old Waller asked you what state we were in, why didn't you let him know I'd been knocked out?"

"It was more instinctive than logical, sir. I was trying to put myself in your place—well, naturally, in the circumstances—and I'd say the reasoning was that if I'd reported you were out of action, Captain Waller would most likely have felt obliged to keep us with him. It would have slowed them down a lot. Also, Surabaya being so much closer seemed to me the place you'd have chosen to make for."

"Has it occurred to you that your decision may have saved all our lives?"

"No, it hasn't."

"We'd have gone with them to Batavia. Then Sunda Strait. I don't think anyone stands a dog's chance through Sunda."

Exeter . . .

He was anxious for news of the American destroyers too. It was about time one heard something. There'd have to be a deadline, some time this afternoon, for Jim Jordan's decision about which way he'd go. Nick lit a cigarette. "Is Leading Seaman Williams still in sickbay?"

"Yes. Out of concussion, but he's immobilized by his leg wounds."

"I'll go along and see him, presently. And the others. D'you have a list of them, and their injuries?"

Williams said, "Can't keep a good man down, sir; isn't that what they say?"

Nick told him, "You can if you shoot him in the legs."

"I wasn't shot, sir. Splinters. Commander Sibbold's dug 'em all out."

"Painful?"

"You wouldn't do it for a lark, like."

"But you'll be on your feet again soon, now."

Williams's vague expression showed the drift of his thoughts. Nick thought, *That's how I've been looking . . .* The killick asked, "No answer to the signal you sent, I suppose, sir?"

He'd signalled Colombo, a week or ten days ago, asking the welfare people whether a Mrs Williams was among refugees arriving there.

"They'll be up to their eyes in refugees, you know. Not only from Singapore, either. It's bound to take some time, to—"

"Take a lifetime."

"What?"

The close-together eyes were calm. "I reckon she's dead, sir."

Sibbold had changed the dressings on Nick's various injuries. Nick had also been talking to the other patients, and he was leaving now. Sibbold murmured, "You should be resting, sir. Really, it's very *important* that—"

"All right, PMO, all right . . ."

Forbes, the chaplain, joined them. "Is he bullying you, sir?"

"Doesn't like to see anyone getting out of his clutches. Probably a hangover from the days when his patients used to pay him."

They both came outside with him. He asked them, "Is Williams as gloomy as that all the time?"

"I don't believe he really *is* so gloomy, now," Forbes said. "He's convinced himself the girl's dead. What was torturing him was the possibility of her being alive in Japanese hands. He *wants* her to be dead."

"In his shoes, padre, one might feel the same."

The chaplain sighed. Sibbold stared at Nick. "As I was saying, sir—about *you*—in all seriousness—"

"I know. I'll turn in soon."

After, he thought, some news arrived about the Bali Strait destroyers. He didn't think he'd sleep until he knew what had happened to those Americans. He could shut his mind to *Exeter.* She was doomed. It was hideous and tragic but he knew that at this moment she'd be fighting her last action, and thinking about it wasn't going to make the slightest difference to the outcome. But he did need rest: for *this* ship's sake, which was what Sibbold, he guessed, had been talking about.

"Captain, sir."

PO Morris, the yeoman of signals, saluted. A square, pale face with a short nose and a blunt chin. Pale blue eyes blinked once. He muttered, "*Exeter,* sir."

Nick took the signal log from him. He'd come out from under the foc's'l break into the heat of the upper deck: the steel of the bridge superstructure was a hot grey wall on his right. The signal told him that four heavy cruisers and an unspecified number of destroyers were closing in on that fine old ship. It was now—he checked his wrist-watch—just on ten, and this signal's time of origin was 0940.

She'd have been trying for the last two hours to get past them, and now they'd encircled her.

"Anything else?"

"No, sir."

"I'll be in my cabin."

Charles Rowley, the first lieutenant, was on number four gundeck with CPO Raikes, the chief shipwright; they were deciding how they'd rig the stays for the dummy funnel. Nick climbed up to the gundeck and joined in the discussion. As the funnel would have its base this high up, it needed to be only twenty-six feet tall for its top to be level with the others. But it was still a bulky object to accommodate in the space available, and the best idea seemed to be to stow it slantwise across the ship between that six-inch gun and the pompom mounting just abaft it.

Rowley pointed out that in either the raised or stowed position it was going to obstruct the six-inch, and when it was raised it was also going to blank off the pompoms from firing on any for'ard bearing. In addition, it seemed the wire stays supporting it would be in the way of both guns.

"It can't be helped." Nick explained, "The object will be to avoid action. If we have to open fire, the camouflage becomes pointless anyway."

Raikes suggested, "So we want to be able to ditch it good and quick, if we're going into action?"

"Yes. The gun's crew could handle it."

The last thing he wanted was a fight. One shot, and all hopes of escape would vanish. He wanted to be silent and invisible. If he was seen at all he wanted to be taken for a Jap.

In his imagination he could hear the thunder of big guns from five hundred miles away, the other end of Java and the Sunda Strait . . .

Chevening stopped him as he went on aft.

"Have a word, sir?"

He'd been working out details for tonight and the night after and for the long run south to Australia after that. Nick had told him to have some notes of it on paper, a copy for Jim Jordan. Whichever way the Bali Strait cat jumped, Jordan would be coming aboard later for a final conference. Chevening had a rolled chart under his arm, and some queries and suggestions. They went into the cuddy—past the late AB Gladwill's noisy canaries and through to the dining cabin, where the table had room for chart display.

Chevening murmured when they'd finished, "I'm afraid *Exeter*'s chances aren't good, sir."

"They're non-existent."

Chevening had improved, Nick thought. To start with he'd seemed a bit of a stuffed shirt. He asked him, "You've no ill effects, pilot, from that smash-up?"

"None except I'm a bit deaf, sir."

"Have you reported it to the PMO?"

"I think it'll just wear off, sir."

"Go and see him. Tell him I sent you. But first get that signal off to *Sloan*."

The signal was to check that the American destroyer had enough fuel for two thousand miles. It wasn't quite that mileage to Perth, but they wouldn't be taking an entirely direct route. Also, the first part of the trip would have to be made at maximum speed, which consumed oil faster. Nick wanted to start by putting as great a distance as possible between themselves and the Japanese, and it would mean steering due south and later making a dog-leg southwestward to get round North West Cape. If Jordan's ship didn't have the range to reach Perth, an alternative might be to make for Port Hedland, at about half the distance.

Perth was the obvious place, though. It was the nearest major port. The fact that Kate lived not very far from it was coincidental. "Not very far" meant, in any case, not far by Australian standards, and it was more than likely that even from Perth—if he got to Perth—she'd be as far out of his reach as she would have been on the moon. Besides which, when one thought about Kate Farquharson, Fiona's image intruded . . . He told himself, pausing at a scuttle and looking across flat water at the heat-hazy shoreline, that it wasn't really a very urgent problem. Very soon the soldiers on that waterfront and in those buildings would be Japanese. In two days? Three?

He sat back in an armchair, and shut his eyes. The plan was set: he was sure of it, in the sense that there was no other way to get out. If he'd had to quote odds on it, he'd have put its chances at about evens. There were quite a few imponderables, and it was going to depend on luck—at least, on an absence of bad luck—at all stages. Which was a lot to ask for.

He dozed, waking occasionally to the familiar noises of the ship's routine. There were waking thoughts as well as snatches of dreams. One dream—it came back to him now with the shock of something horrible that he'd forgotten about and suddenly recalled—was that Paul was out there in *Exeter*. He shook it out of his mind, thankful that it had turned out not to be real. There was something he had to do, that he'd thought of earlier . . .

"Captain, sir?"

He focused on PO Harkness. Harkness told him, "Made you some more coffee, sir. Petty Officer Morris says there's a signal you'd want to see."

"Send him in." He remembered what it was he'd been thinking about in that half-sleep: "Harkness—pass the word to the captain of marines that I'd like a word with him, will you? And let's have another cup here for him."

Morris had two signals to show him. The first was an answer from *Sloan* to his question about fuel for the long haul south. Jordan had replied, "Your 10:31, affirmative." The other was from *Exeter* to Admiral

Helfrich at Bandoeng. She was stopped and on fire and taking repeated hits. Time of origin 11:20.

Haskins clicked his heels. "Wanted to see me, sir?"

"Yes. Come in, soldier. Sit down, and don't let's be too bloody military."

The marine grinned. "Sorry, sir."

"Help yourself to coffee. Is your landing organization all geared-up?"

"Top line, sir. Do you mean—d'you want us to stay behind?"

Nick looked at him. He shook his head. "No. Even if any such thing had been suggested . . . No. The object is to get out of here, *save* our skins, not throw more of them away."

He thought of *Exeter,* and of *Perth, Houston, Electra, Jupiter, Encounter* and *Pope;* and of *de Ruyter, Java,* and that Dutch destroyer, *Kortenaar* . . . All gone, in the space of a couple of days. He was appalled at the waste, the pointlessness, the sheer stupidity . . . What he had to think about now was how not to add to the list. He told Haskins, "As you know, we'll be sailing at dusk. But before daylight we'll be tucking ourselves into cover behind an island called Sepanjang, which is in a small group called the Kangeans about seventy-five miles north of the Lombok Strait."

He described the plan to him, and the reasons for it.

"We'll be there from before dawn until it's dark enough to move. If you ask Chevening, he'll show you a description of the island's topography, in the Pilot. It mentions that there are two villages on Sepanjang, and local trade between it and the larger island, Kangean itself. We'll be on the north coast, up some creek—I mean literally, for once, and let's hope not figuratively as well. Mangroves and so on. The south coast has a sandy beach and that may be where the inhabitants keep their praus. Anyway, read what it says, and study it on the chart. I'd advise you to make notes, and a tracing of the island—the ship's office could run off copies for your NCOs."

Haskins nodded. Nick went on, "The object of putting you ashore will be to maintain security in the vicinity of the ship, and prevent any of the locals leaving the island while we're there. So word doesn't get to the Japs. Remind me now—how many men have you got?"

"Colour Sergeant Bruce, two sergeants, four corporals, forty-one marines, sir. And me, making total strength forty-nine."

"Organized how, for landing?"

"Five sections of eight men each, plus Platoon HQ. Sections one, two and three form a rifle group, four and five are the Bren group. Platoon HQ includes a two-inch mortar section and one PIAT."

"What the hell's that?"

"Projector infantry anti tank, sir."

"I think we can assume there won't be any tanks on Sepanjang."

"Quite. We could leave the mortar on board too, I should think . . . The marines carry P-14 rifles, and section leaders have Lanchester sub machine-guns."

He thought about it . . .

"I should imagine that to police the shoreline near the ship, plus both villages and whatever beaches they keep their praus on, you'll need every man you've got. I want a lookout post established on high ground, too, but we'll use sailors for that . . . All these weapons of yours—obviously you must be armed, but let's not make a show of it. If the natives are friendly, or even just not obviously hostile, let's keep it like that. No rough stuff, women strictly taboo, and arak is not to be so much as sipped even if it's forced on them. See your men understand it."

The marine said grimly, "They'll understand it, sir."

"They must also understand it isn't any kind of picnic. It's a very tricky operation and we'll be lucky to get away with it. One shot at the wrong moment could ditch us all. Make sure they don't load a single gun unless they're about to be attacked. Even then, I'd sooner there wasn't any noise. They're not to be seen, either—there are bound to be Jap aircraft passing over. Everyone keeps under cover and dead quiet all the time. Any sign of the enemy landing, you fall back on the perimeter around the ship. We'll discuss that contingency after we see the lie of the land, though . . . What else?"

"Rations and water for one day, I suppose?"

"Yes. And medical equipment? Snake-bite, etcetera?"

"Goes with Platoon HQ, sir. If we had an RM band, it'd be their pigeon."

"Why don't we?"

"Very few of these small cruisers do have, sir."

Defiant's band was a volunteer group of bluejackets. They were pretty sound on the National Anthem and on "Hearts of Oak," but they were capable of some fairly extraordinary sounds when they strayed from that beaten track.

Nick said, "Mosquitoes are likely to be a problem. Make sure every man has his tin of the smelly stuff . . . And I think that's about all the direction I can give you. Do your homework, brief your troops and have the gear ready . . . Did you say P-14 rifles?"

Haskins nodded.

"They had them in '14–'18!"

The marine said, "We're lucky they don't give us pikes."

At 11:40, *Exeter* had sunk. *Encounter* followed her a few minutes later. The report came from the American destroyer *Pope,* who at the time of her last message had been under attack by dive-bombers.

It was 12:30. A midday air-raid which had started just as the ship's company were being piped to dinner had again been driven off by the Dutch shore gunners. Work on the dummy funnel hadn't stopped, and it was still in progress now although the ship's company were at lunch. Nick had a look at it on his way for'ard: despite the promise to Sibbold that he'd turn in, he knew he wouldn't have been able to sleep. In any case, he'd have his own lunch before long. He went in through the screen door under the foc's'l, and up the ladderways to the reconstructed bridge.

He even had a reconstructed bridge seat, he saw. A solid timber job rather like the one he'd had in *Tuareg*. Up here, where so short a time ago men had died and he'd lain unconscious in his own blood, the work was finished. In fact there were improvements: his own telephone to the director tower had been sited in easier reach from the chair than it had been before, for instance. He went into the chartroom: chart 1653c was spread out on the table, with a track drawn in on it and notations of times and courses; Chevening's navigator's notebook lay open on it, with neat lists of data such as shore bearings at the turning points.

"There you are, sir!"

He looked round. "Hello, Bob."

"Been scouring the ship for you, sir. An SDO messenger went down to your cabin and reported you missing. And Harkness didn't know where—"

"I think you'd better stop regarding me as some kind of helpless idiot, Bob. I'm back to normal. Apart from this arm, which is a minor inconvenience—"

"You'll feel better still when you hear the news, sir. About the Yanks who were trying the Bali Strait?"

"Well?"

"Bandoeng sent out a Beaufort reconnaissance flight. It's back on the ground now. At 10:30 it found all four destroyers well clear to the south and on course for North West Cape at thirty knots."

"Ah." He nodded, restraining the urge to cheer. "That was news worth waiting for."

Sloan would be all right. Even if Jordan's engine spares didn't arrive— the railways were being bombed, and you couldn't count on it—his prospects for a fast exit via the Bali Strait were a lot better than the obstacle race *Defiant* had ahead of her. Nick wondered again about transferring his wounded to the American.

CHAPTER TEN
·   ·   ·

The *Montgovern* was alone, down by the bows, making eight knots southward through a milky dawn. Her pumps had been slowly losing their battle against the inflow of sea, and she had ten feet of water in number one hold now. If her engines had been stopped it would have eased the pressure on cracked frames and leaking bulkheads. But you couldn't stop—the destination was still Malta, and a stopped ship would get sunk anyway.

The light was growing. It was only in the last few minutes that Paul had realized the heavy dampness they'd been steaming through was a sea-mist. When it lifted, she'd be exposed—to her obvious enemies, and also to the Vichy French in Tunisia, who might object to an intruder in their territorial waters.

The wind was down. There was a low swell, and the sea was loud, thumping and swishing around the damaged bow, banging in the cavity where the torpedo had hit. She sounded, right up there in the bow, like an old sow guzzling with her snout down in the trough.

The Vichy coast, he guessed, would be only a mile or two to starboard. He wondered if they had a hope in hell of reaching Malta. Or whether they'd just keep going as long as possible and then turn and run for the beach. If they ended up ashore here, the French would intern them all. A Vichy prison camp would be a truly rotten place to spend the rest of the war.

Well, you'd be able to catch up on some sleep.

He decided to go and find out, or try to find out, what was going on. It had been hours since Mick McCall's last visit, and even longer since the last flare-up of action. All through the first part of the night there'd been explosions, leaps of flame, outbreaks of gunfire and the rumble of distant battle. One ship, so heavily on fire that she'd been unrecognizable, had crossed about a mile astern of the *Montgovern,* heading for the coast and incapable of answering signals. And in the early hours of the morning a Hunt-class destroyer had appeared, exchanged shouts with Mackeson and then sheered away again into the dark, towards the running fight to the north of them. They'd stood to the guns when she'd first appeared—a small, menacing bow-on shape that could have been an E-boat, at that distance—and several other times when they'd heard the throb of engines, E-boat or aircraft.

On his last visit McCall had told them that one of the merchantmen sunk during the night attacks had been the *Blackadder,* the commodore's ship.

Beale was a dark mound recognizable as human only because you happened to know there was life inside it. Paul went over and told him he was going aft for a few minutes.

The mound grunted. Withinshaw mumbled, " 'Ave one for me too." Withinshaw was a mound with a shine on it, because he was wearing an oilskin over his other gear. Like a great seal, slumped against the ammo bin. Wally Short was horizontal under a piece of old tarpaulin hatch-cover, and McNaught was stamping about and slapping his arms against his sides, whistling between his teeth.

In the saloon Paul found Brill asleep, and Woods, the Army gunner, gulping coffee. He poured some for himself, and Woods gave him a cigarette: he'd only come down here for a moment, he explained, to thaw out.

"Are you lot paddling, up front?"

"We'll be swimming before long, I dare say."

"Well, I don't know." Woods yawned. "We're still afloat and moving. If we hadn't been knocked out of the convoy we might have been cinders, by now. Real firework show, wasn't it?"

His hands were shaking, Paul noticed. Or perhaps he was only cold, still shivering.

Thornton stirred, and sat up. The cipher expert had been flaked out on the sofa. He stared at Paul as if he was wondering who he was, or about to challenge his presence here. Then he flopped down again and shut his eyes. Paul yawned, and told Woods, "When I've drunk this I'm going up to see if Bongo's feeling sociable."

"And I'm going back to my useless gun."

"Useless?"

"Low-angle, so it's no good against bombers. And it's on the stern, so E-boats or what-have-you had better not attack from ahead . . . But I'm looking after a Bofors and some Oerlikons as well, so it's not a total waste of time, I suppose."

The door opened, and the RAF man blundered in, the grey-haired flying officer. He was too old-looking for the rank, Paul thought, and now he was grey-faced as well as grey-headed. He stared at the coffee urn, then shook his head and turned away. He muttered, "What a way to earn a living . . ."

"Seasick?"

"What do you think?"

Paul suggested, "Try tightening your belt, and lying flat."

"Can't lie flat, I'm on lookout. Does a tight belt help?"

He nodded. "And don't drink any liquid."

"Why don't they tell one these things?"

"Perhaps you didn't ask." He put down his cup still half-full. He thought he really shouldn't have left the foc'sl. He told Woods, "I'm off. Good luck."

"I'd better go too," Woods muttered as they left together. "Sort of spooky, isn't it. Alone, and this fog . . ." He went aft, and Paul went for'ard and up to the boat deck, unaware that he and the Army man had had their last off-duty conversation. He was right, it was spooky. It was like being in a ghost-ship, dead men lost to the outside world. It was the fog, the enclosed, *hidden* feeling it gave you, and the lack of sleep, and the surrounding threat . . . Daylight was noticeably stronger as he made his way up to the bridge, but it was a woolly sort of light, a cocoon of it that hemmed the ship in on her patch of grey, heaving sea. Her motion was peculiar, like the lurching of a man with a heavy limp: the result of the water inside her forepart, of course, but you noticed it more up here because of the swaying of the superstructure.

Mackeson was in the front of the enclosed bridge, and Pete Devenish was in charge of the watch. No sign of the master. Devenish asked without turning his head, "Who's that?"

"Everard, sir."

Mackeson looked round, lowering binoculars. "Problem?"

"The gunners are wondering what the future holds, sir. Thought I'd try to find out. I'm sorry, I suppose I shouldn't—"

"I'm no soothsayer, Everard. Anyway, no, you shouldn't. We've got twenty lookouts posted around this ship, and you're one of them."

"Sorry, sir, I'll—"

"Need every pair of eyes we've got, in this muck. But since your father's a *very* old friend of mine, we'll overlook it this time. Eh, Pete?"

Devenish muttered, with binoculars at his eyes, "Please yourself."

There were lookouts in both wings, Paul saw. Gosling was one of them. There'd been others on the boat deck, he'd noticed on his way up, and of course McCall would be up in his Bofors nest. The fog was like cobweb all around the ship and the shine on the sea's humpy surface was visible through it over a radius of perhaps two or three hundred yards. Mackeson murmured, "Wonder where he is now? If he's in the Java area, he won't be shivering like we are. And it'll be something like early afternoon, out there . . . Well, look here." Thinking about Paul's father seemed to have made his mind up for him. "I'll tell you what's happening, then you can go into the chartroom and take a look, and after that you can make yourself useful by going round the ship and giving them all the gist of it. All right?"

He nodded. "Sir."

"We're about two and a half miles off the Tunisian coast, off a place called Kurbah, which means we're inside the Kurbah Bank. Our course is two hundred and twelve degrees, and in another ten miles—just over an hour—we'll be off Ras Mohmur. That's the point at the top of the

Gulf of Hammamet, and it's near the port of Hammamet, which is a Vichy French base inside the curve of the Gulf. Are you with me so far?"

He was using his binoculars all the time he was talking. He didn't move his lips much when he spoke, and you had to listen carefully to hear what he was saying.

"At that point we'll turn to port a bit and steer due south, straight across the entrance to the Gulf, for another ten miles. We're taking this inshore route for two reasons: one, to avoid the Pantellaria-based E-boats and torpedo-bombers who made hay with the convoy last night, and two, because the French have a swept channel here inside the minefields, and we hope we're in it."

"Did the convoy lose much, sir?"

Mackeson hesitated. Then he murmured, "Going by the signals we've seen, and what the captain of the Hunt told us—well, there may be three survivors on course for Malta."

"*Three* . . ."

"That seemed to be the state of things a few hours ago. But there are also some other stragglers, like ourselves. The Hunt's trying to round us up and get us together. But information's scanty, at the moment, and obviously nobody's using his wireless much." He took his glasses away from his eyes, blinked, put them back again. He started a slow sweep down the starboard side. "Now. Halfway across the Gulf of Hammamet, in about two and a half hours' time we intend altering course to the east—actually to one hundred degrees—for the straight run to Malta. It'll take us just to the north of Linosa—that bit'll be after dark—and we'll be taking our chances as far as minefields are concerned. We'll be close to Lampedusa, too. At our present speed of about eight knots—well, call it twenty-four hours. If nothing gets any worse, we ought to stay afloat that long. Barring further enemy action, of course. So, all those things being equal, ETA Valletta some time after dawn tomorrow."

"But that's marvellous!"

"It's also highly improbable, Everard. It's what we're aiming at, that's all. I did say, 'barring further enemy action.' You can't bar it, can you? We're in an extremely vulnerable state—you can see that for yourself. Once this fog goes—well . . ."

"It might not, sir?"

"Then we'd be *bloody* lucky!"

"You think it's going to lift, then?"

"My dear boy, I'm not God!"

"Steady there." Humphrey Straight pushed up past Paul. "Royal Navy officer admitting he ain't God?" Devenish laughed. Straight growled, "Better watch it, Commander. They'll 'ave you for bloody sacrilege. Hey, what's—"

"Ship, green eight-oh!"

The signalman was shouting from the starboard wing, outside. Mackeson rushed out there. Straight slid a side window open and raised his glasses, cursing at Paul to get out of the way. Paul went out into the wing behind Mackeson.

Narrow, bow-on, trawler-like. A little upright ship with a small gun on its foc'sl, like a harpoon gun on a whaler. It had come from the direction of the land—from the bow, in fact, which suggested it might have come from Hammamet—and now a light was flashing from its bridge. In English, slowly spelt-out morse. He read it: *"What ship are you?"*

From the bridge window Straight bellowed, "Tell the little bugger we're Noah's Ark!"

Mackeson told the signalman, "Make to him: *Please identify yourself.*" He called to Straight, "Better turn away, captain. We're half a mile inside his territorial waters. I'll try to stall him while we do a bunk."

The signalman had passed that message, and the Frenchman was flashing again as the *Montgovern* began her slow and cumbrous turn to port. Paul read: *"You are in the territorial water of France. Stop your engines or I fire."*

Mackeson said, "Make to him—slowly—*I am in international waters and I have a destroyer escort within call. Keep clear of me.*"

He added, as the signalman began calling at about half his normal speed, "In other words, piss off *s'il vous plait.*" He looked round. "Everard, nip aft, tell the pongo to stand by with the four-inch and man his telephone."

"Aye aye, sir!" He flew—down to the boat deck, down the length of it and down again at its after end to the well deck, across that— skirting the crated deck cargo—and up another ladder to the poop. "Captain Woods?"

"Yup?"

"Commander Mackeson says close up the four-inch and man the telephone!"

"We *are* closed up. Try the phone, Reynolds." He told Paul, "We're loaded too. What's it about, anyway?"

"Vichy patrol. Told us to stop engines or it'd fire."

Woods laughed. The soldier at the telephone shouted, "Stand by to fire one shot under his bows, sir!"

"Set range two hundred yards, sergeant."

"Range two hundred set, sir!"

"Report ready!"

"Ready!" Then: "Fire!"

The gun roared, and recoiled. The breech thudded open and the empty shell-case was a yellowish streak that flew out, clanging on the steel gundeck. Another shell had gone in, the breech was shut and number two had slammed the intercepter shut.

"Ready!"

The splash of the shot they'd fired went up about twenty yards short of the Frenchman's stem. And the little ship was already slewing away to port. The soldier at the telephone barked, "Cease fire!"

Woods muttered, "Spoilsport." The *Montgovern* was under helm again, coming back to her course down-coast.

Soon afterwards course was altered again, to one hundred degrees. Visibility was still low, but patchy; sometimes you could see half a mile. Attack was expected—awaited, even *wanted,* almost. To end the waiting, which was mind-wearing, exhausting . . . It was odds-on that the Frenchman would have reported their position. Most of the Vichy people were said to be pro-German, but on top of that the patrol boat's captain had been made to look silly, which had never been the way to warm the cockles of a Frenchman's heart.

On the other hand, the French had only seen the *Montgovern* forging on southward across the Gulf. They hadn't seen the subsequent turn to port, so the enemy couldn't know where she was now. With the surviving ships of the convoy fifty miles closer to them—closer to Malta, too—and with this bad visibility as well, the Luftwaffe might not be inclined to waste time searching for stragglers.

Not that this meant the *Montgovern* could have any real chance of getting to Malta, Paul thought. Mackeson had been talking sense. A ship alone, making only a few knots, already sinking and with the best part of two hundred miles of enemy-infested sea to cover . . . You'd back a donkey to win the Derby, he thought, if you'd back those chances.

Withinshaw said, "Once fog lifts, we've fookin' 'ad it."

Nobody argued with him, because that was also true. The *Montgovern* was carrying out a clumsy zigzag, altering about twenty degrees each side of the mean course to make submarine attack less easy. It reduced the speed of advance, of course: but what tidal stream there was here— according to McCall—was running in their favour. McCall reckoned they'd be making-good about seven and a half knots; so ETA Malta, given some sort of magic wand to keep enemies away, could still be tomorrow forenoon.

Like an owl and a pussycat went to sea in a beautiful pea-green boat. Malta tomorrow forenoon was about *that* believable. He began to sing about the owl and the pussycat, and Beale was looking round at him as if he couldn't stand it, when they heard an aircraft engine. The droning German kind, the note with the throb in it. Paul, startled, shouted "Stand by!"

He'd yelled it without thinking; it hadn't been at all necessary. Being tired made one stupid, and jumpy. Withinshaw had thrown him a look of mock alarm, and Beale, hunched at his gun, looked round and grinned sardonically. The sound of the plane was drawing ahead. He thought it had flown up the starboard side, and it was moving from right to left now as it crossed ahead. Then it was in sight—ahead—a big float plane, a Dornier, he thought. It could see them too, of course. Withinshaw opened fire, aiming out over the port bow with about fifteen degrees of elevation on the gun. The ship was under helm, swinging to a new leg of the zigzag, and the Dornier was already on the beam. The midships Bofors, McCall's gun, began firing at it. You saw it sporadically, flying in and out of fog patches. Then it was out of sight, and Withinshaw's gun fell silent.

Beale muttered. "Recce plane." The Bofors amidships and aft were still firing. Paul went to the starboard rail to look back, expecting it to appear on that other quarter, but it didn't and the after guns ceased fire now, having lost it in the fog astern.

Beale muttered, "Know where to find us now, don't they?"

An hour later, the Ju88s came.

All hands had breakfasted. Devenish had set up a cafeteria system, so each man collected his own food from the galley and ate it at his action station. Short was the last of the foc's'l-head gang to return with his mug of tea and mutton sandwiches, and he informed them that the depth of water in number one hold was now more than eleven feet. Harry Willis, fourth mate, was the ship's officer responsible for that hold, and he'd just been along with the bosun to take soundings. They'd been in the food queue at the galley, and the bosun had said the leaking into number two was getting worse.

Everyone looked gloomy as well as tired. Paul said, echoing Woods's earlier remark, "But we're still afloat and still moving. If we'd been with the convoy last night—"

"Ah." Beale nodded. "Reckon they took a clobberin', all right."

Paul hadn't told them about there being only three ships left in the convoy. When you remembered that at sunset last night there'd been eleven . . .

McNaught grumbled. "There's nae sugar in this fuckin' tea."

"Sugar?" Withinshaw looked round at him. "You're lucky there's *tea* in it, y' Scotch twit!"

He glanced at Paul, winking, inviting him to share in the joke, but Gosling's whistle shrilled from the bridge wing. They were at the guns in a rush of movement and a Ju88 from wave-top level was lifting over them in a scream of engine-noise, bombs tumbling from its racks as it swooped across the ship and banked away to the right with the mist already folding round it. One bomb struck somewhere aft, and the others went into the sea to starboard, the first one very close and the other two farther out. The guns on the ship's stern had got off a few rounds but these Oerlikons hadn't fired until the attack had been over and that first bomb had burst on her. Now a second Junkers, again from sea-level and the direction of the Tunisian coast, was roaring over with all the guns at it this time, tracer pastel-shaded in the fog and one of the bomber's engines smoking: flames too, that engine and the wing on fire, black smoke trailing, rising in the machine's own upward-curving path. Beale's and Withinshaw's guns were blazing at its tail as it tilted away to starboard: its bombs had gone into the sea. The *Montgovern* was slowing: her engines had stopped, and smoke was pouring up astern— from the area of the boat deck, he thought. That second bomber had gone into the sea nose-down and then toppled over on to its back, spray raining down in a white circle around it. Everything seemed quiet, suddenly; the regular thud-thudding of the engines had stopped, and although you hadn't noticed it before you missed it now. You were left with the noise of the sea against the ship's hull, the sound of flames as the fire took hold amidships, and the fading engine-throb of the Junkers that had done the damage.

•   •   •

Mick McCall was dead. Splinters or blast from that bomb had wiped out the crew of the midships Bofors, and he'd been with them at the time.

Fighting the fire would be easier now the engineers had got the ship under way again. It had been the near-miss, the second bomb in the stick, that had stopped her. She was making about six knots now. The fire would be more easily controllable, and a lot less dangerous, because the wind from ahead would hold it back. Until they'd got her moving it had been touch-and-go whether they'd manage to keep the flames from spreading into the bridge deck where the cased aviation spirit was stowed. Devenish was in charge of the fire-fighting.

Astern, smoke rose to a height of a couple of hundred feet, hung there like a marker telling the enemy where they'd find an easy target. Obviously they *were* looking for stragglers, or those two Junkers 88s wouldn't have been hunting fifty miles away from the convoy's track.

Fog hung around in patches, but visibility averaged about two miles.

The boats amidships, those near the for'ard end of the boat deck, had been turned out on their davits. Not because anyone was think-ing of abandoning ship—yet—but to get them clear of the fire. Devenish had men hosing them down, so their timber wouldn't catch from sparks. Paul had seen it when he'd been back to the bridge to offer his services as a fire-fighter, but he'd been told to stay on the foc'sl-head: Mackeson had warned, "That won't be the last attack we'll see today, you know."

You could forget about arriving in Grand Harbour tomorrow morn-ing. Even if there were no more attacks, at this speed it was going to take more like thirty-six hours than twenty-four. And as the ship was on fire, with twelve feet of water in her forepart, it was difficult to look far ahead.

Paul told the DEMS men, "We're lucky, in one way. If it had been a clear day like yesterday—without this fog to cover us?"

"There's some as like to look on the bright side." Beale said it to Withinshaw, and they both laughed. There was no malice in it: he was labelling Paul an optimist just as he'd labelled Withinshaw a bigamist. As far as Beale was concerned, either was good for a laugh. Paul passed his cigarettes round, and Short gave him a light for his own; he said, standing back from it, "I wonder what we'll get for lunch?" Withinshaw suggested, "Soup an' a mutton fookin' sandwich, o' course." He added, "Mutton-bone soup, an' all."

There was some excitement in the bridge, activity out in the port wing. They all stood up and moved so they'd have a view of what was happening. Mackeson was out there, with his signalman. Then the signalman was out of sight but you could hear the rattle of an Aldis lamp. Humphrey Straight appeared, with binoculars at his eyes: behind and above that sturdy silhouette, smoke still billowed up.

"Some bastard's flashin'!"

McNaught was pointing out on the port bow: there was a flash there just as Paul turned to look. An answering flash—to a message that was being passed from the *Montgovern*. From down here you couldn't see what sort of ship it was, but Paul guessed it would be the Hunt which had visited them before. But then, in a patch of better visibility, he made out the outlines of a freighter, and he thought he recognized her.

"Is that the Stars and Stripes?"

It was. Which made her the *Santa Eulalia*.

Beale said, "Got on fire, didn't she?"

She'd been on fire at one time. According to McCall, she'd been in danger of blowing up. Last night, it must have been. One memory of convoy action in the last day or two was very much like another, they'd merged in Paul's mind into a montage of guns, bombs, aircraft, dusks and dawns and stolidly plodding ships, with a mental image of Malta in the distance like a mirage . . . But it would be good to have company now, and the DEMS men were immediately much happier. As the ships drew closer to each other they were waving and cheering, and Americans on the *Santa Eulalia*'s upper deck were waving back. You could see the blackened area where the fire had been.

Mackeson sent Gosling round with the information that the American ship had been directed to this rendezvous by *Ainsty,* the Hunt who'd been looking for stragglers in this area. She was now looking for a third one, and hoped to get them all together before nightfall.

Gosling looked ill. Paul asked him, "How about our fire, or fires?"

"Getting the better of it, they say. But my God it stinks, back there." The smoke did seem to be thinning. But so was the mist: the circle of visibility was growing rapidly. Paul said something about it, and Gosling left, to return to his lookout job. He was seasick, Paul guessed, like the airman. This quite gentle but continuous rhythmic rolling was probably worse for them than a really rough sea might have been. As he turned back, he found Beale watching him with a peculiar, half-suppressed grin. Beale said, "Fog's about gone. Be clear as a bell soon."

"So?"

"Well—lucky, aren't we? I mean, we can see where we're going, like." He began to let the laugh out: and the others, catching on, were also sniggering. Beale spluttered, choking with amusement, "Gawd, ain't we bloody fortunate?"

Paul said, "I don't know about fortunate, but you're a bunch of idiots, all right." Over Beale's head, high up and still a long way off, he saw the Stukas. It was just the first glimpse of them that told him they were Stukas: there'd been nothing he could have explained in terms of shape or features, and they were no more than specks; but they were, undoubtedly, Stukas. Withinshaw was saying, "Don't mind Ron—'e likes to 'ave a go, like."

"He can have a go at *them,* in a minute." He put two fingers in his mouth, and whistled. It was a better noise than Gosling could have produced. The signalman appeared at the front of the port-side wing. Paul shouted, and pointed. Then someone else was blowing a whistle; but the American was ahead of them, there was a red warning flag at that yardarm already, and men were ready at her guns. The two ships were steering the same course, parallel to each other and four hundred yards apart, and the *Montgovern* seemed to have built up her speed to

something like the previous eight knots. He wished, as he pushed the
strap of his tin hat under his chin and watched the *Staffel* of ten or
twelve Ju87s growing very slowly up the sky, that he had a gun he
could use himself.

But they were changing direction. They'd appeared on a course that
would have brought them from Sicily, and now, with some miles still
to cover, the mosquito-like objects were altering away . . . No—they
were dividing. Some going left, some right.

"Splittin' up." Beale glanced round from his gun. Paul nodded. They'd
circle, he supposed, anyway separate, so as to attack from different directions. Against two slow-moving, virtually helpless merchantmen. The
bastards had it made, the way they liked it. Nazi schoolgirls could have
done it, but that lot would go home and be given Iron Crosses . . . It
seemed odd, all the same, to be starting their deployment at such a
distance.

Whatever tactics they adopted, a few of them were bound to land
bombs on these ships. When there were only close-range weapons to
fight them off with.

"Twelve, d'you make it?"

Withinshaw, to Beale. Beale answered, "Too bloody many, any road."
He looked round at Paul again: "Fam'ly man 'ere can't swim. Would
you credit it?"

The far-off Stukas were now in two entirely separate groups, flying
in opposite directions. It didn't seem to make sense. Nor did what
Beale had just said. Paul asked Withinshaw, "Is he joking again?"

"Not a fookin' stroke, I can't."

"Did you ever try to learn?"

"Never seemed to take to it. I reckon me bones is too 'eavy."

Beale said *"Bones!"* and laughed. Then: "What's *this* monkey business?"

Paul was wondering, too. The Stuka group to the left had seemed
to be motionless, static in mid-air: then he realized—they were circling, turning yet again, way out there over the horizon. He wondered

if they might be waiting for other forces to join up with them—more of their own kind, or torpedo aircraft, for the sort of multiple attack they'd mustered once or twice before this. It would make sense, he supposed: this close to Sicily they were in enormous strength, and after their successes of last night they mightn't have so many targets left, so they could afford to make sure of each one they found.

It struck him for the first time as a serious proposition that perhaps not even one ship out of the sixteen who'd passed through the Gibraltar Strait three days ago would reach Malta. Such a huge effort, for a total loss. And what happened to Malta, then? Surrender?

It was unthinkable. He found he was looking at Withinshaw, and angry with him for not being able to swim. If that was true, and not another childish leg-pull. He told him. "If you really can't swim, and we look like sinking, you'd better hightail it aft and make sure of getting a place in a boat."

"These lads'll 'old me up." The fat man's eyes stayed on the Stukas. He'd meant Short and McNaught would hold him up. McNaught said, "Aye. Wi' a block an' tackle."

Two of the Stukas, tiny at that distance, were plummeting like hawks. Beale shouted, "Some other bugger they're after!"

Soundless, and remote. At the bottom of their dives they were out of sight, either over the rim of the horizon or in the haze obscuring it. More going down now. None of them reappeared: they must have flown off at low level, Paul guessed. That area of haze was darkening and swelling, like smoke.

Beale said, "Some poor sod's copping it."

"Bastards." Withinshaw spat. "Dirty fookin' *bastards.*"

The smoke-cloud rose, black, mushrooming. After what seemed to have been a long interval they heard the deep rumble of an explosion.

That quick, he thought. That easy for them. A ship alone, probably. Stopped, broken down, the easiest of targets. This one and the *Santa Eulalia* wouldn't be much different.

"Us next, d'you reckon?"

Beale was asking him. Half-turned from the Oerlikon, with a fresh cigarette in his mouth and one hand feeling for a match. Withinshaw pointed: "Us *now,* Ron, could be." The group of Stukas who'd separated to the right were still up there, still circling. Their movement at the moment was from right to left. Watching them, Paul saw that movement stop. They were flying either away now, or towards: from such a distance it would be a minute or two before you could be sure.

Withinshaw, his bulky frame resting against the shoulder-pieces of his gun and his eyes fixed on the Stuka formation, was mumbling a private litany: "Fookin' soddin' murderin' *bastards* . . ." Paul detected the small upward tendency, the slight lift of those bombers against the greyish background which told him they were approaching, not departing. Beale had seen it too. He took one long drag at his newly-lit cigarette, and flicked it arcing over the starboard rail.

Mackeson counted five Stukas. In the haze out on the port beam there was nothing to see now. There'd been a glow, just before the explosion, but no outline of any ship. After the explosion, black smoke had hung there, slowly changing shape as it broke up. Now there was nothing—except five Stukas who hadn't emptied their bomb racks yet.

Straight had asked him a few minutes ago whether he still thought the Hunt, *Ainsty,* would be coming back for them. He'd answered that if she didn't he doubted if it would be her captain's fault . . . The Stukas were close now, rising overhead, as menacing and unpleasant as vultures. Any second now, the leaders would be tipping over into their dives, and he'd have given a lot to have had that Hunt here with her high-angle four-inch.

One was diving on the *Santa Eulalia.* By the sound of it, another might well be coming down on the *Montgovern,* but he couldn't see it from inside the bridge. The Oerlikons on the foc'sl-head were both engaging the American's attacker, but the guns aft had opened up as well. He muttered to Straight, "Going to have a look at this," and put his tin hat on as he went out into the wing. The American's guns were all in action, a roar of noise and tracer flooding up through smoke to meet the diving Junkers. Junkers plural: there were two going for her now. And there *was* another coming down astern; he'd noticed that the leading edges of its wings were painted yellow, then his attention was on the single bomb that looked as if it was rocking, wobbling in the air as it fell away, slow-moving at first as the pilot began to drag his bomber's nose up. He didn't see how it could possibly miss. Another bomb had burst in the sea ahead of the *Santa Eulalia:* her guns— rocket-launchers too—were barraging under the nose of the second attacker. Mackeson felt the shock of the bomb hitting and bursting aft. He called to Straight, telling him the ship had been hit at the after end of the boat deck. Devenish was sprinting for the ladder, and Straight had taken over the conning of the ship. A Stuka was spinning, in flames, off on the far side of the American, but two were still to come and it looked as if both had picked on the *Montgovern.* They always went for the one that was already hurt. It was the jackal mentality, and one's contempt for it was the greater for being on the receiving end of it. In fact the Stuka pilots weren't being stupid: the *Santa Eulalia's* defensive barrage was twice as effective as this ship's. The rising note of the first bomber's engine-scream rose above the cacophony of Bofors, Oerlikons, Brens and whatever the American's light guns were: those were adding to the umbrella above the *Montgovern* now. There was a fire aft, he knew, but he was watching these last two bombers coming, and one bomb was already on its way. Staring up under the rim of his tin hat and through a mass of tracer-streams roofing the ship in a lattice-work of explosive brilliance, he saw the slant of the falling mis- sile and shouted, "Miss!" The shout was inaudible and he had his hands in his reefer pockets with their fingers crossed, in case he'd misjudged it. He hadn't—not that one—and it went into the sea thirty yards clear, to starboard. But the second one was a different matter: he knew in the last second before it hit that it was going to, and its bone-shaking explosion was in the after well deck. The possibility of reaching Malta changed in that moment of impact from being remote to non-existent. It was the chance of the ship's survival even until nightfall that became remote. The Stuka had been hit; it was trailing smoke and its engine was coughing in uneven bursts as it banked away to starboard, away from the American guns on the other side. The foc'sl Oerlikons followed it, and he thought one of them was hitting too. At any rate the Junkers was done for: it had jack-knifed downwards, and the sea flung up a white shroud around it as it hit and cartwheeled. The *Montgovern*'s afterpart was solid flame, the roar and crackle of it taking over as her guns and the American's fell silent.

The gunner's "wingers" had refilled all the Oerlikon magazines; the bin was full and there were several on the deck beside it. They'd also brought up several cases of loose ammunition for late refilling operations. A bosun's store in the foc'sl had been in use as a magazine, but it had now been sealed off, like other spaces for'ard, so as to provide some buoyancy as the flooding pulled her down. So they'd got their stuff out of it while they'd had the chance.

Paul said to Withinshaw, "Should've had some of that wheat down there."

"Ah." The fat man nodded. "We'd 'a been laffin', then." He began to tell him again about the trip he'd made from Halifax. The bulk cargo of wheat had shifted, apparently, but it hadn't stopped him laffin'.

They'd been unmolested for several hours, but dusk wasn't far ahead and nor were the island bases of Lampedusa and Linosa. *If* the ship floated long enough to get that far. Devenish and his fire-fighters had kept the fire away from the high-octane stowage, and on the starboard side they'd actually got it out, but the full-scale dousing operation meant diverting pump-power from the flooded spaces for'ard, and the rate of inflow had substantially increased. It seemed to Paul a rather silly arrangement of pumps and plumbing, that you couldn't do both jobs at the same time, but a ship like this one hadn't been designed to cope with action damage, simultaneous fire and flooding. As the third mate, Pratt, had commented, you couldn't have it both ways—"as the bishop said to the actress"—and the choice, anyway, wasn't likely to be either the bishop's or the actress's or their own, but the Luftwaffe's. The bombers would be busy elsewhere, he supposed, but they'd surely be back. When they arrived, the only opposition they'd meet would be from the *Santa Eulalia's* many guns and from the *Montgovern's* foc'sl Oerlikons. All the after guns had been knocked out and their crews killed either by the bombs or in the fire that resulted from them. A few survivors, alive but suffering from first-degree burns, were in the hands of Dennis Brill in the saloon. Harry Woods was among the missing—who would have gone over the stern, Paul guessed, if they hadn't been killed outright. They'd have been either killed, or incapacitated and caught in the flames, or they'd have jumped. Jumping would have meant drowning, because nothing had been visible aft during the worst of the fire, but most men, he guessed, would choose drowning in preference to burning. It brought you back, if you had a sense of humour like Beale's, to Pratt's Alternative.

Paul hadn't been aft. He remembered very clearly, from Narvik, what the results of battle looked like, and he couldn't have helped or done anyone any good. But he felt stupid. Everyone had told him and the others how slim the chances were of getting through to Malta. You'd listened, not doubted the facts about previous convoys or that on the face of it the hazards on this trip would be the same. But you hadn't really taken it in, not in real and personal terms, you'd never recognized the *probability* that you'd burn or drown. Beale had known, though: Beale, with his dark-sided humour, knew *now.*

When he thought about Woods, he saw it very clearly. Woods had expected to be in Malta in a day or so. Right up to the last second he'd still have been expecting that. There'd be this danger, that danger, but eventually you'd get through it and you'd *be* there. But Harry Woods would *not* be there. Most likely Paul Everard wouldn't either. He told himself, *That's real, it's true.*

So there'd be no letter to his father. And that, he told himself, was the
only truly ill effect his death would bring.

The weight of water in the ship's forepart, the flooded bow's resistance to forward movement, had cut her speed to about five knots. The
Santa Eulalia had reduced speed to stay with her, and was still abeam.
It was generous of the American, he thought, to be doing this. Her guns
would help to shield the *Montgovern,* who was otherwise more or less
defenceless, and it was comforting to know she was close by in case
they had to abandon ship. (*When* they had to, Paul corrected.) But from
the *Santa Eulalia*'s angle the *Montgovern*'s company was now a liability.
There was smoke coming out of her, there might be a glow from her
fire still showing after dark, and there was the fact that moving faster
would get one out of the enemy's back yard more quickly . . . He
thought that if he'd been Mackeson—or Straight, whichever of them
had the decision to make—he'd have suggested to the American captain that he should push on at his best speed, leave the *Montgovern* to
take her chances. It ought to be a matter of judging priorities, he
thought, cutting your losses; there'd surely be a better chance of getting
that one cargo into Malta if the faster, undamaged ship pressed on alone.

The smoke wasn't rising, as it had earlier, only lying in a spreading
trail above the wake. There wasn't as much swell now, and there was
hardly any breeze at all, but it was still extremely cold.

McNaught muttered, "Here's y' whatyacall 'im."

Mackeson. Old Bongo, coming for a visit. Paul stood up. Withinshaw
was asleep, swathed in tarpaulin, but Beale came aft from the bow
where he'd been smoking and staring down at the froth.

"Well, Everard!"

"Hello, sir."

Mackeson nodded to Beale and the others. His eye fell on the slum-
bering mass that was Withinshaw. "That one all right?"

Beale said, "It's 'ow 'e likes to be."

"No accounting for tastes. Deck must be damn cold." Mackeson
nodded towards the Oerlikons. He looked exhausted, ten years older

than he'd looked two days ago. "These are all we've got between ourselves and perdition, now. We're relying heavily on you chaps."

"Reckon we'll get there, do you, sir?" Beale's grin had something behind it, Paul noticed. He'd grinned like that when he'd been taking the Micky out of *him:* it was the same line, the same amused contempt for false optimism. Mackeson said, "The thing is, we have to keep going. As long as we're afloat and moving in the right direction, we *are* getting there." He noticed Beale's wag of the head, wordless sarcasm saying something like *That's the stuff to give 'em* . . . "I'm not saying we *will* get there, but I *am* saying we still have a chance."

Withinshaw sat up, staring at him. He transferred his blinks to Beale. "What's this, then?"

Paul said quickly, "This is the other Oerlikon gunner, sir. Withinshaw."

"Sorry to disturb you, Withinshaw." Mackeson nodded to him. "What I came for really was to say we've seen the pair of you doing some nice shooting, a few times."

"That would 'a been me." The fat man jerked his head, indicating Beale. "Killick's no fookin' use."

Mackeson laughed. He and Paul walked for'ard, up into the bow. The liaison officer stood looking down at the foam pushing out around it. "Not much freeboard now, is there?" He was right: when the time came to leave her, it wouldn't be much of a jump. Mackeson added, "Frankly, there's very little chance she'll last the night through. We've got to try, that's all."

"Yes."

"Every cargo's so darned important. And miracles *do* happen. I know, I've seen some. What seemed like miracles, anyway. So we'll stick to her as long as she'll float and move."

"Isn't it surprising they've left us alone this long, sir?"

"Probably got targets nearer to them. Anyway at sunset, pretty soon now, we'll be less than thirty miles north of Lampedusa . . . Those fellows seem sound enough?"

"They're—very individualistic . . . Sorry about the gunners aft, sir. Woods and all his—"

"I think the only way to look at it is that the rest of us are bloody lucky, Everard."

He thought, *So far . . .* He asked, "Any more news of the Italian cruisers that were reported at sea, sir?"

Mackeson glanced at him sharply. Then, with a shake of the head, away again. "No. None."

Sunset came in technicolor: pink and gold and lilac, the pink deepening to blood red and the lilac to mauve and black. With the day fading and the air getting still colder, what had been a smoke-trail was only vapour, a shimmer against the light. There was an exchange of signals. A long message from the *Montgovern* was answered by the *Santa Eulalia* with "Negative, and let's just keep praying."

"What's that about, then?"

He told Withinshaw, "I wouldn't know." All you could know was as much as you could see around you. He didn't even know whether the fire was still a danger, aft, but he could see for himself that she was about six inches lower for'ard than she had been at the time of Mackeson's visit. He came back to the Oerlikons, from another visit to the bow. The light was leaking away and the colours astern were deepening, but the two gunners were still lounging around, smoking and chatting with the younger men. McNaught chewed steadily. Paul didn't want to have to tell Beale and Withinshaw to stand-to. Contrary to all the precepts and principles that had been dinned into him during his training, lectures on such subjects as "Power of Command" and "Leadership," it was plain to him that his relationship with these DEMS characters depended largely on not giving orders. They accepted him because he didn't try to, and if he'd ignored the tacit agreement they'd have responded by ignoring *him*. Then his usefulness here, small as it was, would disappear altogether.

It was a relief when Beale stood up and stretched, and told Withinshaw through a yawn, "Best start lookin' like sailors, Art." He threw Paul that same half-smile, the sardonic look, as he moved to his gun and unclamped it.

•   •   •

Mackeson heard Gosling shout, and then the whistle. He went out quickly into the starboard wing. "What's up?"

"Surface craft—green eight-oh, sir!"

The spark of a white bow-wave caught his eye, and he settled his binoculars on it. E-boat. There was another to the left of it and both were bow-on, attacking. E-boats if they were German, Mas-boats if they were Italian, and it made not a shred of difference. He shouted at Humphrey Straight through the bridge window, "E-boats attacking, starboard beam. Will you come hard a-starboard, captain?" Then— "Signalman!"

"Sir?"

"Make to the Yank: *E-boats starboard.*" Over the front barrier of the wing he saw the foc's'l-head gunners standing by, alerted by Gosling's whistle. Everard looking up this way to see what was happening. Until she'd swung her bow towards the attackers, only one of those Oerlikons would bear. The *Santa Eulalia* had all the firepower: these bastards should have come from the other side. But they'd come from the Lampedusa side, of course. Even closer, just a few miles away, was the smaller island of Linosa. They'd quite likely been lurking there all day, anchored inshore in the knowledge that some easy kills were coming right towards them.

She'd begun to swing, at last. It was to avoid torpedoes as much as to bring both Oerlikons to bear that he'd suggested the turn to starboard. He had the E-boats in his glasses again. No—only one of them: and it was mostly bow-wave he was looking at. But where the hell . . . "Ah. There you are." He'd said it aloud. From behind him Humphrey Straight bawled: "Midships the wheel!" He had Pratt, third mate, in there; Devenish was still occupied below decks, getting that fire out. The second E-boat had shot away eastward in a wide, sweeping turn: moving across the line of sight as it was now, you could see it was doing about forty knots.

The Oerlikons opened fire. The first E-boat was moving slightly right. It had altered to port, to put itself on the *Montgovern*'s starboard bow. The other—he swivelled, and focused on it—was creaming round on the other side, to the east. That one would be out ahead of the *Santa Eulalia,* who'd held to her course and was consequently on the *Montgovern's* port quarter. The first one opened fire. A machine-gun firing tracer: yellow, twin streams of it lifting, slow-moving as it reached towards them, then accelerating to meteor-like flashes as it passed—at bridge level, for'ard. It fired in short bursts, not a continuous stream like the *Montgovern's* starboard Oerlikon was spouting. Straight had ordered another turn to starboard, to avoid any torpedo that might already have been fired and also to bring the other gun to bear. The E-boat jinked, came on again, coming in almost on the beam. Unless its skipper was dim-witted he must have realized by now that this ship had no weapons anywhere except on her foc's'l-head. Mackeson heard the *Santa Eulalia's* guns in action, as the *Montgovern* began responding to her rudder: slowly, and the damage for'ard wasn't making her any easier to handle. The E-boat was tearing in to close quarters, *two* double streams of tracer leaping from it. The *Montgovern's* starboard Oerlikon found the range and began to hit. You could see the explosive shells bursting, and one of the two guns stopped firing—and so did the Oerlikon. Jammed . . . The enemy's bow-wave high, brilliant white, wide-spreading on a surface turning black with the fading of the colour in the west: the E-boat swung hard a-port, dipping its gunwale to the sea as it spun around, one machine-gun slashing viciously at the foc's'l-head at point-blank range and unopposed, and at about that moment the torpedo hit the *Montgovern* in her starboard quarter. The crash of the underwater explosion like a kick in the belly of the ship triggered a voice in Mackeson's tired brain. It was his own, and it said, *End of the road, old son* . . . The Oerlikon had started up again but the E-boat, roaring from left to right down the ship's side as she still swung, was already escaping from the field of fire. He heard water drenching down across the stern—it would be from the torpedo's explosion—then tracer was bright in his face, the glass side of the bridge shattered, Gosling collapsed and flames were licking round the paintwork at the back end of the bridge. The foc's'l gun had ceased fire, and so had the E-boat after that final, vicious burst. It had turned away, swinging its stern towards the *Montgovern,* a pile of foam moving at forty knots. At Mackeson's elbow the signalman shouted, "One's on fire, sir. The Yank must've got it." The *Montgovern* was listing to starboard, and her engines had stopped.

Paul was at the port-side Oerlikons, leaning into the shoulder-rests with the gun cocked, his fingers on the trigger and the weapon's long, slim snout trained out to where a feather of white had been his last glimpse of the E-boat. It might be finished, going home, but with any luck it might come back, too. The list on the ship made his stance difficult. He was a couple of feet higher than Beale was on the other side, and the slanting deck was also slippery. The listing process seemed to have stopped, for the moment: half a minute ago he'd been expecting her to carry on, roll right over. This was Withinshaw's gun. Withinshaw's head had been smashed in in that last but one burst of machine-gun fire. The fact that the E-boat had still been hanging around out there gave him hope that it would come back to finish them off. He and Beale were waiting for the flicker of bow-wave to show up again. He wanted the pleasure, the relief, the deep joy there'd be in blasting it. McNaught, at his elbow, complained that it was *his* job to take over this gun when the number one gunner copped it. Paul told him, "Sure. Hang on. You can have it, in a minute." He thought, *Come on, come on, or we'll sink before you get here!*

Gunfire, out there on the bow. Biggish guns, percussions cracking hard across the water. But the American was astern somewhere. Surely, this ship had reversed course and was pointing west, back the way she'd come from, and the *Santa Eulalia* had held on? Ahead, there was a flash, a yellow streak that shot upwards from sea-level and then died down into a glimmer of burning on the sea. Gunfire had ceased. Now a white light sparked, expanded, lengthened into a long, harsh finger that swung and fastened on the *Montgovern*'s bow. From the north: a ship from the north, with a searchlight on them. He didn't think E-boats had searchlights, not of that size. It swung aft, touched the bridge, came back for'ard. At that moment, blinded by its glare, he felt the ship move, her stem rising in a sudden jolting lurch as the list became a steady roll to starboard.

CHAPTER ELEVEN

. . .

In the southwest Pacific it was about ninety minutes short of dawn. It was pitch dark, and Nick could smell the mangroves. He said into the telephone, "Steady as you go."

"Steady, sir. Oh-six-oh, sir."

"Steer that." He was using this telephone, not a voicepipe, because the wheelhouse was out of action and there was no voicepipe now, only the telephone line, to the lower steering position on the platform deck. Down there the new acting chief quartermaster, Petty Officer Riley, was wearing a telephone headset. Nick asked Chevening, "Depth?"

"Eight fathoms, sir." Chevening was in the front of the bridge, watching the echo-sounder. Nick asked him, "Two point two miles, on this leg?"

"Yes, sir."

"Tell me when we've done two."

It would show up on the log, which was also under Chevening's eye, another indicator glowing softly in the dark.

"Course oh-six-oh, sir."

"Very good."

Very quiet, too, although at this slow speed there was more vibration than there would have been at higher revs—as well as some extra rattles from the damaged area below the bridge. And very dark, because the moon was down. It had been shining when they'd been off the Madura coast, earlier in the night, and the chances were that watchers ashore would have seen a three-funnelled light cruiser steaming eastward. Earlier, a two-funnelled one had come out of the Surabaya Strait and turned west, and the Japs might well be looking for that one at dawn, on course for the Sunda Strait.

This was going to be a very, very tricky bit of pilotage. He had the islet called Sasul in sight to starboard, but against the darker background of Sepanjang itself you wouldn't have seen it if you hadn't known it was there and looked for it. It was only a mile, two thousand yards, to starboard, and during the next five minutes that distance would be lessening. There was a reef extending all along this side of it. Ten minutes ago, from a different angle and with sky and stars as background, he'd even been able to make out the shapes of coconut palms along its spine. He had to take *Defiant* right around Sasul: steering northeast now, then southeast, to the place where he'd stop to put the first of the boats into the water. Before that he'd have to take her clear of the rocks which abounded off the islet's northern extremity, then guide her in between other rocks to starboard and a confusion of reef to port.

Reefs were self-perpetuating, self-extending. The chart showed him their positions and extent as they'd been when the last hydrographical survey had been made, but the coral could have grown out anywhere in recent years. Nobody came in here except fishermen—Kangean fishermen, at that.

The land-smell was a stench, and he guessed that before long mosquitoes were likely to become a problem.

Chevening called sharply, "*Four* fathoms, sir!"

The tone of alarm was irritating. Nick countered it by murmuring his acknowledgement, the traditional "Very good," so gently that it might have come from someone half asleep. The sudden drop from eight to four fathoms was drastic, all right, but in fact it would have been more worrying if the sounder had produced any different reading. The figure matched chart data, and was what he'd expected. It would be fractionally *less* than four fathoms in a minute, and then it would increase again, and when they reached the turning-point they'd have about six fathoms showing. But Chevening didn't think this was going to be tricky, he thought it was going to be impossible. Chevening, Nick thought, was a bit of an old woman, and being knocked about in that engagement had *not* improved him. He'd come to see Nick last evening, half an hour before sailing time, bringing with him the chart, the Sailing Directions, and a very nervous manner.

"There's a point I seem to have overlooked, sir, about this place Sepanjang. In fact we all seem to have missed it . . . You want to get in here, on the north side: so we have to come past this off-lying bit—Pulau Sasul—then turn in here. But it says positively—here in the Pilot, but it's in the next column and I hadn't read that far—that the whole area between Sasul and Seridi Besar—that's this bit—is foul."

"Foul" in that context meant that it contained reefs, rocks or other underwater dangers that weren't specifiable or predictable and were therefore to be given a wide berth.

Nick had looked carefully at the chart again. There was a contradiction between that statement and the soundings that were shown. He knew there'd be foul areas which he'd have to negotiate, but this entrance point *had* to be open. He wasn't going to throw the whole plan away for the sake of three lines of small print and Chevening's worried frown.

"Whoever wrote this was simply clearing his own yardarm. All right, in general terms the whole area's rock-strewn. But look here—in here, steering clear of this lot, we've got six to eight fathoms. And right inside all this muck—reef—we've *still* got water enough to float in—right up to the bloody mangroves . . . All right?"

Chevening had licked sweat off his upper lip. He'd asked diffidently, "Do you think we'll be able to follow that channel in the dark, sir? With no lights, and nothing to fix on?"

"What d'you mean, nothing to fix on?"

"The moon'll be down—"

"So it will, thank God."

The navigator cleared his throat. "You're thinking of taking bearings on this high ground—Paliat? But that's only one feature, and it's at quite a distance, and on Sepanjang itself there are no heights marked, sir, no features as such, or—"

"Pilot, tell me this. Where would you like us to go instead?"

There wasn't anywhere else that was suitable. They both knew it. The only other island they might have considered using would have been the big one, Kangean, but the one place there for *Defiant* to have berthed would have been in Ketapang Bay on its northwest coast. The objections to it were that if any Japanese were thinking of landing in the Kangeans, that was where they'd arrive. In the whole group of islands it was *the* anchorage and landing-place. Also, unlike Sepanjang's north coast, it offered no cover. In fact the bay was visually open to ships passing southward en route to Bali or Lombok. Third, Kangean was more densely populated: the Pilot listed half a dozen villages. As Nick had pointed out, exaggerating somewhat, in an earlier discussion, it would be like tying up in Piccadilly Circus. And what it came down to was that they were extremely lucky that Sepanjang existed. Also— he'd mentioned this to Chevening—the fact that nobody would have expected anything bigger than a rowing-boat to have been able to get in through those various hazards was a distinct advantage, because the Japs were unlikely to be looking for them there.

"What about these bays, sir, on Kangean—Hekla or Gedeh?"

"Look at the Pilot. The land on that coast's dead flat. Paddy-fields. Barely enough cover for a tapeworm."

Remembering from his own earlier days how ridiculous senior officers' tantrums had often seemed, he'd tried to stifle his annoyance. And Chevening was perfectly correct, anyway, in coming along and pointing out the dangers. It was his duty, as navigator, to ensure the navigational safety of the ship. Besides which he might yet find himself in a position to shout "I told you so!" Because the dangers were real, unquestionably so. It was only a matter of seeing the wood as well as the trees—the wood being the fact that this was the only way to get *Defiant* out of the Java Sea.

"Five fathoms!"

"Good." He lifted the steering-position telephone again: "Nothing to starboard."

"Nothing to starboard, sir!"

That meant, not one yard's latitude to starboard of the ordered course. He had the chart photographed in his mind. *Defiant's* pencilled track at this point was tangential to a dotted line surrounding Sasul's fringe of rock, and the line meant "Keep out." Sasul was eight hundred yards to starboard but most of that eight-hundred-yard gap was rock-strewn.

One mile to go, before the turn to starboard.

"Five and a half fathoms, sir."

He checked the bearing of the high ground on Paliat, an island just this side of Kangean. That summit was marked as being four hundred and twenty feet high, and it was clearly distinguishable against the stars. Behind it by a distance of about five miles, and twice its height, was a peak in the spur of hills which ran along Kangean's north coast. If while the ship was on this course Paliat should fall into line with the higher, less distinct summit, he'd know he'd come too far, that he was running into danger.

He was running into danger anyway. But there was another metaphor, after the woods and trees one, about omelettes and eggs . . . Perhaps he *should* have transferred the wounded to *Sloan*. He hadn't, because Jim Jordan had made a proposal of his own which Nick had turned down, and after that it would have been difficult, to say the least, to have suggested it. *Sloan's* spares had arrived, but by truck instead of by rail, and in the same convoy of Dutch army vehicles about forty refugees, who'd been on their way from Bandoeng to Tjilatjap for evacuation by sea, had turned up. Some railway junction had been bombed, so the Dutch had brought them to Surabaya instead. Jordan's idea had been that *Sloan* and *Defiant* should each take half of them. He'd had them all, when he'd made the signal about it, because his ship was alongside a jetty and the Dutch had found it convenient to dump them at his gangway. They were all civilians, and they included women and children. Nick had declined to take any of them, mainly because it was obvious that *Sloan's* chances of getting away were a lot better than *Defiant's*. A year ago in the Aegean he'd seen ships being loaded with troops only to put to sea and be sunk. He thought that if *Sloan* couldn't take them all, they'd be better left in Java. Besides, he had a day to spend lying-up in the Kangeans, and it was going to be tricky enough without having a load of women and children to complicate matters internally.

Jordan had thought Nick's attitude was unreasonable. *Defiant* was twice the size of *Sloan* and had far more room for passengers than the destroyer had. When the American had come aboard for a final conference before *Defiant* sailed, his manner had made his feelings plain. It was a pity, because Nick liked him and they'd got on well. Nick thought it was only a matter of seeing the issue clearly and objectively, and that for some reason Jordan wasn't able to. But at the last minute, everything changed. Jordan had made some remark about the passage down the Australian west coast to Perth being a hell of a long one, sixteen hundred miles, especially with overcrowded messdecks. Nick had suggested that when they were away and clear, say by the evening of the day after they cleared their respective straits, they might stop and transfer some of the refugees from *Sloan* to *Defiant*.

"In fact I'll accept three-quarters of them."

"Well, now. That sounds like a very fair solution, sir."

"*If* we're there to take them from you. If we aren't, you'll know I was right not to embark them."

He and Jordan had parted on good terms. *Sloan*'s ship's company had cheered the British cruiser on her way, and *Defiant*'s sailors had returned the compliment as she'd left the anchorage. *Sloan*'s men were going to blow up the destroyer that was in the graving dock, before they themselves left. The job was to be left to the last minute in order not to signal too clearly to the Japs that a naval evacuation was in progress. There'd been two enemy reconnaissance flights over Surabaya during the day, as well as one bombing raid.

"Two miles run, sir!"

"Depth?"

"Six fathoms, sir."

He checked the bearing of the Paliat hill again. Three degrees to go. The course after this coming turn would be a hundred and thirty-five degrees. On these revs *Defiant* was making five knots, so one-fifth of a mile would be covered in two-point-four minutes. At the turning point there should still be six fathoms. He asked Chevening, "Log reading?"

"One cable's length to go, sir."

A cable's length was a tenth of a mile. Just over one minute. If he turned too early he'd put her on the rocks, and if he left it too late he'd be on a reef. He sighted again on that hill, and the bearing was *just* about—

"Stand by, sir!"

"Stop starboard."

"Stop starboard, sir . . . Starboard telegraph to stop, sir."

It would be hot, airless, really bloody awful, down in that lower steering position.

Chevening called, "Now!"

"Starboard fifteen."

The bearing was exactly right. Wiley confirmed over the telephone that he had fifteen degrees of starboard rudder on her. This was to be a seventy-five-degree turn, but starting it with that screw stopped she'd fairly whistle round; which was what he wanted, as opposed to letting her drift outwards on the turn.

"Midships."

"Midships, sir."

"Slow ahead starboard . . . Pilot, one-point-five miles to the first stop, that right?"

Chevening confirmed it.

"Steer one-three-five. We're in a narrow channel now, quartermaster."

"Aye aye, sir. Steer one-three-five, sir. Starboard engine slow ahead."

"Bob?" Gant moved up beside him. Nick told him, "Man the starboard cutter. They'll be slipped in eighteen minutes' time."

"Aye aye, sir." Gant went to the after end of the bridge, to shout down to Charles Rowley. Haskins was down there too, and the thirty-foot cutter on the starboard side, abreast the second funnel was already turned out in its davits and ready for lowering. One section of Royal Marines would be taken in it to land on the southeast corner of Sasul; when Nick stopped the ship, she'd be opposite the landing point. There was a village on Sasul for the marines to keep an eye on, and the northern end of it, which they were rounding now, commanded this channel; the section was landing with a Bren and the two-inch mortar, and with those they'd be able to sink anything that tried to get by. (Nobody in his right mind, Nick thought, would try to come through the channel in anything bigger than a canoe, anyway.)

The cutter was an oared boat, "double banked," with six oars a side. *Defiant* did have two thirty-foot motorboats that might have been used, but oars were quieter and more reliable: also, this inshore water was, as Chevening had pointed out, foul, and a pulling-boat was less likely to rip her bottom out on a rock.

The cruiser was moving into the crescent-shaped hollow that was Sepanjang's northern side. Land-smell, mangrove-smell increasing, enveloping. Sasul was easily visible to starboard, its palms starkly black against the sky. The only connection between it and the main part of the island was a reef enclosing both of them, rather as if the larger island had arms tightly enfolding the smaller one. There were several smaller islets in the lagoon between them, between those coral banks. In a hundred years, or perhaps much less, the whole thing would quite likely be filled in solidly, a coral extension to Sepanjang. Kangean itself, according to the Pilot, was made of coral—coral lime erupted by volcanic action.

One and a half miles at five knots meant eighteen minutes from the last turn to the point where he'd arranged with Haskins that he'd slip the cutter. After it had landed the RM section that boat would follow on inshore, to the place he'd picked for *Defiant's* berth. At this next stopping-point, in just a few minutes now, Sasul's southeast coast would be in a straight line to him so that it would look like one clear-cut edge of land, and there'd be a gap visibly open between it and the islands in the lagoon. From any other angle, they'd all overlap. The cutter had to make for that spot on Sasul because it was the one place with no reef to bar its approach. It was also the site of the village, and where the villagers would berth their praus. So landing the section here would kill several birds with one stone.

He settled his binoculars on it. There was no gap visible yet.

Chevening warned, "Two cables' lengths, sir."

He said into the telephone, "Stop both engines."

"Stop both, sir!"

The ship's momentum would carry her on into position. The quarter-hour had passed so quickly that he felt his thoughts might have been wandering. It was still a danger to watch out for. So far, he believed his mind had been working normally, responding normally to the stimulus of danger and tension. Anxiety, too. The knowledge that with one small act of carelessness, or one piece of bad luck over which he'd have no control, he could put his ship on a rock or across a reef: the prospect was so shocking that the mind, fit or sick, rejected contemplation of it. But it was there, it existed . . .

He saw the gap, just as Chevening called to him that the ship was in position. "Slow astern together." He said over his shoulder, "Away cutter."

Gant shouted. And from down aft Nick heard Rowley's order, "Lower away!"

"Stop together." He'd taken the way off her. He could hear the squeaking of the blocks as the boat was lowered, with two dozen men in her, to the black water. At the next stop he'd be sending away both whalers, but that would be a quicker process because, being seaboats, the whalers had quick-release gear on their falls. The heavy cutter had to be lowered right into the water and the falls slacked off before they could be unhooked.

He checked the compass. The ship's head was at rest, on course: there was no drift or wind in here, and Wiley had held her steady while the screws had been running astern. He heard the clatter as the falls were unhooked, and then the orders, low-voiced but reflected from the water's surface: "Shove off for'ard . . . Oars down!" The thumps of the oars' looms banging down on the boat's gunwales. Then: "Starboard side oars, one stroke back-water . . ." And finally, "Give way together!" That was Wainwright, an RNR lieutenant: Gant had detailed an officer to take charge of each boat. There was also a leadsman in the cutter's bow, to take soundings as it moved in towards the landing-place.

Gant murmured, returning, "Cutter's well clear, sir."

"Slow ahead together."

The screws churned, and dark water swirled away under her counter. A mile and a half again now. He'd have preferred to have sent the whalers away here and now, but time was limited, and if he was going to have her hidden before the light came he'd have to get closer inshore before he brought her down to the speed of oarsmen. In less than an hour the sun would be dragging itself up over the eastern extremity of the island, that long spar of land with a fishing village called Kiau on the end of it. By that time he wanted to have her tucked away, and there'd still be some camouflaging to be done. Also, he wouldn't know until he got there whether the inlet he'd picked was as suitable as it looked on paper. It might be silted up, or too narrow, or someone might have felled the trees and destroyed the natural cover. It was pot luck, a gamble: and meanwhile you had also to accept this further period of risk navigationally. It was an exceptionally heavy risk, but here again he had no choice.

"Petty Officer Wiley."

"Yes, sir."

"Nothing either side. Steer as if you were on a tightrope."

"Do me best, sir."

"Depth, pilot?"

"Eight and a half fathoms, sir."

When they stopped, *Defiant* would have her forefoot on one of those dotted lines which, on the chart, enclosed foul ground.

He thought, *I'm mad, and Chevening was right* . . .

He saw it, quite suddenly, as his navigator must have seen it—as an attempt at the impossible. The evidence, the words printed in the Sailing Directions and the patterns and symbols on the chart, all declared it. They didn't *suggest* it, they declared it unequivocally. Only an idiot could have embarked on this—could even have considered it . . . An idiot, or a desperate man, a man at his wits' end for a way out. He'd clutched at the straw and now he had it in his hand and there was nothing he could do except carry on, attempting the impossible but no longer believing it to be anything else . . . Again, it was like looking back on the workings of a mind that was not your own. He thought he must have seen the risks and subconsciously decided to ignore them, push on as if they didn't exist. But they did. They were *here*. And having come this far he had to go on with it, acting as if he'd assessed the risks and accepted them, expected to come through it . . .

If he bungled it, and got her stuck here, the Japs would bomb her into scrap.

Chevening called sharply, "Five fathoms, sir!"

According to the chart there should have been eight, all the way through!

"Stop both engines."

"Stop both, sir!"

The whalers' crews were going to have to pull farther than they'd expected. He was sweating. Before he spoke he paused, getting hold of his nerves, ensuring that his voice was steady.

"Bob. Pass the word to Ormrod and Brown that I'm slipping them a mile farther out than we'd intended. Man and lower both whalers, please."

Each boat would have a leadsman taking soundings. Lieutenant Brown's boat would be *Defiant*'s guide, immediately ahead of her, while Ormrod's ranged farther ahead and from side to side across the bows to locate the channel and lead Brown to it. Each twenty-seven-foot whaler had five oars and a coxswain, so there'd be eight men in each, and the officers in charge of them had blue-shaded signal lamps for communication. *Defiant* was going to have to follow at no greater speed than the boats could be rowed, and she'd certainly be late in getting to her hiding-place. It would be a race with the sunrise, now, but it would be just a little less dangerous than it would have been to have gone ahead without having the boats down. The echo-sounder wouldn't be much use from here on. You needed to know what was ahead of the ship, not what was already under her.

She was slowing, and Gant reported that the two whalers were manned and lowered, ready to slip. There was no need to stop her this time. You could drop a seaboat from the disengaging gear even when you had quite a lot of way on. He'd only slowed her now because she'd be moving like a snail from here onwards in any case, and to start with the boats had to be allowed to get up ahead of her. He told Gant, "Slip both whalers," heard the two crashes as they hit the water, and moved to the front of the bridge, beside Chevening, to see them both pull ahead. Like black water-beetles down there . . . It was Gant who'd picked Ormrod and Brown for the boat-work. Nick had told him he needed level-headed, steady characters who were experienced seamen and who'd use their initiative and find ways round problems when they came up against them. His own brain here would be operating through theirs—extensions of his own, well out ahead.

Brown had positioned his boat dead ahead of the cruiser: his orders were to keep about thirty to fifty yards ahead. Ormrod's whaler was pushing on, five oarblades swirling the dead-flat water at each stroke. He was to keep about fifty yards ahead of Brown, and to range over a channel-width of a hundred feet, marking it when it was narrower than that and reporting and marking hazards. He had a dozen white-painted spar-buoys under his boat's thwarts, and Brown had more in case he needed them.

Nick told Wiley, "I'll be using one screw only now, with an occasional touch ahead and then stopping. We'll be following our own boats through foul water."

"Aye aye, sir."

It might have made things easier if they'd had normal conning, with the wheelhouse in action and the quartermaster able to look ahead through his small window and see where he was going. From this upper bridge, Wiley and his assistants were six decks down.

"Slow ahead starboard."

"Slow ahead starboard, sir . . ."

"Steer one degree to port."

Down there, they'd still follow courses on the compass card, but Nick would only be keeping her stem pointing at Brown's whaler.

"Cutter's inshore, out of sight, sir."

"Good." Gant had been at the back end of the bridge, watching the cutter through binoculars. Nick said into the telephone, "Stop starboard."

"Stop starboard, sir . . . Starboard telegraph to stop, sir."

"If you think you're losing steerage way, let me know at once."

"Aye aye, sir."

Creeping in. A touch ahead, then stop, drifting forward until the boats had increased their distance again. Then another shove, to push her along behind them. He wondered what he'd do if they came up against a solid barrier of coral, if the channel came to an end. It was quite possible that it would. Anchor, hope for the best, send the boats inshore for camouflaging materials? It would be a very awkward hole to be in, and even more awkward to get out of. Turning her, for instance, in this narrow channel would be quite a problem. *Defiant's* waterline length was four hundred and sixty-five feet. He realized he'd probably have to take her out astern. God Almighty . . . But then, if you got stuck to that extent, you'd be lucky if you got as far as facing that particular extra problem, the one of getting *out* . . . Sweating again. From ahead, faintly across the water, he heard Brown's leadsman call, "And a quarter five!"

Five and one-quarter fathoms, they had there. The mark on the leadline at five fathoms was a piece of white bunting. There was no mark at six, and such unmarked depths were called "deeps." In-between soundings were reported as references to the five mark, or to the seven which had red bunting. At four there was no mark on the line; at three, there were three strips of leather. How, or how long ago the peculiar system had become established, would be a question for historians in the National Maritime Museum; but Drake in his voyage of circum-navigation probably had leadlines marked like these.

"A quarter less five!"

The report was to Brown in the sternsheets of the whaler, not to Nick back here. But it was reassuring to hear it, even though they'd lost three feet of water between the last two soundings. There was still a depth of twenty-seven feet there, and *Defiant* only needed sixteen to float in.

Gant slapped his own neck, and cursed quietly. "The bloody things . . ."

"A half less five!"

"Slow ahead starboard."

Creeping in. So far so good, but you might be stopped at any moment. Land-smell foetid, thoroughly unpleasant. Mosquitoes were getting to be a nuisance, and all the repellent stuff they had on board had been issued to the marines. *Defiant* trembled as one screw churned, pushing her up closer to the boats. Fine on the bow, Ormrod's blue lamp flashed dot-dash-dot, "R" for rock. He'd put a marker over it, then prospect for a wide enough, deepwater passage round it, if there was one . . . Nick wondered again what Gant would have done, if he'd been the man to decide it. Whatever he'd said when Nick had asked him, you could be fairly sure he wouldn't have tried *this* way out. On the face of it, he'd have had more sense; but even if he'd considered it, wouldn't Chevening's quiet hysterics have persuaded him to drop it? Then *Defiant* wouldn't have been in this knife-edge situation. But where *would* she have been?

Spending a day at sea, the first idea he'd had? That would be much more dangerous. And as for the idea of going west to Sunda—

"Stop starboard."

"Stop starboard, sir!"

Stop *thinking* . . . It was something foreign to him, this doubting introspection. It was also pointless and potentially destructive. The result of that bang on the head, and high time he got over it. He thought, one hand up feeling the bandaging around his head, *You're in it, just get on with it* . . . Beyond that rock, which he'd buoyed, Ormrod was leading round to starboard. Making the buoy a starboard-hand mark, as it were. If this was the point for the turn in towards the creek, or inlet, there wasn't such a vast distance to be covered now. About—perhaps three thousand yards; something like that. But even three thousand yards at rowing pace, in boats that were also sounding as they went, would take some time to cover, and meanwhile a faint radiance eastward and overhead was a warning.

He checked the ship's head: it was on a hundred and forty-six degrees. Then the bearing of Brown's whaler. The course, he reckoned, would be about due south, and she'd need more steerage-way to make the turn, even if it brought him up a bit close behind the boats.

"Slow ahead port."

"Slow ahead port, sir. Port telegraph slow ahead, sir."

"Starboard five."

"Starboard five, sir . . . Five degrees of starboard wheel on, sir."

You felt the gentle push from that screw. And then the cruiser was bringing her bow around slowly to follow in the whaler's path.

"Midships."

"Midships, sir. Wheel's amidships, sir."

It was very quiet in the bridge. Chevening, Nick thought, was probably holding his breath. Not a bad idea, in this hothouse stink. He sighted across the compass again, on Brown's boat, and told Wiley to steer one-seven-eight. There was no absolute guarantee of safety in having boats out ahead, all this creepy-crawly stuff. There could well be a rock pinnacle which neither leadsman would pick up, and it wouldn't be their fault if they didn't: no one's fault, everyone's disaster. Sepanjang rose darkly ahead, blotting out a section of the lightening sky. To port, where the land was lower, the brightening was more evident. It was the first showing of the dawn, and they were running neck and neck with it. Running like a tortoise runs when it isn't in a hurry; and it was anyone's guess how long the berthing process would take.

Gant murmured, "Another rock ahead, sir."

Ormrod flashing "R" again. Right ahead. So the channel leading inshore had a hazard smack in the middle of it. It could even be a reef, a barrier right across it which the chart didn't show.

"Stop port."

Defiant was very close behind Brown's whaler, since he'd had to keep a screw going all through the turn. He said into the telephone, cutting across Wiley's acknowledgement, "Steer one degree to starboard."

If he couldn't find a way past that rock, Ormrod would flash "S" for "stop." Or, until he was sure of it, "W" for "wait." Nick focused his glasses on that more distant boat. He could see the spar-buoy in the water, and the whaler was under oars again, pulling away to the right. He could see the leadsman's upright figure in its bow.

Gant murmured, "Getting lighter, sir."

"Yes."

Did Gant imagine he was blind?

Ormrod's boat was still moving to the right, oars sweeping slowly. Stopping, holding water . . .

The blue lamp flashed "R."

Another rock. It would be thirty, forty yards from the first one. Thirty yards was ninety feet, and *Defiant*'s beam was just on fifty. He muttered in his mind, *Check the depths between them and beyond* . . . He'd seen the second marker buoy go over the whaler's stern; the port-side oars were backing water, to turn her back across the channel. He said to Gant, "Glad *I* don't have to pull an oar in this fug."

Silence: the silence of surprise, he hoped. He'd wanted to show Gant that he was relaxed and confident. Brown's boat was edging across to starboard.

"Slow ahead port." He added to Gant, "God knows how we'll breathe when the sun gets up." Ormrod's whaler was crossing the gap between the two spar-buoys, sounding as it went. The leadsmen weren't actually heaving their leads, only dabbing them up and down, feeling the bottom as they went along. A boat's lead weighed seven pounds and was shaped like a thin leg of mutton. It had a cavity in its end into which you could put tallow wax so as to bring up a sample of the ground and know whether it was sand or mud or what. That was important, so as to know whether or not it was good holding ground for an anchor. There was a lot to know about leadlines: that you measured them, for instance, when they were wet, and stretched a new line by towing it astern of a ship. Drake had probably done those things too, in his time: but he wouldn't have tried to get in behind Sepanjang in a ship drawing sixteen feet.

Well, he *might* have.

"Stop port. Steer three degrees to starboard."

Ormrod's boat had found the channel clear between the markers; it was moving on between them towards the shore. There was a veining of light overhead and a gleam of treetops, palms, along a high slope leading upwards towards blackness. Brown's boat was under way again, pulling after Ormrod's and aiming to pass exactly in the middle between the two spar-buoys. Nick heard the leadsman's hail: "And a half, three!" Twenty-one feet. At that point, forty yards ahead, the ship would have five feet of water between her keel and the mud. Ormrod's whaler was almost impossible to see against the land's shadow; it was easy enough with binoculars, though. They were close in now, really *very* close. The picture of this bit of the chart which he had in his visual memory was of a line of reef indented like a funnel leading to the inlet, and *Defiant* would be entering it now, or soon, moving slowly towards its narrowing inshore neck. Out here the edges of the funnel were banks of coral, but right inside where he wanted to hide her—if he could get her in that far—they'd merge into mudbanks and the mangroves.

From right ahead, a blue light flashed "W," meaning "wait."

She was virtually stopped already. Forty yards ahead Brown's whaler was taking soundings. The signal to wait might mean that Ormrod had come up against some obstruction, or it could mean he'd found the inlet and was investigating it. There'd be some exploration to be done. You needed the depth of water to get in there, and the length of navigable water from the mouth inwards so as to berth her right inside, and at the inner, bow end they'd have to land and find a tree stout enough to take a cable from the foc'sl. The hemp cable would be passed out through the bullring, and when it had been secured ashore the inboard end would be brought to the capstan, to warp her in.

"Boat coming up astern, sir!"

Number three lookout on the starboard side had reported it. Gant went back to take a look, but it could only be the cutter. It had made good time, but it had had the spar-buoys to follow. It would lie off now, close astern, until it was called for.

The sky in the east was turning pink and silver, and fissures of colour were like cracks spreading into the darkness overhead. This part of the island was still shadowed, four-fifths dark.

Ormrod's light flashed "A." A dot and a dash. "A" stood for "accessible."

Incredible. You had to make yourself believe you'd seen it. If it was true, there should have been trumpets, a fanfare of triumph, celebration. There wasn't so much as a whisper until Nick said into the telephone, "Slow ahead port." You had to believe it, because it was happening. As well to postpone self-congratulation or thanks to the Almighty, or any told-you-so to Chevening, until you'd dealt with the dozen-odd problems that would be cropping up during the next half hour . . . Brown's whaler was pulling hard, heading inshore to catch up with Ormrod's. *Defiant* could now move in and wait where Brown's had been. And meanwhile, at the risk of spoiling one's luck by counting unhatched chickens, there were arrangements to be put in hand.

"Bob. Go aft now, please. Check that Greenleaf's ready with the stream anchor. I want it ready for letting go, and the quarterdeck telephone manned, *now*. Hail the cutter and tell Wainwright to keep clear of the wire. When you're satisfied with Greenleaf's arrangements, go for'ard and see Rowley's making sense on the foc's'l. I'd like you to gravitate between the two. All right?"

"Aye aye, sir."

"Lieutenant Flynn?"

Flynn answered from the back of the bridge: "Sir?"

"Stand by the depth charge telephone, Flynn, and don't leave it."

That was the communication line to the quarterdeck. The stream anchor—the stern one—would by now have a steel-wire rope shackled to its short swivel-length of cable; it would be let go more than a ship's length outside the inlet, and the wire would be paid out as she nosed in. When they were ready to sneak away tonight it would be brought to the after capstan and the ship would be eased out stern-first.

"Stop together . . . Pilot, how much water?"

"Two feet under the keel, sir."

In that inlet, he guessed, she'd crease the mud. He told Chevening to stand by the foc's'l telephone. He had no other work for him now, and in this operation co-ordinating the actions on the foc's'l with those on the quarterdeck, getting the right orders and information to and fro, was vital. He said into the quartermaster's telephone, "Slow astern together." To take the way off her, hold her where she lay now. The cutter would wait astern until the ship was in and secured, and then it would be used for landing the other sections of Royal Marines. Brown's whaler would be coming out to the ship in a minute, paying out a light line to measure the right distance for letting go the stream anchor; they'd only need to measure the distance to her stem. The same line would be passed inboard, up to the foc's'l and in through the bullring, and it would then be used to haul a heavier line from ship to shore. On the end of that one the mooring cable would be dragged over.

"Stop together."

"Stop together, sir . . . Both telegraphs to stop, sir!"

Wiley had done an excellent job, Nick thought. So had Ormrod and Brown and their boats' crews. Now, apart from some back-breaking work ashore, the kingpins of the mooring effort would be Rowley and Greenleaf, with Gant looking over their shoulders.

Gant. Nick had been doing some thinking about Bob Gant. Not now, though . . . He glanced round as Flynn reported, "Commander says all's ready aft, sir. He's on his way to the foc'sl."

Dawn. With binoculars he could make out—just—the darker area that could only be the indentation in the wall of mangroves. There was a whaler halfway out, pulling towards the ship, a glistening of water flying from the dipping oars. Brown's. Behind the flat coastal mangrove area the hillside rose quite steeply: it was still in shadow and would be for some time yet, but he could make out the shapes of palms where they grew thinly or on their own. In about ten minutes it would be more or less daylight. What was needed now, he thought, was half an hour without any Jap aircraft over. She'd be hidden, by that time; in an hour, she'd be invisible.

By the afternoon it was very hot indeed. Nick had slept for an hour, after an early lunch, and he'd been woken by PO Harkness with a message about a Jap seaplane circling over the islands. He'd turned out and come for'ard, up to the director tower, to see it for himself. As he heaved himself up through the lubber's hole entrance—it was awkward, with only one arm in use—Charles Rowley turned a surprised but genial smile on him.

"Give you a hand, sir?"

He shook his head. "This seaplane—"

"Gone, sir." Rowley could have done with a haircut. His shaggy, gingerish head gave him the appearance of an Airedale, Nick thought. Fortunately he rather liked Airedales. Rowley gestured, encompassing a steamy area of reef-broken, shimmery sea: "Circled round and went down low over the eastern end there, then climbed and bumbled off that way."

Towards Kangean . . .

Rowley, as senior watchkeeping officer, had reserved this lookout job for himself. It was the only place in the ship you could see anything from, but also, slight as the breeze was, you were out of the clammy stillness of the swamp below.

The seaplane pilot would have needed hawk's eyes to have spotted them, Nick thought. Branches of mangrove festooned this tower, masts, yards, upperworks and upper deck. After the ship had been secured Gant had mustered all hands and sent them ashore in teams to cut and bring back the foliage. To be sure, you'd need to fly over her yourself, but she had to be pretty well invisible. Meanwhile the marines were in control of the villages of Tanjung Kiau and Mandan, three sections were patrolling in the palms behind the long southern beach and another manned a lookout station on the hill. A field telephone had been rigged from there to a guard-post in the trees abreast the ship. This was the landing-place. Both cutters, side by side, supported a gangway which ran from the ship's side to the mudbank, and all of that brow and the boats had been strewn with foliage.

The view from the lookout hatches (one each side of the main-mast) in the after bulkhead of this tower was restricted by the shore-line to a quadrant between northwest and northeast. Blue sea, reefs and islands in the distance, shimmery in the heat-haze as if you were looking at it all through rising steam. Above the land to the left, just about exactly northwest, a bluish hump trembled in the sky. It was the hill he'd used to take bearings on during the early stages of the approach. Rowley asked him what it was.

"Island called Paliat. That's a hill, four hundred and twenty feet high. It's—roughly—fifteen miles from us."

"Would any sea routes pass close to us here, sir?"

"Close to the islands." He nodded. "Anything coming down to the Lombok Strait from the Macassar Strait up north—or from Borneo or the Celebes—would pass to the east here. Fifteen or twenty miles clear, probably, because of reefs to the northeast. So we wouldn't see them— or vice versa."

"What if they took it into their heads to land on the big island, Kangean?"

"I'd guess their hands are a bit full, at the moment. But they'd go for Ketapang Bay, on the west coast, and that's a good forty miles away."

"So we're pretty safe from being stumbled on."

He nodded, reaching for a cigarette. It was quite pleasant up here. He said, "Except for aircraft. And with any luck—"

A face—head, shoulders—appeared in the open hatch, the lubber's hole entrance in the deck. The face was reddish—brown, and seamed. Able Seaman Bentley. Gant had produced him this morning as a replacement for Gladwill.

"Sorry, sir, I didn't know you was on the move. Else I'd 've—"

"It's all right, Bentley. I don't need you." He checked the time. "I'll be going down to turn in again in a minute, and I suggest you get your head down too. We'll be up all night and there'll be no rest tomorrow."

A nod. A very solid, seasoned three-badger, was Bentley. "Seen them monkeys, have you, sir?"

"Monkeys?"

Rowley pointed. The monkeys were on the cable that ran to the ship's bow from a palm-tree ashore. There were three of them, swinging around and doing acrobatics on it, hanging upside-down. Bentley said, "I got nippers just like them."

Rowley asked him, "D'you mean they look like that, or behave like it?"

"Both, sir." The AB slid feet-first into the tower and into the rate-clock operator's seat. "Spittin' image. I could take two o' them home and switch 'em with the little 'uns and the missus'd never know no difference." He looked at Nick: "Wanted to say, sir, off-duty like, I'm happy to get this job, sir."

"Fond of cage-birds, are you?"

"Ah." He frowned. "If I *got* to take them birds on—"

"Find another home for them, if you like, sell them and send the money to Gladwill's widow."

"Wasn't never married, sir."

"Nor he was . . . His mother, then."

"Orphan, I b'lieve he was, sir."

"There'll be a next-of-kin on record, Bentley."

"Ah. That's a thought, sir."

"I'm told you were cox'n to the C-in-C on the China Station at one time."

"I was, sir. In thirty-six, that was. But I got in a spot of bother in Shanghai, and they drafted me up the perishin' Yangtze. In the old *Aphis*. We was at Chinkiang when the Japs started bombing the Chinks in thirty-seven . . ." He pointed suddenly, squinting round over his shoulder, out through the lookout hatch: "See there, sir!"

Floatplane: it was coming from the direction of Kangean, and it looked as if it would pass over Tanjung Kiau. Rowley said, with his glasses on it, "Looks like the same one, sir."

"Very likely. Been snooping round the big island, I expect." He told Bentley, "*Aphis* is in the Med, now."

"Turning towards us, sir."

It was over the islet called Seridi. It was banking, making a slow turn to starboard . . . And steadying now, heading directly towards the inlet and the ship. Nick put his glasses down, and motioned to Rowley to do the same. One flash of sunlight on a lens would be enough to invite inspection . . . He asked Bentley, "What kind of bother, in Shanghai?"

"Russian woman, sir. Holy terror, she was."

He nodded. That expression might have described his own ex-wife Ilyana very aptly. He said, "You have my sympathy." He recognized surprise in the first lieutenant's quick glance at him. But you could hear the drone of the seaplane's engine now. Nick looked down through the starboard-side embrasure, down at his mangrove-smothered ship. Nobody was in sight, nothing moved. But if one man, one white cap appeared now among that greenery . . . The noise was growing as the floatplane bore in towards them.

"Think he could have spotted us, sir?"

"Unlikely."

It might be just shaping course to pass over the centre of the island. It had looked at the other islands, so it was reasonable that it should have a look at Sepanjang as well. That it was heading for this inlet could be coincidental: and the flight-path would be about right for Bali, if that was where it was now returning. On the other hand—he woke up to this point suddenly—it was flying at only a couple of hundred feet, which would barely clear the hill at this point . . . He suggested to Bentley, "Chief and petty officers might like to have those canaries in their mess. So might the warrant officers, come to think of it."

"I wouldn't let the WOs have 'em, sir." The creases deepened in the sailor's face. "Serve 'em up for breakfast, soon as look at 'em."

Rowley chuckled. With an anxious eye on the sky, though, as the engine-noise still increased. Nick said, "No looking out, now."

Deafening racket. They sat or squatted with their faces turned downward, as if the steel roof with its burden of branches might be transparent. The noise lifted to a peak: the machine couldn't have been even as much as two hundred feet up. But sound was falling away again, pulsing back from the hillside. Nick suspected that it had been losing height, actually coming down as it approached. Rowley was looking out through the for'ard observation slit that ran from beam to beam in that side of the DCT's armour. He said, "Circling to the left now."

"If it didn't, it'd be flying into the hill."

Waiting . . .

Rowley shifted his position, to keep the seaplane in sight. "Still circling. Might be coming round for another look."

If the pilot *had* seen the ship, he'd be using his radio to call up an air strike. Vals, probably, from Bali: and they could be here in about as long as it would take to recite the Lord's Prayer. Meanwhile the seaplane would hang around, and show the bombers their target when they arrived.

If it came over for another check—shoot it down? Close up a pom-pom crew? But then, if you failed to knock it down—and if you were wrong and it *hadn't* seen the ship, or used its radio . . . He heard Greenleaf mutter, "Still circling."

So it *was* hanging round.

Bentley growled, "Prob'ly only takin' a bit of a look-see, sir."

This had been the only way to get the ship out. But he'd had a pretty good run of luck. There'd been at least as much luck as good judgement. It could have run out: it could be that this was as far as they were going to get.

On the other hand . . .

Forget the pompoms, he decided.

"Turning the other way. Going round to starboard."

He joined Rowley at the hatch. The floatplane was out over the reefs to the north and banking to the right, to fly eastward. Rowley said, "I don't believe he can have seen anything."

"One section of marines is at the village where he's heading now. You said he came in over that point, didn't you?"

If Haskins's men had allowed themselves to be seen? Going back for another look at *them,* now?

But there were leatherneck sections at Mandar in the southeast, and on Sasul, and along the south coast as well. Wherever that thing flew you could imagine the worst, give it unpleasant reasons to be there.

"Turned south, sir."

"To fly over the island where it's lower. Home to Bali."

Or to swing back this way. The Vals would be lifting from their airstrip about now. Rowley told the pilot through that aperture in the armour, "Go on home, you disgusting object."

Able Seaman Bentley stirred. "Well, seein' you don't need me, sir . . . What time we turnin' to, sir?"

"Sunset, or about then."

"Aye aye, sir." Bentley let himself down through the lubber's hole. A ladder from it led into the HACP—high angle control position—and from another manhole in the deck of that a longer ladder ran down the foremast to the rear end of the bridge.

"Can't have seen us, sir. He's gone."

For a few minutes, things hadn't looked at all promising. Nick told Charles Rowley, "I'm going down. If anything worries you, just let me know."

With just one arm, the climb really was quite difficult. But you had to manage, get used to it. Much worse was the fact that his nerve wasn't as steady as it had been before he'd been wounded. When that seaplane had passed over and then begun to circle round again, he'd really thought they'd had it. It wouldn't do. He needed to pull himself together, get back to normal quickly: in fact *immediately*, because tonight wasn't going to be without its problems.

Thinking of wounds, though, reminded him that he had to visit the sickbay and get his dressings changed. Now might be as good a time as any.

"Captain, sir!"

He was on the third down-ladder from the bridge level, and the sickbay flat was close to the bottom of it. But the yeoman of signals, Morris, was rattling down the ladder after him. "Signal to us, sir. Us and the *Sloan*."

Nick took the clipboard one-handed, and leant against the steel handrail. "Who deciphered this?"

"Sub-lieutenant Carey, sir."

Carey was a paymaster. Schooly Hobbs had been in charge of decoding, but Hobbs was dead. Nick saw that the signal, addressed to him and to Jim Jordan, was an Intelligence report from Bandoeng. It read: "Enemy naval movements southward through Lombok Strait are now heavy and continuous. Units passing through are deploying westward along south coast towards Tjilatjap. A destroyer guardship is reported to have been anchored in the Alas Strait since first light this morning."

Destroyer guardship in Alas. The cork was in *that* bottle, then.

No question of fighting your way through, either. If you fired a shot, they'd have you on toast at dawn, if not before.

Take a chance on Lombok? Trust to the dummy funnel, try to slip through without being challenged?

He took the signal off the log.

"I'll hang on to this, yeoman."

He wanted time to think about it, before he had to discuss it with Gant or Chevening.

CHAPTER TWELVE
· · ·

Next time I'm sunk, Paul thought, *I'll drown.*

Brill had made it at the first attempt. And Mackeson had gone with him. The *Montgovern* had sunk, and Paul was on board *Ainsty,* the Hunt-class destroyer: he hadn't even got his feet wet. And at Narvik, two years ago, he'd been sunk in *Hoste,* and lived: so next time would be the third time *un*lucky . . . It was reasonable to suppose a man's personal luck couldn't last for ever; in fact it was a thought which had bothered him a few times when he'd been thinking about his father, when he'd got the feeling that that worst-of-all news was, in the long run, inevitable . . . Paul was standing, looking down at Beale, and Beale had made a remark about Withinshaw. Withinshaw's stout, dead body had been in the sea for two or three hours now, and it had been through remembering how it had looked when he'd last seen it that had triggered the presentiment, virtual certainty of his own turn coming—let alone his father's. It was logical to expect it: you couldn't go through this sort of experience often and expect to stay alive. To be alive as he was now, on board the destroyer, was something to be surprised at and grateful for. His last sight of Withinshaw's body had been after it had slithered down to the starboard side of the foc's'l-head. The sea had already been lapping across the scuppers although the ship seemed to have halted her long slide over and to be hanging, hesitating . . . The pause would be temporary, of course, and at any moment she'd decide to move again. Paul and Beale, clinging to the rail and stanchions on the high side—knowing by this time that the ship with the searchlight illuminating them was the Hunt and that she was closing in, coming to take them off the sinking freighter—had both been looking at the body, each thinking his own thoughts about it, and then happened to meet each other's eyes. Beale had shrugged, and Paul had

understood him to be saying that it wasn't worth trying to do anything about it, that Withinshaw was dead and what happened to his
corpse didn't really matter. Paul had been considering sliding down
there after it and trying to drag it up: for what purpose, what good,
he couldn't remember.

What Beale had just said was, "Soft as butter, was old Art."

"Is it a fact he had two wives?"

Beale nodded. They were on the port side of *Ainsty*'s iron deck,
abreast the pompom, which was perched up on a raised mounting abaft
the funnel. It was about midnight. *Ainsty*'s wardroom, which was below
the bridge, in the forepart of the ship, was stuffy with the crowd of
survivors in it, and he'd come up for air; he'd walked aft down the
starboard side of the ship to the quarterdeck, then back up the port
side, and found Beale sitting here with Short and the Glaswegian and
some other DEMS men from the *Montgovern*. Beale told him, in answer
to the question about Withinshaw's marital complications, "On account
of bein' so soft. Couldn't say no to 'em, poor old sod."

Paul put one hand up to the stem of the whaler in its davits, to
steady himself. There wasn't all that much motion on the sea, but it
was getting livelier. The *Santa Eulalia* was on the quarter, a dark bulk
with white foam along its waterline. She'd sunk one of the E-boats,
and the destroyer had bagged the other—which was cheering news,
but no swap for the *Montgovern*. A ship became a home, and you grew
fond of her without realizing it, and in this case the feeling of depri-
vation concerned people too—Brill in particular, and Mackeson as
well. They'd been inside the ship when she'd slipped under. They and
the wounded gunners, and four engine-room hands who'd been killed
when the torpedo hit, and little Gosling who'd been shot through the
throat, were the only non-survivors.

They'd known it was *Ainsty* floodlighting them, because after that
first inspection she'd begun signalling. He'd read the flashing light:
*When my boats are in the water I intend putting my foc'sl alongside yours.
Boats will pick up swimmers.* Boats had to be careful about getting too

close to a ship that was about to sink and might roll over on them. The Hunt had slipped hers, then manoeuvred her bow up beside the freighter's stem. By that time other men were crowding for'ard, and among them was Thornton, the cipher expert. He'd told Paul that the order had been passed to abandon ship, and Mackeson had sent him up here to make them leave her quickly; the destroyer's captain had been issuing similar instructions through a loud-hailer. *Ainsty's* foc'sl was higher now than the *Montgovern's* partly submerged forepart. They let two jumping-ladders down, and the survivors began to swarm up them, destroyer sailors reaching down to help. Paul shouted to Thornton, while they were waiting for the others to go first, "What about the doc and his patients?"

Mackeson was trying to get a boat alongside for them, Thornton had told him, and Brill had been trying to find a way of moving them. They were very badly burnt, and it wasn't easy; there was no possibility of getting them up to this end of the ship.

The *Montgovern's* own boats had been incinerated, but there might have been some rafts intact, and the wounded could have been floated off in them, Paul thought. Fit men would be all right: the sea was low, the ship was taking her time about going down and the destroyer was close at hand. As long as no fresh attack developed, while they were in this vulnerable condition . . . He'd wondered about going aft to lend a hand: he was a very strong swimmer and might have made himself useful. But only the wounded needed help; Mackeson was taking charge of it and his orders to everyone up here were to clear out as fast as possible.

Thornton said, "Go on, Everard."

Action, emergency, had seemed to improve the cipher man. Paul had climbed over, stood for a moment with his heels hooked over the second rail and the top one against his calves, and judged his moment to jump for the ladder. A few seconds later he'd been on the destroyer's foc'sl, with Thornton clambering over behind him. They'd been the last and the destroyer had already been backing off, getting clear.

Brill and old Bongo must still have been with the wounded in the saloon when the *Montgovern* had tilted her bow up and slipped down. The doped-up wounded mightn't have known all that clearly what was happening to them, but Brill and Mackeson would have. They'd be inside her still, in several hundred fathoms. People you'd talked to only a few hours ago . . .

He said, "The doctor drowned, with the guys he was looking after."

Beale looked surprised. "Doctor?"

"Army man."

He strolled aft again, getting a good ration of fresh air before returning to the stuffy wardroom. Beale's surprised query, "Doctor?" was a new sore in his mind. As if Dennis Brill had never existed.

There were some *Montgovern* survivors hanging around on the destroyer's quarterdeck; and torpedomen were hunched, muffled in coats and balaclavas, on watch near the depth charge chutes. The crew of the after four-inch gun was one dark mass trying to keep itself warm inside the gunshield: and it wasn't so very long ago that he, Paul Everard, had kept a watch on deck like that. It did *seem* a long time ago . . . There was quite a lot of rise and fall on the ship: here on the quarterdeck you saw it as well as felt it, as the destroyer's counter rose and fell against the pile of white froth astern. Aboard the *Montgovern* he'd been thinking of the sea as more or less flat: except, remembering again, for the way it had come slopping over into the scuppers, like a live creature reaching to get at Withinshaw's body. Poor old Withinshaw, who couldn't swim and wouldn't have had to, either . . .

He went back up the starboard side, in through the door in the foc's'l break and through to the wardroom. The same crowd was in there, and the air was heavy with cigarette and pipe smoke. It was a space about twenty-seven feet long—the full width of the ship at this point—by twelve wide: the starboard half of it made a dining area, the rest was furnished with chairs and a sofa. Paul saw Pete Devenish, John Pratt and Harry Willis, and Cluny and Harrison, both engineers. Most of them had had to swim, and were in borrowed gear, dressing-gowns and blankets, while their own clothes dried out on the engine-room gratings. Thornton was here, and the RAF man, and some others. He guessed that Humphrey Straight, who'd been given the captain's day cabin, would already have turned in. When Paul arrived they were all listening to a young, cheerful-looking RN lieutenant: and he'd just said something about joining up with the *Caracas Moon* at first light.

But the *Caracas Moon* was the tanker, which when last seen had looked more like a floating bonfire than a ship.

"Excuse me, sir. Did you say the *Caracas Moon*'s afloat?"

"Astonishing, isn't it? After she left the convoy she was torpedoed, and it let in a rush of water that put the fire out. Then she was near-missed again yesterday, when we were with her, and it stopped her, but her plumbers are reckoning to get her fixed up during the night . . . Anyway, we left her to it, and came to round up your ship and the Yank. Who are you, by the way?"

He'd glanced at the single wavy stripe on the shoulder of Paul's greatcoat. Paul told him, "My name's Everard. Taking passage to Malta to join HM Submarine *Ultra*."

"Submariner, eh? Well, I'm Simpson, first lieutenant of this tub. How d'you do." They shook hands. "Did you say your name was Everard?"

He nodded.

"Any relation?"

It was ridiculous, really. The middle of the night, enemies thick all round them, and a few miles back men who'd been your friends were dead, drowned . . . Mackeson saying, *Bongo, they used to call me. I dare say he'll remember* . . . Simpson had turned back to the others: "Now here's the point I was about to raise, gentlemen. The *Caracas Moon* people are just about dead on their feet. I suppose you've had a rough time too, but you can get a few hours' rest now, so—my CO suggests—how about some of you, or better still all of you, volunteering to move over to her when we find her?"

•   •   •

Dawn: with *Ainsty* zigzagging ahead of the *Santa Eulalia*, both ships rolling to a sea that had risen during the past few hours. The wind was force four gusting five, still from the northwest. White wave-crests streaked the darkness, and spray flew over the destroyer's port side and bow as she dipped her shoulder into them. Paul was on the upper deck, on the lee side of the funnel, with a group of the *Montgovern's* officers. Thornton and the RAF man were both prostrate with sea-sickness, and had refused breakfast. It didn't matter: the meal had been laid on early for the benefit of those who'd be transferring to the tanker when they found her. Finding her shouldn't be difficult—if she was still afloat—as *Ainsty* was equipped with RDF.

Simpson had told Paul last night that *Defiant* had, indeed, been sent out to the East Indies. A friend of his had been in Alexandria when the cruiser had left for Port Said and the Canal.

"I didn't know your father had become a cruiser captain, though . . . Bad luck for you, anyway—you'd have been hoping to see him, I imagine."

"Yes. I'd hoped to."

Nobody could count on seeing anybody. From time to time, things happened to remind you of this simple truth. You had to register it, be aware of it, and then shut your mind to it. He'd woken with the uncertainties in his mind, though: uncertainties here in the Mediterranean, others more distant. The sleeping or half-sleeping mind had no defence, it was only the waking one you could hope to take charge of.

He asked Harry Willis, "What odds, d'you reckon, on getting *Santa Eulalia* and the tanker into Malta?"

Willis shifted his feet, balancing against a sudden bow-down lunge. In a destroyer, particularly a little one like a Hunt, when the wind got up you really felt it. That was something else Paul had forgotten about lately. The fourth mate suggested, "Three to one against?"

"Steeper than that, I'd guess." John Pratt chipped in, "You're for-getting the Eyetie cruisers."

Paul asked him, "Eyetie cruisers?"

"A bunch of them's supposed to be coming to head us off from Malta. Now there are so few escorts left I suppose they reckon it's safe for them."

Out of Cagliari, he remembered. But that had been days ago, and Mackeson had said they were probably going east, lured by some dummy convoy. This was the worst of being a passenger: you heard only bits and pieces, scraps of information that happened to come your way. The sense of ignorance and confusion was annoying and frustrating.

"You mean the two cruisers that were seen leaving Cagliari, Sardinia?"

"They've joined up with others." Pratt said, "Your pal Simpson was telling us."

Willis said, "Call it *five* to one against, then." From above them, the pompom deck, an alarm rattler was sounding. And someone was shouting at them from the foc'sl ladder. It was a sub-lieutenant shouting through cupped hands over the racket of wind and sea, "Passengers go below, please! Clear the upper deck!" Paul joined in the unwilling shuffle to the screen door, into the enclosure of the foc'sl. If it was true that an enemy cruiser force was coming, you could reckon the chances of reaching Malta as nil, he thought. Another thing Simpson had mentioned last night had been that the third cruiser, the last of three who'd been intended to escort the convoy on to Malta, had been knocked out on that night when the *Montgovern* had been hit and left the convoy. The cruiser had been torpedoed, and he thought they'd had to abandon her and sink her. So there was only a handful of destroyers now—most of them Hunts, escort destroyers with no torpedo armament. The sort of odds Italians might rather go for, he thought . . . In the wardroom, Devenish was just hanging up the telephone: he told them, "Air attack coming. They've got the bastards on RDF."

Paul realized, looking around for somewhere to sit—and seeing Humphrey Straight arriving, standing glowering in the doorway because there was nowhere for him to sit either—that he'd never been below decks during an action before.

Ainsty began to heel to port: and stayed there, hard over. Altering course, under a lot of rudder, jolting and thumping her way round against the sea. He grabbed a cushion and sat down on it, on the deck in the corner near the pantry hatchway. Straight had done better: someone had surrendered the best of the armchairs to him. Devenish was stooping with a hand on the arm of it while he and Straight talked. Then he'd straightened, glancing round, and he was coming over to this corner.

"You with us, young Everard?"

"What d'you mean?"

"The old *Caracas Moon*. About half our DEMS blokes are coming over to her, but we'll be a bit short-handed. Might be useful to have you help organize 'em."

He nodded. "All right."

"Fine." Devenish looked round at Straight, and nodded. Straight, pleased-looking, nodded to Paul.

Christ. I've joined the Merchant Navy.

The four-inch opened fire. The mounting on the foc's'l was above this wardroom and only about thirty feet for'ard. When the guns fired, you *heard* them. There was no reason, he thought, not to go over to the tanker. Being a passenger with no job to do wasn't enjoyable. It was highly unenjoyable here, now, sitting and guessing at what was happening. It would be far less unpleasant in the open, and *much* less so if one was busy. Behind that feeling was a sense of enclosure, of being trapped—as Brill and Mackeson had been . . . There was a lot of gunnoise now, shaking the ship, but it was still all four-inch. He saw a new face in the doorway, hesitating, looking round genially as if it was about to introduce itself. It was a red face under brown curly hair, and the uniform had RNVR lieutenant's stripes on it. Then he saw there was red between the stripes. A doctor, surgeon-lieutenant.

"Hello . . . Captain Straight, is it? I'm Grant. I'm the sawbones."

The pompoms had joined in now. Grant was a Scot, and he'd be about thirty, Paul guessed. Those thumps had been bombs bursting in the sea not very far away. The doctor was telling Straight, pitching his voice up over the noise, "Well, we have *three* twin four-inch, you see, because we're a second-generation Hunt. The group one variety only had two twin mountings, you're right, they had a four-barrelled pompom where our number three gun is. Our pompom has its own deck up by the funnel. We have Oerlikons too, though, one each side of the signal bridge. You're safe as houses, you see, with us!"

She'd heeled again. You could hear the Oerlikons, as well as the pompoms and the four-inch. On the port side more bombs were exploding: he'd counted five, probably one stick. The doctor said, "These are Junkers 88s annoying us. But there's good news too—we've a surface contact on the RDF and the skipper's pretty sure it's the *Caracas Moon.*"

One isolated, very loud explosion, somewhere astern. Grant said, "Missed again. Never seem much good in the mornings, do they?" He looked at Straight: "Rotten luck, sir, losing your ship."

Straight glowered at him, and didn't answer. Humphrey Straight might not have been at his best in the early mornings either. And he *had* just lost his ship. Also, this doctor was a garrulous, socially ebullient type of man, the complete opposite to Straight, whose reaction to chitchat was to clam up, back off. The doctor had obviously been told by the destroyer's captain to come down here and entertain the passengers, and he was working hard at it too . . . Only four-inch now, and *Ainsty* was on an even keel for once, steering a more or less straight course, bucking and plunging to the sea. Straight was thumbing shag tobacco into his pipe: it wouldn't improve the quality of life for the seasick members of the party.

The four-inch ceased fire. The silence was ominous, leaving the imagination loose with no guidelines for guesswork. Then she was beginning to heel again: right over, turning in a tight circle with her starboard gunwale in the sea, by the feel of it. Juddering round: and everything suddenly letting loose again—four-inch and close-range guns all opening fire at once. Devenish yelled at Grant, "Do they get air and surface contacts on the same RDF set?"

"Different set for each job." The doctor leaned towards him. He looked glad to have something to talk about. "The type 271's for surface work, finding submarines and so on, and the 279's for aircraft. They had a type 79 to start with, but it didn't give ranges, only bearings . . . There are new types being developed every week now, you know."

She'd steadied, level-keeled, with all her guns still blasting. Straight blurted suddenly, "D'ye know as much about doctoring as you do about bloody RDF?"

"Lord, no." The Scotsman raised his hands imploringly. "*Please* don't get anything wrong with you."

Gunfire slackening. Grant was looking across at Paul. "You must be the submariner, I take it?"

It was a surprise, ten minutes later, to find the *Santa Eulalia* still afloat and apparently unhurt, butting along at seven or eight knots while the destroyer zigzagged through grey-white sea a couple of hundred yards ahead of her. A new day had been born while they'd been listening to the guns. The sky was high grey cloud, wispy and fast-moving, and the wind was whipping the wave-crests into flat white streamers. Harry Willis tapped him on the shoulder: "Other side. *Caracas Moon* herself!" Paul followed him in through the screen door and through to the other side of the ship: the weather side, wind gusty and laced with spray. Willis pointed: "Load of old iron. Our new home, mate."

The tanker was under way, but listing heavily to port. She was more than a load of old iron, though, Paul thought, she was a load of high-octane spirit, the stuff the Malta fighters needed, and diesel fuel for submarines as well. According to the late Bongo Mackeson. A light was flashing from her bridge, and he read "Master and chief engineer will remain on board but assistance welcome and relief of crew members and gunners will be appreciated. Stopping my engines now." The destroyer was under helm, heeling as she swung to pass under the tanker's stern. Paul heard the shrill of a bosun's call and the yell "Away motorboat's crew!" It might be a damp crossing, he thought. But there was too much movement on the ships for them to approach each other closely. The boat would have the benefit of the bigger ship's lee. The *Caracas Moon* would provide a very solid barrier against wind and sea.

"Everard?"

Turning, he found Simpson, the first lieutenant, in seaboots and duffel-coat. "You've volunteered to go over with the DEMS gunners, that right?"

"Yes, sir."

"Well done." Simpson looked round at the others. "Better stand by, now. Motorboat's starboard side. We'll be turning that side to her when we get up in her lee, but it'll take several trips." He said to Paul, as they filtered away aft, "You're a glutton for punishment, Everard."

Paul didn't see that it made much difference. This destroyer could be split open by a single bomb, torpedo or mine and go down in seconds. Tankers, being full of inflammable liquid, were feared: but the *Santa Eulalia*'s cargo—Pratt had told him—included fifteen hundred tons of high octane, five hundred tons of kerosene and two thousand tons of explosives including torpedo warheads. He didn't see that it could make much difference which deck you sat on.

Ainsty had hoisted the red warning flag, and gunners on all three ships waited, watching the sky, ready for whatever had appeared on the destroyer's RDF screen to come into sight.

In the boat—he'd come over to the *Caracas Moon* in the second boatload—he'd met Beale. Now, as the little convoy got under way, he had Beale in charge of all the guns aft while he himself looked after the four Oerlikons on the bridge deck up for'ard. He'd got one of them for himself, and fourth mate Willis had another. On the raised deck aft, around the funnel, there were two Bofors and two more

Oerlikons. Beale had put Short and McNaught on the Oerlikons, and he was operating one of the Bofors and supervising the other one. From Paul's point of view, since he knew nothing about Bofors, it was a good arrangement.

The tanker was fire-blackened, her paintwork scorched and blistered. She was also listing, several feet lower in the water than she should have been, and there was some talk of her back being broken—or that there was a danger of it, if she was shaken by any more near-misses. Boarding her amidships, on to her after section of tank-tops in the low part between bridge and funnel, had been simply a matter of jumping over from the boat's own level.

However, she was making about five knots now. She and the *Santa Eulalia* were abeam of each other, with *Ainsty* weaving ahead.

Malta sixty-five miles away.

High on the port beam—Stukas. Paul had only just spotted them when *Ainsty* opened fire at them with her four-inch HA guns.

Sixty-five miles at five knots: thirteen hours. It was now just after eight. So ETA Malta—Stukas and others permitting—might be 2100 hours this evening?

Stukas permitting . . . *Ainsty*'s time-fused shells, opening black against pale grey sky and turning immediately into brown smears on the wind, lined the Stukas' approach. Eight—no, ten of them, all in one group. He'd looked round, checking that all the other guns were manned and pointing the right way. Now he settled at his own, straddling his feet and pressing his shoulders into the curved rests. He pulled back the cocking lever, felt and heard the first round slide and click into the breech. Eight o'clock here, he thought—remembering what Simpson had told him about *Defiant*, that she *had* gone east—would be eight hours plus six, therefore 2:00 in the afternoon, in the Java Sea. The mind reached to what one knew, in sober recognition of reality, Beale-style reality, might very soon be unreachable.

Come on, Stukas . . .

•   •   •

By noon he'd lost count of the number of attacks. Nearly all had been
by Ju88s, only three by Stukas. There'd been plenty of near-missing. All
three ships, at times, had been hidden from the others by bombs bursting around them. The red flag had just run up the *Ainsty*'s yardarm
again, and Paul was remembering Jack Everard telling him that in the
Crete battle there'd been occasions when ships had been under air
attack continuously, with no intervals, from dawn to dusk. By that
comparison, he told himself, this wasn't anything to write home about.
You did get moments in which to draw breath, look around, smoke a
cigarette.

It was bad enough, though. The attacks got into your mind, after a
while. You had the images of diving aircraft, noise of guns and bombs
there all the time, like some internal film running which you couldn't
stop. Like the kind of replay-dreaming that you got sometimes, after
some daytime task of a repetitive nature, the half-asleep brain playing
it over and over . . .

Low on the port bow: torpedo aircraft. Real, not imagined. Italians:
Savoia Marchetti 79s. Withinshaw's voice croaked in his mind, *Bastards.
Fookin', soddin' bastards* . . . *Ainsty* was cracking on speed and heading
straight out towards them, a mound of foam piling under her stern as
she charged at high speed towards the closely-grouped flight of torpedo-
bombers. Her for'ard four-inch opened up. She looked small from here,
stern-on and with all that foam around her, twin four-inch hammering and shell-bursts opening, low to the sea, under the attackers' noses.

One was in flames, slithering down; a sheet of water sprang up
where it went in. Another was banking away, its torpedo falling askew.
Two others bearing away to port, getting the hell out . . . Another torpedo toppled in all wrong, wasted—from any Italian way of looking at
it—and there was only one Savoia left now. It had turned away to port,
but not running away like that other pair. It had by-passed the destroyer
and was now swinging in again to approach from the starboard bow,
the *Santa Eulalia*'s side. *Ainsty* was turning back, and all her guns were

concentrating on it. It was on the American freighter's bow, steadying on a low, attacking approach with the American obviously its target. The *Santa Eulalia*'s Bofors had judged the range right and opened fire. The *Caracas Moon*'s guns weren't going to get a look in, because by the time the range was short enough the *Santa Eulalia* was between them and the attacker. Frustrating. But there'd be time yet. Nine, ten hours, for sure . . . *Ainsty* was swinging hard a-starboard and her guns were cocked up, firing at maximum elevation.

Target overhead?

Ju88s were coming in shallow dives from astern: four of them, a pair going for each of the merchantmen. They'd sneaked up when everyone had been concentrating on the Italians. They were at about two thousand feet, in dives that would bring them over at about fifteen hundred, and almost right on top of their targets already. Paul aimed well ahead of the leader of the pair on this side, and opened fire, heard Beale's two Bofors banging away at about the same time. The bastards had been pretty smart, he thought, his gun deafening him and his head back from the sights now, watching the other end of his tracer-stream and hose-piping it towards the bomber's nose.

Hitting!

Bombs slanting down. All the guns in all three ships working hard. An explosion—away to starboard somewhere. Torpedo, he guessed: *Santa Eulalia?* The front Junkers was streaming smoke but he'd left it, to concentrate on the second. A bomb went into the sea close off the tanker's starboard quarter: a second and a third—horribly, unbelievably—burst on her, somewhere aft. He heard and felt the explosions, then almost immediately felt heat, flames behind him. The second Ju88 had let its load go. He knew, in physically sickening disappointment, that this would be the end of it—for the ship and for himself personally . . . There were no targets now except for that bomber leaving, the *Santa Eulalia*'s second one departing too and bomb-splashes subsiding right ahead of her. He thought—from just a quick glance—that she'd stopped. The gunners aft—where flames roared, heat so strong that even right up here you wanted to take cover from it—were his responsibility, and on the port side it might just be possible to get through to them. With a coat over one's head—might be . . . Harry Willis yelled at him, but he didn't hear the words. He ran to the ladder and started down—it led down in two flights, with its base at the walkway over the after tank-tops—going down it backwards, on that port side of the ship, his back to the heat and the fire's noise. One-handed on the ladder's rail as he reached with the other for a handkerchief to hold over his nose and mouth to act as a filter. Halfway down he thought, *I shan't make it. It's impossible and they must be dead.* He'd heard of people plunging bravely into fires, but he'd just begun to appreciate that there were degrees of heat into which the human body could not be forced. He went on down. He had to, because something might change, it might become easier down there. And there could be a man or men not dead. Two more steps backward, dragging himself down into the inferno, *knowing* he wouldn't make it, paint that was already black from an earlier fire beginning to run and blister on the bulkhead and the ladder's handrail already hot to hold.

"Bloody idiot, *here!*"

Willis had come down after him. He was grabbing at his arm. They were halfway down, where at the level of the accommodation deck you had to switch from one flight of ladderway to another. It made sense. Sense mightn't have prevailed if the fourth mate hadn't been here bawling it in his face. They were off the ladder, in the after promenade of the accommodation deck, when the fire got into an after tank and the *Caracas Moon* blew up.

He didn't know it, at the time.

It wasn't clear what was happening, or had happened. He'd go on down in a minute, he thought, and get Beale out of it. The other way about, Beale wouldn't have left *him* to burn. Beale was a hard nut in a way, but he was absolutely straight, a man to count on. One knew that, instinctively, it was a basis of—he hoped—mutual respect. His father had said, "I really do have to marry Mrs Gascoyne, old chap.

Very kind of you to be so concerned, but—" Beale had laughed. "Soft as butter, that's his trouble. Can't say no to 'em." When Paul came out of the dream-world he was flat on his back and staring up at a steel ceiling on which paint was bubbling and turning brown. Something was on fire beside him, the smoke of it in his eyes and throat; and Harry Willis was crawling towards him on his hands and knees but with his head up and his eyes fixed on Paul, his mouth opening as if he was shouting but no sound coming out. He looked either furious, or mad. Willis was on fire; the nearer burning was Paul's own great-coat. There'd been some kind of cataclysm in which personal responsibility had ended, everything had cut off, finished. Willis was totally on fire: didn't he know it? Paul was crouching beside him, beating at flames with his bare hands. Then he'd wrenched his own coat off—it was only smouldering—and he tried to wrap it around Willis, to smother the flames with it. Willis struck out at him. He was a big man and he *did* seem mad, screaming like a character in a film with the sound cut off. He'd pushed Paul clear, throwing him back, and broken free—to the rail, sliding his body over it horizontally and then letting go . . . He *had* been screaming, Paul realized; because he, Paul, had shouted at him a second ago and not heard his own voice either. He was stone deaf. Burst eardrums, probably. There'd been an explosion, she'd blown up . . .

But—afloat, still . . .

Where the ladder had been, the ladder he'd come down from the deck above, flames licked over paintwork on the blackened vertical bulkhead. The ladder itself was scrap, twisted iron, and the bulkhead ran straight down to the sea. Down there now was no fire, no ship. Sea washed soundlessly six feet below him. A littered sea, all sorts of rubbish floating. No heads, no swimmers. The stern half of the ship had gone, sunk: she'd broken in two, he realized, and he was on the for'ard half, which was still afloat. It was conceivable, he supposed, that this half might *remain* afloat . . . He'd have been dead by now, he thought, if Harry Willis hadn't pulled him off the ladder. Willis: he went back to the side rail, where the fourth mate had gone over, expecting to see him swimming, getting clear of the ship's side. But he wasn't, he was close to it and spreadeagled face-down, motionless except for the sea's own movement. He'd have a lifebelt on, under his coat—should have—and for the time being the coat and his clothes would be helping to hold him up. But face-downwards in the water, unconscious, he'd drown even before they were sodden enough to drag him under. Paul climbed over the rail. Hesitating for a moment, he saw *Ainsty*—to his left—coming up astern through patches of burning oil and a scattering of wreckage. She had scrambling-nets down, and a whaler just leaving her side. But from there they wouldn't see Willis, not in time anyway. He jumped, feet-first and well out, away from the ship's side and Willis who was still close against it.

Under water—for a long time after he'd thought he ought to be coming up—he wondered about Beale and the others who'd been aft. Whether they'd got over the side. If they had, the destroyer might find them, somewhere astern. The light was blinding and his stretched lungs were hurting as he broke surface and let breath go, gulped air, tried not to gulp sea or, worse still, oil. Willis was within arm's reach. Paul got hold of the large, heavy body and turned it over: it had already begun to sink. And the forehead was bloody, pulpy. He'd hit the ship's side on the way down—because of the list, the slant, and just letting himself drop like that. He'd been on fire, for God's sake . . . Paul got behind, under him, began to swim with his legs, towing Willis backwards away from the tanker's side. Above him, in the bridge wing, someone was leaning over, pointing downward and waving either to the destroyer or the boat. Probably shouting, as well, but Paul still couldn't hear anything at all. Be no damn use in submarines, he knew, if he was deaf. No use anywhere. He stared up, through the water and salt in his eyes, at the figure on the tanker's bridge—two men there now. He was wishing he could hear a shout, hear *anything*—when, up beyond them and against pale grey sky, he saw four Spitfires in tight formation circling above the ships. He couldn't hear *them*, either.

•   •   •

On board the destroyer—whose whaler had picked him and Willis up, after which they'd been inboard in what had seemed about five seconds —Paul assured the doctor, Grant, that he was perfectly all right except for the fact that he couldn't hear. Grant examined him, then wrote on a signal-pad, "Temporary flattening of the eardrums. Should correct itself quite quickly." He didn't look as if he believed it, though. Paul took the pencil from him and wrote, "Willis?" The answering scrawl read, "Unconscious. Head injury. You rest now." Willis had been in the sickbay, and Paul had been lent the navigator's cabin. He wasn't sure, and couldn't remember drinking anything except a mug of coffee, but the doctor might have given him some kind of sedative, because he did go out like a light; and Grant had been right about the eardrums, because after a short, heavy sleep he was woken by the ship's guns firing at more aircraft. Either he'd dreamt about seeing Spitfires, or they must have left . . . Wrapping himself in a blanket, he went into the wardroom: its sole occupant was Thornton, reclining on the sofa. The cipher expert woke up, and asked Paul why he wasn't on board the *Caracas Moon*.

He didn't mind Thornton now. When the *Montgovern* had been sinking he'd seemed quite human. Thornton asked him, "Why are you wearing a blanket, for God's sake?"

"D'you have a cigarette?" He had to explain it all. While he was doing so, he smoked the cigarette and got dressed. There was a heap of gear in the corner, stuff that had been borrowed while the borrowers' clothes had been drying out, as Paul's were drying now. He selected grey flannel trousers, a collarless shirt and a white submarine sweater, and seaboots with seaboots stockings in them. The boots were tight, so he discarded the stockings, and the trousers were short but it didn't matter, they were tucked into the boots anyway. There was an oilskin coat on a hook outside the wardroom door, and he borrowed that too on his way out. The guns had ceased fire, by this time.

He went to the sickbay first, to check on Harry Willis, but the fourth mate was still in coma. And no other swimmers had been picked up, so far as the doctor knew. Simpson, whom Paul ran into in the lobby outside the cabins, confirmed this. There'd been no survivors from the *Caracas Moon*'s afterpart. Simpson said, "But the good half of her's in tow now. Did you realize?"

Half a tanker: in tow from the *Santa Eulalia*. Simpson told him, "Apparently she has seventy-five per cent of her total cargo in the for'ard tanks."

It had taken an hour to get the tow passed—a manilla hawser from the *Santa Eulalia*'s stern to the tanker's bow, and a wire linking the *Caracas Moon*'s after end—which was now just behind her bridge, where she'd broken in two cleanly at the bulkhead, which was holding—to *Ainsty*'s foc's'l. The wire, with the destroyer's weight judiciously applied from time to time in this or that direction, made towing possible by holding the misshapen hulk on course; without it, the half-tanker swung around and pulled the *Santa Eulalia* off *her* course. The art, *Ainsty*'s captain's expertise, was to use just enough drag and no more: clumsy handling might part the bow hawser. Meanwhile, they were making-good three knots.

Simpson added, "Except for interruptions. In the last Stuka attack we had to cast off the wire, to get room to manoeuvre. Then it takes a while to get connected up again."

"So what speed are we averaging?"

"Well—up to now—about a knot and a half."

"How far to go, now?"

"Thirty-eight miles."

At a knot and a half, that would mean twenty-five hours' steaming.

His ears still felt muffled, and one of them had a persistent ringing noise in it . . . Simpson said, "You'd better come up top. Skipper wants to say hello, anyway."

Ainsty's captain was an unshaven, exhausted-looking man: bloodshot eyes stared at Paul from under a woollen hat with a red bobble on it. He nodded. "I've met your father. You've got something to live up to there, sub. Glad they fished you out so you'll get a chance to." He was watching the wire and the hulk of the *Caracas Moon*. He told Simpson, "Let him stay up here if he wants to. Out of the way somewhere."

Paul settled at the after end of the bridge, behind the starboard look-out position. He saw that the *Santa Eulalia*, who was towing the tanker, was herself listing about ten degrees to starboard. She'd been hit by a torpedo from a Savoia, Simpson told him. He remembered: he hadn't seen it but he'd heard it, just as those Ju88s had been coming at them. But a cripple towing a wreck, he thought, watching the two ships lumbering ahead: how the hell anyone could think it possible to keep this lot afloat and moving for a whole day, or even half a day . . . But the American freighter's weight, her momentum through the water, did make her a far better towing vessel than the lightweight Hunt could have been. It still seemed futile—inevitable that pretty soon one or both ships would be bombed and sunk. But on the other hand it was also impossible just to give up, go home, admit defeat . . . He remembered a passage from a novel he'd read a few months ago, when he'd been in *Ultra* in and around the Clyde. It was a book called *The Empty Room* by Charles Morgan, and he'd re-read the lines until they'd stuck in his memory, and with an effort he could recall them now: "Because the security of tomorrow was gone, the long, binding compulsion of past and future took possession of the English mind. Not to yield ceased to be heroic because to yield had become impossible." It was exactly like that: you were in it and you had to go through with it, as long as there was strength to move. This convoy operation seemed to have become disjointed and haphazard; but this was only one fragmented section of it, there'd be other struggles elsewhere, ships like badly wounded men just managing to crawl on, with Malta like a magnet drawing them. Morgan's words hit the nail on the head: there was no question of heroics, only of a one-way street and a driving impulse.

He asked Simpson about the Spitfires. And they *had* been here—Spitfires from Malta. Simpson thought they'd be back again in the morning, probably. It had almost certainly been due to their presence earlier that there'd been an hour's respite from attack while the tow had been passed and the ships had got themselves under way again. Since the Spits had flown off there'd been two attacks, and the Stukas had come with an escort of fighters—Messerschmitts—over them. Stukas on their own made easy meat for fighters: but on that evidence, when the Spitfires did return these ships couldn't count on anything like total protection, because the bombers would probably have *their* escorts.

RDF had hostile aircraft on the screen. Simpson muttered, "Here we go again. Keep your head down, sub." He moved away, into the forepart of the bridge.

"Aircraft red three-oh, angle of sight one-five, Junkers 88s!"

The guns would be swinging to that bearing and elevation. He heard the captain tell Simpson, "I'll try to keep the tow intact this time, number one."

"Aye aye, sir."

"Messenger—give Sub-Lieutenant Everard a battle-bowler."

"RDF reports second formation right ahead, closing!"

Two lots of attackers now. They'd want to end it before sun-down, Paul guessed. They'd be alarmed by the possibility of the ships getting under the Malta fighter umbrella by first light, perhaps. Not that it could be done, in fact—unless the *Santa Eulalia* was sent on alone?

Get one ship in, rather than lose two?

"Green nine-oh, torpedo-bombers!" The lookout in the bay below Paul had half risen from his seat, pointing. He yelled, "Angle of sight zero!"

Someone in the bridge announced, "They're Heinkels, sir."

"God damn and blast it." The skipper told Simpson bitterly, "Slip the bloody wire."

It might have been a month, by the feel of it, since the *Montgovern* had steamed through the Gibraltar Strait. And he'd changed, he felt, in that time. Passing Gib, he'd been younger, too hopeful, too blithely confident, too bloody ignorant.

Hadn't Beale seen that, and laughed at it?

No *laffin'* voices now. Just guns' voices, all of them familiar. The destroyer's four-inch alone, at first, and then the American freighter's heavy defensive barrage. Her gunners were US Navy men, Pratt had said at some stage. The half-tanker had only the four Oerlikons on her bridge now, but every little helped. One Heinkel III went into the sea, and the torpedoes from the other two weren't seen after they hit the water. The formation right ahead turned out to be Malta Spitfires: they arrived too late to break up the Junkers attack but shot two of them down as they flew away towards Sicily. No damage done, only time lost. Time, ammunition, fuel. That much less aviation spirit for the fighter defence of Malta: that much more time to be spent at sea— tonight, tomorrow . . . Considering that he'd had a few hours' sleep last night and another sleep after his swim, Paul felt extraordinarily tired. Perhaps Grant *had* given him some sedative. He didn't want to go below, though; he'd sleep up here, he thought, when it was dark and the dusk attacks were over. He thought he might even be able to sleep standing up, if he had to. Like a horse: lean on the back of the lookout bay, lift one foot on to its toes behind you, lower the head and sleep. Even the guns mightn't wake you.

"Hello, there. Everard, isn't it?"

Ainsty's RN sub-lieutenant shook Paul's hand. "I'm Carnegie. How goes it? Ears okay now?"

Carnegie looked younger than Paul thought *he* looked. He also looked, if anything, more tired even than Paul felt. Everyone you looked at was in a state of near-exhaustion. These people would have been at action stations continuously, he guessed, for the last four days.

"Hear about the Italian cruisers?"

"I heard some were on their way south, or—"

"They've turned back. RAF recce planes fooled them into believing they were guiding some powerful force of battleships to intercept them. By putting out a lot of phoney signals, and so on. So the Eyeties have turned tail and they're legging it for home."

"That was smart work."

Carnegie nodded. "*Mare Nostrum* is Italian for Naples harbour. The *inner* harbour, actually . . . Now I've got to go down and see to that frigging wire. See you later."

He'd gone. *Ainsty's* gunners were training their weapons fore-and-aft and ditching empty shell-cases as she returned to her station astern of the *Caracas Moon's* fore section. She'd nose up close, and a sailor on her foc's'l would lob a heaving-line across for the eye of the wire to be attached to it. (In the tanker they'd have hauled the wire up inboard, while the attack had been in progress.) Then the wire would be hauled in and made fast; and then on again, Malta-wards, waiting for the next assault to come in, and with possibly only thirty-*seven* miles to cover now.

CHAPTER THIRTEEN

· · ·

"Stop together." Nick Everard put the telephone down and lifted his glasses for a look at the motorboat, which was lying waiting a cable's length on the port bow. Through gathering darkness he could see three men in its sternsheets: they'd be the boat's coxswain, and Lieutenant Wainwright, and probably the sergeant of that marine section. The rest of the Sasul RM party would be inside the cabin. *Defiant* was losing way, sliding up towards the stopping-point where he'd embark the marines and hoist the boat. He'd sent it over from the mangrove inlet just before he'd started to move the ship out; it had been reasonable to use the powerboat instead of a cutter this time, because the channel's hazards were marked with spar-buoys and Wainwright, who'd been in charge of the cutter this morning, knew his way in and out.

Nick wished he knew *his* way out. He'd weighed it up and made a choice, but the spin of a coin might have been as good a way to decide it. The Alas Strait or the Lombok Strait, both of them almost certainly patrolled. Heads or tails . . .

He'd begun extracting *Defiant* from her mud-hole just as the light was going. Breast-wires to the shore, hand-tended on both sides of the foc'sl and with the capstan running so they could apply tension this way or that as necessary, had kept her bow middled in the inlet while the wire to the stream anchor was being hove in on the quarterdeck. That part of it had been an awkward, inch-by-inch progress, but as soon as her stern had been out of the creek, and a leadline had confirmed that there were a few feet of water under it, he'd given her a touch astern on one screw, and she'd come out like a cork from a greasy bottle. A short churn of the same screw running ahead had stopped her then, while the stream anchor was weighed—a hose playing on it over the stern to wash half a ton of mud off it as it rose.

It hadn't been possible to turn her until she was out through the gap where, on the way in, Ormrod had buoyed a rock on each side of the channel. Nick had conned her out stern-first, very carefully and slowly, with Ormrod showing a fixed blue light from a whaler to guide him down the middle. When he'd got her out and clear of that gap he'd turned her inside her own length, using one screw ahead and one astern, while Chevening watched the bearings on the two spar-buoys to ensure that in the process of turning she remained over the same safe spot. Then the whaler shot alongside and was hooked on; as soon as it was clear of the water he'd had his ship under way, both screws slow ahead, following the marked channel to this point off Sasul.

Gant called from the after end of the bridge that the motorboat was out of the water.

"Slow ahead together. Steer three-one-five. And—Wiley—steer as fine as you did this morning."

"Aye aye, sir. Both telegraphs slow ahead, sir."

"Pilot, is it one and a half miles now?"

"One-point-four, sir. We overshot a little."

"Tell me at one-point-three."

Rounding the Sasul island and its rock surround, now, on the same track he'd come in by but in reverse. He was tempted to cut the next corner, and according to charted information he could have, but it would only have saved a few minutes. He'd been very lucky, he knew, to have got away with so much already. One should thank God for it, he told himself, not get over-confident and start taking risks that weren't essential.

There'd be risks enough that would *have* to be accepted, in the next few hours. Tonight, either the gamble paid off, or you lost everything. "Everything" being a cruiser and her company. The personal side of it, his own, didn't count for much and wasn't an element in his thinking; except he'd like to have seen Kate again, and Paul. He'd like to have talked a lot with Paul, tried to steer him clear of some of the family complications. Paul would make out all right, though. By tomorrow's sunrise he might have become Sub-Lieutenant *Sir* Paul Everard RNVR, but he'd wear that all right too, once he got used to it.

Sunrise here tomorrow would be only midnight in the Mediterranean. By sunrise there, it would be midday here, and by that time *Defiant* would be either in the clear—or getting on that way— or under a lot of water.

Cross your fingers . . .

He could do that with his *left* hand.

"We've run one-point-three, sir!"

"Stop port."

"Stop port, sir . . ."

The bearing on Paliat was all right. But on this course, heading almost straight towards it, the bearing didn't change much anyway. The log-reading was what you had to go by.

"One-point-four, sir!"

"Port ten."

He had to bring her round to two hundred and forty degrees now, for a leg of two and one-fifth miles. Then due south for six miles, which would take her clear of Sepanjang's southwest corner. And *then* . . . Well, that was the crucial decision. He'd made it, for better or for worse; and he'd used Gant and Chevening to help him in the process.

He'd sent for them to meet him in the chartroom at half an hour before sunset, when the marines had been recalled to the ship and were on their way from the two villages, the hilltop and the southern beach. He'd shown Gant the signal from Bandoeng about the heavy naval traffic in Lombok and the destroyer on guard in Alas.

Gant murmured, passing it to Chevening, "Seems to put the kybosh on both exits."

"What's your view, pilot?"

"Don't know, sir . . . It's—well, it's not *good*, is it . . . Might we go west, try the Bali Strait?"

He shook his head. "I don't even think much of *Sloan's* chances there now. With a stream of enemy ships through Lombok, turning west—they're all cutting across the exit from the Bali Strait, aren't they? If they're still coming through, that is . . . Another point, though—if they've bothered to put a patrol on the Alas Strait, the odds are they'll have done the same elsewhere."

You could just about spit across the Bali Strait. You could guard it with a rowing boat.

Gant was rubbing the small of his back, where the pain was. He asked, "I imagine you've formed an idea or two already, sir?"

"Nothing hard and fast. That's why I'm enrolling your brains as well. As I see it, we have a straightforward choice between the Lombok Strait and the Alas Strait. This signal's time of origin was just after noon. We don't know what time the observations were made—by aircraft, submarine, or shore observations, whatever—but we must assume, I think, that it describes the position as we're likely to find it. And on that basis, Bob—what would you do?"

"I'd forget Alas, sir. Because it's narrower than Lombok and we do know it's guarded. I'd go for Lombok—with your dummy funnel up, and hoping to be taken for one of their lot."

"Pilot?"

"I think I agree with that, sir."

It had been his own first reaction, too, when he'd first seen the signal. It was an attractive idea because Lombok was the nearest of the straits, and the widest, and the direct, head-on approach appealed to him. But there were some aspects of it he didn't like. He said, "The traffic through Lombok can't go on indefinitely. I imagine they're sending forces through to take Tjilatjap, cut off any evacuation and any ships that may be there. Perhaps put some troops ashore somewhere; but it's a phase that could well be over."

He hoped it was, for Jim Jordan's sake. But he was only prodding, looking for aspects he hadn't thought about already.

Chevening nodded. "It might be wide open, now."

"Would you leave it wide open, if you were a Jap? While you were taking the trouble to block Alas?"

"Fair point, sir." Gant said, "The fact is we *know* they're blocking Alas, and we can give Lombok the benefit of a doubt. If they've been rushing ships through there, they may not have got as far as putting a watch on it yet. You'd tend to watch the holes you weren't using, wouldn't you?"

"Perhaps . . . You'd just dash through, Bob, would you?"

"Well—if one went through at about twelve or fifteen knots . . . Not too much dash, but not looking too sneaky either."

Chevening said, "My feeling too, sir."

"And you may well be right." His own mind was open to the idea, at that stage. Baulking still at the thought of all that traffic, the prospect of having Jap ships challenging him, or sending other signals that he wouldn't know how to answer. Except by shining a light on their beastly flag, which in any case he wasn't keen to fly. The thought of a challenge and having to identify himself was the real snag. There were advantages too, though. It was close, and he could travel fast through it and be a lot farther south by first light than he'd be if he took the longer route via Alas.

But the wide-open, easy-looking Lombok Strait still gave him the shivers, for some reason.

"Do we have a large-scale chart of the Alas Strait?"

The folio for these waters was in the top drawer of the chart table. He lit a cigarette while Chevening thumbed through the labelled front edges and then pulled out chart 3706.

Nick leaned over it, smoking and ruminating. After a few minutes, he thought he might have found the answer.

"Right. Pilot—you're captain of a Jap destroyer, and your orders are to anchor in the Alas Strait where you can cover anyone like us trying to break out of the Java Sea. Where'll you drop your hook?"

The requirements were for water shallow enough to anchor in, and to be able to see right across the Strait. He thought there was one place more suitable than any other; and two other possibles that you'd discard in favour of the first.

Chevening said, "Either in this area—here, or here—or on this patch just north of Petagan."

"You can only be in one of those places, though."

"The Petagan area's ideal, sir. Good view across the entrance, ten fathoms or a bit less, and you'd be covering this Sungian Strait as well."

"Why not here on the east side, your other possibles?"

"Because a ship could slip into the Strait through the Sungian backwater and you wouldn't see it."

"That's true, you wouldn't. But if you were lying there near Petagan, what if a ship came hugging the east coast, down inside all these islands? Bob?"

Gant had been nodding, agreeing with the navigator's choice of anchorage. He answered, "Because that's a complicated passage. It's not even labelled as a channel, the way the Sungian route is. Also, I think if I was a Jap, I'd be expecting any Allied ship to appear from the west, not from that way."

"Exactly my own thought." Nick was studying the chart again, looking for anything he might have missed. But this did look like the answer. He might kick himself when at dawn tomorrow he found himself not very far south of the islands—because it *would* take longer . . . Petagan: he felt sure that no destroyer captain in his senses and with that purpose would pick any other anchorage.

Steering south now, at twenty-five knots. In five minutes he'd be bringing her round to a hundred and twenty-five degrees, which would take her across the northern approach to the Alas Strait at a distance from it of about thirty miles. After three hours on that course, he'd turn south. An hour of that, and *Defiant* would be slipping in between the islands of Pandjang and Seringgit, then turning southwest to follow a zigzag route between the mainland of Sumbawa and the island that fringed the northeast entrance to the Alas Strait.

Nothing about this plan was foolproof or guaranteed. By now there might be a whole flotilla patrolling the strait. Or there might be Japanese ashore in Sumbawa—in the act of landing, perhaps, in Labu Beru Bay for instance, which was an inshore stretch he meant to sneak through. If there was anything like that going on, he'd run right into it—just as *Perth* and *Houston* had run into an invasion force in the Sunda entrance . . . But so far as he knew, there were no Japs on Sumbawa yet, and while they were so busy with Java they probably wouldn't have time or forces to spare. Also, Gant had been right about an approach from the east being unexpected. That destroyer would have been out there to thwart any escape attempt by one British cruiser and one American destroyer, which the Japanese had known to be in Surabaya. The cruiser had sailed yesterday at sunset—heading west—and disappeared, and the destroyer had still been in Surabaya at this last sunset. The Japs would be looking for the cruiser, and waiting for the destroyer to make her run for it, but they wouldn't be looking for anything to show up from the east.

So the cruiser that had departed westward, and since grown another funnel, *would* be slinking into Alas from the east.

And *Sloan* would be on her way now. Jim Jordan's ship would be in the Madura Channel, going flat out for China Point, then Cape Sedano and the Bali Strait. In which, please God, there would be no guardship. Fervently, Nick wished Jordan luck.

But he needed some more luck for himself too. *Now.* It wasn't only the passage through that strait that he had to worry about. If there was a lot of stuff passing through the Lombok gap, at least some of it would be coming down past the Kangeans. So right now, and at any time in the next few hours, *Defiant* might find herself in the middle of it.

Chevening warned him, "Coming up to the turn, sir, for course one-two-five degrees."

Guns and tubes would be closed up all night. The last thing he wanted was any kind of action, but he wasn't intending to be caught napping, either.

"Now, sir!"

"Port fifteen." He called over his shoulder: "Yeoman?"

"Sir?"

"I want the Rising Sun hoisted aft, Morris."

"Rising—"

Morris had gagged on it, for a second. Recovering, he muttered, "Rising Sun, sir, at the main gaff—aye aye, sir."

Lack of enthusiasm: Nick shared it. Survival before scruples, though. It hadn't made him feel nearly so uncomfortable a year ago to fly the Italian ensign for a short while. It was perfectly legal, too, provided you hauled it down before you opened fire. He still thought, *Ugh* . . .

"Midships."

"Midships, sir!"

"Steer one-two-five. Have yourself relieved at the wheel now, Wiley. I'll want you on it again in four hours' time."

"Aye aye, sir. Steer one-two-five, sir . . ."

Nick looked round for Gant. "If we run into anything, Bob, which God forbid, I may need to floodlight that rag. Warn them on the search-light platform. But let them have an Aldis ready for it, not the big light."

He didn't want to light up the whole afterpart of the ship, which would draw attention to at least one obvious difference between *Defiant* and a Japanese Natori-class cruiser.

Gant came back. "That's organized, sir." He added in a flatter, quieter tone, "And we're flying the Rising Sun."

"Not for a minute longer than we have to."

"Course one-two-five, sir!"

"Very good."

"If you feel like a rest, sir, I could take over."

"Kind of you, Bob. But we'll let Chevening have her. Pilot?"

Chevening took over at the binnacle. Nick went to his new high seat, and struggled up on to it. Not too easy, with only one arm in use. Binoculars weren't easy one-handed either, for any length of time. Another source of irritation was that the wound in his face was sensitive, like a bad bruise, and he had to take care not to let the lens on that side bang against it; with one-handed clumsiness it did happen, and it hurt.

Gant moved up to the front of the bridge near him, and raised his glasses to look out ahead.

Stars, and their reflection in the water, and the phosphorescence in the ship's bow-wave and wake, were all that relieved the darkness. The ship's engines rumbled steadily, a constant thrumming that you felt as well as heard. From below this bridge, in the space that had been a wheelhouse and a plot, rattles seemed to be getting louder.

This first hour was the period when they were least likely to run into an enemy. Southbound ships steering for Lombok from east of the Kangeans wouldn't be likely to cross *Defiant*'s track until she'd covered the first thirty miles of it, on account of the wide spread of reefs up north of the islands. If there was any safe time at all, or near-safe time, this was as good as they were likely to get for quite a while.

"Bob. I'd like you to make a tour of the upper deck. Check they're all on their toes and understand our situation."

"Right, sir. I'll go round now."

"Good man. Ormrod there?"

"Here, sir." Lieutenant Ormrod had taken over the torpedo officer's job. Swanson's. Nick asked him, "Tubes on a hair trigger, are they?"

"Pretty well, sir." He added, "And Mr North's all-about, down there."

"You did a first-class job in the whaler, Ormrod . . . Who's that?"

"Me, sir. Bentley. Brought you a cup of coffee, sir."

"You must be psychic, Bentley."

Sandilands, the engineer commander, had protested about the twenty-five knots that Nick was again insisting on. He'd had his men working in the boiler room all day, while *Defiant* had been in the mangroves, and as usual he'd been working with them.

"Two-six-oh revs is putting an awful strain on our temporary repairs, sir. It really is a lot to ask for, after such a—"

"I know it is, chief. But tonight and all tomorrow, the only speed that's acceptable is flat out. If flat out's two-six-oh revs, two-six-oh's what I want. After dark tomorrow—if we live that long, and we *won't*, chief, if you fail to produce those revs—we'll ease down a bit. Twenty knots, perhaps."

"Make it fifteen, sir?"

"This isn't an Egyptian market, chief."

Sandilands blinked at him tiredly. He said, "It's a very old, cranky ship, sir, and she's been knocked about pretty badly. If we can't slow down, the odds are we'll *stop.*"

He'd nodded. "A lot will depend on *Sloan*. She'll need to conserve oil even more than we will. Let's talk about it tomorrow evening, chief. Meanwhile, I'd like you and your men to know that I appreciate you've been doing a bloody marvellous job."

Engine breakdown would be fatal, now. It was one of several things which, if any of them happened, would wipe you off the board.

It was 10:40. They were out of the partial-safety zone and the island of Lombok was about forty miles due south, on the starboard bow. And *Sloan*, he guessed, would be something like halfway to China Point.

Sloan's refugees were on his conscience. Partly because he couldn't put Jim Jordan's prospects any higher than his own now, and partly because he hadn't thought of asking whether there might be a Mrs Williams among them. He should have. Even if it was a thousand-to-one chance, when you'd been sending enquiries to places as far away as Colombo you ought surely to look at what was right under your nose.

He'd ask *Sloan* about her—he crossed mental fingers—when they joined up tomorrow. What a fluke it would be if the answer should come as affirmative. What a marvellous fluke, for Williams!

He *should* have asked about the girl. But his mind had been full— the Kangean plan, doubts whether his brain was working properly, engine repairs, the trouble with Jordan over the refugees themselves. That was what had really obscured the Williams problem . . .

Williams was mending well, anyway. All but two of the wounded, Sibbold had reported, would be back to duty before long. The other two would survive, but would need to be landed to hospital in Australia.

If . . .

To some hospital with Kate in it?

Kate: her eyes smiling at him. Eyes very much like Ingrid Bergman's. But they were better than that, they were Kate's eyes. She did have the Bergman look, though.

There was a change in himself—one, anyway—that he'd taken note of. He thought about Kate now, and hardly at all about Fiona Gascoyne. He'd wondered about this during the day, when he'd been half-sleeping in that oven of a cabin. It might be explained—unflatteringly—by the fact that the ambition now was to get to Australia: even to Perth, which was vaguely in the direction of Kate's home. Perth—Fremantle—same thing . . . So the mind—if this *was* the explanation—fastened pragmatically on what was—might be—within reach. Another possibility, less unattractive, was that when survival appeared uncertain your thoughts went to the things or people that mattered most to you. He was committed to Fiona—he *was*, he knew it and so did she—but if he was unlikely to live to do anything about it, then he could forget it because it didn't matter, he could let his thoughts loose to wander where they felt happiest.

He had one foot up on a projection in the front of the bridge, and his right elbow rested on the raised knee as a support to the hand holding the binoculars. Gant, Ormrod, Chevening, the yeoman and signalman of the watch, three lookouts in the bays on each side, the PO of the watch and a messenger and a bosun's mate, were all looking out, straining their eyes into the dark. Above all their heads were Greenleaf in the DCT and Haskins in the ADP, and their assistants. It added to a fair number of eyes.

Haskins had done a good job ashore on Sepanjang. No trouble, no casualties. Haskins was one of several officers and men who'd merited commendation in any report of proceedings that might come to be written. In the personnel area, the only problem was Bob Gant. In all respects except one, he was a very competent second-in-command. Because of that one deficiency, though, Nick had come to the conclusion that he'd be more suitably employed ashore. His damaged spine would serve as a good reason for recommending it, but—

"Ship, green one-oh!"

Gant's voice—low, urgent. And the DCT telephone buzzed. Nick had it at his ear and Greenleaf reported, "Cruiser green oh-eight steering north, sir!"

"Stop together. All quarters alert."

He couldn't use his glasses now because he needed the hand for the telephone link with the tower. Chevening had called down to stop engines: vibration ceased abruptly. *Defiant* still slid ahead, still showed bow-wave . . .

"Stand by all port-side tubes."

He heard Ormrod, at the torpedo control panel, pass that order down to Mr North, the gunner (T). Down on that side of the upper deck they'd be turning out the two triple mountings. If he had to engage, Nick intended to swing the ship to starboard and fire on the turn.

"Keep her stem pointing right at him, pilot."

"Aye aye, sir."

The Jap cruiser was crossing the bow from starboard to port. As it crossed, Chevening would have to apply port wheel, the object of doing so being to present a small, end-on view of *Defiant* for the Jap lookouts to continue not to see. It was contradictory and inconvenient that if he had to engage he'd need to reverse the direction of the turn, but it couldn't be helped because that was the way he'd want to be pointing after he'd fired.

"Tell them on the searchlight platform to be ready with the Aldis, but not, repeat *not*, to switch on without my order."

Ormrod reported, "Tubes turned out and ready, sir."

"Enemy is right ahead, course north, speed sixteen, range oh-three-eight." Three thousand eight hundred yards. Less than two sea miles. Greenleaf added, "I think he's Kako-class, sir."

Eight-inch guns, twelve tubes, about thirty knots.

"Pilot. At the first sign he's seen us, I'll want port screw full ahead and wheel hard a-starboard. If I shout 'Go!' that's what I want. Ormrod,

you'll fire six fish on the turn, spread from half a length ahead to half
a length astern."

As we turn, we'll be showing him his own flag . . .

"Yeoman, have the port-side ten-inch manned."

"Leading Signalman Tromsett's on it, sir."

To give a delaying, gibberish-type reply to any challenge that might
come flashing. The first spark of a light would be the signal to engage:
as *Defiant* swung to loose-off her torpedoes there'd be a Rising Sun
lit-up aft and something like *Knees Up Mother Brown* rippling out in
fast morse from that lamp. Every second's bewilderment of the enemy
would increase one's chances of hitting and escaping.

Chevening said quietly into the steering-position telephone, "Port
five." To keep her bow pointing at the enemy. Greenleaf muttered
through the DCT phone, "No indication he could have seen us, sir."

Not yet. But he might, at any moment . . . Nick thought, *I'll have
to be damn quick on that turn. Get the fish on their way, then hell for leather
out of it . . .*

No. You wouldn't get out of it. Not far out, anyway.

One-handed, he'd got his glasses on the enemy cruiser. Long, low,
two raked funnels. He thought, *I could have blown him out of the water,
by this time.*

Turn now, and fire?

No chance of getting away with it, of course. You'd never get
· through the straits. Or if you did, they'd nail you at first light.

Still—a seven-thousand-ton Jap cruiser for a five-thousand-ton
British one?

But there'd be no certainty of hitting with torpedoes. Hit or miss
Defiant would pay for it with her life and with the five hundred lives
in her. No strategic balance would be changed, no tactical advantage
gained. And the orders were to get *Defiant* out of the Java Sea.

Chevening had increased the rudder-angle to ten degrees, because
the ship had lost way and was less responsive to her helm now. The

enemy cruiser was hard to see, even with binoculars. It was still dead
ahead but almost stern-on to them now as it continued northward and
the darkness swallowed it.

Half an hour after midnight, he turned her south. By that time they'd
passed across the northern approach to the Alas Strait, and at a steady
twenty-five knots it would be one hour's run down to the islands that
lay off Sumbawa.

At 0115 hours he moved to the binnacle and took over the conning of the ship.

"Stay here, pilot. I'll need your eyes. Can't manage glasses and the
telephone at once."

They hadn't considered the complication of his being one-armed,
when they'd decided to forgo the refitting of a voicepipe.

Navigation was likely to be slightly hit-or-miss, this next bit. He
had to find and identify two islands, Pandjang and Seringgit, and pass
through the half-mile gap between them. Both islands, according to
their descriptions in the Sailing Directions, were low, without hills or
other distinguishing features. Pandjang was all mangroves, Seringgit
scrub-covered; and a number of other islands to the east of them were
equally featureless. Depths were said to be less than those shown on
the charts, and in the middle of the passage between the two islands
there was a nineteen-foot shallow patch.

"According to this, it could be less than nineteen feet. So let's keep
closer to Seringgit than to Pandjang. Not *too* close, mind you."

Because Seringgit's encircling reef extended a third of a mile from
its southwest corner.

"Bob. Chevening and I will be concentrating on pilotage. Looking
out for Japanese is your pigeon now."

"Aye aye, sir."

Chevening suggested, "Run the echo-sounder, sir?"

"Might as well. Ormrod—you look after the sounder and the log."

At 0120 he cut the revs to a hundred and forty, ten knots. A minute after that, Chevening had land in his glasses, on the port bow. And then ahead, too; and to starboard. It was all low, unidentifiable: a rotten place to have to make a landfall in the dark.

Chevening said, "I think we should come round to starboard, sir. If my guess is right, we're too far east."

And if it was wrong, they'd now head out towards the top of the strait, where the guardship was thought to be . . . He brought her round, leaving all the land on her port bow. Chevening had his glasses on it, muttering to himself as he tried to sort it out, spot gaps and match the sizes of different islands to the chart-picture in his memory.

It was now 0126. Meeting the Jap cruiser had put them ten minutes behind schedule. Schedule being simply the need to get through as fast as possible, as far south as possible before day-break. Now they were losing *more* time.

Sloan would be just about approaching the entrance to the Bali Strait. Jim Jordan would tear straight in at his full thirty knots, Nick guessed. The Strait was too narrow for any possibility of getting through craftily, unobserved. He'd take it head-on, and ready for a fight.

"On red two-oh, sir—must be it, I think! The gap's about the right size, and on the other side the land seems to go on for ever, flat as a pancake, so—"

"Pandjang." He said it flatly, to counter the navigator's excited tone. He must have been getting worried, he realized. He was sighting across the dimly illuminated compass: "We should come round to two-one-oh, sir."

"Port ten."

"Port ten, sir. Ten of port wheel on, sir."

"Steer two-one-oh."

"Then we'll have to turn due south to get through it, sir. Say half a mile after we cross the hundred-fathom line."

"You'd better check that."

Chevening went to the covered bridge chart table, and confirmed it, and Ormrod at the echo-sounder reported crossing the hundred-fathom line at 0141. Land to port, on the beam, was visible to the naked eye by this time, and after the next half-mile it was also in sight on the starboard bow. Nick brought her round to south, to put her through the gap. This was another half-mile run, and by the end of it the coastline to port, Seringgit's, looked dangerously close. But if you turned too soon you'd run into trouble presently with the reef that extended south from Pandjang's eastern end.

Chevening came back from another refresher at the chart.

"Time to alter to two-three-oh, sir. For seven and a half miles."

"Starboard ten."

"Starboard ten, sir . . . Ten of starboard—"

"Gets easier now, doesn't it?"

"Should do, sir." *Defiant* was swinging to her new course, which would take her down to Kalong Island. Chevening added quietly, "Please God."

"Amen." He said into the telephone, "Two-six-oh revolutions."

An end to dawdling. And they were only a few minutes astern of where he'd expected to be, so it wasn't too bad, so far. It was likely to be easier down there because there were some prominent hills to fix on, on the islands of Kalong, Namo and Kenawa. *Defiant* would be passing inside all three of them in the process of rounding Labu Beru Point, which was Sumbawa's northwest cape, and thus entering the Alas Strait proper. If there was a Jap destroyer anchored where he'd guessed it would be, there'd be seven or eight miles of open water between them as she rounded the point.

He'd slow down again, for that stretch. The bow-wave of a ship moving at speed was the real give-away, in the dark.

Sloan would be right in *her* strait, now. In the top of it where it was only three thousand yards or less from shore to shore.

•   •   •

"One-two-oh revolutions."

Eight knots seemed about the optimum speed. Minimal bow-wave but acceptable progress, less than twenty minutes in the open. If there was an enemy there to see them . . . He glanced over towards the hunched figure that was Bob Gant: "Bob, ask Greenleaf whether he can see anything like a Jap destroyer at anchor on bearing—what bearing would it be, pilot?"

"About three-three-five, sir."

He raised his voice: "Nobody else need waste time looking for it. Could be a patrol anywhere, from here on."

The echo-sounder was switched off now. Pilotage *was* easy. They'd had the hills on those islands, and there was another right on Labu Beru, like a big pimple on a nose. Also, off the north end of Belang Island, which was flat, was a two-hundred-foot rock pinnacle called Songi. All the way down the Sumbawan west coast, which *Defiant* would be keeping close to, the chart showed hills and headlands; and a bonus was a southward-running two-knot tide.

It was time, he thought, for some *bad* luck. So be ready for it . . .

For a signal, perhaps. An enemy report, from *Sloan*. He and Jordan had agreed that if either of them ran into trouble, they'd let out a squawk, to let the other know. Then the survivor, if there was one, wouldn't waste time tomorrow looking for a partner who wouldn't be capable of keeping any rendezvous.

The DCT telephone had buzzed, and Gant had answered it. He said, "PCO reports two ships at anchor on that bearing, sir. They do look like destroyers."

Two, now. How many might there be elsewhere by this time? Patrolling, or waiting at the southern end. He hoped those destroyers had the same standard of watchfulness as the Kako cruiser had demonstrated . . . He said to Chevening, "You guessed right, pilot."

"With some prompting, sir."

Chevening had been doing rather well, Nick thought. Finding the gap between the islands an hour ago hadn't been at all easy. Chevening had made a judgement, stuck his neck out, and he'd been proved right. He had the makings of something after all, it seemed. Nick called over to Gant, "Tell Greenleaf to keep an eye on the destroyers and report any sign of life."

There was a small island called Paserang to the north of Belang, and they'd have that between them and the guardships before they got behind the bigger one. A few minutes' less exposure . . . Songi, the tall rock, was abeam now, about one mile to starboard. Chevening suggested, "We could come round, sir."

"To what?"

"Two-one-oh, sir. It would take us all the way down to that lower point—Belusan."

He told Wiley, "Starboard five, steer two-one-oh."

With the tide to help her, *Defiant* was making ten knots over the ground. In five minutes' time, when she was behind Paserang, he'd increase to revs for twenty-five knots, and she'd make twenty-seven. There'd be no cover after they left Belang Island astern. He'd just hug the coast, holding his ship against its blackness. He asked Chevening, "Off that point we're now heading for—"

"Belusan, sir."

"There's a small island to look out for, isn't there?"

"Just south of it, sir. If we turn to one-six-three when Belusan's abeam we'll be all right."

They reached that turning-point within a few minutes of 0300. Two minutes later the little island was abeam to starboard. In fact as they passed it it turned out to be twins. The course of a hundred and sixty-three degrees led them into a bay called Talliwang, which had a good hill just behind it to take bearings on. The turn was to starboard now, for a five-mile run to the next headland, Tanjung Benete.

Sloan would be in widening water now, the opening funnel-shape of the Bali Strait as she pounded southward. If she ran into opposition Jordan's signal would be addressed to Bandoeng, but primarily for

Defiant's information. The same would apply the other way about. Codes could be broken, and you didn't want to advertise the fact that another ship was on the run.

"Course two-two-oh, sir."

"Very good." Nick told Gant, "It gets narrower ahead. Tell Greenleaf that if there's a patrolling destroyer anywhere, this is where I'd expect it."

It was probable that there would be. By a miracle, they'd escaped being sunk by that cruiser, and miracles were rationed. At any second, gunfire could split the darkness. You had to be on your toes, geared-up. A few seconds' hesitation, when the moment came, could finish you . . . He was taut, tense with readiness: the wound on his face itched from the irritation of sweat running down inside the dressing.

Tanjung Benete was abeam before 3:30. Right opposite it, eight miles away, was the southeast corner of Lombok. And nine miles ahead, after he'd brought her round to a course of a hundred and ninety degrees, was the southwest corner of Sumbawa. At that point, in another nine miles, *Defiant* would emerge from the Alas Strait. In fact she'd be leaving the Pacific, entering the Indian Ocean.

Nine miles could look like ninety, when they lay ahead of you.

"Pilot. If you had the same job down at this end—to anchor as guardship—where would you do it?"

"It's all deep water, sir."

"No little bays inshore?"

"I'll check it, sir." He went to the chart. There was a canvas hood over it, and a light you could switch on inside when the hood was lowered behind you. New, stiff canvas now. Nick guessed that those destroyers would probably have been anchored to save fuel. The Japs had come a long way south in a very short time, and until they got their fuelling arrangements set up in places like Sumatra—where the installations had been wrecked and set on fire—they'd be wanting to conserve supplies. Chevening came back and told him that there were three suitable inshore anchorages, three bays in the strip of coastline that lay immediately ahead of them.

They'd all be within two miles of *Defiant*'s track down-coast, and only after she'd passed each headland would it be possible to see into the bay. Unless Greenleaf, with the tower's extra height, might see over any of the promontories. Nick told Gant to warn Greenleaf about it.

To starboard, a sea-mist clung to the black surface. To port, the first of the headlands was already looming close. He ought to have considered this possibility before, he realized, been prepared for it. Not that there was much preparing that anyone could do. But he should still have seen it: seen those bays open to the strait, with clear views across it . . .

"DCT reports this bay's empty, sir."

Two to go.

"What's that hill, pilot?"

"It's called Maloh, sir. Same name for the headland." It was the next one, on the bow. Chevening added, "The bay on the other side of it's about the most likely one, sir. Good wide entrance."

"Be ready with torpedoes either side, Ormrod."

"Standing by, sir."

Overdue bad luck didn't *have* to be an ambush behind that headland. It could come from patrolling ships out to starboard. The straits were about nine miles wide at this end.

Maloh loomed black against the stars to port. It was about a thousand feet high, massive-looking on its steep-to, craggy headland. About half a mile away. *Defiant*'s wash, which was powerful at this speed, would be following in a rush of wave-action along those rocks. Passing the headland: the blackness of it abeam to port—now . . .

"Can't see anything in there, sir."

"Bay's empty, sir!"

One more to go. The next headland was clear to see. As you passed one, there was always another. And beyond it was the third potential anchorage. The headland—Chevening said it was called Tanjung Amat— was coming up on the beam at 0342. Its rocky cliff-face was pale, yellowish-looking in the dark; and there was a group of hills behind it, a corrugation against the sky. To the south—opening to them suddenly as the light-coloured rocks drew aft and vanished in the dark—was the last of the three bays . . . Gant had his glasses trained into it. In the tower, Greenleaf's much more powerful ones would be probing too.

Gant answered the telephone. He muttered, "Very good," and told Nick, "This one's clear too, sir."

Incredible . . . But there, two miles on the bow, was the last headland, tall and stark against blue-black sky, the last landmark in this Alas Strait. Relief was tinged with a feeling of surprise amounting to suspicion: the feeling that there had to be some snag, something still in store . . . That point—it was called Mangkung—formed the southern arm of the wide bay, this third one in which he'd been expecting to find enemies. Who, evidently, must have their hands full elsewhere, he thought—probably on Java's south coast . . . He said into the steering-position telephone, "Port five. Steer one-eight-oh."

Due south. The course to the rendezvous with *Sloan*—of whom no news was good news . . . You had first to survive the dawn, and then to live through several hours of daylight that would be spent within a few minutes' flying distance of the Bali airstrip. He'd foreseen this moment: the moment when it would occur to him that if he'd come down through Lombok he'd be twenty or thirty miles farther south by now.

Jim Jordan, by this time, ought to be right out of the Bali Strait. He'd be about a hundred and twenty miles away, steering southeast at thirty knots. The two ships' courses were converging and they'd meet at about noon, two hundred miles south.

There'd been no signal. The American destroyer *must* have got through.

Dawn, now, would be the danger time. Sunrise, and then every minute after it until the damn thing went down again tonight. For *Defiant* and for *Sloan* too, it was going to be a nervy day.

"Course one-eight-oh, sir!"

"Very good. You can hand over the wheel now, Wiley."

"Aye aye, thank you, sir!"

Chevening said quietly, diffidently, "I'd—like to congratulate you, sir."

He glanced, surprised, at the tall, angular silhouette of his navigator. Chevening was congratulating him, he realized, on having brought *Defiant* out through the strait. As if that was the end of it—or *an* end, on its own. It had seemed like the biggest hurdle, of course, the real gauntlet, when they'd been on the other side of it. He'd forgotten, because that stage was done with and one's thinking moved on, ahead of whatever was happening at any given moment—let alone what had *already* happened . . . He told Chevening, "Could be a little premature, pilot. Say it again at sunset, will you?"

Forty miles farther south, he rested in his high chair and watched a faint paling in the eastern sky. The fingertips of dawn's left hand. How did it go? "Awake, my little ones, and fill the cup . . ."

Splice the mainbrace tonight, if the good luck lasted?

But—he thought—if it held, if they were still afloat and plugging south when the sun went down again, would there be cause for celebration? For the fact that *Defiant's* and *Sloan's* names had not been added to the heartbreaking list of ships and ships' companies who'd been lost—to no good purpose—in the Java Sea? Would that be a reason for self-congratulation?

It was a time for mourning, he thought. And for anger. The names of those ships ran through his mind. The destroyers whom he'd known well, shared actions with in the Mediterranean; and *Perth* and her captain, Waller, to whom the same applied; and Rooks of *Houston* . . . When he thought of *Exeter* it was like remembering someone who'd been very close, someone you'd loved who'd died.

Might that be why he'd dreamt of Paul being in her, that night?

Overhead, the director tower trained slowly round, watching the horizon as it became hard, definite. Nick had just put his own glasses up—resting that elbow on a raised knee, the only system that seemed to work—when Gant spoke quietly beside him.

"Stand-to at the guns, sir?"

Guns' crews were still closed up, but they'd been relaxed to the second degree of readiness, allowed to sleep around their weapons with one man at each mounting keeping watch. Now—Nick glanced to his left again, at the threatening dawn—Gant was right, it was time to stir them up.

"Yes, please, Bob."

Not that you'd be able to do much about it, if the Vals did come. Except make it a bit harder for them. He sat back in the tall chair, and watched the light grow.

CHAPTER FOURTEEN

· · ·

They came in low on the dark surface, and from the west so as to have their fat, slow target silhouetted against the first bright streaks of dawn. Savoias. Paul couldn't see them, but the director tower's crew could. There was shouting, down for'ard and back aft, as the wires securing *Ainsty* to the tanker were slackened and cast off, and *Jouster*, the fleet destroyer who'd turned up during the night, was wheeling, on her beam-ends in a froth of sea as she turned under full rudder and increasing power to get back there and meet the bombers.

"All gone for'ard!"

Banshee-like cry from the foc's'l. And a man at a telephone reported, "All gone aft, sir." *Ainsty* had been secured alongside, towing as well as guiding, helping the *Santa Eulalia* with the tanker's weight and adding a knot or two to the rate of progress. But she needed her freedom of movement now. Paul heard her captain order, "Two-seven-five revolutions!" He'd need to have her clear of the hulk before he could put his wheel over, for fear of swinging his stern into it.

The Hunt was surging ahead, diverging.

"Port ten!"

Astern, *Jouster* opened fire.

"Hard a-port! Full ahead together!"

Ainsty's four-inch opened up while she was in the turn. But the tow would slow virtually to a standstill now. The *Santa Eulalia* couldn't hold that stubby hulk to a straight course without assistance.

"Midships!"

Guns drowning other noise: voices, orders, were fragmented, sandwiched between their crashes. Pompoms were at work from *Jouster*, and Oerlikons' tracer arcing back, slow-moving, streaking the gloom. *Ainsty* picking up speed, hurling her slim hull jolting across the sea. Paul hadn't yet seen any of the attackers. He was trying to, using the tracer-streams as pointers.

Explosion: brilliant, dark-splitting, dark-into-daylight splitting. He thought—momentarily blinded by it—*Jouster* . . . And—still blind—*Don't count on seeing Malta* . . .

He'd woken half an hour ago with the question in his mind: Malta, today? He'd probably been dreaming about it. No memory of the dream, though, as he woke. His first waking thought was a realization that the motion of the ship had been entirely different. What had roused him—he believed—had been gunfire, but there'd been no more of it as he slid off the bunk—the navigator's, the same cabin he'd been allowed to use before—and groped around for boots and sweater. Thinking about the ship's changed and peculiar motion—it was jerky and unnatural—he wondered if she'd been damaged while he'd been asleep, might be under tow. But her engines were going strong . . . Might she have taken over the tow from the American? Maybe the *Santa Eulalia* had come to grief?

Shivering cold . . . He might have dreamt that gunfire, too. There'd been quite a lot of it last night, bombing attacks continuing until well after dusk and then two separate assaults by torpedo aircraft, the last one around midnight. He'd gone below and turned in at about 1:00, four hours ago. He'd been out for the count, and he was still heavy-headed now . . . *Ainsty* had just lurched to port and come up hard, as if she'd crashed into something. She definitely was towing, he'd thought. He buttoned the borrowed oilskin on his way up to the bridge. Time, somehow, inverted and upside-down: through sleeplessness, long periods of action, uncertainty, total absence of routine, regular mealtimes and so on. Also, time was relative, if it existed at all. Time was the distance to Malta, how long since the last attack, how long before the next one.

Earlier, there'd been a moon, but he'd found that it was down now. And the reason for the strange motion became obvious as soon as he got up to bridge level and into the cold pre-dawn air: *Ainsty* had put herself alongside the hulk of the *Caracas Moon*, her starboard side against the tanker. From the place he'd occupied before, behind the starboard lookout bay, his downward view had been on to the flat tank-tops: a short way aft, the tanker's bridge was ten or twelve feet higher than the destroyer's. At about this level, back there, was the deck he'd jumped from after Harry Willis had saved his life.

That was a truth. If Willis hadn't pulled him off the ladder he'd have been either spread like jam across the bulkhead or tangled into its twisted steel. He wanted to know how Willis was. There'd been no news of him last night when he'd gone below to turn in.

It was the strain on the wires linking the destroyer and the tanker that had been producing the jerky, tugging effect. He stared aft at the black rectangle that was the *Caracas Moon's* bridge, and imagined Humphrey Straight standing there beside the useless wheel, sucking at his pipe, thinking about whatever wordless men like Straight did think about. Gardening, or greyhounds, or something quite unlikely . . . There wouldn't be much for Straight to do, except see the wires here and up for'ard were tended, and the four Oerlikons manned and ammunitioned, and he'd have Devenish to help him with that; but he was the only master of the *Caracas Moon's* remains now, since her own captain had been transferred to *Ainsty* last night in a condition of total exhaustion. He was below, in *Ainsty's* captain's cabin.

"Kye, sir?"

"Why, thanks!"

Exactly what he'd needed. The sailor—it was a bridge messenger or a bosun's mate—brought him an extremely hot enamel mug. "You're the officer as was in the 'oggin, ain't you?"

He nodded. Sipping, burning his lips. "Was there some action, short while ago?"

"Aircraft, sir. They was on the 279, then we could 'ear 'em, but never got a good look at 'em. When we opened up they buggered off like." He'd added, "Be dawn soon. We'll 'ave 'em all back then, I reckon."

They'd got them back *now* . . .

But *Jouster* was all right. The explosion had been beyond her and it had been a bomber going up, or rather the torpedo in its rack under a bomber's fuselage. The effect of a torpedo warhead exploding in the open was spectacular, and that plane's pilot wouldn't have known much about it. Paul's eyes were only just back to normal. There was another aircraft in trouble, a shoot of flame along a tilted wing, heavy-looking body stalling, tracer flowing at it in smooth bright curves and a Savoia rising across *Ainsty*'s bow, turning away to port and straining for height—there'd be a torpedo in the sea, somewhere or other. Probably several. They wouldn't do much good—or harm—from astern though; if the Savoias hadn't been picked up by RDF, or seen from the director tower—whatever had happened, he hadn't heard the start of it— they'd have turned out on to the quarters, he guessed, flown up and then turned in to launch their fish from somewhere near the beams. Perhaps, if they'd seen *Jouster* guarding this side, from the south. She was over on that quarter now, still in action. *Ainsty*, lacking any target, had ceased fire, and her captain was bringing her round to port.

"Two-four-oh revolutions. Midships."

He'd have to catch up before he could take her back alongside and get the tow moving again. They'd been making something like four to five knots, Paul thought, when he'd come up, and depending on how much ground had been covered during the night there couldn't, surely, be more than about twenty miles to go.

Jouster had ceased fire. So that was one more attack beaten off. But it wouldn't be long before the light came.

"Slow together. Steer one-oh-two."

Ainsty was sliding up into the black shadow of the tanker. Simpson came to the back of the bridge and leaned over to shout down, "Stand by, you down there!"

"Ready, sir!"

"What about the bloody fenders, then?" Turning, muttering angrily, he peered to see who Paul was. Then, recognizing him: "You all right?"

"Fine, sir, thank you. Do we have far to go now?"

"About twenty-two miles. They might be bloody long ones, though."

Six thousand miles east-southeast, Nick reached for the telephone to the director tower. It was just on 1100. If everything had gone exactly to plan, as agreed between himself and Jim Jordan, *Sloan* would now be twenty-five miles away and roughly on *Defiant*'s beam.

He asked Greenleaf, "Still not in sight?"

"No, sir. Nothing."

He put the phone back on its hook. Gant said, "May have found he couldn't make his thirty knots after all, sir."

"That could be it."

There was no reason, he assured himself, to think the worst. Not yet. Plenty of things could have happened to cause slight delay. As Gant had suggested, *Sloan*'s engine repairs might not have come up to expectations. Or if there'd been Japs around—south of the Bali Strait, ships coming out of Lombok and heading west across Jordan's track—he might have made a detour, or had to creep out slowly, or—

Or this, or that. The trouble was, if he'd been *much* delayed, one might conclude that he couldn't have come out of the Bali Strait by sunrise. You couldn't have it both ways, unfortunately. If he hadn't, he wouldn't be coming out of it at all.

One should be able to switch one's mind off, at times like this. Go back into what Sibbold had called a "coma." Specialist's word for "unconscious" . . .

"Bob."

"Yes, sir?"

"We can dispense with the dummy funnel now. Lower it, and have it dismantled."

At first light, as soon as he'd been satisfied that the sky and the sea were clear, he'd told them to strike the Japanese ensign. Petty Officer Morris had asked him eagerly, "Permission to shove it in the galley fire, sir?"

"If it'll give you any satisfaction, yeoman."

Hardly an approved manner of disposing of Admiralty stores . . . But he should have got rid of the extra funnel sooner, he realized. American submarines were likely to be operating in these waters now, and if one of them got *Defiant* in its periscope and mistook her for a Natori . . .

Sloan. It was quite possible that a ship could be hit so suddenly and devastatingly that she'd have no chance to get a signal out. A W/T operator could bungle it, or panic, not stay long enough to tap it out . . . A mine or a torpedo: sudden, overwhelming, and immediate destruction . . . In his memory he saw Jim Jordan's shrug, and heard that laconic dismissal of all the disasters that had lain ahead and which both of them had foreseen: *However* . . .

How long ago, that conversation over a glass of Laphroaigh? Ten days? A lifetime?

Gant said, "The funnel's coming down now, sir."

Poor old Bob. It was rotten to like a man, have him with you, and be intending to ditch him. Bob Gant was a reliable, efficient officer, as well as a thoroughly decent character to have around. The only thing that was wrong with him—apart from his cranky spine—was this fear of responsibility, the reluctance to take command. A number two had to be equipped and ready to become number one; it was part of his *raison d'être*. Gant wasn't up to it, for some reason. You couldn't let it pass, once you knew it. If you were Nick Everard you could turn a blind eye to the burning of a flag worth a few shillings, but you could not connive at risking a ship and a ship's company, risking their being left in the hands of someone who might let them down. To be kind to Bob Gant, you'd have to endanger others.

That back trouble of his was a liability anyway, entirely valid as a reason to recommend shore employment. Besides, he'd get used to it, and his family would be pleased. Bob had a wife and children in Hampshire somewhere.

Extraordinary that one could begin to think about this sort of thing now. Of a future, and places like Hampshire, and next month, next year . . .

Could Jim Jordan?

Not a thing in sight. Only an enormous circle of blinding-bright blue sea under a dome of clear blue sky . . .

"Captain, sir?"

He looked round: Sibbold, the PMO, told him, "You're about due for a change of those dressings, sir. Could you possibly come down—"

"No, I could *not!*"

Sibbold was taken aback. Gant met his eyes and very slightly shook his head, warning him to lay off. Sibbold, with his job to do, didn't see it. He suggested, "May we do it up here, then, if you—"

"For Christ's sake—"

This time he saw the PMO's startled surprise. He told himself, *Steady, now* . . . He shook his head. "Sorry, doctor. This isn't a good moment. I'll—contact you later. How are your other patients?"

He'd made himself ask the question. Now he made himself listen to the long and detailed answer. Thinking about *Sloan*, and the refugees he'd refused to take.

It was 11:20 when Sibbold left the bridge. Nick asked Chevening, "Where would she be now, precisely, if she was up to time?"

Chevening went to the chart, and worked it out. He came back and told Nick, "She'd bear two-five-five, fourteen miles, sir."

So she'd have been in sight from this bridge, let alone the director tower.

The *Caracas Moon* was entirely hidden behind bomb-splashes. *Jouster* was alongside her now, with the *Santa Eulalia* still tugging doggedly ahead, *Ainsty* off the leash and placing herself wherever the current threat was coming from. Malta was in plain sight: low stone-coloured, stretching from north to northeast seven or eight miles distant. It was now 0800: the ships had been under attack sporadically since dawn, but it would have been a great deal worse if Spitfires hadn't been taking a lot of the pressure out of it. *Ainsty* was astern now, barraging over the linked ships with Ju88s overhead, diving, bombs coming like slanting rain and the sea rising white-topped all around the tanker's stern and starboard side. Around what *had become* her stern . . . There was a Spitfire patrol around somewhere, but these 88s had somehow avoided them. When enough approached at once, the RAF couldn't stop them all. One last bomb-load coming now, from a bomber trailing the first five. The guns were at maximum elevation and rapid-firing, *Ainsty*'s and *Jouster*'s and the Oerlikons on the tanker. The American freighter would be part of it too, but from here all you could see was the haze of gunsmoke over her. Paul was squinting up under the rim of a borrowed tin hat, but that Junkers was hidden in shell-bursts. Then he saw it again suddenly, a glimpse just as the bombs left it.

"Full ahead together! Port thirty!"

This destroyer, not the tanker, had been that last one's target. The Hunt was heeling to full rudder and trembling to her screws' thrust as she cracked on power. *Ainsty*'s silent now, no targets left. Astern the sea blossomed, lifting in dark humps that broke white-topped, the Junkers' Parthian gifts. She was heeling right over, twisting away from danger. Paul heard "Midships!" Third bomb . . . fourth . . . The fifth went in close to starboard, where seconds ago the ship had been. He felt the explosion through his feet, and the spout was so close that her stern swung into it as it folded, drowning her afterpart in foam. Her engines had stopped. Gunfire from the other ships—from the *Santa Eulalia*—petered out. *Ainsty* was back on an even keel, losing way as quickly as if she'd had brakes and slammed them on. The brake was the sea's pull, sucking at her. On her compass platform there was a lot of telephone and voicepipe talk going on: *Ainsty* wallowing, slumping in the sea as she lost all forward motion. There was already quite a distance between her and the group of ships plodding away eastward and making about six knots. But they needed her guns, the high-angle four-inch, to shelter them. They were cripples helping each other along. The American had been torpedoed, bombed, and at least once she'd been set on fire, and the *Caracas Moon* was more corpse than cripple. A corpse worth a lot more than any other ship, though, to that island . . . *Ainsty* and

Jouster had changed places earlier because *Jouster* was a bigger and more powerful ship than the lightweight Hunt, better suited to the towing job. She was about twice *Ainsty*'s displacement, in fact. They'd swapped round after the first series of Stuka attacks, just after first light. During that Stuka raid there'd been a near-miss on the *Caracas Moon*'s starboard side, and she was leaking oil, a long trail of Malta's life-blood discolouring the sea right back to where they'd been at dawn.

A signalman had gone to the starboard ten-inch lamp. *Jouster*—whose captain was senior to *Ainsty*'s—must have been waiting for a report, because at the first dot-dash of the call-up signal she flashed a go-ahead. The message that went over to her was "Expect to get going in about thirty minutes." *Jouster* acknowledged. The stern-on view of her with the blocky shape of the half-tanker beside her would have been baffling if you hadn't known what it was, and it was further complicated by an occasional sight of the *Santa Eulalia*'s upperworks beyond it. A haystack leaning on a Baby Austin, against a background of telegraph poles? The whole assembly was dwindling as it hauled eastward. It had to get right round the island's southern coast, then turn to port, northward, up towards Valletta, which was on the southeast coast.

Even that short haul, and with Spitfires helping, seemed more than one could hope to accomplish, with so much damage done already . . . A roar of engines overhead was sudden, startling: but they were Spitfires. Two of them, swinging to their left now to pass over the tow as well. As the racket faded, Simpson spoke beside him: "Minesweepers are on their way to meet us, and we're told we'll have Spits over us all the way in now. Things are looking up, sub!"

And he'd just been thinking the opposite . . . He asked Simpson, "How about us? The engines?"

"Not to worry. Some sort of blow-back, from that near-miss. I don't know, but it's fixable." He patted Paul's shoulder, and grinned: "You'll soon be safe and sound in your little submarine, Everard!"

It was now 8:35. And there were—roughly—eleven miles to go. He wondered if Simpson could be right, if one should allow oneself to

believe in what he'd said. If the tow could continue to make five or
six knots, with Spitfires to protect it and minesweepers coming out to
help—might make it in about two hours? Into Grand Harbour, in *two
hours?*

Bewildering. He was *believing* it. And thinking of Beale laughing,
winking at old Withinshaw, telling him, *There's some as like to look on
the bright side . . .*

He wondered what he'd do about getting new gear, uniform and
other stuff. All he possessed were the clothes he'd been wearing when
they'd pulled him and Willis into the whaler. They'd be dry by now,
but they'd also be salt-stained and shrunk, and scorched too, some of
them, and he had nothing else at all, not a razor or a toothbrush even.
Presumably one would be able to get an advance of pay, and a Slops
issue—"Slops" being stores you paid for, Admiralty-issue stuff. You could
get a battledress uniform from Slops, and socks and things. He wondered if there was a branch of Gieves in Malta. Simpson had gone back
to the for'ard part of the bridge, so he couldn't ask him. He hadn't
asked him about Willis either.

Spitfires were busy in the distance. Several times there were patches
of action, smoke-trails plunging seaward, as attacks were intercepted
and broken up. At 9:20, *Ainsty* got under way and worked up to twelve
knots, steering east to catch up on the tow. Fighters still up there, wing-
ing around at a few miles' radius. Filfla Island—a rock, three miles off
the coast—fell astern to port. Fifteen knots now: it took half an hour
to overhaul the others, joining them just as they reached the position
for the turn north, rounding the corner of the island. By this time the
two minesweepers had arrived, and were turning in to take station
ahead. Each of the stubby little ships had a three-inch AA gun and an
Oerlikon.

Hour and a half now? No—surely—*less* than that . . . He checked
the time: then glanced up, looking for'ard, where something was going
on. Binoculars were being trained astern: and he heard the report,
"Large formation, closing, sir!"

RDF report. He couldn't see any Spitfires now. Perhaps Malta's
fighter-direction people had already vectored them out to meet this
assault.

"Port fifteen!"

Ainsty's captain was bringing her round to cut the corner and close
up on *Jouster* and her charges. The *Santa Eulalia's* and *Jouster's* joint
efforts had dragged the *Caracas Moon* around. They had only to follow
the sweepers now, the local boys. *Ainsty* with her fifteen knots and the
short cut was closing the gap very rapidly.

Cutting the corner might be taking her through mined water?

"Alarm port, red one-five-oh, angle of sight ten, Junkers 88s!"

A quieter report added, "Fighters above them. Messerschmitts, I
think."

Lacking binoculars, it was a minute or two before he saw them. Then
the picture was a confusing one. Like midges in a distant haze . . . Well,
those were the fighters: ours or theirs . . . He found the bombers now,
and he was watching the familiar, target's-eye view of oncoming Ju88s.
He wondered if he'd seen any of this particular lot before: had seen that
one, or that, overhead yesterday or this morning . . . Withinshaw could
have named each one of them, he thought, the same string of names
for each. He counted two groups of four and another of about eight,
all at roughly five thousand feet. The Spitfires obviously had their hands
full with escorting fighters, and the Junkers were about to get a clear
run in. *Ainsty* had cut her speed as she came up astern of the others.
Guns elevated, loaded and ready, gunners' eyes slitted under the hel-
mets' rims. Tanned, tired, unshaven faces, red-rimmed eyes. Grey sky,
weak sunshine filtering through high cloud, grey-green sea, dun-
coloured island . . . The front-running party of bombers were pushing
their noses down, starting into their attacking dives. *Ainsty* weaving
across the stern of the tow, two cables' lengths clear of it. Over the
island more fighters—Spitfires—were climbing, heading south. *Ainsty's*
four-inch crashed: the for'ard mounting was trained to an extreme after

bearing to throw the shells up over her shoulder as she slanted across the tow's broad, swirling wake. *Jouster* had opened fire, and *Ainsty's* pompoms joined in too, then Oerlikons and Vickers adding to the din just before the attackers pulled out of their dives. Bombs started on their way: in slow motion, tumbling, then speeding into streaks, invisible. The splashes went up to starboard and ahead: *Ainsty* under helm, turning back to recross the wake the other way. At this moment her stem was pointing directly at the tow but you couldn't see it for the bomb-splashes. The entire area of sea between this ship and the bunch ahead seemed to be erupting. *Ainsty's* four-inch had shifted target—to engage the second wave of the attack, another group of four: but behind that foursome, Spitfires were dropping on the larger group. The Junkers back there were shedding bomb-loads and turning away, running for it: one spiralling, trailing smoke. Gunfire at crescendo again as the next four bombers came droning over: and releasing bombs *now* . . .

Most of them went in to port. One stick fell close enough to *Jouster* to qualify as near-misses. Then ahead, an explosion, a gush of flame, smoke pluming vertically: like a gas-jet igniting.

Santa Eulalia.

"DCT reports tow parted, sir!"

Smoke, tinged with the colour of flame, billowed skyward. The guns had ceased fire. The tow was broken, stopped, *Santa Eulalia* burning. *Ainsty's* captain had his bearded face at the voicepipe shouting orders that were inaudible as a Spitfire screamed overhead through dissipating shreds of shell-bursts.

By the dog watches, afternoon growing into evening, it had become certain that *Sloan* had gone.

One more name on that list of ships: with the difference that in this case he, Nick Everard, felt largely responsible. He should have foreseen that they'd have clamped down on the Bali Strait, when they'd known there were still two ships to get away from Surabaya and the Bali gap was the nearest exit. Even if they hadn't been alerted to the fact that four US destroyers had already slipped away by that route; and the odds were they *would* have caught on to it.

From as much as one had known in Surabaya, the Madura Channel and the Bali Strait *had* looked like the best route. So it could be argued that this retrospection was a judgement based on factors which had emerged later. But mightn't clearer thought, logical analysis, have pointed to this outcome?

He'd have taken *Defiant* out by the Bali route if she'd been able to get over the Madura shallows. It had been the discovery that she couldn't make it that had provoked that brainstorm, panic . . . The fact she was here now, well south and within a few hours of safety, was sheer luck. Luck, not good judgement.

Bentley asked him, "Coffee, sir?"

"Thank you." He took the cup, put it on the ledge beside him, lit one of his last cheroots. Chevening met his glance: grimly, with no trace of the congratulatory mood in which he'd started this long day. Everyone felt the same: the failure, loss.

And only he, Nick, knew about the forty refugees who'd have been embarked in *Sloan*.

However . . .

It didn't help. He could see Jim Jordan's wry expression, the slight twist of a grin on that wide-jawed face. He could hear him saying, "It'll be a great moment, making that rendezvous."

It would have been, too.

It had been a risk—he and Jordan had both recognized it—deciding to let the American wait that extra day. He should have insisted on her sailing the night before. It had seemed like a calculated risk, one well worth taking, for the sake of those few extra knots, but the entire situation had been so fraught with risks to start with that one had had no business adding to them. Twenty-four hours earlier, the Bali Strait might still have been wide open; and the big movement south through the Lombok Strait hadn't started.

You had to face up to it, accept your own share of blame, learn the lesson. In war, lessons tended to be expensive.

Face up to a courtmartial too, for not having engaged that Kako cruiser?

It wasn't inconceivable. There were individuals in certain quarters, hangers-on in high places, whose main concern was to make damning judgements from their armchairs. And it *had* been a close, difficult decision.

The DCT telephone buzzed. Greenleaf was still up there, although Nick had relaxed the ship's company to cruising stations a couple of hours ago. Greenleaf told him, "Ship's foretop on green seven-oh, sir—"

"*What?*"

He'd started, spilt coffee. Greenleaf said, "Looks very much like *Sloan*, sir."

The *Santa Eulalia* was stopped, low in the water and listing danger-ously to port. Smoke oozing from her internal fires drifted southeast-ward, a heavy blanket on the sea. *Ainsty*, secured alongside the *Caracas Moon's* starboard side, was sixty yards to windward of the American as they forged slowly past her. They were just getting the deadweight of the half-tanker under way again, *Ainsty* on this side and *Jouster* on the other, steel-wire ropes bar-taut and quivering with strain. You kept well away from wires in that state of tension. If one parted, it could slice a man in half.

Moving, though. Just . . .

It was getting the movement started that took most time and effort. The strain had to be applied carefully, increased slowly and steadily and the two destroyers had to synchronize their efforts. To hold the hulk on course, you had to continue to strike a balance.

Tugs were said to be coming out from Valletta. They'd been com-ing anyway to take over the tanker, but now they'd be redirected to the *Santa Eulalia*. One of the minesweepers was standing by her mean-while.

Looking down at the sea alongside, Paul guessed they were making about two knots. With about five miles to go. That was a guess too. But they had to get up-coast a bit and then turn to run down the swept channel to the harbour entrance, and it couldn't be much less than that.

Three knots, perhaps. Two and a half, anyway. And it was now just past noon.

Spitfires—several groups of them—were flying north, all seemingly heading in that one direction. He turned to look astern. At the end of the long shine of the oil-leak from the tanker, the *Santa Eulalia* lay motionless, bleeding smoke. It was the Spitfires' departure northward that had reminded him of her: the fact that she was alone and in very bad trouble, probably not far short of sinking, and that she seemed now to be losing the fighter cover as well as the protection of these destroyer's guns. He thought the minesweeper had gone alongside her, but it was on the other side of her, and he still didn't have binoculars. She looked very much alone, back there.

"Tugs are passing, t'other side."

A signalman had said it, leaning over to address one of the look-outs. Paul asked him, "How many?"

"Three, sir. Reckon it'll be a race who gets in first, them or us. If they can 'old 'er up, that is."

In the north, a tail of smoke extending downward was a fighter destroyed. It had the look of a Spitfire, but it was too distant to be sure. Astern now he saw the three tugs from the Malta dockyard chugging down the oil-path towards the *Santa Eulalia*. It would be filthy luck, he thought, if she sank right there, after as much as she'd come through. The signalman said, nodding towards the sky ahead, "88s. Sods don't give up easy, do they?"

There were dogfights in progress, Spitfires versus others, in the northern distance. This side of that action, lower in the sky, he saw the Ju88s. But off to the left again, climbing towards them, was another batch of Spitfires. He pointed them out to the signalman.

"They aren't going to bother us this time." Then he asked him—because signalmen saw signals, which a passenger did not—"Have we been told anything about any other ships arriving?"

"Only them two, sir."

"Which two?"

"The *Miramar* and the *Empire Dance*. They're both inside an' unloading."

"And that's all?"

"Well. There's this lot, now." He looked astern. "Except I wouldn't bet on the Yank making it, would you, sir?"

The tugs were getting their lines into her, back there. And this tow, meanwhile, was making a good four knots. Paul said, looking back at the American and crossing fingers on both hands, "She'll make it."

One hour before dusk, six thousand miles away. Checking the time and glancing at the position of the sun, Nick recalled that this was the sunset he certainly had not counted on seeing.

"Message passed, sir."

"Very good. Bring her round, pilot. And come down to two hundred revs."

Jordan had signalled, an hour ago: *I decided to maximize my distance from the Bali Strait by holding to a more southerly course before turning east to join you. Sorry if this departure from our original intentions has caused you concern.*

Then later, in answer to a question from Nick, he'd sent: *There is no Mrs Williams among my passengers.*

Nick hadn't thought there would be. And Williams, not having known of there being any refugees in the American destroyer, would have no reason to be disappointed.

Sloan was abeam to starboard: turning inward now. A handsome, fine-looking ship, Nick thought. He was putting her astern of *Defiant* so as to make night station-keeping simpler; and both ships were cutting speed now to sixteen knots.

"Course one-nine-two, sir!"

"Very good."

To call it "very good" was putting it rather mildly, he thought. A hundred and ninety-two degrees was the course from here to North West Cape, the top-left corner of Australia. A run of about seven hundred and fifty miles: at sixteen knots, two days. Then south down the Australian west coast for about the same distance, two more days, to Perth.

Perth—or Fremantle—close to where Kate was. Or where she had been . . .

Kate, my darling, please be there.

Tugs had charge of the *Caracas Moon* now. *Jouster* was leading them and *Ainsty* followed, while four tugs dragged half a tanker into the Grand Harbour.

Just minutes ago a Ju88 had crashed in flames right in the harbour entrance. Spitfires had driven others off: Spits circled now, on guard above Valletta.

That noise: as *Ainsty* nosed in around the point, Paul suddenly caught on to what was making it. Brass bands, and people: about three-quarters of the island's population—going mad. He could see them, as the view unfolded: bands, people, playing and cheering the ships in. Wherever there was a foothold—on roofs, balconies, walls, ledges, ramparts, the terraces and battlements of ancient fortifications, the Maltese had massed to welcome them. Hordes of people: waving, shouting, howling, clapping.

Astern, the *Santa Eulalia*, with smoke still gushing out of her, was entering harbour with two tugs ahead and one alongside. She was very low in the water, and listing so hard that you'd guess she was on the point of foundering. The tugs were hauling her around to port, close in past a rocky promontory. The noise was indescribable: and it was moving, you could feel it in your throat. *Ainsty*'s crew were fallen in, in ranks for the drill of entering harbour. Two ranks of sailors on her foc's'l, some amidships on each side of the iron deck, another platoon on the quarterdeck: they'd become parade-ground sailors, suddenly. Up here on the compass platform the captain had exchanged his woollen hat for a uniform cap, and the two-and-a-half stripes on each of his reefer's sleeves were bright, new-looking. From a distance, nobody could have guessed he hadn't had more than a brief doze in a bridge chair for the last five days and nights. Paul was looking into the forepart of the bridge. Simpson saw him, and came aft to tell him quickly, "They're taking the *Caracas Moon* into Dockyard Creek—round that next point on the left. Fort St Angelo, that heap is. The next point after it's called Senglea, and we'll be berthing in the creek—French Creek—beyond it."

The *Empire Dance* was alongside a wharf, stern-on to them as they passed. She was unloading, all her derricks busy and men swarming all over her, a mass of cargo streaming out of her to the wharf on one side and into lighters on the other. Beyond her, higher up the creek, he had a brief glimpse of the *Miramar*, the centre of an equally frantic discharging operation.

The *Santa Eulalia* had stopped. She'd grounded, close to the rocky shore in that first bay. He guessed they'd got her into shallow water just in time. All three tugs were alongside her now. If they could contain the fire they'd most likely unload her there, into lighters. The noise of cheering and clapping and the blare of the brass bands never slackened, it was a constant roar of excitement and joy: it was marvellous, he thought, but it was also crazy. How many people here—ten thousand? More? But what they were getting was half a tanker, maybe three-quarters of that American freighter's cargo, and two other ship-loads. At the cost of twelve merchantmen, an aircraft carrier, three cruisers and some destroyers: and those were the ships he *knew* about . . . The band they were passing was playing "Rule, Britannia!". A hand fell on his shoulder. Turning, he found the doctor, Grant, where Simpson had been a moment ago. Grant shouted, "Bad news, sub. Your pal Willis. I'm extremely sorry."

"Dead?"

The doctor nodded. The band had switched to "Scotland the Brave." Paul hadn't known Harry Willis well, but Willis had saved his life and now he was dead. So were Ron Beale, and Art Withinshaw, and Dennis Brill and Mick McCall and old Bongo Mackeson and young Gosling. And God knew how many others. The bands played and the people cheered and it made you want to cry: for the thrill in it, and pride, and sorrow too. But also, surprise. He wondered, *If they act like this now, what in hell will they do when we start winning?*

POSTSCRIPT

· · ·

There was no cruiser *Defiant* or destroyer USS *Sloan*. In other respects the description of the Java Sea battle (27 February, 1942) and subsequent events is drawn from history. The Japanese landed in Java on 1 March.

The Malta convoy is more thoroughly fictional. There was no convoy from the west in February: that month's attempt to supply the island was from Alexandria, and no ships at all got through. So it was necessary to invent one—in order to get Paul to Malta. The fictional convoy story is based loosely on the facts of Operation Pedestal, which took place a few months later. Pedestal opened with the loss of the carrier *Eagle*, and two cruisers and the tanker *Ohio* were hit in one (Italian) submarine's torpedo salvo at the entrance to the Skerki Channel. Among the fourteen ships in convoy was an American freighter called the *Santa Elisa*, but she was not among the five ships—two of them sinking—that reached Malta.

More Action, More Adventure, More Angst . . .

McBooks Press invites you to embark on more sea adventures and take part in gripping naval action with Douglas Reeman, Dudley Pope, and a host of other nautical writers. Sail to Trafalgar, Grenada, Copenhagen—to famous battles and unknown skirmishes alike.

All the titles below are available at bookstores. For a free catalog, or to order direct, call toll-free 1–888–BOOKS–11 (1–888–266–5711). Or visit the McBooks website, www.mcbooks.com, for special offers and to read excerpts from McBooks titles.

ALEXANDER KENT
The Bolitho Novels

DOUGLAS REEMAN
Modern Naval Fiction Library

Royal Marines Saga

____ 1 Badge of Glory
       1-59013-013-8 • 384 pp., $16.95

____ 2 The First to Land
       1-59013-014-6 • 304 pp., $15.95

____ 3 The Horizon
       1-59013-027-8 • 368 pp., $15.95

____ 4 Dust on the Sea
       1-59013-028-6 • 384 pp., $15.95

____ 5 Knife Edge
       1-59013-099-5 • 304 pp., $15.95

DUDLEY POPE
The Lord Ramage Novels

____ 1 Ramage
       0-935526-76-5 • 320 pp., $14.95

____ 2 Ramage & the Drumbeat
       0-935526-77-3 • 288 pp., $14.95

____ 3 Ramage & the Freebooters
       0-935526-78-1 • 384 pp., $15.95

____ 4 Governor Ramage R. N.
       0-935526-79-X • 384 pp., $15.95

____ 5 Ramage's Prize
       0-935526-80-3 • 320 pp., $15.95

____ 6 Ramage & the Guillotine
       0-935526-81-1• 320 pp., $14.95

____ 7 Ramage's Diamond
       0-935526-89-7 • 336 pp., $15.95

____ 8 Ramage's Mutiny
       0-935526-90-0 • 280 pp., $14.95

____ 9 Ramage & the Rebels
       0-935526-91-9 • 320 pp., $15.95

____ 10 The Ramage Touch
       1-59013-007-3 • 272 pp., $15.95

____ 11 Ramage's Signal
       1-59013-008-1 • 288 pp., $15.95

____ 12 Ramage & the Renegades
       1-59013-009-X • 320 pp., $15.95

____ 13 Ramage's Devil
       1-59013-010-3 • 320 pp., $15.95

____ 14 Ramage's Trial
       1-59013-011-1 • 320 pp., $15.95

____ 15 Ramage's Challenge
       1-59013-012-X • 352 pp., $15.95

____ 16 Ramage at Trafalgar
       1-59013-022-7 • 256 pp., $14.95

____ 17 Ramage & the Saracens
       1-59013-023-5 • 304 pp., $15.95

____ 18 Ramage & the Dido
       1-59013-024-3 • 272 pp., $15.95

ALEXANDER FULLERTON
The Nicholas Everard WWII Saga

____ 1 Storm Force to Narvik
       1-59013-092-8 • 256 pp., $13.95

____ 2 Last Lift from Crete
       1-59013-093-6 • 272 pp., $13.95

____ 3 All the Drowning Seas
       1-59013-094-4 • 320 pp., $14.95

DEWEY LAMBDIN
Alan Lewrie Naval Adventures

____ 2 The French Admiral
       1-59013-021-9 • 448 pp., $17.95

____ 8 Jester's Fortune
       1-59013-034-0 • 432 pp., $17.95

JAN NEEDLE
Sea Officer William Bentley Novels

____ 1 A Fine Boy for Killing
       0-935526-86-2 • 320 pp., $15.95

____ 2 The Wicked Trade
       0-935526-95-1 • 384 pp., $16.95

____ 3 The Spithead Nymph
       1-59013-077-4 • 288 pp., $14.95

JAMES L. NELSON
____ The Only Life That Mattered
       1-59013-060-X • 416 pp., $16.95

C. NORTHCOTE PARKINSON
The Richard Delancey Novels

____ 1 The Guernseyman
       1-59013-001-4 • 208 pp., $13.95

____ 2 Devil to Pay
       1-59013-002-2 • 288 pp., $14.95

____ 3 The Fireship
       1-59013-015-4 • 208 pp., $13.95

____ 4 Touch and Go
       1-59013-025-1 • 224 pp., $13.95

____ 5 So Near So Far
       1-59013-037-5 • 224 pp., $13.95

____ 6 Dead Reckoning
       1-59013-038-3 • 224 pp., $15.95

____ The Life and Times of Horatio Hornblower
       1-59013-065-0 • 416 pp., $16.95

continues . . .

V.A. STUART

Alexander Sheridan Adventures

___ 1 Victors and Lords
    0-935526-98-6 • 272 pp., $13.95

___ 2 The Sepoy Mutiny
    0-935526-99-4 • 240 pp., $13.95

___ 3 Massacre at Cawnpore
    1-59013-019-7 • 240 pp., $13.95

___ 4 The Cannons of Lucknow
    1-59013-029-4 • 272 pp., $14.95

___ 5 The Heroic Garrison
    1-59013-030-8 • 256 pp., $13.95

The Phillip Hazard Novels

___ 1 The Valiant Sailors
    1-59013-039-1 • 272 pp., $14.95

___ 2 The Brave Captains
    1-59013-040-5 • 272 pp., $14.95

___ 3 Hazard's Command
    1-59013-081-2 • 256 pp., $13.95

___ 4 Hazard of Huntress
    1-59013-082-0 • 256 pp., $13.95

___ 5 Hazard in Circassia
    1-59013-062-6 • 256 pp., $13.95

___ 6 Victory at Sebastopol
    1-59013-061-8 • 224 pp., $13.95

___ 7 Guns to the Far East
    1-59013-063-4 • 240 pp., $13.95

___ 8 Escape from Hell
    1-59013-064-2 • 256 pp., $13.95

PHILIP McCUTCHAN

The Halfhyde Adventures

___1 Halfhyde at the Bight of Benin
    1-59013-078-2 • 224 pp., $13.95

___2 Halfhyde's Island
    1-59013-079-0 • 224 pp., $13.95

___3 Halfhyde and the Guns of Arrest
    1-59013-067-7 • 256 pp., $13.95

___4 Halfhyde to the Narrows
    1-59013-068-5 • 240 pp., $13.95

___5 Halfhyde for the Queen
    1-59013-069-3• 256 pp., $14.95

___6 Halfhyde Ordered South
    1-59013-071-5 • 256 pp., $14.95

___7 Halfhyde on Zanatu
    1-59013-072-3 • 192 pp., $13.95

DAVID DONACHIE

The Privateersman Mysteries

___ 1 The Devil's Own Luck
    1-59013-004-9 • 302 pp., $17.95
    1-59013-003-0 • 320 pp., $23.95 HC

___ 2 The Dying Trade
    1-59013-006-5 • 384 pp., $16.95
    1-59013-005-7 • 400 pp., $24.95 HC

___ 3 A Hanging Matter
    1-59013-016-2 • 416 pp., $16.95

___ 4 An Element of Chance
    1-59013-017-0 • 448 pp., $17.95

___ 5 The Scent of Betrayal
    1-59013-031-6 • 448 pp., $17.95

___ 6 A Game of Bones
    1-59013-032-4 • 352 pp., $15.95

The Nelson & Emma Trilogy

___ 1 On a Making Tide
    1-59013-041-3 • 416 pp., $17.95

___ 2 Tested by Fate
    1-59013-042-1 • 416 pp., $17.95

___ 3 Breaking the Line
    1-59013-090-1 • 368 pp., $16.95

NICHOLAS NICASTRO

The John Paul Jones Novels

___ 1 The Eighteenth Captain
    0-935526-54-4 • 312 pp., $16.95

___ 2 Between Two Fires
    1-59013-033-2 • 384 pp., $16.95

Classics of Nautical Fiction

CAPTAIN FREDERICK MARRYAT

___ Frank Mildmay OR
    The Naval Officer
    0-935526-39-0 • 352 pp., $14.95

___ The King's Own
    0-935526-56-0 • 384 pp., $15.95

___ Mr Midshipman Easy
    0-935526-40-4 • 352 pp., $14.95

___ Newton Forster OR
    The Merchant Service
    0-935526-44-7 • 352 pp., $13.95

___ Snarleyyow OR The Dog Fiend
    0-935526-64-1 • 384 pp., $16.95

___ The Phantom Ship
    0-935526-85-4 • 320 pp., $14.95

___ The Privateersman
    0-935526-69-2 • 288 pp., $15.95

RAFAEL SABATINI
___ Captain Blood
         0-935526-45-5 • 288 pp., $15.95

MICHAEL SCOTT
___ Tom Cringle's Log
         0-935526-51-X • 512 pp., $14.95

WILLIAM CLARK RUSSELL
___ The Yarn of Old Harbour Town
         0-935526-65-X • 256 pp., $14.95
___ The Wreck of the Grosvenor
         0-935526-52-8 • 320 pp., $13.95

A.D. HOWDEN SMITH
___ Porto Bello Gold
         0-935526-57-9 • 288 pp., $13.95

Military Fiction Classics

R.F. DELDERFIELD
___ Seven Men of Gascony
         0-935526-97-8 • 368 pp., $16.95
___ Too Few for Drums
         0-935526-96-X • 256 pp., $17.95